MATCHSTRIKE

Book 2 of the Apex Society Trilogy

Rhone Atleshen

LONE SPIRE PUBLISHING

SERIES LIST

APEX SOCIETY

MATCHSTRIKE

RHONE ATLESHEN

Published by Lone Spire Publishing
www.LoneSpirePublishing.com

ISBN:
eBook: 979-8-9934362-0-3
Paperback: 979-8-9934362-1-0
Hardcover: 979-8-9934362-2-7

Cover design by Candlelight Creative LLC
Interior design by Lone Spire Publishing

Library of Congress Control Number: 2025922946

Printed in the United States of America

First Edition: November 2025
10 9 8 7 6 5 4 3 2 1

DEDICATION

Dedication

For every woman who ever wished the karma fairy had a
taste for blood—I brought the tarp and shovel.

CONTENT ADVISORY

BEFORE YOU BEGIN...

I write thrillers designed for emotional intensity. The characters and events in these pages aren't real — but the stakes are meant to feel real. My villains do bad things. My heroes are flawed, layered, and not always altruistic.

I hope you enjoy the ride, but your mental and emotional health matter more. In these stories, you'll encounter adult language, violence, and at times sexual content.
If you need to step away–*please do so.*
My characters will still be here when you're ready.

For a list of potential triggers, visit the book's page at www.rhoneatleshen.com before you dive in.
Protect yourself.
Never stop reading.

CONTENTS

PROLOGUE

LILA: 3 MONTHS AGO

I WAS WALKING INTO the lion's den.

My boss, the Captain of my New York PD Precinct, wasn't known for his patience. His temper was legendary, and I'd been known to push his limits from time to time with my 'ask for forgiveness later' approach. But if the sidelong glances I received passing through the pit were any indicator, I was in for one of the worst ass-chewings of my life.

"Sit down, Rivera." My Captain growled, fingers smashing the keys on his laptop.

As I waited, I steadied my nerves and mentally crossed my fingers that I could convince him to give me the remaining week of my planned PTO. So I could return upstate to finish what I started. I knew if I did, I could return with evidence in hand.

I knew it, deep down in my bones; Marcus Brinks was dirty. His hands were in every dead prostitute case I tracked, his name flagged as legal counsel to over half a dozen high-profile perps for charges from

1

drug possession to money laundering and even racketeering. You could feel the slimy filth every time he opened his mouth, and not a single client on his roster was earning their wings in the great beyond for good deeds—fat cats who avoided jail via red-tape loopholes and paperwork mistakes.

His name–synonymous with the term mistrial.

At least once a week, behind closed doors in some judge's chambers, Brinks had a trial thrown out on a technicality. He was infamous at my midtown police station. When the man walked in, cases practically closed themselves.

Every time I tried to interview Brinks, he was unavailable. Every time I wanted to investigate him officially, my Captain would drop the hammer on me for some complaint that had been lodged.

It was maddening.

"Cap," I cocked a nonchalant chin, trying not to provoke the vein-throbbing frustration I saw pulsing in my Captain's neck as he popped a Tums and slapped his laptop shut.

"You told me you were taking some time off." Not a question, but a statement delivered with aloof matter-of-factness. I bristled at his overly calm demeanor.

I was prepared for yelling.

"I did," I confirmed, wondering why a coffee cup hadn't been thrown yet and trying to decide if I should back away slowly. I knew I'd taken a pretty ballsy step outside the lines, and if I was busted, I was surely done.

Despite repeated warnings, I'd kept tabs on Brinks. Where he lived, what clients he handled from his prestigious high-rise office overlooking Central Park, and even who he slept with. That's how I knew when Brinks took off to represent an arsonist in upstate, NY. An outlier that had me calling in my saved-up paid leave to follow the breadcrumbs. Captain happily granted me the PTO, having already nagged me to 'get my head on straight' after everything that had happened.

I told myself my Captain was glad to be rid of me.

I reasoned I could work faster out from under his scrutiny to connect the loose ends I'd been scrambling to tie together like a noose around Brinks' neck.

So why did my neck suddenly feel the squeeze?

"You said you were using your leave to..." He paused and eyed me over his shoulder. "Clear your head?" I willed my face into neutrality, fighting the rising adrenaline that told me I was really screwed if he was this calm.

I'd used my time to 'volunteer' my skills to the Lake Placid PD, where Brinks was named counsel for the defendant in an arson case. I didn't love the pretense. I'd allowed the lead officer to believe I was on a loan from the city, but I was desperate. On my own, I was no closer to finding the concrete proof I needed to hang Brinks. I was banking on this oddity of a case to give me what I needed. While assisting, I uncovered a short money trail in which Marcus funneled client funds through a non-profit organization into several Lake Placid municipal branches—maybe greasing new palms by helping out a fireman who'd done a real number on some poor woman. She'd barely escaped with her life.

I felt for her, I did.

But I couldn't get distracted.

Time was limited.

I shared what I found with Sergeant Wilder, the local who seemed on the up-and-up, and hid the details I needed for the case I'd been building at home.

Then I received an angry call from my Captain, demanding my return.

"Yeah... You'd been on me to take some time off for months." I kept my voice casual, even as anxiety pressed in around me. "I figured it was as good a time as any." Then I made my fatal mistake, adding a smile and a light, "You called me back early, though. What gives?"

His expression deflated to disappointment.

"What gives?" Captain huffed, half mumbling to himself as he pulled a freshly printed document off the printer. "You know, kid... I've always been on your side." His voice was stone-cold calm. "I hired you right out of the academy despite the lack of professional recommendations because of your blue-blood family and your tech-savvy."

He was too calm. Shit shit shit.

"And I've had your back on countless cases when you rolled off half-cocked to get some electronic evidence before the warrant was in because I *trusted* your instincts. You always came through in the end."

My chances of flying under the radar grew slimmer by the second.

"Yeah, Cap. You've always been good to me." I appeased, offering another smile and hoping to build on his memory of my better outcomes and his goodwill with my family name. "You've been a good boss...a mentor even. My brother always said so."

Come on, heartstrings...do your thing.

"You got talent, Rivera. You know it, I know it," he waved a hand around the room. "The whole goddamn department knows—no one's better at the tech side of investigations than you." He held the paper in front of him, tapped it neatly into a small stack of other documents, and stapled them together before sliding it across the desk with a resigned sigh. "That's why this kills me."

I leaned forward, grabbed the paperwork, and slid it into my lap to read.

OFFICIAL NOTICE OF TERMINATION
To: Officer Delilah Rivera
From: Internal Affairs Division – NYPD

Subject: Termination of Employment – Effective Immediately

This letter serves as formal notification that your employment with the New York Police Department is hereby terminated, effective immediately, pursuant to multiple sustained violations of departmental policy and procedure.

"Wait...no..." My heart dropped into my stomach as I continued reading.

A comprehensive review by Internal Affairs determined you have demonstrated a consistent pattern of misconduct, including but not limited to:
-Failure to adhere to departmental protocols and codes of conduct
-Persistent insubordination and disregard for supervisory directives
-Unauthorized use of law enforcement credentials and inter-agency resources

-Unwarranted targeting of an officer of the court, contributing to a hostile and unprofessional work environment

These actions constitute a breach of the standards expected of NYPD personnel and are grounds for immediate dismissal under Article 764.b-3 of the Departmental Code of Conduct.

My brain couldn't comprehend what I was reading, and I hunched forward as I read the final paragraphs, as if sitting over them would allow the words to sink in better.

Enclosed please find:

-Personnel Action Form documenting the change in employment status.

-Property Surrender Checklist detailing the required return of all department-issued equipment, including badge, uniform, firearm, and identification

-Final Compensation Summary, which includes any outstanding pay and benefits owed, contingent upon signed receipt of the department's Non-Disclosure Agreement (NDA) and release of liability

The NYPD acknowledges your prior service and commitment. Should you have questions regarding the terms of separation, you may contact Human Resources.

This action is final and non-negotiable.

Sincerely,

Agent 7382649

Internal Affairs Division

New York Police Department

No, no, no, no, NO!

I read the letter a second time, then a third, my mind reeling as this final sliver of normalcy slipped through my fingers.

"I couldn't protect you this time, Rivera. You waltzed into an upstate precinct, logging unpaid hours on a case without due process."

"Cap. I was - "

"What the hell did you think would happen?" He sat back in his chair, lacing his fingers together across his stomach with a scowl. "As is, you're lucky I kept the half-dozen code and ethical violations off your permanent records. And that's after I did some serious fucking tap-dancin' to talk down Brinks from adding Conflict of Interest, Breach of Confidentiality, and Neglect of Duty so you can keep your bennies."

"Brinks!" I stood, rage rising at the mention of that vile bastard's name. "He was the reason I went up there—"

"And he's the goddamn reason I'm losing a good officer to a half-cocked obsession!" The Captain stood, matching my posture and pointing his finger in my face as his volume rose. "Jesus Christ, Rivera, you were my best officer's daughter. I've known you since you were knee-high to a cricket, but you went too far." He pulled back, anger and disappointment warring in his eyes. "Frankly, I hadn't done you any favors letting this drag on like it has."

"I'm close, Cap," I begged, ignoring my fracturing heart at the loss of my last hold on my family's memory, and maybe my sanity. "I know it. That's why Brinks wanted me fired. He *knew* I was—"

"Enough!"

His voice boomed—silencing the department cacophony. I imagined the entire pit straining to hear as my career plummeted into the abyss.

"Internal Affairs gave the official order after Brinks caught you digging around in that arson case from one of his clients...Jesus, Rivera!" The Captain started pacing behind his desk. "First, it was dead prostitutes you tried to pin to district attorneys, then it was nefarious hedge funders you swore were running drugs, and now you're looking at arson cases outta your jurisdiction."

"Ask yourself why a Manhattan attorney would be in a shitty upstate town defending some rando firefighter in the first place?" I argued, unable to accept that my time was well and done.

"Maybe it's a friend of his, or a former client." He fired back.

"The only thing Brinks ever defended was fucking white-collar garbage!" I bellowed, emotion steamrolling better judgment as I grasped onto my last anchor in life.

"The fuck business is it of yours why he's there!" Captain roared as he ran his hand over his face before leaning his clenched fists back down to his desk and mumbling to the floor. "That's the whole point, though, isn't it, Rivera? You don't even see how off-base you are 'cause of this goddamn obsession. I hardly recognize you anymore." He opened his desk drawer, pulled out a pen, and held it before my unbelieving eyes. "If he were alive, this'd break your father's heart."

"Okay," I whispered—panic rising as the walls closed in around me. "I'll see the station counselor like you wanted me to. I'll finish the therapy sessions. I'll—"

He clicked the pen to life, face frozen in resignation.

"I'll take unpaid leave...jump through *whatever* hoops IA wants. I can even—"

"Sign the papers, kid." He dropped the pen into my pleading hand. "And be glad I kept Brinks from pressing formal charges against you."

"Cap." My voice cracked as reality caved in. "I can't leave the case unsolved. Not when my dad and my brother -"

"There is no case, Rivera...there never was," Captain whispered as he sat down in his chair, his face showing all the resigned determination of a brick wall. "Leave your badge and gun. Box your shit. Get the fuck outta here before you lose your severance."

"Please." Desperation stung before traitorous weakness spilled down my cheeks.

"My hands are tied." His face flashed a glimmer of sadness. "I can't help you now."

Just like that...the last of me that was...was gone.

I had nothing left.

Nothing left of my father and brother, and nothing left to lose.

1

SAM

"**I**'M AN UNCLE!" I shouted over the din of my favorite bar. "Drinks are on me!"

Loud and raucous cheers followed me through the place, congratulatory shoulder smacks ushering me to my barstool at the back corner of Scaled Back's long bar.

A seedy joint off an old logging highway out of town, Scaled Back served as the unofficial outer line of the county. Once a truck stop and weigh station, hence the punny name, it became a glorified watering hole when the state opted for automated weigh stations. Its use dwindled to a convenient spot to rest a rig overnight before crossing into Canada.

"Congrats, Sammy boy. Boy or girl?" Marge, the owner, had been a friend since I responded to my very first 911 call as a probationary paramedic –a bar brawl gone south.

We arrived to find two unconscious men and a baseball bat-wielding Marge standing over them, smoking a cigarette with a bloody forehead.

She refused to leave, making me stitch her up right there in the bar, so she could 'keep the booze and money flowing'. I returned after my shift ended to find her serving shots to the men she'd knocked unconscious earlier. My shocked face gave her the 'best laugh of her life', so she poured me a drink on the house, explaining that the men were fighting over hockey when their good sense took a backseat. She intervened, but no hard feelings.

"NIECES!" I accepted the mug of on-tap lager. "Can you fucking believe it!"

"Both girls!" Marge exclaimed. "How's Mama doing?"

"Moira's great. Chase said she was amazing. You should see the girls... they're absolute dolls." I took out my phone, showing a picture of my teary-eyed brother, Chase, holding one of the girls as he sat beside a besotted Moira, who held the other baby, both of them beaming. "They take after their mother...thank God." I swiped to another picture – me holding both my nieces at the same time. "That's River," I pointed to each baby in turn. "And that one is Blue."

"River and Blue?" Marge scrunched her face at the monikers.

"Yeah...I don't get it either. Chase came up with the names." I flipped through a few more pics of Troy, and then one of Chase's face when we announced the girls' arrival. "Chase is just gone over 'em."

"And did you lose your marbles holding those babies?" Marge prodded. "Blowing in here and buying a round for the whole fucking house?"

"C'mon, Margie girl." I teased the nickname she hated. "You know I gotta celebrate."

"You mean blow money in this shithole...Yeah, I know." She whipped her towel at me before strolling to serve a few patrons, leaving me to scroll through my photos.

The twins hadn't been here 24 hours, and I was utterly smitten.

After Nonna passed, my brothers and I had no steady female presence in our lives. We exited the Marines, launched our real estate company, and settled into our respective careers in town emergency services as unsupervised bachelors.

Then came Moira, by far the girliest thing I'd ever met, who proved to be the perfect match for my tatted-up biker brother, Chase. He now smiles every damn day. Then came the twins, and just like that, our little band of brothers was forever changed with three beautiful little women.

I swear, watching the bulkiest, tatted-up guy in town give googly eyes to two tiny bundles of pink made my heart ache. I envied him a little.

Of the three of us, I was the Wilder brother voted most likely to grow into a full-on man-whore. I subscribed to the 'work hard...play harder' school of thought. While at work, nothing distracted me from caring for a patient, whether stitching up an angry bartender wielding a bat or comforting a woman pulled from a burning building. I was never rattled and never backed down from doing what was needed to take care of the person on my rig. I loved helping someone when they were hurt, broken, and scared. I loved being an EMT.

But off-duty, I wanted to party with some soft curves.

Or rather, I used to.

Snagging the eye of some hottie passing through Marge's bar for a hook-up was easy. I rarely saw any of them more than once, and never did sleepovers. Outside the bar, my job as an EMT meant I saw the nurses and doctors regularly. I tried not to dip my pen in company ink, but hook-ups happened.

At some point, though, it lost its appeal.

It was subtle at first. I'd be too tired or a shift too bloody. Closing down the bar took a backseat to a hot shower and a soft bed. Soon, I preferred spending time with my brothers over random women asking the same tired questions. *'What do you do for a living? Oh, you're an EMT? How brave! Wanna play doctor?'*

Don't get me wrong. Women, in general, were awe-inspiring. Beautiful to behold and fierce and complicated. I loved getting to know all the nuances that women brought to the table. But the monotony began to wear. Being alone was easier than scratching an itch that went more dormant by the day.

If I let myself think too hard about it, I might worry I was broken. Hell, if I were counting the days since my last good lay, I'd schedule a physical to make sure my dick still worked. But the issue was me, generally dissatisfied with the notched-belt lifestyle.

"Hey, Uncle Sam!" Marge's voice snapped me out of my revelry. "You serious about buying a round for the whole place?"

I glanced at Marge, who was talking to a few long-haul truckers.

"Absolutely!" I shouted up to Marge. "Beer's all 'round in honor of my nieces!"

The bar erupted again, the two newcomers tipping their hats in appreciation.

"It's like you don't like keeping your money, Sam." Marge sauntered over, grabbing my credit card. "Figured I'd taught you better."

"How many times am I gonna become an Uncle?" I asked, tossing the last of my beer back. "Troy's wound so tight he'll never marry. If that control freak sat on a lump of coal, he'd shit a diamond." I palmed a fresh mug. "Did I tell you the girls are identical?"

"How can you tell them apart?"

"Doc said little differences will emerge as they grow, but they were painting their toenails different colors when I left." I got lost in pictures of my growing family, laughing at one of Troy awkwardly holding the girls. "Check it."

I turned the screen to Marge, who lifted her reading glasses and laughed.

"He looks damn near terrified."

"100%." I swiped through a few more pictures. "It's hysterical."

The bell jingled over the door, pulling Marge's attention.

"You want me to cut off that tab now or wait 'til you come crying over the bill?"

"Go ahead and close it out after..." My response trailed off as I got an eyeful of the newest patron to walk in, door bouncing off the rounded ass of the hottest woman I'd ever seen.

2

SAM

WEARING SKY-HIGH BLACK LEATHER knee boots over shredded jeans, she couldn't have been taller than 5'4. Her ass and thighs were luscious and round, serving to escalate the soft belly sitting below full tits that stretched the top of her worn-thin t-shirt to its absolute limits. Though half-hidden under a black leather jacket that couldn't possibly keep her warm in freezing temperatures, I got a peek at her rock-hard nipples when she turned slowly, scanning the room.

She had a body built for sin, and my dick awoke from hibernation with a roar.

The pint-sized goddess walked with confident steps to the only available stool, which, thank the merciful heavens, sat next to me. Hopping up to the seat, she stood on its rail and reached for the bowl of stale peanuts while shouting down to Marge.

"Bottle of Medelo, please.... bourbon chaser." Her New York accent fit the leather and heels look, but her beer and liquor chaser added a surprising twist to the picture. Most women I'd met liked fruity cocktails or frozen blends.

She plopped back to the stool, flicking back a wayward strand of honey-brown hair that cascaded halfway down her back like a fiery lion's mane. The move gave me a better look at her coppery skin and the adorable elf-like nose.

I shifted my gaze to admire her through the bar's mirrored backsplash.

Long, thin fingers, a narrow chin, and beautifully full lips that my dick screamed to have wrapped around it. I considered starting a conversation, if only to see the color of her eyes. But before I could so much as utter a word, a guy made a beeline across the room and, in one smooth move, leaned against the bar—effectively becoming a wall between the goddess and me.

"Hey there, sexy, I hadn't seen you in here before." I rolled my eyes at his opener, but her expression in the mirror piqued my curiosity.

"Yeah, well...now ya have...lucky you." Her voice held all the enthusiasm of a tax audit; her eyes locked on the bowl of peanuts in front of her for another second before adding, "I'm not gonna be here long, so..." Her words trailed off, and her gaze lifted to the TV.

She didn't spare the guy so much as a glance.

"Can I buy you a drink?" He leaned in, and I snickered at his dense insistence when she squeezed her shoulders together, pulling away. "I'd love to get to know you while you're here."

This guy was not picking up what she was putting down, and as much as that shit tended to grate my nerves, the ire in her expression told me I was in for a helluva show. Looking down the bar, I caught Marge's knowing expression of bemused boredom before she turned back to some guys in suits chatting her up. We'd both seen his douchey type before. But the goddess on the barstool seemed unruffled as she took a swig of beer, tossing the bourbon in one fell swoop.

"Like I said, I'm not gonna be here long." She waved the empty shot glass at Marge, who cocked her head in response. "And as you can *see*," she waved the beer bottle in front of the guy's face. "I don't need a drink. So...no thanks."

God, it was awesome seeing women maintain their power when assholes couldn't take a hint.

"Name's Carl." The douche held out his hand, and I had to cover my mouth to stifle my laugh as she grimaced like he offered her a fistful of shit.

"Look.... Carl," She cut her eyes up at him. "I appreciate how hard it is to walk up to a woman. I applaud the effort. But... I'm. Not. Interested."

Carl stood a little straighter, maybe getting the message, but also eye-fucking her tits, which had me more than ready to upend the guy on the spot.

"In fact...Carl," The fiery goddess drawled his name on a sugary breath. "I'm meeting a guy here from Tinder." She waved her phone around for Carl to see. "I swiped right and we're supposed to meet and well...gee," she gave a toothy smile and a shrug before adding in, "how would it look if I started talking to some other guy when I should be," she waved her phone so close to Carl's face pulled back to avoid being hit, "Waiting on Mr. Tinder?"

She was savage.

She'd said no to this asshat about four different ways and now used a syrupy sweet voice and a heaping side dish of fake-date-meetup to get the job done. High impact, non-aggressive, non-confrontational, and concise.

Fucking. Goddess.

"Well, uh...maybe you and I can get a table instead." Through the barback mirror, I watched Carl's face curl into a snarky smile as he leaned in to shoot his shot one more time. "I bet you're a *real* hellcat in the sack, aren't ya?"

My amusement with shit-fisted Carl officially ran its course.

"Look...pal," her back went ramrod straight, and she spat her words with the quiet venom of a woman unhinged as she stood on the rails of her stool. "I've told you no about every way I can, and..." She gripped the beer bottle in her hand as if preparing to smash it over this idiot's thick skull.

Marge clocked it too, eyes locking on mine in a silent request.

"I already told you! I'm waiting on Mr. Tinder. So...Off you fuck." She flicked her wrist at the door as if swatting a fly, then dismissively turned and gave Carl her back.

He inhaled for another pitch, but I decided to shut him down.

"I thought that was you!" I interjected loudly, enjoying Carl's startled expression. I reached around him, extending a hand to the woman and simultaneously nudging Carl out from between us. "It's me...Sam, from Tinder." I waved my cell phone in shit-fisted Carl's face with a smile. "Thanks for keeping her company, pal."

He was forced a step back, his face flashing through confusion and irritation before embarrassment gave way to anger.

"Can I buy you a drink for my appreciation before you *leave*?" I laced the last word with a hint of unmistakable violence.

God knows I'd seen enough assault calls to have zero tolerance for jerks who couldn't take no for an answer. But finally, shit-fisted Carl backed away, snarling a half-intelligible insult under his breath as he went.

"Thanks for keeping my date entertained for me!"

My parting shot wasn't necessary, but I couldn't help shouting it loud enough for others to hear. Douche-canoes who couldn't take' No' as a complete sentence deserved no respect.

I turned on my stool, locking eyes with the woman who looked so mad, I thought steam might come out of her ears. Dammit if those honey-brown eyes shooting daggers at me didn't have my cock begging for mercy.

"Don't worry," I said, turning towards the TV and fighting to keep my outer cool despite the screaming desire to take her on the bar top. "I just wanted to avoid the broken glass from the baseball bat."

3

LILA

"**D**ID YOU SAY, BASEBALL bat?" I questioned the do-gooder whose attention seemed to be back on the blaring TV.

"Yeah." He looked almost disinterested despite his role as over-eager Mr. Tinder. Honestly, it was a relief considering my hours of driving and utter lack of fucks to give.

"Marge has this big-ass baseball bat for when shit hits the fan. The way you gripped that beer," he pointed at my fist, still white-knuckling my bottle, "I figured you were about to clean Carl's clock. I mean, he's harmless, but even the best of men could lose their shit if they took a bottle to the face, and then I spend my night stitching up people instead of celebrating."

I only wanted to be left alone, but this guy's casual assertion that I could clock a man over the head for being an ass was mildly amusing. The fact that he paid such close attention to how I held my bottle, though...that had me appreciating that this guy had shoulders like a linebacker and a beard I could ride.

In another life, perhaps.

I was starving, utterly exhausted, and all I wanted was a quick drink before collapsing at the nearest motel, which I still needed to find. There was literally nothing else that I cared about.

Especially after losing everything.

With my shield gone, I sold my dad's place and stored or donated his and my brother's belongings. I sublet my apartment to a rookie on the force, bought a used Jeep Wrangler, and hit the road. The freedom to walk away from old ghosts and refocus my Brinks investigation became the silver lining to unemployment. I had almost nothing to go on beyond this small dot on the map in upstate New York. I hoped to sweet-talk one of the Lake Placid cops to help me, and I knew my efforts could land me in jail, or worse, but I stopped caring the moment I put my family in the ground.

Tonight, I wanted to drink until I couldn't remember what I came here to forget. Then I wanted the sweet release of sleep to take me til dawn. Tomorrow, I'd set up my tech, make a connection with Sergeant Troy Wilder, and learn what I could before doing a dark-web dive on Brinks' connection to this tiny little town. Of course, I would walk into the one bar full of creeps looking to score, so instead of quality time drowning my demons, I got to fend off a jackass who couldn't take no for an answer. As a bonus...I got a barstool lumberjack who thought I was a damsel in distress. Nothing irritated me more than someone thinking I needed saving.

"I wouldn't have, you know," I said without thinking. "Hit the dude in the face."

"When he called you Hellcat...I thought you'd make his asshole a beer koozie with the way you shot fire out of your eyes." I caught his wink through the bar mirror as the mental picture his words conjured had a surprising laugh bubbling up.

"Holy shit, that's graphic," I huffed, noticing my empty bottle. Just as I looked for the bartender, she appeared with another beer and a bourbon chaser—a mug of whatever tap swill the lumberjack was drinking found his hands.

"Thanks, Sam." She addressed the guy before turning her attention to me. "I'm Marge, this is my place. Don't mind Carl back there," She waved her towel towards the pool tables where Carl leaned over another woman. No doubt offering a stale line to a fresh crowd. "He's harmless if not overeager. I was stuck with a chatty suit and gave it to Sam to get rid of him."

"It's why I get the *free* drinks, right, Marge?" Sam lifted his glass with a broad smile.

"Fuck you...I like keeping *my* money." She whipped her damp towel across the bar, plopping Sam in the face before walking off with a gritty laugh.

"Yep," Sam wiped the booze-juice that sluiced off his face with his sleeve. "Saw that coming."

"I had it under control," I felt the need to clarify for some unknown reason. "But...thanks anyway." I tipped back the cold beer and tried to push off the nagging need to explain myself when the lumberjack, Sam, wasn't asking. He'd returned his attention to the TV.

"I'm sure you did," he mumbled before gulping his beer. "You just seemed exhausted, so I figured I'd help. No big deal."

He saw me.

He didn't hit on me.

But he did try to help me.

Exhaustion must have been clouding my judgment, because Sam's unexpected kindness felt unusually warm. I felt a sudden urge to explain my clipped attitude to him.

"I'm just tired from the drive," I said on a shrug. "And I don't have a lot of bandwidth for–"

"The fuckery of asshats?" Sam cocked an eyebrow, shifting a playful gaze to me in the mirror's reflection.

Another laugh erupted out of me at his turn of phrase–this one even bigger than before. I couldn't have rubbed two laughs together in the past year, and yet this guy conjured two in a single night. It felt so good that I leaned into it, resisting the urge to cover my mouth or stifle it with sarcasm or irritation. In doing so, I caught his attention. Sam turned on his stool, giving me more focus, and I mentally prepared for a come-on.

But he didn't speak.

He just watched me laugh until I stopped, his eyes glinting with what could've only been mischief. He didn't look away, but he didn't lean into my space either, and I appreciated the distinction.

"I have *zero* time for the fuckery of asshats." I nodded. Then, as if I had forgotten my soul focus was booze and sardonic, existential dread, I extended my hand. "I'm Lila."

"Sam." He answered, reaching his giant mitt and giving me a gentle but confident shake.

I wish I'd stopped the entire moment right then and there; Thanked him, maybe bought him a beer, and left. But damn if my brain didn't look at his giant meathooks and wonder what else was as big, and might feel as nice, as that sprinkle of laughter in the desert of my life.

23

"Glad I could help you lighten up a little. You seemed wound so tight that you could spring right off the ceiling. No one needs to be that stressed sitting in Margie's place."

His observational skills on full display, I felt the room grow a little smaller under his gaze.

"Did uh...did I hear you say you were celebrating something?" I asked, turning the would-be rescuer's gaze off me...even if his eyes were easy on mine.

"That's why I'm here." He whipped out his phone and flipped to the photo album filled with tiny pink bundles.

"My new nieces were just born. This is River, and that one is Blue."

"Aw, cute babies?!" I admired. "And River and Blue...*great* names! I appreciate a parent who can think outside the box a little on names, especially after being saddled with a name like mine my whole life."

"Lila isn't so bad." He quipped, scrolling through photos

"Ah, but you don't know the full story." I tipped back my bourbon, feeling the warmth of it settle in my gut. "Dad was a huge Tom Jones fan. Lila is short for **Delilah**. Not a bad name overall, except all anyone ever thinks is the bible hussy who took down a demigod with a haircut." I tossed back another swig of beer. "I got *endless* shit for it growing up in catholic school."

"Well then, allow me to reintroduce myself for the trauma bond." Sam pocketed his phone and extended his hand with a mischievous expression on his face. "I'm Samson."

"Shut. Up!" I shouted. "You are not named Samson."

"Yes, and if the fates are lining up for us, Delilah, I'm suddenly happy I got a fresh haircut so I don't have to worry about you doing it." He ran his other hand back through his tousled hair. "Just promise me you won't shave my beard in my sleep. This thing took forever to grow."

"Deal," I laughed as I took in the man next to me with a little more focus.

He sat tall, broad, and built like he worked with his hands—not a gym rat, just solid in all the right ways. God, I loved a beef-cake. Shaggy brown hair swept off his face, eyes that crinkled when he smiled. He was distractingly observant, which made his sex appeal that much more distracting. Even his olive skin was nearly perfect, if not for the scar slicing through one eyebrow, adding a fuckable menace to his stupidly handsome Lumbersnack vibe.

I couldn't deny it — he was my type.

A year ago, I might've let myself enjoy the view. As it was, I needed to pound back my drink and leave before he tempted me into bad decisions.

"You mentioned you were tired from driving." He studied me as he spoke. "What brings you into town?"

"Oh uh," I scrambled to find the answer to cut the conversation short.

Here on business? Nope, I didn't want to invite questions about my not-job.

Here on vacation? Didn't need the do-gooder thinking I needed a tour guide.

Here on a wild goose chase fueled by a vendetta against a corrupt lawyer who...

Nope, that ugly truth wasn't ready for the light of day.

"I'm passing through to friends up north. Pit-stopped here for some shut-eye."

"Oh God." He cringed, "Please don't tell me you're staying at any of the motels along the highway. They're all disgusting."

"Well, that was the plan...But-"

25

"There's a few hotels further in town that stand-up people run." He pulled out his phone and clicked on his contacts. Hitting Air-Drop, he gave me an expectant glance. "They will be a little more expensive, but you'll be a lot safer and more comfortable than any shithole out here."

"Oh...uh," I accepted the contacts without thinking. "Thanks...I guess." My mind wandered to what this guy did to have a hotel manager's contacts saved in his phone.

Then I wondered why I cared what this guy did.

Glancing at the list, I noticed he'd slid his contact file in. 'Sam, the man, call if you need help. '

A very smooth move.

"Pimp...or travel agent?" Sam spat out his beer, and I heard the bartender let loose a raucous belly laugh.

"What?" Sam asked, eyes watering as he wiped beer from the end of his nose.

"Not many people hang out in dive bars, know the bartender like family, and have half the town's hotels saved in their phone. You don't scream mayor with all that flannel, so unless you're a lumberjack travel agent, I'm assuming pimp."

Sam coughed and sputtered a few more times before answering.

"That phone number move usually goes over better." He smiled at me and downed the rest of his beer. "I'm an EMT. I know about the shithole motels 'cause I take calls from them all the time. Trust me when I say you do NOT want to stay at any of the locations around Marge's place."

"I gotta agree with Sam here." The bartender strolled up and leaned on her elbows. "If you plan on staying more than a night or two, almost any place is better than these rat traps." She gave Sam a serious look as she rapped her knuckles on the bartop. "I could use some of your expertise, Sammy. Got time to chat after closing?"

"I'm beat, Marge. I've been at the hospital all day. Is it important?"

"It can wait 'til tomorrow. Before opening? Come around noon?"

"It's a date, Margie girl." He gave her a wink and dodged another playful swing of her towel.

"Another round, you two?" She asked, and Sam nodded yes before glancing at me and adding.

"Maybe a couple of burgers and an order of cheese fries too, eh, Marge?"

4

SAM

HER CONSTITUTION WAS IMPRESSIVE.

I'd seen bigger men fall off their barstools after rapid-pounding as much booze. Still, she was a little glassy around the eyes, and I decided some food would help soak up the alcohol.

I also gave Marge the signal to slow the next round.

I couldn't leave this gorgeous mess buzzed in a bar full of idiots.

"I didn't know they sold burgers here." Lila spun on her stool, her back leaning against the bar, elbows propped on either side.

Her shirt stretched tight across her tits, and my cock started planning its future.

"Thanks for ordering, though. I'm starving."

"It's standard bar fare, all deep-fried and salt-filled," I answered, willing my body to calm the fuck down. "It's got zero nutritional value, but it'll fill you up."

Lila gave me a quick once-over with an unexpectedly amused expression.

"Yeah. I guess nutrition would be important to you...what with all *that* going on." She opened her palm, fingers splayed wide, as she waved her hand in my body's general direction.

"All.... that?"

"You're a big guy," her eyes rolled into the same mildly bored expression from before. "But dumb ain't a good look, ya know."

"Admiring my muscles, eh?" I couldn't help my knee-jerk response, given our proximity and my level of alcohol. And it was a hell of a lot more attention than she'd spared for poor shit-fisted Carl.

I decided to blame it on the booze and the sheer volume of fuck-me pheromones I was pumping to get those spike-heeled boots around my neck.

"Working out helps with the job. But I'm not a full-on musclehead if that's what you mean. My brother gets that title. Before his wife, that dude was in the gym more than he was at home."

"He the one with the babies?" Lila asked without so much as glancing my way. "He looked pretty swole."

"Yep. Bulky, protective, and a big softy." She turned to face me, lifting one leg to fit her knee in between my thighs in a sexy as fuck move.

"Your voice changes when you talk about them. Did you know?" Her sudden, intense eye contact and grazing knee had my cock twitching at the attention.

"Changes?"

"Your eyes, too...they smile when you mention the babies. I've seen it like three times now. And just now, when you mentioned your brother, your voice took on this warm, kinda gooey sound to it." She gestured with her hands while she spoke, and I found myself oddly mesmerized by the way her fingers moved in rhythmic cadence with her words. "It's clear you love your family."

The sentiment was sweet, but her voice shifted. Her face momentarily flashed a faraway look, as if she were sad. I wanted to know what it meant, but more than that, I wanted to see her smile again.

What the hell happened to a celebratory drink and home to bed?

"I'm not sure how my voice goes 'gooey'...but you aren't wrong about loving my family." I contemplated pulling out my phone and showing off a few more pics, but Lila's face went neutral again, biting her bottom lip—her eyes darting over my shoulder to the far corner.

"Pool tables free!" She jumped off the barstool and made a beeline to the back corner with nary a stumble in those heels.

The slingshot was jarring.

So far, this woman looked bored, irritated, momentarily checked out, all up in my business before disengaging, and now gleefully bolted for the pool tables.

I should have turned my ass around, eaten my burger, and gone home.

No denying, something about her had me thoroughly intrigued. The way she handled shit-fisted Carl made it clear she didn't 'brook any fools' as Nonna would've said. Lila seemed insightful enough to pick up on subtle things, such as voice inflection and facial expressions, but disengaged enough to keep an eye on the room while having a conversation. She wasn't some chick looking for a hook-up, even though she was fucking sex-on-heels, and she sure as shit wasn't passing through town.

I clocked that lie right off the bat.

The way these old back highways ran, unless her friends were Canadian Mounties or park rangers, there was nothing and nowhere to go beyond my town. She wasn't dressed for hiking the frigid Adirondacks with that ridiculous leather jacket, and even if I overlooked her sexy as fuck fashion choices, how she ended the lie sealed the deal.

'Pit-stopped here for some shut-eye.'

What...a load of bullshit.

It was damn near midnight. Anyone driving up here would have stopped a solid hour earlier down the highway, where cleaner rest-stops and well lit signs boasted brand-named food and hotel options that would've felt safer for a woman 'just passing through'.

"Hey, Uncle Sam!" Lila shouted across the room. "I can't kick your ass if you're way the fuck over there, can I?" She leaned on the pool table with one arm, the other cocked up on her hip, accentuating the ridiculous ratio between her generous hips and the short-ass waist that supported what promised to be an award-winning set of tits. Nearby men ogled her, and it made my blood boil.

This confirmed I couldn't leave until I saw her safely in a hotel.

My dick saluted the sound reasoning.

"I'll rack 'em." She said, deftly setting the balls into place with a wry smile that made her eyes sparkle. Her brazen assumption that I would join her without argument was hot as fuck.

I loved a confident woman.

"You break." I hid my smile as I watched her tiny frame stretch across the table.

"Didn't you start the conversation tonight by pontificating the merits of drinking a bedtime cocktail before hitting the sheets?" I grabbed a stick off the wall and scanned the table for chalk.

"But the fuckery of asshats." She cocked her chin over to Carl, cozied up in a corner booth with a woman. "He pissed me off. I've got adrenaline to burn." Then she cocked an eyebrow at me, her half-curled smile burning right through me, "But you do make hitting the sheets appealing." .

My dick stood...in applause.

"You shooting or what?" She gestured to the table, snapping me out of my reverie.

"Right," I scowled at the table, forcing myself to focus on the game and not the emotionally slingshotting sex-bomb now blatantly flirting with me.

Despite how fuckable she was, I didn't do one-night stands.

I'd play a round, make sure she ate, then dip.

Any other night.

Any. Other. Woman.

My cock had other ideas.

5

LILA

S AM LOOMED OVER THE table, giving me a front-row seat to forearm porn courtesy of the Henley scrunched up below his impressive biceps. When he pulled his arm back to break, his hands splayed on the table, fingers spread under his stick, it was hot.

Then there was that cocky smirk.

The dingy bar with dim lights and loud music provided the exact white noise my brain craved for turning off the symphony of pain that played on a loop. While dumb-ass Carl did nothing but piss me off, the lumbersnack gave serious big-dick energy, and I found myself warming to the idea of him in a hotel room.

Not that I needed to take home strays tonight.

I shook my head back to the present as he smashed the cluster of balls into chaos.

"Solid Break," I huffed, feigning low-level disinterest. "You play a lot?"

"My first call as an EMT was stitching up this wild woman's forehead while she leveled a boot on some asshole's neck." He nudged the passing shoulder of Marge as she placed two baskets of food on the ledge along the wall.

"He's a damn liar." She gave a wry smile. "It was a scratch." Then she popped Sam on the butt as she walked away. "That asshole deserved my boot."

For a second, I hated how safe he looked with a bar wrapped around him like a damn blanket—familiarity dug at a painful memory.

A family in a town full of families.

I used to have that.

Before Marcus Brinks snatched it from me in a flash of gunfire and blood.

"I was a wet-behind-the-ears probie shaking in my boots." Sam went on. "Marge was calm, cool, collected...and offered a free beer after my shift."

"Awwww," I drawled, stalking around the table. "You made a friend."

"Margie's good people. And despite this shithole's questionable clientele..." He scanned around the room and finished, "I've been coming here at least twice a week since."

I leaned over and aimed down the stick before banking the cue off the side and sinking the 6-ball in the corner pocket.

"You play a lot?" Sam asked, eyebrows raised to his hairline.

"Do I have to answer your question with my entire life story?" I asked, chalking my stick. "'Cause this game is gonna take all night if I go on like you do with every question you ask."

I half expected a snarky comeback, but instead, the man stood there, unmoving, unyielding, with an unreadably neutral expression on his face. I stood a second, expecting him to crack a smile and make some witty comeback, but no. Instead, the human wall eyed me down like a lion waiting to pounce. My skin prickled with an odd mix of arousal and irritation at the realization he wouldn't banter but...expected me to answer.

The rude mother fucker.

"Yeah." I huffed, irritated that I caved to avoid the stare-off. "I play a little."

"Excellent." He clapped his hands and swaggered over to where I stood.

He stood shoulder to shoulder, or rather, my shoulder to his mid-arm, since the man was huge. Directly at my side, almost no space between us, he gazed down at me with his face unflinching and his massive bicep flexing. The unwanted visual of him lifting me with one hand and mounting me to his cock without breaking stride woke my long-neglected vagina from her self-imposed dry spell, screaming, *'Take me, giant lumber-beast, I'm yours!'*

"All yours." He grumbled, a hint of delight twinkling in his eyes

"What?!"

"The table," Sam clarified. "You sunk the 6-ball... table's yours."

Fuck me sideways, why did I pick a game where this man worked his stick, and I played with his balls?

"Right." I snapped my eyes to the table and grasped for a way to get my brain out of the lusty gutter. "Let's make this interesting. Loser buys the next round?"

"Easy pickings. You sure you wanna squander your money on cheap beer?"

"Awful cocky for a guy who admitted he was exhausted and is only hanging out to make sure I eat that burger."

A flash of surprise coursed across his face before he settled back into his playful demeanor.

"Deal," he said, a different edge to his voice. "Loser buys next round."

One game turned into three, and hours passed by in a whirl. We drank as we went and, burger be damned, I ended up good and drunk. This explained how I let this giant hunk of Lumbercock distract me from my mission.

Bourbon always did make me do dumb shit.

6

SAM

FUCKING HELL.

I wanted to drag out the game until the food had a chance to hit bottom, but it was clear she was playing me. Hell, if I didn't love it. By the end of the second game, the flirty glint in her eyes had my beer-soaked cock standing at attention, and every time she walked past me, her ass grazed the front of my jeans. Then she started with that leaning shit, and I began unravelling.

Leaning across the table, cleavage on full display.

Leaning against the side rail, her tits strapped under her snug t-shirt.

Then the little minx leaned against a guy at the neighboring table with what I swore was a wink. She laughed off the oversight, grazing his arm, but his heated glare down her tits, while grabbing her ass, snapped my patience.

"We're done here." I dropped my stick on the table and tugged her towards me.

No way I was leaving her tipsy, with this guy leering at her like a walking fuck-hole. No way some pissant got lucky with a goddess that I'd spent the better part of the night enjoying.

This was my goddess...and we were leaving.

"Aw," Lila teased, a little louder than necessary–the bourbon breaking her volume control. She fluttered her lashes at me, hooking a thumb back at the other guy. "Don't tell me you're jealous of *that* dumb shit."

"Dumb shit?" The guy took understandable offense. "Looks who's talking, you drunk slut."

My hands flew before I realized what I was doing. A single hit sent the guy across his table.

"Holy Shit!" Lila exclaimed.

"Holy shit is right!" Yelled Marge, stomping over, bat in hand. "Tell me you're not starting this shit, Sam?"

"Guy's gotta mouth on him, Margie-girl," I growled, clenching and releasing my fist to fight the tension building in my knuckles and wondering what the hell had gotten into me. "He's getting grabby."

To his credit, the guy jumped up and began rounding the table.

Ballsy idiot, I'd give him that.

"Don't worry, Margie-girl," he sneered. "That lucky shot will be his last."

He lunged for me, but Marge was quicker.

"No one calls me Margie-girl." She socked the end of the bat in the guy's gut, doubling him over with an 'OOF'. Standing back, she snapped, "Now...you can *all* get the fuck outta my bar." She grabbed the doubled-over asshat by his ear and leveled a glare at me. "Get gone, kid." I prepared an apology, but she waved the bat towards Lila. "And take trouble with you."

Marge meant business, so I grabbed Lila's hand and headed towards the back door, ignoring the big-mouthed asshole Marge dragged out front to a soundtrack of rising applause.

What. The. Hell. A bar fight, really?

"Wait..." Lila straightened, trying to pull her hand free and ignoring my glare. "I'm not done shooting pool."

"Yeah...you are." I turned back and continued walking, hearing her boots click out two steps to my one and gaining no small measure of cavemanly pride knowing the trouble-maker nearly ran to keep pace.

"My car is out front, Jackass." She yelled as the steel door slammed behind us. "Let me go!"

Again, she yanked on her hand, and I turned to narrow my eyes at her.

"You're drunk. You started a fight. You are in no condition to drive. You don't need your car." I started mentally counting down from five, trying to cool off and praying she'd calm the fuck down before I lost control of whatever primal thing was trying to claw its way out of me.

"I'm not drunk...*Jackass*." She pointed a finger at my chest to punctuate her words. "YOU started the fight. Not me. And I can drive just fine. So, fuck o-!"

As if karma delivered on demand, her final insult ended with a yelp when her heel dipped into a crack in the asphalt, sending her careening forward. I used the momentum, leaning down and letting her topple right over the top of my shoulder. As I turned to my car, she began yelling about the injustice of it all, using the word fuck like a comma.

Given her incapacitated state, it made for an adorably filthy protest. When her feet began kicking, however, my free hand found its way up to slap her ass with a sense of pride like I'd bagged a prize lion.

No..not a lion.

"You're gonna hurt yourself if you don't calm down...Hellcat."

I couldn't fight my smile as my use of Shit-fisted Carl's nickname sent her into a tizzy.

"Sit down... I'll take you to the hotel before Marge calls the cops." An empty threat. Marge avoided calling the cops at all costs, but it settled Lila enough for me to buckle her into the passenger seat.

"I don't *have* a hotel yet, Jackass," she flung her arm out, gesturing to god knows what. "And all my shit is in my Jeep." Cross-armed and fuming, her tits pushed up under her shirt like she won arguments on cleavage alone.

"Fine. We'll check you in somewhere, then I'll come grab your Jeep for you." I started my SUV while doing a mental check on my faculties.

I'd been drinking, but the adrenaline and my size burned through it fast–I was clear.

Making sure she was settled somewhere clean and safe was all I had to do. I didn't know the woman's budget or last name, but it hardly mattered since I realized we had left her purse at the bar and with it...her ID.

"I didn't start that fight." I could feel her daggers blazing through me as I drove. "That was you and your burly lumberjack testosterone."

"Sure, it was," I deadpanned, the memory of the handsy asshole spiking my blood pressure.

"I could've handled the guy on my own!" Damn, could the woman rant.

Even as I pulled into the parking lot of the hotel, she was still going. I begged whoever was listening to shut her up before I decided to shut her up with my tongue, or my cock, which was rock, fucking, hard. Rounding the front of the SUV, I opened the door to her continued lecture.

"You gotta bad habit of swooping the fuck in, rescuing a damsel who can fucking take care of her damn self."

Jesus...the balls on this woman.

"Mm hm." I agreed, grabbing her hand and half-dragging her to the front desk of what I only then realized was the most expensive hotel in town.

Just perfect.

"I'll need a room for a couple of nights," I said, noting Lila's eyes widening in outrage.

"Wait." Lila snapped, her eyes laser-focused on the scrawny, pimple-faced kid working the front desk night shift. "No way am I staying a—"

"Listen, honey," I cut her off with a glare, half-whispering so the kid behind the counter wouldn't think I kidnapped her. "I know you didn't want to stay here that long, but better safe than sorry." I kept my face neutral, but Jesus, this woman was a tantrum wrapped in a snackable ass, and those fiery eyes were sinking their claws deep. "It's fine. I'll grab the room for a few nights, and if we don't need it for that long, you can check us out tomorrow." I released her and reached into my pocket. "Why don't you get our bags?"

I dangled my keys at her and sighed with relief when she yanked them from my hand and stormed out the door, undoubtedly to steal my car.

"Um, sir?" The kid behind the counter pulled me away from watching her fine ass stomp away. "Here's your room keys, and," he leaned forward and whispered, "Good luck. When my wife is that angry, I usually end up sleeping on the couch."

I couldn't hide my shit-eating grin that this scrawny guy had a wife—good for him.

"She's not half as pissed as she'll be when she realizes I handed her the house keys and not the car keys."

7

SAM

I WALKED OUT TO her leaning against my SUV, shooting angry daggers from those gorgeous eyes.

"You're a real asshole, you know that?"

"So, we've moved past Lumberjack and Jackass," I smiled, calmly holding out my hand to her. "Glad you've broadened your vocabulary."

"I'm not fucking taking your hand." She sneered, eyebrow cocked into a fucking hot arch that sent lightning straight to my balls.

"Keys...." I cocked up an eyebrow of my own as she reared back to throw the keys at me when again her foot slipped, and she fell...right into my arms.

Easy as breathing.

I tossed her, kicking and screaming, over my shoulder–my inner caveman grunting approval at the capture of a lifetime–Hellcat. Even as the feeling came, I reasoned out the unsustainability of it all. I didn't want one-night stands anymore. I was done with all that fucking around.

43

She was temporary; I was not.

She was passing through. This town was my world.

Was she hot as fuck when mad? Yes.

Did that change the fact that she lied and had more issues than the New York Times? No.

It was time to cut and run. If my dick had eyes, I'm pretty sure it rolled them at me.

To her credit, Lila never stopped ranting curses at me up to the third floor, down the corridor, and into the room. Her vocabulary was filthy, but extensive, and cut short only by the huff of air when I flipped her unceremoniously onto the bed.

"Are you done yelling at me now?" I didn't bother hiding the growl in my voice. "'Cause your little Hellcat routine was cute at first, but frankly, you're making my ears hurt, and I'm pretty sure the people in the next county can hear your foul mouth."

"Don't. Call. Me. Hellcat." Lila emphasized every word by wriggling herself into standing up on the bed, putting us eye to eye.

If my irritation wasn't so high, the move would've been adorable as she attempted to level the playing field between us. I should've left her then, having secured her a safe landing for the night, but damn if pushing her buttons wasn't my new favorite hobby.

"You know, most women would be thrilled with a guy willing to foot the bill for a nice hotel...maybe a little gratitude would be nice to sprinkle in between the screaming curses."

"Yeah, well, assuming I was like most women was your first mistake, Jackass."

Oh, yay, Jackass is back.

"What the hell do you expect me to do now that you've kidnapped me, trapped me here with no car and no purse..." The effort to stand on the wobbly mattress put her slightly out of breath, and her chest heaved so close to my face that I could have buried myself in her tits. Instead, to answer her accusation, I whipped out my cell phone and began dialing. "What are you doing now...who are you calling?"

"Shhhh...sweetheart," I raised my finger and the most patronizing whisper I could muster. "Daddy's making a phone call."

I knew it would piss her off...I wanted it to piss her off... but I was wearing thin trying to hold back how much she turned me on.

"Making a phone ca - DADDY! "I silenced her with a swift shift of my hand over her mouth.

"Marge...yeah, it's Sam," I said into the phone, seeing Lila's eyes roll. "Yeah, I know... I'm sorry. I got her a hotel room, but we left her purse behind." Marge confirmed she already put it behind the bar and would hold it for her, which I expected. "You're the best. I'll swing by and pay for any damages." Marge ended our call by reminding me I left my tab open, and she'd be buying rounds to offset her irritation until I got back.

Just awesome.

"See," I removed my hand from Lila's mouth and lifted my arms in surrender, trying to gain composure and self-control with a half-step backwards. "I'm not trying to fuck you over. But I meant what I said." Lowering my hands, I noticed how she glared, her breath whooshing in and out in deep huffs. "You drank too much. You had no business driving. I don't budge on safety."

I could see the moment her anger cooled, tugging her bottom lip between her teeth as if considering my words, and fucking hell, did I want to suck on that lip.

"You can stay here and sleep it off." I lifted her cell phone from my back pocket and let her see me place it on the bedside. "Your phone is here. When you wake up in the morning, you can call an Uber back to

Marge's. She's there at 11 to set up and will come to the front door if you ring the bell twice."

Lila watched me for a brief second, and a quick exit suddenly felt possible, and more disappointing than it should have been.

"Thank fuck, she sees reason," I mumbled in resignation.

Then her eyes narrowed, shoulders squared–Oh shit, spoke too soon.

"So, I'm stuck here paying for an Uber while you leave as you please, and I'm supposed to what...*swoon* with appreciation?" Her anger rubbed at the last shred of control. Mentally, I counted down to keep my shit together while watching her fiery eyes blaze.

10, 9...

"God forbid you acknowledge you needed a little help back there," I growled at the memory of the guy's hand sliding to her ass. "I wouldn't have taken a swing at the guy if you hadn't thrown yourself at him."

8,7,6...

"So it's MY fault I wanted to have some fun?!" She roared. "The fuck do you care if I find a willing dick to blow off some steam?! Lemme guess, *you* get to fuck anything you want while *I* play nun...that it, Jackass?!"

5, 4, 3...

"I don't give a goddamn red cent who you fuck or don't fuck. But if you're with me, you sure as shit aren't rubbing up on other guys like a Hellcat in heat!" I stepped to the edge of the bed, using every ounce of restraint not to reach out and grab her.

2...

"And who," She lowered her voice to a whisper and leaned in, nose to nose, as she punched her finger into my chest, "said I," She stepped to the edge of the bed, her body shaking as her heels wobbled.

One more word and I'm gone—or I'm gone in her.
"Was with you."
Snap.

8

SAM

I PULLED LILA INTO me so fast she latched onto my shoulders to keep from falling. Before so much as a hint of venom could slip out, I claimed her lips with a boiling desire as the taste of bourbon filled my mouth. Reaching my free hand around her hips, I squeezed her ass until she relaxed into me on a moan, eagerly sucking on my lips and tongue.

That submission melted my inner turmoil away. One night or not, I had to have her.

I might have kissed her for hours, but she tossed off her coat and yanked at mine. My hands found the edge of her shirt, lifting it over her head as her hair came cascading down her dark, honey-brown shoulders. Getting to see those gorgeous tits spilling over the top of a barely-there lacy bra became the high point of my life.

My dick nearly leapt from my pants and offered itself as tribute.

Burying my face in the cleft of her hot mounds, I reveled in kissing, nipping, and sucking from one barely exposed nipple to the other.

Pulling her bra down, I swirled my tongue around the outer edge of her nipple before sucking hard enough to earn another gasping moan.

So damn responsive.

I popped the clasp of her bra and pulled back to take in the sight of her.

"Look at those perfect tits." My mouth watered as I stared my fill, and I swear if I were a drowning man, her tits would be the air I begged for. Removing my shirt and stepping back into her waiting arms, I let my hands carry the weight of her breasts.

"You gonna admire my boobs all night?" She mumbled into my mouth, tugging my hair, sending a sting rushing down my spine. "Or are you gonna do something about that raging hard-on...Jackass."

"Fucking hell, woman," I growled, grabbing the back of her knees and pulling her legs into the air so she plopped on the bed with a yelp. "Do you ever stop sassing?" I trailed kisses up from the edge of her jeans, back between her breasts until I reached the soft skin just below her ear, where I growled. "Or did you hope to make this a hard, angry fuck?" I ground my cock against her core, and she shivered beneath me, gasping and panting, and holy hell, her arousal was intoxicating.

I damn near came in my pants like a prepubescent asshole at the smell of her want.

"You better fuck as good a game as you talk, Lumberjack."

Laughing, I trailed kisses down until my teeth snagged the zipper of her jeans. With a slow tug, I dragged it down, inhaling more of her intoxicating scent–earth and jasmine and a tang of want that shot straight to my balls. I couldn't wait to be inside her.

Grabbing the waist of her jeans, I yanked them down until they bunched just below her knees.

"Wait, my boots." She panted

"Leave 'em on," I commanded, flipping her onto her belly. "You'll need the traction."

Slapping her ass, I pulled her back off the edge of the bed, wedging my feet between hers until the tension of her jeans locked her legs into position. Sliding a hand around, I slipped one finger between her folds and found her dripping, swollen, and ready.

"Oh God, Sam."

My name on her lips was a goddamn firing pistol.

"You are a needy little thing, aren't you?" I bent her over the bed, gripping her hips and squeezing. The heat coming off her pussy, my new drug.

"Condom!" She yelped, her body tensing.

"Never leave home without 'em," I growled, ripping the condom from my back pocket and sliding the head of my wrapped cock against her even as I rolled it to the base.

"What a wet little hellcat you are."

She lifted at the use of my new favorite nickname and tossed her head back, sending that wild hair splaying across her back. I eased my tip into her, then pulled back to graze her clit before slipping the first inch back inside. She tried to push against me, arching her back and angling her hips to draw me deeper, but I gripped her hips.

"Nuh-uh, Hellcat. I've been wanting to do this ever since you first grazed that fine ass against me earlier tonight." I gave her another inch. "I'm gonna take my time and savor it."

Sliding another inch, then another, her cunt squeezed around me, and it was the sweetest feeling in the world. Every inch back and forth drew out more moans, more gasps, and the most magnificent little whimpers. I was dying to rearrange her lungs, but her noises sounded good enough to delay gratification longer than I would've thought possible. Finally balls-deep, I let one hand slide up to her shoulder, stilling for one final moment.

"Let me know if I get too rough with you, baby." She could only half glance over her shoulder before I pulled out and slammed to the hilt in one sweeping motion.

"Fuck!" Lila screamed, her walls quivering around me. "Yes!"

Shoving in again and again, I watched as every thrust sent ripples of tension waving across her perfect cheeks. I held her shoulders for leverage, smirking when her arms gave out and she fell against the bed. The new angle felt amazing, but having her moans buried in the blanket wouldn't do. Sliding my hand around the front of her, I pulled her up against my body, keeping my cock buried as I shifted us both up towards the headboard.

"Hold on, Hellcat." She gripped the railing of the headboard as I settled my knees outside of hers, pressing her thighs together.

Moving more slowly, I groaned at the way the new angle squeezed her tighter around my cock, teasing us both until Lila pulled at my hips, needing more, and I felt like a damned sex god. When I finally set about slamming into her over and over, she sounded feral. Lila tried using the headboard as leverage to buck against me, but the brutal force of my thrusts had her barely holding on.

"Fuck, Sam, Oh god." Her walls fluttered around me, and the sound of her voice calling my name would haunt me for the rest of my days—each breathless hitch that escaped her perfect lips—music to my ears.

"Need me faster, deeper, or harder?" I asked, slowing my pace to let her catch her breath.

Her moans turned to whimpers, but she never answered—just wiggled that fine ass against me in a tempting plea. Slowing a little more, I held deep, but barely grazed her inner walls. My balls screamed in protest, but I loved the growing frustration in her too much to yield. She grunted, pressing and releasing her muscles around me, but I gave her nothing to work with as we all but stilled.

Denying this brat an orgasm for no other reason than to show her who was boss was fan-fucking-tastic.

"I need an answer, Hellcat." I twitched my cock for added incentive and slowly slid back as if to leave her wanting.

"No." She reached a hand back to my thigh, nails scratching to pull me back in. "No, please. Don't stop." I pinned her between me and the headboard, locking her into place with my legs. She would get no pleasure until I decided to give it to her, but fuck if those nails dragging me to her didn't set my blood on fire.

She needed me as bad as I wanted her, and that was everything.

"Come on, baby." I grazed my beard against her ear. "Use your words." Sliding a hand around, I pressed my fingers against her mound, knowing the pressure would drive her wild. "Tell me what you need."

My balls pulled tight, barely holding on, when she mercifully groaned an answer.

"Harder...God, please. Fuck me hard. Make me cum." I could almost hear a tear in her voice before I drifted a hand into her hair and gently pulled her face back to me.

"Good girl." I swallowed her moan as I pinched her clit and snapped my hips forward.

Slamming into her again, and again, alternating long, punishing thrusts with pressing the outer edges of her swollen clit, I made her walls clench, and her screaming climax pushed me right over the edge. Roaring to a finish, I thrust a final penetrating jerk before my head fell against her shoulder, riding the aftershocks as she milked me dry.

"I thought you would never answer me," I muttered with a shit-eating grin on my face. "You...are such a brat, Hellcat."

"Just not your brat." She answered with a breathy laugh. "Jackass."

WILDER FAMILY GROUP CHAT

-1-

Chase: APB, guys.

Troy: What's the emergency?

Moira: NOT an emergency… geez.

Chase: We're almost out of diapers. It is an emergency.

Troy: You realize it's after midnight, right?

Moira: Sorry, Troy. I tried to stop him.

Troy: My dear sister, the only voice of reason.

Chase: HOW do two babies go through so many diapers?

Troy: I see my nights will be sleepless too, thanks to my nieces.

Moira: We got this. Ignore Chase. He's spiraling.

Chase: It's like 2 an hour. DO THE MATH.

Troy: Deep breath, brother.

Chase: That's 48 in a day! We'll be out by this time tomorrow night!

Moira: I'm taking his phone away.

Troy: Bless you, good woman.

Chase: Where's Sam...he'll understand.

9

LILA

*"D*AD...DADDY.... DADDY....No, no, no....STAY, daddy, STAY!"

I woke up the same way every day since the funeral: Sweating, heart racing, with tear-stained cheeks and a cold, damp pillow. I lingered there, eyes shut, to practice breathing as instructed. As if breathing exercises would do anything beyond giving me an excuse to wallow in bed–remembering I was here, and they weren't.

Therapy was crap.

My captain forced me to see the shrink, hoping I'd find courage to keep existing. Box breathing couldn't undo watching your family die in the line of duty. It's why I stopped going to the shrink after two obligatory sessions.

Groggy, I lifted my head to look down and find myself neatly tucked under the covers...naked. The man from the night before, Sam...his name was Sam, must have covered me before leaving.

Descent of him.

I slept hard, nightmare be damned, and my body let me know precisely how heavily with each achy throb. The sunlight blaring through a crack in the curtains felt like the spotlight of God. I squinted around the room until I found my cell on the nightstand along with a travel packet of aspirin, a bottle of water, and a note that read, 'You're going to need both of these, Hellcat.'

Fucking do-gooder lumberjack, and that goddamn nickname ta-boot.

My memories of the night weren't gone, just fuzzy. I remembered getting into town late, hitting up the first bar I found, and drinking.

Some guy made a lame ass move.

The do-gooder cut him off.

He was hot and genuinely seemed like a nice guy. He tried to keep his hands to himself at first, but damn me and my fucking warped brain. The more he kept his hands clean, the harder I tried to wear him down.

More booze, a little grazing, a little flirting.

I picked a fight.

I didn't know territorial pissing contests would trigger Sam's particular brand of machismo. Still, I aimed for a reaction, and well...punching a guy across the room was a reaction.

Things got a little hazy after that, but I recalled being bodily tossed around like a sack of potatoes, then thrown against the headboard and fucked until I saw stars. Reaching for the bottle of water, a flash of soreness brought vivid pictures of how hard Sam railed me.

Holy hell, could that man lay pipe.

He was a fucking savage in bed, and I loved it. Intense but unhurried; focused, but not selfish. He dropped me, flipped me, pounded me, moved me, and gloriously rutted into me like he won me at the fair.

Stretching, I smiled at the tight muscles in my lower back and my achy hips.

After our first round, he cleaned us both up, laid me back, stripped my boots off, and feasted on my pussy until I begged for mercy before he took me a second time. That last climax exhausted me to the point of losing all measure of common sense and passing out with a stranger still in my bed. I mentally chastised myself for the poor judgment of that one as I stood to take a shower, noting with relief the two discarded condoms tied off in the trash can.

At least one of us responsibly adulted last night.

Then I remembered I had no clothes, no jeep, no purse, and grimaced. Grabbing my phone, I checked the time, trying to remember the name of the bar. It was nearly 1 o'clock, but maybe it served lunch? Surfing my memories, I could see the bartender's face...weathered, but kind.

Was it named after her? Barbs? Or Darla's? Hollys?

I waded through everything while I put on my clothes. Grabbing my phone and hotel room key, I went down to the front desk to see if the manager could help jog my memory.

"Good afternoon, ma'am." Said a chipper girl behind the counter. "Can I help you?"

"Yeah, I checked in late last night and -" she cut me off before I could finish my question.

"Room number?" She started typing on her screen, then stared at me for an answer. I glanced at the card in my hand, grateful the room number was written on it with a marker.

"312," I answered. "And I wondered - "Ms. Chipper cut me off again as she eagerly tapped her nail against the computer monitor.

"Ah, yes, your husband came by earlier and left your bag. I'll grab it for you."

She flitted off before I could ask the obvious question: What husband?

Then I recalled Sam half-dragging me here, pretending we were a couple and not some caveman with a drunk hellcat. Then I remembered his little trick with the keys, and again, he threw me over his shoulder and hoisted me up three flights of stairs.

My irritation with the man was rising sharply when the woman returned.

"Here you are." She handed over my purse, my duffle bag, and my laptop bag.

"Thanks," I mumbled, wondering how he got all my stuff as I rummaged through my purse and found my Jeep keys. Walking outside, I pressed the door lock button a few times before the lights flashed and the horn beeped–my car waving from the far end of the lot. Slightly mollified, I returned to my room and checked my belongings, finding everything intact. Relief, tinged with regret, settled in my chest.

I'd used a decent man as a quick lay and a distraction.

Pushing it aside, I stripped for the longest shower of my life in a bathroom far nicer than anything I'd ever seen. Standing in the heat and steam, I began filling in the gaps on all my poor decisions from the previous night, starting with how long I drove despite being exhausted. Followed immediately by letting a guy put me up in a fancy hotel like a whore.

My big brother's voice echoed in my head, *'dammit, Lil D...you know better. What the hell are you doing?'*

Flashes came like snapshots on shuffle.

I saw all the million happy times my brother and I shared. Like when I joined the force and we celebrated at the same cop bar our Dad had once celebrated with him. Then my traitorous lock-trap photographic memory flashed darker.

Dad shot down, splayed across the concrete.

My brother, reaching, blood seeping from his nose and his mouth as he tried to speak.

Me...floating above their death...watching myself scream, and scream, and scream.

I'm not sure when I sat down, nor how long I rode the merry-go-round of despair, but shivers of icy cold water cleared the fog. Crawling up the wall from my huddle on the floor, my legs throbbed with pins and needles as the last of the water went down the drain.

I let my pain go with it.

There was work to do.

Stepping in front of the mirror, I used my finger on the steamed glass to draft my to-dos.

Set up tech.

Connect with the cop.

Connect dots to Brinks.

Burn motherfucker to the ground.

A cheerier checklist never existed.

Rummaging through my duffel, I threw on fresh clothes and headed to my Jeep, grabbing the boxes of extra laptops and files stowed beneath the rear bench. Carrying them back in, little Miss Chipper cleared her throat with pointed force.

"Ma'am.... Ma'am?" I paused and propped my box on the desk with an audible huff. "I um..."

"These ain't getting any lighter, ya know." I gestured to the boxes balanced between the counter and my hip, irritated at the delay and her hesitation.

"Right," she said apologetically. "It's just that, well, your husband called and instructed me to extend your room to the end of the week while he was...away on business? But said if you needed it longer than that, you'd need to," she leaned in and whispered, "use your own card." So many thoughts flew through my mind as her shameful little secret sank in.

This ain't the dark ages.

Why would my using my own card need whispering?

And why would the do-gooder pay for a week after a one-night stand?

I never told him I planned to stay...did he want a repeat performance?

I sure as shit ain't a high-paid call girl in need of a keeping!

"Ma'am?" The woman cleared her throat to catch my attention again. "Did you want to set a check-out date now, or did you want to put another card on file? For incidentals...that is?"

"Incidentals?"

"Yes, ma'am. Room service, laundry service, things like that." Miss Chipper suddenly sparked a wicked idea.

I didn't know where this guy got the idea that I was staying, nor did I care to ask him, but if he wanted to throw his card down on a gamble that I might offer a repeat performance, then I might as well teach him a lesson about assumptions.

"I'll be checked out by the end of the week. No additional card will be needed," I answered with a smile. "What time does the kitchen close?"

"Our full kitchen is open til 10 pm; after that, we have a limited menu of drinks and cocktails, and whatever food items are in our Guest Service store." She gestures to a small bodega-looking area in the corner of the lobby.

"Excellent." I grabbed the boxes and added. "Can you have laundry come to my room and grab some things for me while I order room service? And send up a selection of snacks and beverages from the store as well. Just add it to my husband's card." I flashed a wide, toothy smile as I toted my things to the elevator, practically twirling the evil mustache in my mind.

If he thought he could afford another ride, I would make it hurt.

10

SAM

R EACHING BLINDLY TO MY bedside, I flopped my hand around to
silence the annoying sound of my morning alarm. Unable to find
it, I cracked an eye open to see my living room...not my bedroom.

Nice job, dumbass. You drank so much you couldn't make it to bed.

Still fumbling to shut off the god-forsaken techno-noise, I contemplated being too old for this shit, as my head pounded, and my mouth
tasted like something died in it. My guts rolled like I'd guzzled a vat of
grease alongside the...how many pints?

Standing to stretch, my muscles pulled as if I'd completed a fresh
workout at the gym. Moreover, my right hand throbbed. Looking down,
I saw tell-tale purple splotches blooming across my knuckles, and the
embarrassment of clarity washed over me.

How long had it been since I'd started a bar fight?

Shaking my head at my stupidity, I grabbed ice from the freezer,
rolled it into a dish towel, and wrapped it around my fist. Resting the

cooling hand against my forehead, I chugged some juice out of the fridge and noted the clock. My shift started at 8 am, and even though I had 2 hours to go, I was moving way too slowly for a full workout. Still, I needed to clear my head, so I opted for a quick run to burn off the haze. Changing clothes, I replayed my evening, like a laundry list of bad decisions.

Shouldn't have drunk when I was so tired.

Shouldn't have bothered with shit-fisted Carl.

Shouldn't have started at pool and that gorgeous mess of a woman.

Shouldn't have cold-cocked some guy out of a misguided sense of what...jealousy?

Definitely shouldn't have taken her to that hotel and...

Nope. I could second-guess a lot of choices last night, but I couldn't bring myself to regret a single second of bedding that fiery goddess. Our time together played through my mind like a movie as I ran—her tipsy smile that made her eyes sparkle, her wild hair fisted in my hands, that luscious ass bouncing as I pounded into her. The glance I allowed myself when I brought her things to the front desk, sneaking up to check on her, laying out painkillers and water, was painfully etched in memory. It all made my pulse race a little faster, which didn't help my run. Hell, even her voice as she begged me to fuck her harder got me a little lightheaded from the sudden rush of blood to my groin.

She was the wildest thing I'd seen in...ever?

The wintery air burned off my hangover as I rounded back to my street, finding my brother on my porch, fresh mug of coffee in hand.

Steady, unflappable Troy.

"Morning, Brother." He stood, offering the mug. "Thought you might need a little help this morning." Troy didn't just look awake—he looked... prepped. Posture perfect. Shirt crisp. Clean-shaved head polished to a shine and goatee in sharp relief, like he just walked out of a military recruitment ad.

"Yeah..." I panted, pacing in circles with my hands on my head before taking the cup. "Thanks."

"From the smell of you, it would seem you also need something to soak up the rest of the booze." He turned toward my door. "Any chance you have anything remotely edible?"

Troy had a way of making you straighten up—even when your body begged to lie down.

It was no surprise that Troy knew what happened at Scaled Back last night. His intuition seemed otherworldly at times. I used to think it was a cop thing, but lately, I wasn't so sure. If Chase and I both had layers...surely the walking monolith did too. Either way, my nosey-ass brother made a damn good detective, and I was in no mood to be grilled.

"The maid doesn't stock the fridge until Wednesdays." I snarked, hoping to hasten the point of his visit. Unnervingly attentive, Troy didn't typically interfere in our lives as adults. Still, there were times he'd interject himself, and it was almost always annoyingly helpful if not terribly timed. I prepared for one of his lectures about the bar fight, but he just walked into my house and headed for the kitchen.

"Hm." Troy shut the fridge and returned to where I lay splayed out on the couch. "Dear God, you are sweating all over the leather." He slapped my foot, nudging me off the couch. "Hit the shower. I have time to grab a bite with you before that damned town committee meeting...but make it quick."

"Jesus, TJ." I groaned off the couch, my limbs sludging through mud. "Why are you here?"

Breakfast sounded wholly unappealing, but I couldn't deny my unsettled stomach needed something.

"With barely 3 hours sleep to spare, the man-child denies a free breakfast?" He mocked, eyebrow raised. "You're getting too old to party like that."

"Yeah, yeah," I headed towards my room, flipping him the bird. "Last night kinda got away from me."

I spent most of my perfunctory shower eyeing the bruised knuckles with frustration at my juvenile actions. Annoyed that somewhere out there, the fiery goddess I left naked in a hotel suite was probably plotting my death—or my return.

Or had she put me entirely in her rearview?

Shaking it off, I dressed quickly, grabbed my gear, and followed Troy to a diner in town that served decent pancakes.

"Ugh," I leaned against the empty coffee mug. "I think Marge poured triples."

"Now now," Troy said, his tone setting up one of our Nonna's sayings. "She poured...you drank. Let's not blame the bartender for the sitting fool's thirst."

Yep...there it was.

"Heard from Chase?" I asked as the waitress filled our cups.

"Only the midnight panic about diapers...while still in a hospital full of diapers." Troy smiled over the rim of his coffee mug. "Our nieces are draining his cool already."

"Damn," I glanced at my phone, only then realizing I'd missed an entire family text interchange. "Need me to run some to the house? I got time."

"I have it in hand." Troy waved a hand at me. "Besides, they haven't left the hospital yet, and you will need to get to work a little early today to get *that* looked at."

I cocked an eyebrow in question at his meaning until I noted his gaze falling on my colorful knuckles.

"It's nothing," I dropped my hand to my lap and attempted to side-step interrogation with a subject sure to draw him away from my misstep. "Any updates on Apex or Jensen?"

Dean Jensen was the monumental asshole who tried to kill both Chase and Moira. Her several times over. His coma, courtesy of my sister's badassery, spared him a trial, but he drew breath. None of us loved that. We'd learned his attorney worked with a group calling themselves The Apex Society, some supposed humanitarian brotherhood bent on 'Bettering the world by fostering confident leaders.' At least that was the generic bullshit their propaganda shoveled. Troy's specialist, on loan from NYC, was recalled before finding more for us, but his Captain met with Chase's fire chief, and everyone agreed there was more here than what was advertised. Troy was given unofficial approval to conduct research within the boundaries of legal searching. The latter a pointless distinction since Troy never did anything that wasn't strictly by the book.

The man practically oozed hall monitor.

"The law firm that Jensen's attorney worked for declined to comment on his employment status, making me think he no longer works there." Troy's irritation was palpable. "While I haven't seen anything about him visiting Jensen in the hospital, I also can't locate him."

"So, he's in the wind?"

"I'm now working on the angle of our small-town administration, hoping our real estate and family goodwill can provide more information. I want to know why Apex is at our doorstep."

"You mean the library donation Moira mentioned?" I asked, remembering the day the library caught fire, and Chase came unhinged about his feelings for his wife, leading to a second proposal and a grand romantic wedding so sweet it made my teeth hurt.

"If the Apex is all about fostering leadership," Troy spat the last part out like he'd tasted something rotten, "then what possible interest could they have in Jensen, his questionable attorney, and our Library, or," he leaned forward and lowered his voice, "the four other local businesses I've connected Apex to."

"No shit?" I motioned for the check.

"Zero shits." Troy agreed. "The Board of Education reported a sizeable donation to the high school, earmarked for after-school programs to underprivileged boys needing career guidance."

"Noble..." I let the word trail off, knowing a program like that would be received with positivity around town.

"On paper." Troy agreed. "They have also begun to pay the back taxes on local establishments."

"Well, those two dots don't connect at all."

"Indeed. However, if the county allows Apex to pay back taxes, they could use it as leverage to force cheap sales."

"The fuck?" I said, shaking my head at how nefariously random it seemed. "They could take people's businesses from them?"

"A small-town hostile takeover."

"Which businesses?" I shuddered to think what poor sap was being bullied by shady New York City misogynists.

"That's my main reason for visiting you this morning." Troy handed his credit card to the server. "One of the ones on the list is Scaled Back."

11

SAM

"**M**ARGE'S PLACE?" I ASKED incredulously. "You gotta be kidding me." Even as I spoke the words, I remembered her chat with the guy in a suit last night and her request, 'I could use some of your other expertise, Sammy. Got time to chat with me...'

"I figured you'd want to know." Troy stood, and we headed towards the door. "I'll let you know what I find out."

"Margie asked me to come see her...what are the chances it's about the same thing?"

"Depends," Troy slid his aviators on with a smirk, "Did she ask before or after you knocked a man across the bar?"

"Quit busting my balls, Grandpa." I mocked. "The guy had it coming."

"No doubt, Brother," Troy called across our cars before adding. "And I feel it's prudent to keep this between us for now. Chase has his hands quite literally full."

I nodded in agreement.

"Moira doesn't need the worry either, and fuck knows Boyscout can't keep a secret."

"It's kinda magical, isn't it?" Troy said with a distant smile.

"Yeah," I mumbled, wondering if Troy longed for a family too. "Think we'll ever have that?"

"You first." Troy joked as he got in his car. "That is, if you ever quit chasing tail in bars."

Flipping Troy the bird, I headed into the ambulance station for my shift, thinking about Marge and her request. She'd never asked for anything. She once bartended with a broken arm for a month without complaint—so how did I not see her request for my expertise as a huge red flag?

Because your dick drove the bus, idiot.

I shoved down the memories of that wild, fiery goddess flashing through me once more and strolled into the ambulance bay, waving at the guys tasked with washing one of the rigs in the frigid morning temperatures.

"Crew Chief." One of the new probies handed me a report. "Here's last night's logs."

"Thanks." I scanned the clipboard – a bathroom fall, a domestic disturbance, and a crank 911 call from a party. "Pretty slow. Nice." I grabbed the binder for the coming month from the desk. "Maybe today we jump into the administrative bullshit and see if we can knock it out early this quarter."

"Want me to grab the guys...team briefing time?" the probie asked, his enthusiasm annoyingly effective.

I liked the kids' go-getter attitude, so I scheduled him as my second whenever possible. I sent him to gather everyone in the kitchen, which served as a de facto conference room.

"Quiet night means you should've all had some good shuteye. Those of you on the last few hours of your shift, focus on vehicle maintenance and then go home." The two men to my left high-fived the cushy assignment. "I'll handle the equipment checks on my own," I continue, "Leaving probie to handle scut."

The room erupted in teasing barbs for the new kid, who tried to conceal his notable disdain behind a resigned smile. Paperwork, incident reports, and compliance regulations were, by and large, the most tedious tasks assigned. However, they gave the new kid a chance to get a handle on call codes and information flow.

I ended the meeting by showing off my new nieces to the crew until their eyerolls and teasing laughs gained legs. Once everyone scattered, I palmed the tablet housing our equipment logs and began the mundane task of inventory. A mindless task, but it kept me from thinking about a wild-haired woman in a hotel bed with my name on it. Determined to forget her, I immersed myself in my task and lost track of time. Looking up again at noon, I remembered I promised Marge I'd come before opening. I couldn't leave the station a man short, and I'd already sent the other two guys home. I reached for my phone to call Marge, but my boss entered the supply room.

"Yo, Wilder." John, my Supervisor, greeted me with an easy smile as he leaned against the door. "You realize it's barely the beginning of the month and you got the whole station handling red tape like it's the last day and the pope's coming?"

"I'm not your favorite for nothing," I smirked.

"The fuck happened to your hand?" He grabbed my tablet, and I couldn't hide the audible hiss when he squeezed my knuckles. "You get that looked at?"

"It's fine." I willed my voice into boredom to mask my rising embarrassment. "Bruised at best."

"Screw that. Let's see what the machine says." My boss walked off as if the conversation was final, and I followed him like a chump. Strolling into the ambulance bay, he yanked out the portable ultrasound machine and dropped a blob of goo on my hand. "Hold still, kid."

With no small amount of pressure, he rolled the wand around my knuckles.

"I'm 100% fine." My wince belied my words as he pressed into my knuckles.

"Shut it. You see here." He pointed to the screen and the fluid around the middle joint. "Your metacarpophalangeal joint is a fucking mess."

"Really... we're using the big words now?" I teased, trying to sidestep his next question.

"4th and 5th carpels too. Maybe a boxer's fracture. The hell you hit?" He asked, cleaning and reseating the machine on the rig. I contemplated the odds that anything I said would appease him and decided a redacted delivery of the truth was my best bet.

"I was at a bar last night; this guy got handsy with a woman." I tried to look disinterested despite my growing urge to see if she was still in town.

"That's it?"

"That's it."

"She your woman?" his question caught me off guard, and I knew by the way he shook his head at me that my face gave me away.

I should have stopped talking.

I should have played it off.

Then again, if last night established anything, it was that I was an idiot.

"Just a chick I met last night. We played pool, a guy got grabby, that's it." I returned my attention to the tablet in my hand and grumbled, "I iced it, I'm taking anti-inflammatories, I'm *fine*."

"I've known you since you were the green probie, excited to wash all the rigs in below-freezing temps just to impress me." He thumped a finger in the middle of my chest, and I started to wonder if there was a target there. "You trying to tell me you walloped a guy so hard your hand looks like it found the wrong side of a brick wall...over a random piece of ass." I had to count past my temper...again.

Yes, that's what I was saying.

Could we please ignore my flawless lack of judgment?

Oh, and I'll wallop you too if you call her a random piece of ass one more time!

Thankfully...none of those things fell from my mouth.

"Look... we're overstaffed today. I'm here. You're off." My boss yanked the tablet from my hand, brooking no protest. "Take a few days, let the hand heal, check back on Wednesday, and if I decide you're fit for duty, I'll let you run the rig through the weekend."

I wanted to argue, but then I remembered I owed Marge a visit. I also remembered I was fucking exhausted, and my hand throbbed like a son of a bitch.

"If it's worse tomorrow, get an X-ray," he added as I grabbed my gear. "Don't be a hero."

With a nod and a goodbye to the crew, I headed to Scaled Back.

12

SAM

I ARRIVED AT MARGE'S a little after one. Walking through the front door to find Marge watching TV and stocking glasses in the otherwise empty bar.

"Hey kid, thanks for coming by." Marge's gravelly voice, courtesy of years slinging booze in a smoke-filled room, was oddly comforting.

"Sorry, I'm late," I strolled the length of the bar to my usual stool. "I had a shift, but ended up getting a few days off." Waving my bandaged hand with an eye roll, Marge gave a low whistle.

"You sure as shit sent that guy flying." She poured a shot of vodka and rounded to sit in the seat next to me. "He must've had a concrete jaw."

"Something like that," I grumbled.

"You get that girl her purse?" Marge gave a wry smile, pouring a second vodka. I just nodded, offering no further fuel for that little jest.

"No booze for me, I'm still paying for last night." I raised my hands in surrender. "What's going on, Margie-girl?"

"This," She slugged back the second shot, "Is also for me. I got a sad tale to tell."

Marge drank two more shots while recounting an almost year-long financial battle.

First, her tax returns were incorrect, then auditors found discrepancies in her receipts and logs, then an accountant filed the wrong reports but swore he'd filed the correct ones. One turn of bad luck after another culminated in tax debt totaling just over $100,000.

"Some big corporation offered to pay my debts, buy me out, and take over Scaled Back." She ended her story with a glassy sheen of tears in her eyes. "The suit last night has been here a few other times, making offers, but I'm running out of time."

"You had no clue anything was wrong until a year ago," I summarized to clarify my understanding. "Just suddenly got a tax bill, penalties, fees, and a year's worth of time lost and fuck all?"

"I love this place, Sammy. I opened it when I was younger than you even. Been running it my whole life," Marge confessed, her eyes wandering over the still-empty room. The bar was not just a business to her, but a part of her life. She slugged another shot and slammed the glass on the bartop. "And I could lose her to some shark making an offer so low-ball it's beyond ridiculous. I'd hardly be able to move, much less retire."

"Damn, Margie." I wanted to reassure her, but even I knew she was shadowboxing at best.

Troy followed up on the tiniest of Apex leads in a million different directions. But reality was, we only felt there was a nefarious connection to all this because of what happened to Moira. Not something I could share with Marge, and not concrete. Not yet, at least.

I tried to pivot the conversation.

"You said you needed my expertise?" I nudged her shoulder with mine, trying to convey confidence and comfort. "I'm just an EMT, so I'm not sure how much help, but I'm here."

"You might've been 'just an EMT' years ago, but don't think you've fooled me, Sam Wilder." She tugged at my beard. "You and your brothers have been flipping real estate all over town. Turning a tidy profit, ta-boot." She then gave my cheek a playful slap. "And before you try to deny your success, I'll remind you that you waltzed in last night and threw down an Amex, buying rounds for the whole fucking bar."

I cringed.

"An Amex *Black*, to be specific." She added, tapping her nose, which had a knack for sniffing out money. "Those ain't the moves of a man living on a civil servant's salary."

"Jesus, don't remind me." I groaned, running my hand through my hair and then down my beard. "Any chance that tab got shut down when I left?"

Reaching over the bartop, she pulled out my card and a receipt so long it could have doubled as a scarf.

"Better if you don't look, kid. Just sign the bottom." Groaning, I signed the slip and vowed never to waltz into a place shouting 'free drinks' ever again. "I need you to see what you can find out...behind the scenes. I'm hitting a brick wall and can't get good information, and I know my place is worth way more than this faceless giant is offering me, but I need proof. Every time I try to call, I get the run-around, and everyone who calls me puts more pressure on me to sell." She slammed her hand on the bar. "I *can't* have my place stolen out from under me, Sam...I *won't*!"

"Whoa, hey," I rested my hands on top of hers, hurting for the anger rolling down her cheeks. "The good thing is, if you are paying anything, the IRS should work with you. You can't be forced to sell to a third party...not yet. All they can do is make you miserable, right?" I hoped I was giving her accurate information, but my gut told me this was so much bigger than Marge's bar. "In the meantime, I'll see what I can find out."

"Thanks, kiddo." She wiped her eyes, poured another shot, and slid it over to me. "Don't let an old woman drink alone... it's tacky."

I winked over the rim of the glass before shooting it back as a couple of truckers walked in the front door.

"Duty calls," Marge spun on her stool, but I grabbed her arm to offer up a warning that I prayed was unnecessary.

"One more thing," I lowered my voice to a whisper. "Until we find out more information... don't make any decisions without me. Don't sign anything or answer calls from unknown numbers, for that matter. Gimme time to research and get back to you so you can work from a more informed position. Okay?"

Marge eyed me for a second before nodding. Then she spun on her heels, waltzing to her patrons like she didn't feel the six shots of vodka filtering through her steel-plated liver.

Walking to my SUV, I fired off a text to Troy.

Me: Just left Marge's

Troy's face immediately filled my phone with a call.

"What did she say?" He asked, direct as ever.

"It's been going on for about a year. One bad money turn after another. She's got a 6-digit tax debt, and she's getting pressure to sell from low-balling suits."

"Apex?"

"Unknown."

"A year?" I could hear Troy's steps as he paced in the background. "That's further back than I've looked."

"There's more," I tell him. "She's getting stonewalled administratively. Can't get a straight answer from the county. She wants me to see what I can find out."

"She knows a good man when she sees one," Troy commented. "What did you tell her? "

"What could I tell her? I told her to keep her head down, don't sign anything or do anything until I get back with her, and that I'd see what I could find."

Troy hummed his agreement.

"Did she mention a name of any realty firm, any other details?" I could hear his pen scratching out notes.

"No." I sighed. "She's scared, TJ. That bar is her whole life. She's got no retirement, no plan B, nothing."

"I'll dig in and see what I can find out. I haven't gone back a year. I'm not sure what I'll have access to, though, since none of this is criminal." Then he added, almost as an afterthought. "Sam? Why aren't you at work?"

Fucking hell.

"We're overstaffed. Boss gave me a couple of days off." I answered casually, praying to all the merciful gods he'd let it go.

"So, it's not your hangover, your hand, or your head still messed up about a woman you bodily hauled out of the bar?"

"Okay, how the hell did you know that?!" I snapped over TJ's chuckle. "You weren't there, the cops weren't called, and Marge doesn't have parking lot cameras. How could you possibly know I tossed Lila over my shoulder?!"

"I didn't," Troy deadpanned. "Not entirely...Lila sounds delightful."

My brother barely dipped a toe into the water of what he knew...and I overreacted and dove in headfirst. Barely catching his 'enjoy your day off' before I clicked to end the call, I couldn't help but sigh in resignation at his immediate text.

> Troy: BTW, Chase and Moira are headed home. He wants diapers. Since you have time now...

In hand my ass.

13

LILA

I MADE MYSELF AT home in the hours since Do-gooder Sam funded my swanky room.

The corner desk was too small, its chair too stiff, and it became relegated to holding my bags. I fashioned a workstation on the second, unused bed for my laptops, using stacked books as a makeshift desk. Then I piled all the pillows from both beds around me and surrounded myself with snacks and drinks from Ms. Chipper's luxury bodega. With everything I owned being laundered, I wrapped myself in the hotel's plush robe and chuckled at the glimpse of my reflection on the TV.

'Quite the rat's nest you built for yourself, Lila-girl,' my dad's voice flitted through memory, rippling love and sadness in its wake.

Shoving emotions back down, I opened both laptops and got to work.

I tracked Brinks' movements North, the first time, based on the arson perp he represented—arrogantly believing I kept a low profile. I was so wrong. Now I planned to locate that arson case and follow Brinks' footsteps from there to see if I could locate him again. Who cares if he found me now? I had nothing to lose.

I attempted to log in to the NY State site that tracks legal actions, only to find my credentials revoked. I expected it, but it still stung. I'd dedicated my entire career to the force, like my family before me, and for them to throw me out so abruptly...

Get your shit together, girl. Stop wallowing.

Using my primary laptop, I initiated a local investigation, digging through courthouse records, press releases, and social media posts. I was surprised to see the original arson case was pending a 'Stay on the Statute of Limitations due to the defendant's medical condition'. A news agency reported a house fire, naming Brinks' client, Dean Jensen, as one of the victims. He was the person of interest in the fire, and also in a coma. I recognized the name of the other victim on the scene from my time before, a woman named Moira Vanderbilt. However, the listed owner of the burning house caught my eye: Chase Wilder.

I worked the original arson case with a Sgt. Troy Wilder.

That couldn't be a coincidence.

I recalled all the corrupt officers Brinks associated with in Manhattan, and I figured he was up to his old tricks again–reaching into deep pockets and pulling out dirty cops.

Hopping onto my second laptop, I pulled up the local PD's personnel files. My shadow system ran multiple anonymizing layers—routed IPs, spoofed credentials, sandboxed browsers—all designed to keep me invisible. It took mere minutes to bypass the department's outdated firewalls and access their HR records.

A toddler with Wi-Fi could've cracked this thing.

I confirmed that I had formerly worked with Sgt. Troy James Wilder. His department record seemed pristine. Graduated from the Academy, top of his class, with a few commendations under his belt, and a military background. A small print news bulletin even announced his appointment as liaison for a community effort targeting Lake Placid's non-profit efforts. Initially listed as the Lead Investigator on the Jensen Arson case, he was downgraded to a contributing officer, a rare occurrence unless extenuating circumstances forced a conflict of interest to take precedence.

Or the golden boy was shady.

I hated the idea that my would-be police contact might be dirty, but I wondered how I'd get the information I needed on Brinks without him. And how was Sgt. Wilder connected to Chase Wilder? The name Wilder wasn't unique, but in a town this small...they were almost certainly related.

With nothing else gleaned from personnel, I delved into the arson case by reviewing the Fire Department files. Jensen was listed as a person of interest in half a dozen arson cases, including the Vanderbilt woman's apartment. Beyond that, the Fire Department records didn't give me much to work with. I almost closed the window on that search until something caught my eye. I knew Jensen was a former fireman here in town, but his official termination date was nowhere near the date of the investigation. In fact, Jensen had been terminated months before the original apartment fire.

So, the pyro psycho wasn't a model employee...shocker.

Apparently, Jensen was put on disciplinary leave for conduct unbecoming. Much of the jargon surrounding his leave was sanitized, written to avoid lawsuits rather than tell the truth, but I pieced together that he'd created a collection of videos of a sexual nature with several other women on the force, without consent. I read several interoffice emails exchanged between employees on the matter, including one directed to Chase Wilder.

'Chase,◻

This email serves to notify you that, effective immediately, you are hereby put on paid administrative leave pending the results of the internal investigation regarding your unprovoked assault of Dean Jensen. I've already sent in my official recommendation on the matter as your immediate supervisor. Until then, hit the gym and keep your head down.◻

On a personal note, I can't thank you enough for what you did for my niece, sparing her the embarrassment of anything getting out the way you did. If it wasn't for you finding those videos, who knows how long he'd have gotten away with sneaking videos at all? You and I both know this board review is obligatory red tape, and your name will be cleared as soon as they convene to review it all.◻

I owe ya one.

FBC - Brandt Jacobs'

Based on my work from before, I discovered Jensen had worked a long con on the Vanderbilt woman, catfishing her to the Adirondacks. I had no idea, however, that he'd been involved with other women as well. All pieced together, this Chase Wilder, also a firefighter, blew the whistle on the whole thing. His boss was grateful for what seemed like honorable actions if the email was accurate. That didn't give me a firm connection to Sgt. Troy Wilder, though, and I couldn't let it go without that trail. Brinks had a long history of getting cops on his payroll. The last thing I needed was to stumble into his hands by assuming one noble Wilder made for a noble Wilders pair.

My list of people to track was growing.

I dug into Chase Wilder's personnel file for a concrete connection to Sgt. Troy, but found nothing. Chase seemed just as upstanding; interning at the fire station in high school, joining the Smoke Eaters out of the military. He is listed as having two unnamed family members, several commendations, and other notable distinctions–Ad nauseam.

I lost hours following these tiny connections between Marcus, this town, and a misogynistic pyromaniac.

Back in the city, Brinks' client list sparkled in their ivory tower of privilege. The whole pack traveled on the smell of old money and handshake deals. The Brinks I had been tracking wouldn't have dared lower his standards to represent a common arsonist in some backwoods town, making this Jensen guy a wild outlier in the pattern.

What was I missing?

I looked at my primary laptop and the public records there, then at my shadow laptop, which held all my hacked data. The only thing connecting Brinks to this town was an arson case. My only real connection to that case was Sgt. Troy Wilder.

Like it or not, if I wanted to dive deeper, I needed Troy Wilder.

14

SAM

I GRABBED THE BAGS from the backseat and used my key to enter Chase's cabin for fear of waking one of the babies by knocking.

"Sam," Moira's sleepy smile greeted me. "Troy texted you were coming."

"I can follow orders," I lifted the boxes of diapers and wipes. "And I brought food." I jiggled a bag of take-out in my other hand.

"I'm STARVING," Moira handed me one of the twins and tugged the food out of my hand. "No clue if it's nursing, recovery, or lack of sleep, but I can't eat enough, and that hospital was stingy with their portions."

She pulled out stew and salad, dragging a thick hunk of dark rye bread through butter before popping it into her mouth.

"Your milk came in, I take it." I snuck a peek at the toes of the baby in my arms. "Pink?"

"That's River," Moira mumbled around the bread. "And YES. My boobs are an alien life force."

"The appetite is normal. Your body is doing what it needs for my nieces." Shifting River in my arms, I held her out, admiring her pretty eyes as she looked around. "Uncle Sam's got you now...Yes, I do." I babbled, mesmerized by her delicate features. "I'm your most favorite uncle ever. You hate grumpy Uncle Grandpa."

"SAM!" Moira scolded with a laugh.

"Make sure you nurse on both sides," I instructed. "Empty 'em completely each time, and hydrate like it's God's work. It'll help avoid mastitis."

As an EMT, I had a fair amount of general practical knowledge about trauma. But once I knew I'd be an uncle, I conducted a thorough investigation into all aspects of pregnancy, delivery, and postpartum recovery. I told myself it was just a diligent spirit, driven to be a good brother and to learn more about the human body to become an even better EMT.

Honestly, the whole process of conception, pregnancy, and childbirth fascinated me.

Women's bodies were nothing short of incredible.

"Stop talking about my wife's boobs." Chase groaned, shuffling into the kitchen holding Blue. "I've read the same books you have, dumbass. I've got this."

"He brought lunch," Moira handed over the container of stew. "I've already eaten half, I'm about to dig into that salad."

"Gimme." I barked at Chase, gesturing for him to place Blue in my open arm. "Go eat, you look wrecked." He put his second daughter in my arms, and my heart swelled to double its size, feeling them lying on me without a care in the world.

"I can't be half as tired as my wife, who's up feeding all night. And yet look at her." Chase gushed a stupidly happy expression.

I was so damn happy for the big idiot, but these little miracles made me ache for something that felt impossibly out of reach.

"Didn't you have work today?" Chase snapped me out of my angsty spiral. "Thought Troy was coming by."

"I injured my hand," I lifted my hand slightly, and wiggled the ends of my bandaged fingers from under the bundle of a burrito-wrapped River. "It's minor, but my boss used it as an excuse to correct an overscheduling and shoved me into R-n-R."

"I'm beginning to see that the Wilder men don't ever stop working unless they are bodily in danger of illness, injury, or a catastrophic life-altering event." Moira quipped.

"When you do what you love," I cooed down to Blue, whose eyes opened momentarily.

"You never work a day in your life." Chase finished Nonna's sentiment between bites.

"I suppose Troy has also never taken a day off work?" Moira mused.

"Are you kidding?" Chase laughed. "He was the kid who asked for more schoolwork during summer break to get the jump on the next school year."

In my arms, River yawned and began to squirm around, grunting as if uncomfortable.

"Is her face tired, hungry, or -" My question died with a muffled drumroll vibrating across my palm. "That would be Uncle Sam's cue to give you back to daddy, little girl."

"Daddy needs to finish eating. I'll take her." Moira stood and grabbed River, whisking her down the hall while talking to her the whole way. I shifted Blue around to get a better look at her, all pink and round with downy hair on her head and the most adorable little nose.

"They totally look like their mother." I smile. "The hell you gonna do when they're hormone-soaked teenagers with their mama's good looks?"

Chase's face went green.

"I hate you so much right now." He muttered.

"Ha, ha," I teased. "You'll be alright." I looked at Blue and added, "Yes, he will. He might be pussy-whipped by Mama and wrapped around your adorable little fingers, but he's gonna be alright as long as he can get you three into a decent house and out of this god-forsaken cabin before boxes swallow you."

"Don't say pussy in front of my girls!" Chase chastised before sighing, "and don't remind me." He ran both his hands over his face briskly before standing and stretching. "This place worked for the honeymoon, but I never planned to be here this long. It's bigger than my old house, for sure, but..." He waved his hands around, and I let my eyes follow them.

The couch was covered in hospital bags, the counters were a mess of bottles and take-out, and the floor was stacked with boxes and baby gear. For a guy who preferred the minimalist side of life, I knew the clutter was making Chase's skin crawl.

"How are you coping with the chaos?" I asked, knowing his previous coping mechanisms were the gym, the Harley, and the fire station, none of which were available to him now.

"Before delivery, lifting." He cocked his head towards the back deck, holding a complete set of weights.

"Even in the snow?" I asked, one eyebrow raised.

"Especially in the snow, cold air is great for clearing my head."

"I hear ya." I nodded, looking back at Blue, dozing again; her tiny, pink fingers gripping my pinky. "What's the latest timeline on the construction?"

The fire Dean Jensen started burned their home to the ground, making their honeymoon cabin a long-term living solution by default. However, our real estate business held all the connections and resources to expedite things, and it had been months. I wondered why Chase wasn't using those now to get his family into something more comfortable.

"The snow keeps slowing shit down, but the builder keeps saying a few more months," Chase groaned as he slid into the chair next to me with a fresh cup of coffee. "I should follow up more, but the days are bleeding together."

"Need me to make some calls and see if I can't push things along?" I asked, kicking myself for not thinking to help my brother out a little sooner. "Maybe the GC needs to use our subs to do the finishing."

"Oh my God, man." Chase leaned his elbows forward on his knees. "How did I not think of that before now?"

"Cause this little lady and her sister have properly preoccupied you," I answered, standing to hand her back. "I'm gonna make a sweep, collect all the garbage I can before I leave, and try to remove the smell of take-out and despair."

Chase took Blue from me and clocked my bandaged knuckles.

"What's the story?"

"A guy at the bar got mouthy," I sighed, circling the kitchen to collect food containers.

"When's the last time you got pulled into a brawl, man?"

"Just a weak moment as I toasted my new nieces with Marge." I moved to the living room, with Chase right on my heels, his annoying enthusiasm in tow.

"You went there to celebrate my girls...and you got pulled into a fight big enough to bust your hand and pull you off the rig?" He cocked his head back with a smirk. "Bullshit!"

"Sounds like a woman was involved." Moira's sing-songy voice came from behind me, and she headed straight to Chase to swap babies. "Was there a woman involved, Sam?"

Don't look at her, don't look at her, don't look at her.

"It's nothing," I answered, noting the full trash bag, thanking the merciful gods for a viable reason to avert my eyes as I tied it off.

Moira's observational skills rivaled those of Troy.

"Better get out of here while my nieces sleep so you guys can nap." Turning towards the door, I called over my shoulder, "I'll call the GC on your house and see what the holdup is, bro."

I heard Chase mumble a thanks behind me, but as I reached the door, Moira's subtle throat-clearing stopped me dead in my tracks...her gaze burning into the back of my head.

"No kiss for Blue from Uncle Sam?" Her question epitomized sweet innocence, but her tone was clear as a bell. The sneaky devil wanted me to turn around.

I contemplated denying her request, but the idea of sneaking a sniff of Blue's soft newborn hair was too tempting, and so, with a sigh of resignation, I turned around to give a quick peck to Blue. Not fast enough, Moira locked on me with a gaze Troy and I dubbed Medusa's Stare.

Sweet, innocent, but utterly paralyzing.

"Get some rest, sister," I flashed her entirely too many of my teeth in a forced smile.

"It IS a woman, isn't it?" She whispered with glee in her eyes.

"You're as nosy as my brothers, you know that."

I turned to leave, heaving a sigh of relief at the chance to escape before I said anything else. The last thing I needed was Chase and Moira digging into my involvement with a woman I was currently footing the bill for, keeping her in town for a whole week for reasons that even I couldn't make sense of. Getting in my car, my mind wandered to the hellcat. Chase was right to call me on it; Moira too. It was because of a woman. I tried to run her out of my system, distract myself with work, and flat-out ostrich myself into pretending she never existed.

And...fucking...yet.

Troy clocked it, my boss clocked it, Margie called me on it, and now Chase and Moira sniffed me out. What's worse, I couldn't do a damn thing about it. She was passing through, her words, and would be long gone by now, and dammit if that didn't low-key piss me all the way off.

I didn't even have Lila's last name—dick move and a stupid oversight.

I was balls-deep in the siren, and that guilty reality had me hating myself a little more. I wasn't thinking clearly then...or now. Whatever magic the woman wielded got under my skin. I told myself that Lila also wanted nothing beyond scratching an itch. That even if I wanted to go back to the hotel, use the second room key I'd pocketed, and demand to know what the actual fuck she was doing in my town, it'd be pointless.

So why in the hell was that the only thing I wanted to do?

15

LILA

M Y HEAD ACHED AFTER hours of chasing dead ends.

My frustration only heightened when I got up to leave the hotel for a drink, realizing that my haste to teach Lumbersnack Sam a lesson had left me nothing to wear. And waltzing into a bar in nothing but a robe would surely get me arrested. Then I noticed the luxuriously appointed bathroom and its giant soaking tub, complete with a collection of lavender-scented salts. My stomach growled a reminder about the room service menu, and thus I opted to stay in and spoil myself.

Thank you, Lumberjack.

I ordered the most expensive steak dinner, complete with mashed potatoes and sautéed mushrooms, and the most expensive bottle of red wine to accompany the meal. I smiled, imagining the look on Sam's face when he got the bill. While waiting, I filled the tub with salts and prepared for a hot soak. My meal arrived just in time for the tub to be ready, and, not wanting to waste the warm water, I took a few mouth-watering bites of the steak before grabbing the bottle of wine and setting it on the floor next to the tub – why waste a glass?

My whole body screamed its thanks when I sank into the water.

Almost too hot, it took a few minutes to relax as I breathed through the burn until every coiled muscle surrendered to the air jets I turned up to high. My legs relaxed, falling each to the outer walls of the tub, and the circulating water lapped up my sore inner thighs in soothing waves. I barely registered how tightly wound I'd been until the salts soaked into my skin and the aches drifted away. My sore back from the rapid packing and moving work I'd done, my hips from the long hours of driving, and the hours today spent sitting crisscross without so much as getting up to stretch or drink a glass of water. Even my forearms ached—and I couldn't think why, until...

'Hold on, Hellcat.'

Sam's growl rang in my head, and at once, the memory of our blazing hot night came flooding back, and with them came a fluttering warmth in my core. I tipped the wine bottle back and let the memory of his kiss—too intense, too consuming—wash over me. A kiss lingering between breath and lips and tongues, sparking an urgent need and growing into a raging fire of uncontainable desire. I let the soft washcloth trace the pattern he used as he kissed down my neck and between my breasts. The memory so fresh, my nipples tighten until their tips broke the surface of the water–a burst of cool air, an erotic jolt as his memory sucked them so hard they nearly hurt. My hands rubbed back and forth across my breasts the way he'd done...Sam. Deftly removing my bra, admiring my figure before diving back into me with both hands, feasting on one nipple at a time before growling in my ear about angry fucking.

If his touch was gasoline...his voice was a match.

Each growl and command was combustible, and the memory sent my hands drifting beneath the surface of the water. Running down my belly onto my aching hips as my core demanded attention. Resting one hand between my thighs, I cupped my mound to squeeze, but resisted the urge to plunge a finger inside. I wanted to make this last as I relived the single best sexual experience of my life. My other hand continued luxuriating around my nipples while I pressed and pinched and rubbed my aching pussy until I panted with need. Sam's voice narrating as I edged myself a little longer.

'I'm gonna take my time and savor this.'

His lusty words only heightened the moment; I could have cum on the memory of his words alone. Mimicking the way he entered me, inch by torturous inch, I slid one finger into my slick channel. Pumping a few times before adding a second, aching for his girth to stretch me again. I continued until the tension began to coil in my belly, and I needed my other hand to grab the edge of the tub for leverage.

I needed stretch and depth.

I needed Sam.

'Let me know if I get too rough with you, Baby'

Baby...the memory of it had me lifting my knees, adding a third finger in the search for the secret spot Sam slammed into over and over again. But where he used my shoulders, my hair, and eventually had me grabbing onto the headboard for leverage, my soap-slick tub offered nothing in the way of traction. I grew so needy I thought I might drown for want of friction. Pumping into myself, grappling with the slippery tub walls, I recalled the way he slowed at the end, forcing me to confess what I wanted him to do.

'God, please let me cum!' I echoed the desire now.

Remembering how we fit together, the ache grew until I was a slippery, frothing, chaotic ball of need. At that moment, my body angled into position for one of the jets to shoot between my hand and my clit, sending sensation scorching across my sensitive bundle of nerves. Leveraging myself to stay in that spot, I angled my hand until the water coursed across my clit, the intense heat almost too much. It took seconds, one or two more pumps, when finally, with a curl of my fingers, I moaned through my climax—stroking through waves of pleasure until tears of release slipped free of my lashes.

Coming down, panting, I hated how I felt.

Not the release I craved, but a haunting and unwelcome hollow.

An intrusion that made my heart stutter.

Loneliness–The kind that creeps in when you whisper the name of a man you barely know.

A man I had no space for with my life already in shambles.

A man who, in a single night, stood up for me, fed me, cared for me, and played my body like a finely tuned instrument before sending me into a deeply sated sleep.

In another life, I might have...but no.

I banished the thought before it fully formed. I swiped away tears I didn't want over a man I'd never see again, hoping the wine would make me forget.

16

LILA

STARING DOWN AT MY dad's *blood-streaked hand in mine, I feel
the moment his soul leaves me. The way his fingers go limp in my
grip. Then I look up and across his body to my brother, who is splayed out,
gasping like a fish out of water, with his hand shaking and raised enough to
still gesture for me with outstretched, bloody fingers. Life... there's life here.
I have to go to him, but that means letting go of my daddy. I look down
and see his eyes, distant and wide and empty. My brother coughs, and I'm
snapped into action, my body moving on its own accord. "I'm here," my
voice scratched out. "I'm here.... I'm -"*

Some memories were harder to wake from than others—details more
visceral.

My shitty therapist explained it as my brain's way of processing the
grief I refused to see. Using my space between sleep and waking to force
the trauma forward in chunks. Sometimes I could pull myself from the
muted flashes and forget it all by the time I showered. Other times, I'd

wake up to the copper penny tang of blood in my nose, feeling the broken glass cutting my knees as my heart pounded the rhythm of flashing blue and red lights reflected in the glassy eyes of my brother.

Those mornings are harder.

This morning was harder.

Opening my eyes, a damp pillow underneath me, my terror lingered. My body moved as if gravity had been turned up on high. The heaviness a bodily response to trauma, so sayeth shitty therapist, causing my muscles to clench in my sleep. I would've called it bullshit if my legs and arms didn't ache like I'd crawled through miles of mud.

In the bathroom, I avoided looking in the mirror. Looking turned into inventory, and every line and shadow would get checked on a list of ways my life circled the drain as my vendetta shredded my soul. My reflection would show disdain, then rage, and thoughts would become fragments of a wounded animal who, when in motion, sometimes required stitches.

I used the blast of icy cold water to clear the fog, sparing a fleeting glance at the tub before pawing through the stacks of delivered laundry for my warmest socks and a pair of jeans so black they could pass as slacks. Next, I donned a simple, lightweight grey V-neck sweater layered under a sleek leather blazer.

A polished look that should give a clean-cut impression to reintroduce myself to Sgt. Troy Wilder and feel out his integrity. My ego was knocked down a few pegs when I failed to find a trail between him and Brinks. I didn't realize how much of my plans hinged on that until it was all but lost, leaving me to rely on polished employment records and a superficial professional interaction.

Caution was paramount

If Sgt. Wilder worked with Marcus Brinks, alerting them that I was in town would ruin everything. If Wilder wasn't with Brinks but was a super 'by the book' cop, my asking for insider information would also destroy everything. I laughingly realized that the same guy I banked on for being shiny and upstanding before, I now needed to be shady enough to help me under the table. My staggering fall from grace as a once-upstanding cop suddenly, painfully clear.

'What a fucking mess you've made, Lil D.'

I planned to 'coincidentally' be at the deli, Sgt. Troy Wilder hit daily during my last stint in town. I would position myself at a table visible from the front door, have my laptop out as if working on something, and wait for him to arrive. Then, I would look up, feign surprise at the serendipity of it all, and strike up a conversation casual enough to make him think he'd stumbled upon me. Using my charm and, if need be, my goddamn tits, I'd get him to spill what information he had.

My dad's admonishing voice sounded in my head, *'God gave you brains, my girl... don't waste 'em trying to draw attention to what your mother blessed you with.'* I always retorted with a slap to my ass, *'I got brains enough to know sometimes you catch more flies with honey, Dad.'* Then he'd groan, and my brother would roll his eyes, and I'd laugh.

Memories burned into armor—a little honey, a little luck, and a whole lotta quick thinking.

17

LILA

I ARRIVED AT THE deli an hour before Sgt. Wilder's truck pulled in at 12:30 sharp. I wasn't sure if his predictability marked him as reliable or neurotic, but the trap was set. I double-checked my screen to make sure it showed what I wanted and then gave my girls the 'ol jiggle and lift to make sure they crested the top of my bra. I had one shot at this, and I had to make it count. As Officer Wilder reached to open the door, I lifted my drink to my lips with one hand and let my fingers drift over my keyboard with the other, scowling in mock concentration.

He went straight to the register, wearing his sunglasses and ignoring the room. After ordering, he leaned his hip against the counter and began scrolling through his phone. I nearly rolled my eyes at his lack of awareness until the hairs stood on the back of my neck.

Under the guise of mindless phone scrolling, sunglasses blocking his eyes from casual observers, thumb rhythmically swiping over his screen, his head made an almost imperceptible sweep of the room.

Clever.

With his gaze nearing me—and my drink long empty—I slammed it down with mock-frustration.

"Argh!"

That got his attention.

"Officer Rivera?" He asked, closing the gap to my table. "Is that you?"

I scowled at my laptop a second more, feigning a focused attention on my task, before turning my face up and shifting my annoyed expression into a smile topped by the bright eyes of welcome.

"Sgt. Wilder?" I offered a hand, which he shook in return. "What a surprise!"

"Indeed." He gestured to the chair. "May I?"

"Yes," I answered with a wave of my hand. "Please, distract me. I've been staring at this screen for hours. A girl could go cross-eyed."

"I was unaware you were in town...again." His face wore expressionless neutrality, but I didn't miss how he emphasized the word 'again'. "You left so abruptly, I assumed you'd been called away on another case."

"Well, yes and no," I tilted my head, as if playing with the answer. "I was called back less for a case and more because of administrative red tape." I let my answer hang for a second, then two, and he didn't acknowledge the statement one way or the other. "You know how it is—everyone wants paperwork ninety seconds ago."

That won me a polite chuckle.

"Ah, yes...the necessary evil of paperwork." He smoothed a hand down his already perfectly ironed tie and added. "If only the wheels of justice didn't require so much of it, imagine the good we could do."

"Cheers to that." I raised my glass. "I'm sorry, by the way, for leaving so abruptly. My Captain was screaming, and I bolted to soothe his feathers. I should've taken a moment to close the circle on my research for you." I kept my statement vaguely open-ended to give him space to spill a few details.

"No apology required." He offered a wave of his hand. "The arson case went a different direction entirely. I doubt I would've had much need of your services beyond what you volunteered."

My stomach flipped at the last word. I allowed him to believe I'd been sent to work on his case, before...not volunteer.

Had Marcus told him I wasn't there on a paid resource-sharing basis?

"Different direction?" I kept my face frozen in the pleasant and passive smile from before, willing my voice to neutrality, and prayed I wasn't stepping right into Brinks' claws. "So not arson?"

"Oh, it was arson," He leaned forward, his elbows spreading across the narrow table. "But the perp turned out to have nefarious connections that *shifted* the investigation."

Another emphasis on 'shifted', had me on alert. His body sat relaxed, non-threatening, across the table from me, and yet his subtext told me there was more here. But damned if I could read his stoic face.

"So, it's not all buttoned up, then?" My question fell out too quickly, and I admonished myself for not pausing a beat. "I only ask 'cause with the woman able to give a statement, it seemed open and shut."

I sat back, sipping my drink to deflect my earlier eagerness. Sgt. Wilder eyed me for a moment, sending my adrenaline soaring as I felt myself on the receiving end of a common interrogative technique: Say less, let the awkward silence pull your perp into blabbing.

I dug in, focusing on my breathing and silently unraveling before he spoke again.

"What brings you into town this time around?" Sgt. Wilder nodded towards my laptop, and I used the moment to slide the laptop around to show a list of vacation rentals I prepared for just this moment.

"Last time I was here, it seemed kinda perfect for a getaway, but I had no time to explore. I was overdue for some PTO, so I wanted to come back for a little mountain air."

I flashed a toothy smile and widened my eyes in fake excitement. A distressed tourist made an easy backstory and made a plausible reason to be in town.

"But your frustration earlier..." He gestured with a casual splaying of fingers, and I mentally high-fived myself that he took the bait.

"Oh, that." I rolled my eyes with a dramatic groan. "I thought I locked my rental down, but I arrived and realized I had forgotten to pay the deposit, and the rental is booked. I'm in a hotel, but trying to salvage my dreamy mountain getaway by finding something last-minute." I mentally applauded my performance, adding a slight shrug and a sigh. "Might be a pipe dream at this point. Nothing is available in my price range on such short notice."

"Hmmm," Sgt. Wilder sat back and considered me, his gaze unflinching, and I again resisted the urge to squirm.

Thankfully, the server delivered a paper bag with his to-go order and Sgt. Wilder excused himself to pay the bill while I returned to fake-scanning the rentals. Mentally, I began sifting through conversation options to try and circumnavigate any suspicions about my previous visit here while still pushing my way back into the station and its resources.

"You know," he said, returning to the table and standing over me, "I happen to own a few vacation rentals."

"Really?" My surprise was authentic. I hadn't found his name attached to real estate in all my research.

"A small side business," he added. "I may have an availability."

"Oh!" The click of a plan falling into place was practically audible. "That would certainly make things easier for me...and I *love* supporting fellow officers," I added the last bit as a measure of goodwill, hoping to foster like-minded generosity on his part while trying to determine–friend or foe.

"Yes, well," He fished a business card from his pocket and jotted a number on the back before handing it over. "That's my cell. I typically get off around 6 or 7, depending on whether I have reports to complete. If you haven't found a place by then, call or text. I can likely have you in something by the weekend."

"Thank you, I'll do that," I smiled, slipping the card into my bag. "Since my vacation plans clearly won't be starting right away," I shrugged in nonchalance, "Meanwhile, I could swing by the station if you needed my services on that case again. It'd be no trouble to dive back into that laptop or any other tech you might need me to sift through."

I stopped talking then, wondering if he'd take the bait or call me out as a big-ass liar.

"Walk with me, Ms. Rivera," He commanded as he turned and walked out the door.

18

LILA

S LAPPING MY LAPTOP SHUT, I shoved it into my bag before stepping in line behind Sgt. Wilder, my brain pulling at every tendril of the 5-word command. He called me Miss, not Officer—a slip or a choice? The uncertainty of his intentions added another layer of confusion to the already complex situation.

Was pulling me out of the diner nefarious or discerning?

Was he about to call bullshit about my vacation?

Was he in Brink's pocket?

I had no time to contemplate it as I scrambled to follow him. His almost imperceptible head nod guided me to his truck, and I willed myself into cool neutrality as I dumbly climbed into the passenger side. The moment the door closed, an alarming realization set in; I voluntarily got into the car of a man who could well be hip-deep in the same shitty waters of a bottom-feeder I was trying to catch.

'The fuck are you doing, Lil D.?'

"Let us dispense with the pretense." Sgt. Wilder began. "When you left, I reached out to your Captain with additional questions for you."

I shut my eyes as nausea took over, my face falling to the useless bag at my feet that held no weapon inside. The weight of my powerlessness in this situation was suffocating.

"Imagine my surprise to have my inquiry stonewalled by Internal Affairs."

"IA?" I snapped my eyes back to him as my worries took a backseat to this new curiosity. "*They* shut you down... not my captain?"

"A question that nagged at me as well. Your record showed an officer in good standing, despite a propensity to...push boundaries." I cocked an eyebrow but didn't speak, wondering where he was going. "The larger question wasn't why IA shut me down, but rather, why the Internal Affairs officer in question was *not* an officer on record."

"Wait...what?" My gears started spinning as I sifted through my IA knowledge.

Internal Affairs functioned as internal babysitters of the police departments. They investigated misconduct allegations and ensured compliance with ethical and legal standards as required by the communities they served. But, above all, IA was always...always...cops.

"What?" I asked again, needing clarification.

"My boss received a phone call from Internal Affairs, notifying me that I should cease any involvement with Officer Rivera, pending her review by the IAD for disciplinary action." Sgt. Wilder continued, ignoring the embarrassed flush of shame he no doubt saw in my face. "I admit, curiosity got the better of me. I logged into your personnel file to see which agent had been assigned to you and found a newly employed investigator. So new, in fact, they'd been appointed to you nearly the same day of employment; their actual name missing from records. Only their employee number available."

"No, wait," my brain was running at 90 miles an hour. "Internal Affairs Agents attach their name and number like it's their goddamn hobby to tag every file they fucking touch to keep 'the accountability of transparency' as they so love to call it." My air-quoted fingers worked in quick succession as Sgt. Wilder jumped back in.

"A practice I admired as a fellow stickler of documentation, and so again, I confess, my curiosity got the better of me. I dug further to find the employee assigned to that ID number."

"And?" I whirled my hand in the air, encouraging him to speak faster.

"Discrepancies." He dropped coolly.

"Discrepancies?"

"Not one record of that IA employee exists in any database, save your disciplinary action.

My termination replayed in my mind nearly daily, Captain's voice echoing—*'Internal Affairs gave the official order.'* It never occurred to me to ask which agent in IA had pulled the trigger much less see if they followed protocol. I was eager to return to the hotel and re-read my termination documents to see if the number was listed there. However, the information would be useless without accessing Internal Affairs, and how far down this road was I willing to go if it got me no closer to Brinks?

"Rivera," Sgt. Wilder's voice pulled me back to the present, my bottom lip still snuggly nipped between my teeth as I stared numbly ahead. "Were you serious about needing a place to stay?" His question felt soft—laced with unexpected kindness.

"No." I answered at first, then added, "I mean...not yet. I've got -"

He cut me off with a wave of his hand.

"My number is yours, but while you are in town, I have the resources to provide you with a...more scenic and relaxing vacation spot for you to stay awhile." His eyes locked on me, and the unspoken meaning behind them became crystal clear.

He didn't want me to leave.

Before my response fully formed, he put on his sunglasses and seat-belt, all but dismissing me from his truck.

"Call me at the week's end. I'll be happy to show you the place personally, and we can have a proper catch-up at that time." His tone was as perfunctory as his body language, and I was in no position to argue for anything different as he nodded towards the door.

I climbed out and ambled to my Jeep, tallying all my new questions about the man himself.

Sgt. Wilder may or may not have a legitimate real estate side gig, but again, why didn't I know that before? Cops usually talk when they are in proximity to a case, and he never mentioned anything. Was he offering a rental to me now, because I'm unemployed? Was this a pity offer or a brag about the place they'll bury my body when he hands me over to the Brinks? Why did he not want to talk in the deli? Why the cloak and dagger to get me in the car? Did that mean he was in league with Brinks, or did his open disclosure about IA's lack of protocol make him someone I can trust?

God...is there anyone I can trust?

As I headed back to the hotel to resume my research, the abundance of new questions began to spiral into a despairing, self-loathing pit of contempt.

My simple plan was now clouded by doubt and suspicion.

Be there, be charming, find out Wilder's allegiance, and make my plans. Instead, at the first hint that he was on to me, I got cagey and impatient, and then I got in the truck with him and sat there like a stone-faced idiot while he unraveled everything. I'd blown my cover with the local PD at best, and handed myself to Brinks at worst.

A little honey, a little luck, and a whole lotta quick thinking, my ass.

WILDER FAMILY GROUP CHAT

-2-

Troy: For clarity... my beautiful niece's arrival qualifies as an acceptable postponement of spaghetti night.

Me: Agreed. We can skip as many weeks as y'all need, Boy Scout.

Chase: Lemme check with Moira—she's nursing.

Chase: quoting here—'what kind of example would we be setting for these girls if their arrival is what derails years of tradition? If anything, we should prioritize it even more so they're surrounded by love and family from day one.'

Me: Damn. Okay. Message received.

Troy: Good. I need a family meeting.

Chase: still quoting...

Troy: Oh dear.

Chase: 'But I just shoved two humans out of my vagina and everything hurts. I'm the gooey carcass of a previously invaded alien parasite, so if anyone expects cooking, place settings, or centerpieces, they can shove it.'

Me: Riiiight... so Family Meeting at Chase's?

Troy: Yes. I have news on the investigation. We need to talk in person.

Me: Back on the rig Thursday through Sunday.

Troy: Sunday night's fine. Sam and I will handle dinner this time.

Me: Do we need to adjust the menu for Moira? Any reflux issues with the girls?

Chase: She wants extra bread, extra butter, and someone better bring chocolate—or there will be blood.

Me: Sounds like nursing is going great. See you Sunday.

Troy: One more thing. I need the rental up the road. A few days. Maybe a week. Starting this weekend. Any objections?

Chase: None... why?

Me: Same.

Troy: I'll explain Sunday.

19

SAM

TROY'S TEXT WAS A welcome distraction. I called him immediately, but he only said, 'Still fleshing out details. Patience, brother.' Of course, he couldn't see how badly I needed a distraction.

And if I pushed, he'd say it was about a woman—and hell, if I jacked off one more time to the memory of that woman, I'd need a banana bag to rehydrate. So I kept busy—deep cleaning the house, checking on our rentals, and even helping with Chase's construction delays.

By Thursday morning, I was itching to be on shift, despite dull, busy work and my boss's snark about the greenish bruises fading on my hand. Restless as hell, I practically lit up when a 6 p.m. call came in—robbery attempt at the Five Points liquor store. By the time we arrived, the scene was already locked down. A uniform took statements from the witnesses.

"She ran up behind the guy, screamed obscenities, and clocked him with that huge bottle!"

"Vigilante's out cold, Wilder." The cop nodded me in. "My partner's with her."

Inside, the place looked intact—minus a few busted bottles bleeding some sweet, heady mix of booze around a sea of broken glass. Boots peeked out at the end of the aisle—and a bolt of recognition hit me. I knew those boots. Praying I was wrong, I rounded the corner—and my stomach dropped. There she was. The woman from the bar. My Lila.

What. The. Hellcat.

"She came to, rambled a bit, then passed out again," the officer said. "Sounds like Xena Warrior Princess gave as good as she got, but took a blow to the head."

Kneeling next to her, I began reciting the ABCs as if from muscle memory; Airway clear, Breathing slowly but steady, pulse sluggish at both neck and wrist—deep unconsciousness. My attention shifted to the head wound—small but deep—needed stitches and definitely concussed. I lifted one lid and flashed the penlight. Her honey-brown eyes fluttered, and my chest pulled tight. I let her lid fall, brushing her cheek with my thumb, silently begging for that fiery glare I couldn't stop dreaming about, and my gut twisted.

I wanted to throttle the perp barehanded.

The rattle of the gurney snapped me to attention.

"Pupils equal and reactive. Head lac needs a pressure wrap." I called out.

"She's probably drunk," my partner said. The comment hit a nerve—my face must've shown it, because his brows pulled together in confusion. "What? Liquor store, Thursday, 6 p.m. What are the odds?" He nodded down at Lila. "Tiny thing like that? Gotta be three sheets to the wind to charge a guy holding a gun."

I couldn't argue the logic—but the idea she was already drunk made my jaw clench. I wanted to defend her—say she wasn't that reckless. But the truth was, I didn't know her, and that had me more than a little disappointed in myself. Maybe if I'd checked on her sooner, this wouldn't have happened.

"Fake gun," the officer pointed to a spray-painted toy on the floor. "Punk kid looking for quick cash picked the wrong woman to scare." The officer's mouth tipped up in pride. "She's ferocious."

"Yeah, well, drunk or not, it'll screw her SATs," my partner muttered, annoyingly accurate. Her being drunk would increase her heart rate and lower O2 levels.

"Let's get her loaded," I said, glancing at the officer still stabilizing her head. "She got a wallet? Purse? Any ID?"

"Just a set of keys and a pocket full of cards." She held up a debit card, a credit card, and the hotel room key. I glanced at them all and smiled.

My Hellcat had a last name—Lila Rivera.

"I'll take 'em." I willed my voice to remain professional as I slipped Lila's cards into my pocket, pairing the twin room keys together once more. "We'll be at the hospital in twenty if you want to send someone for her statement."

"Copy." The officer gently passed Lila's head into my hands and left me alone as my partner went to the rig. My chest clenched—seeing her lying out on a filthy floor, undone by her own damn reckless bravery.

"Jesus, Hellcat," I whispered. "What the hell were you thinking?"

In the ambulance, I started an IV line, and the needle stick brought a scowl on her face.

"Response to pain stimulus," I noted across to my partner.

"She's got a shiner coming in, and did you see this?" He gave me an oddly pinched look, flipping her right hand to show a small cut across her palm that had already clotted.

How the fuck did I miss both of those?

"Looks small." I tried to keep my cool, but my frustration grew by the second at the state she'd put herself in. "That eye won't be that bad, and they'll handle it in the ER."

Why is she still here, still in town, still in the hotel? Why didn't she call me? Why is she at the liquor store, and why in fucking hell would she attack someone with a bottle of booze if she thought they had a gun?

"She got any ID?" the driver hollered back.

"Just a couple of credit cards." I fished them out of my pocket and showed them to my partner, keeping the hotel card for reasons even I couldn't explain.

"I'll add it to the report. Think she's on any meds?" he asked, giving me that stupid look a third time, and I couldn't take it anymore.

"For Fuck's Sake, what's that look for?"

"You know this broad?" he smirked—earning himself a spot on my shit list. "Because I swear to Christ, I've never seen you miss an injury before, and tonight you missed two. Not accounting for the fact that you've seemed hella on edge since we arrived on scene."

"Just focused on the head lac." I huffed

"No...meds." My eyes snapped down to find her eyes clenched tight into a scowl. Lila sounded on the verge of tears.

"Ma'am," My partner moved before me, emphasizing how right he was that I was off my game. "Do you remember what happened?"

She hissed at his penlight.

"Get the fucking light out of her eyes, Jackass." I shoved his arm, ignoring his knowing smirk. "She's concussed. That's not helping." I added, trying to deflect just how far offside I ran.

"Jackass," she whispered, a ghost of a smile curling. "I know you."

"You're in the ambulance," I murmured, listening as her lungs started to quicken. "You stopped a robbery. Took a hit."

Her voice called to something I hadn't felt since I sent a guy flying over a pool table. I waited for the fire—the heat–For her to come back swinging. But just as fast, she was out again—drifting as the ambulance rocked beneath us. My hand lingered on her wrist—steady pulse, soft skin.

Relief warred with rage.

She wasn't a cop.

She wasn't armed.

She was outnumbered and outsized.

What the fuck was she thinking!

"Bastard tried to rob the place." She mumbled. "I couldn't let him...Not again. Fuck...my head." Then she went silent, and my heart sank.

"She's in and out," my partner muttered as we hit the bay. "Ma'am, stay calm. My buddy Sam and I are gonna take care of you."

"Jackass," she whispered, eyes still closed, head tilting my way. "How'd you find me?"

"Gee, Thanks. Now she thinks my name is Jackass." My partner drolled.

I couldn't tell if I was irritated that he thought she was talking to him or relieved that he didn't know she was talking to me. Either way, she remembered me; My voice–our night–the way we fought before we–

The doors to the truck opened with a loud clang, bringing me back to the ER team, who jumped into action.

"All signs point to a concussion," my partner dictated. "Not sure she even knows which way is up." He rattled off stats to the intake nurse, but I was watching her.

Usually, I handed off paperwork and checked the rig's supplies, getting it prepped for departure and the next call. The patient was stable, and the hospital was well-staffed. Unlike gunshot wounds or vehicle accidents, there was no injury critical enough for EMS to remain during hand-off. But this wasn't any patient, as was evidenced when I snatched the Patient Care Report away from my partner.

"I got the PCR," I aimed for casual. "Figured I'd have better luck getting her info than you... Jackass." I gave a quick grin, eyebrow raised in jest.

"Yeah, yeah," he waved me off. "Least you could do is paperwork bullshit since you're the one who stuck me with the nickname."

Relief hit hard—whether because he didn't catch on, or because I gained a few precious minutes with Lila, I didn't know. I turned toward her gurney in the hallway, grateful for a moment alone as I pulled up a stool.

"Lila... it's me, Sam." Her brows pinched. "You're in the ER. I rode with you in the ambulance. Do you remember?" She turned toward me, eyes still shut. "Don't talk if it hurts. You've got a concussion, probably need a few stitches."

"Sam." My name, in her fractured and wispy voice, was the sweetest sound that called me to wrap around her like armor. I wanted to hold her, rock her, comfort her—and I had no clue where that urge came from.

"Yeah, Hellcat. It's me." I squeezed her hand. "Anyone I should call? That friend you were visiting? Maybe a...boyfriend...or husband?"

That question dripped pragmatic masochism. I held no claim on her. Our encounter was unplanned, and why shouldn't this gorgeous creature have someone waiting for her?

If she were taken, I'd 100% walk away despite the growing urge to stay in her orbit. Then again, she hadn't called all week, and if she were single, I was still fucked—because she was under my skin, and I clearly wasn't under hers.

I was screwed six ways from Sunday.

"No." She shook her head, then winced. "Just... you."

Relieved, elated, gutted—she had no one but me.

A nurse rounded the corner, hand stretched out for the paperwork.

"Uh, not much to show." I handed it over, barely filled in.

"You guys never give us anything useful," she muttered, scanning the form. "Name, no meds, no allergies." She looked up. "She woke up and told you that?"

"On the rig...she seemed lucid enough." I realized I was still holding her hand. I let go fast, wondering if the nurse had noticed.

"Any purse, phone, or personal items?" Nurse Protocol held out a bag, and I dropped in the cards and cell phone from my pocket, keeping the keys and hotel room card, which went against every rule in the book.

The nurse glanced from the bag to Lila.

"No purse? No car keys?"

"Nope. That's it."

"So, no address, no insurance, no next of kin, no emergency contact..." She ticked through the gaps, and I fought the urge to list myself as emergency contact.

Everyone needed someone, right?

"Yo, Wilder." My partner yelled from the ambulance bay. "We ready to roll?"

"Alright, alright." The nurse yelled, shooting my partner a glare. "Just sign the bottom so we can take it from here." Without looking at the paper, I John Hancocked the bottom of the form and stood there like an idiot.

Staring at Lila alone on the gurney made my chest ache.

No one should wake up alone in a hospital.

I'd never cared before—not on a hundred other runs. But this time, I white-knuckled the bed rail until the nurse nudged Lila towards triage, and I caught my reflection— standing there like a lost puppy.

That's when I knew... I'd be back.

20

SAM

AFTER MY SHIFT, I followed a hunch and found Lila's Jeep in the liquor store lot—purse and a month's worth of food containers inside. I didn't know how long she'd be at the hospital, but I couldn't have her stuff sitting here exposed either. I left a note with the clerk, then started the Jeep, frustration coiling in my gut and my head all over the place with this infuriating woman.

I gave the front desk authority to charge the room on my card until the end of the week, suspecting even then that she wasn't just passing through town. I walked through the hotel lobby, heading straight up to her floor, remembering her tossed over my shoulder.

My palm tingled at the memory of popping that perfect ass.

At the door, I ignored the "Do Not Disturb" sign and threw caution to the wind, swiped the keycard across the lock, and held my breath. Knowing some hotel chains fail to re-key the cards between guests, I could freak out whoever occupied this room, which would be super fun to explain my way out of. 'Sorry, sir, ma'am, I was obsessing over this insane sex bomb of a woman I fucked ten ways from Sunday in your bed, and was hoping she was still here, though I don't know why, since she's making me crazy!'

Mercifully...the lock turned green with a soft beep, and I entered an empty room, finding only Lila's things. Flipping on the light, I dropped a text to Troy.

> Me: Can you come get me? I'll drop a pin of my locale.

> Troy: Be there in 20.

Pocketing my phone, I inventoried the room.

One bed was a mess of pillows strewn from one end to the other, blankets twisted like a tornado had blown through. Flashes of our night came rushing back—her body, the bed, the headboard, the way I kicked the pillows aside to make space for us. Looking at the state of her bed now, it seemed she was just as wild when she slept. The second bed was still made, except for a pile of books and twin laptops fashioned into a makeshift workstation.

Passing through town, my ass.

I was so drawn to something about her that I let myself ignore the lie. And she begged for more and slept beside me, curled in my arms, before I snuck out the next morning.

Then she ghosted me, so why was I still here?

A need to know more had me snooping through the drawers of the small dresser and then the bedside table, both empty. The bathroom had minimal makeup and hair items. Aside from a pile of freshly dry-cleaned clothes on the chair, the room was barely touched. So Lila wasn't planning to stay long-term, but her Jeep looked lived-in. The longer I stayed in the space, the more agitated I grew.

What the hell was she doing here?

Why play vigilante at the liquor store?

Was all of this avoidable if I'd just come back to check on her?

I ran my fingers through my hair, trying to strengthen my resolve. I couldn't keep obsessing like this. I needed to go back to the hospital, ask her all these questions myself, and clear up the mystery of it all. I had just about made up my mind when my phone chirped a text alert.

> Troy: Here.

I almost made it through the lobby when the familiar voice of the scrawny, pimple-faced kid who had been working the night I checked us in halted me.

"Sir." I turned to see him smiling, and I worried for a moment that he might call me on basically breaking and entering into Lila's space. "I see you and your wife are still here." A statement, not a question, and so I nodded. "Please tell her thank you for me?"

"Thank you?"

"She came by two nights ago, and we started talking. It's quiet in the late hours, and I get a little chatty, what with being usually alone and not having many people to - "

"You asked me to thank her?" I cut the kid's ramble off, eager for him to find the point.

"Yeah, right...Well," He fidgeted from one foot to the other. "I mentioned in passing that my wife was looking for work, and hitting a brick wall here in town since unemployment is kinda..." he paused to search for the right word.

"In the shitter." I deadpanned, knowing full well the state of our town's economy.

"Yeah." He huffed. "Well, your wife asked what my girl did for a living, and well, the next day when I clocked in, a printout of a bunch of legit work-from-home agencies that happened to have openings perfectly matching my wife's resume waited for me. As of now, my wife has *two* interviews lined up!" The kid beamed with pride. "It's the most interviews my wife has had in months. She's excited and relieved and...well, thank your wife for me."

Random acts of kindness didn't match up with the foul-mouthed, wild image I built in my head, and it pleased me to know Lila would help someone unasked. As if this new facet of her repainted the picture in my mind.

"I'll pass the message along." Leaving the hotel, I schooled my face into neutrality as I climbed into Troy's truck.

"Do I want to know why you are stuck at a hotel with no car at midnight?"

"You wouldn't believe me if I told you," I looked out the window, hoping he'd let it go.

"It's a 20-minute ride home, and I'm feeling open-minded. Regale me." He answered, his trademark monotone commanding obedience from his 'little' brother. Grasping for any way to avoid the oncoming lecture, I blurted.

"My car is at the Five Points."

I stared so hard out the window, you would have thought flying monkeys were outside.

"And we've now passed the point of general curiosity and delved straight into 'what have you gotten yourself into'?"

Troy would never let this go.

Groaning, I realized that if the shoe were on the other foot, I'd have had the same questions, so, with a sigh, I tried to appease the beast.

"Okay, I promise, I'll tell you everything when I have it straightened out myself. But I'm still trying to unravel the mess, and honestly, I wouldn't know where to start, right now." Troy considered me for a minute...then two...before taking a deep breath.

"Answer me three questions?" His voice took on the interrogative timbre I'd heard him use time and time again, both on the job and with Chase and me when we were growing up.

"Oh, c'mon, TJ!" I begged. "Gimme a day to - "

"Three." His voice was straight and resolute. "Questions."

Fuck me sideways.

"Fine," I sighed.

"Is this about the woman from the bar?"

"Yes." I sighed. He had me dead to rights if that was his jumping-off point.

"Is she the vigilante from the liquor store robbery tonight?" His eyes never left the road, but I could feel his peripheral gaze.

"Yes."

"Is she worth the trouble?" I turned, surprised by the profoundly simple question.

"She's...a handful," I said honestly, unsure what other answer to give since I hardly knew enough about her to confirm her character, but I was drawn to her nonetheless.

Troy nodded, and we drove in silence to the liquor store. Once parked next to my SUV, he spoke again.

"It's clear that you don't want the family to know about your woman." I started to protest his use of the word 'your,' but he held up

124

a hand and continued. "I respect your desire for privacy." Lowering his hand, his voice softened. "But I have concerns, brother."

"It's not that big a deal," I said, hardly believing the lie.

"A drunken barfight, an interrupted robbery, late-night calls for hotel pick-ups, and cars left all over town...Come now." He sighed and added, "Not your usual fare, would you agree?"

I had no answer for him, stunned at hearing all the shenanigans strung together like that. Equally stunned that he didn't think this level of fuckery was my usual. I knew my reputation.

"You're a grown man, and, loath as I am to admit it, I trust your judgement. You'll do the right thing, always, and so I won't push...for now."

"Thanks," I answered, remembering once again why we treated Troy like the older brother. He was a good man in a storm.

"Promise me, you'll ask for help should you need it."

"I will," I promised, climbing out of his truck.

"*Before* I have to arrest you...preferably!"

21

LILA

*T*HE MEMORIAL TO FOLLOW *was at the precinct's favorite bar. It
would be an endless onslaught of memories and condolences shared
over a never-ending flow of cheap beer and sour whiskey, and I was expected
to go there. But my feet...my feet wouldn't move. I hardly felt my black
dress clinging to my body as cold rain fell, sticking my hair to my face and
masking the tears that fell in time with every drop from the sky. I was
frozen where I stood, a living statue at the foot of the graves I wanted to
throw myself into. I hadn't noticed that the other mourners had gone, and
I was alone. Until his voice...in my ears...in my soul..." My dear Officer
Rivera. I was so grieved to learn of the loss of your poor dear father and
brother." My head turned in slow disbelief, like I was trapped inside a
nightmare. Looking up at the slicked-back ponytail and black suit of the
man I had been trying to pin was more than my mind could register. "I
came too late to pay proper respects; it seems the fanfare has all gone." He
smiled down at me...the bastard smiled...as he waved a limp hand around*

the empty cemetery grounds around us. "Though...a little too late does seem to be a theme with you, does it not, Officer Rivera?" My stomach turned, bile and panic climbing to suffocate me. "Phone calls answered too late, efforts to save the day too late, it's all a bit on the nose." He sighs, taking in the grim scene of their mud-covered graves like he's taking in a lazy sunset. "If only officers these days would be more careful not to meddle in things above their pay grade. So many needless, avoidable deaths." He was here. He was here! HE WAS -

I pried my eyes open, skull pounding with a vengeance as the morning's memory clung to me like a living thing with teeth.

Then came the pain.

I was cold, half-naked, and didn't recognize my room—never a great sign. I had been hitting the bottle a little hard these past few months, but never blacked out drunk. I wasn't that stupid. I drove to the liquor store, stone-cold sober. Then came the night's entertainment on a loop in my brain.

Store...punk...robbery...mind-numbingly poor decision on my part.

Easing into a sitting position, I looked around the sterile surroundings of a hospital room. Hitting the call button, I scanned for my phone and clothes.

"You're awake, Ms. Rivera." A doctor with a tablet and too much enthusiasm stepped to the foot of my bed. "You've been out cold for hours with a concussion. Do you remember what happened?"

"I ducked too slow?" I muttered, fingers grazing the bulky bandage on my forehead as fragments of memory floated up. "How many stitches?"

"Just two. I tucked them into the hairline...they won't even scar. I'm something of an artist, if I may say so."

"Lucky me." I swung my legs over the edge of the bed. "Unhook me and hand over my clothes. I'll clear out so you can dazzle the next unlucky bastard." My head protested my attempt to stand, and I squeezed my eyes shut to stop the spinning.

"It's not advisable for you to be on your feet right now." The doctor lent an arm to steady me. He set the tablet aside and gently pushed me back into a sitting position. Kind of a dick move, considering how hard I'd worked to stand.

"We'd prefer to keep you—monitor the dizziness, maybe run another CT, before discharge."

"Yeah, so," I focused on his badge for his name. "Dr. Rinds. I've had concussions before. I know the signs. And yeah, I've got a killer headache—happy to take a couple painkillers—but I don't need more fluids and I sure as shit don't need a repeat scan."

"I admire your pluck, Ms. Rivera—" he began, but I cut him off, shifting tactics.

"Pupils uneven? Unresponsive?" I held his gaze.

"Well...no." He said, grabbing his tablet.

"Did I throw up...slurred speech?" I pushed, not giving him time to think.

"No. But I still—"

"Then you've got no grounds to hold me. Someone else probably needs the bed more." I stood again, forcing my eyes to stay open and steady.

"So remove the IV and bring me my things before I waltz my sweet-ass outta here with your shitty paper gown showing my ass in the wind." Then, with my most pleasant smile, I added, "Please."

Dr. Rinds stared me down, weighing my resolve, then sighed disapprovingly.

"You'll be signing out AMA," he muttered, to which I gave a wave of acknowledgement. I just wanted to get back to my car, my hotel, a bed, and my work.

"Oh, and the police need a statement now that you're awake."

My pulse spiked before he reached the door, fueling my headache. Of course, there would be a police report. I stopped a robbery.

Idiot!

I couldn't risk my name being linked to a crime in any police database without knowing whether Brinks could find me. Certainly not while trying to gauge whether Sgt. Wilder was clean or on the take. Not to mention, my ploy as a civilian tourist wasn't built for clocking punks over the head with a bottle of Bushmills.

"Ma'am," a nurse came in with a bag. "Here are your things." She turned off the IV drip and clamped off the line, unhooking me from the bag but not removing the canula from my arm. "I'll let you get dressed, and then remove the IV after the police finish their statement. I'll get your discharge forms printed while they are here."

I had to get the hell out of here.

Glancing into the hallway when she left, I noted the stairwell door directly across the hall. I quickly dressed, finding my credit cards but not my room key amongst my things. Looking down at the IV cannula still taped to my elbow, I pushed the room card issue to the back of my mind.

Priority one: get out before this shitstorm deepens.

I considered waiting for the nurse to remove the IV, but didn't want to risk getting cornered. Holding my breath, I pulled at the tape with a yank, removing the whole thing in one fell swoop while repressing ten different curse words. Clamping my fingers over the crook of my elbow, I peeked into the hallway, then darted across to the stairwell to slip out unnoticed.

22

SAM

TROY'S WORDS RANG IN my ears, deterring me from going to the hospital but following me to bed. I usually slept fine, but not with the Hellcat under my skin. I tried working out my issues in the shower, but even that didn't work. My hand made a poor substitute for her delicious curves.

Lying awake, I questioned everything about her, and got out of bed to Troy's words echoing—'Not your usual fare.' In truth, historically, I was drawn to light-hearted encounters, good in the moment, with zero baggage. Anything beyond that was too messy, too time-consuming, and would inevitably turn into something c lingy.

Troy caught on that something had changed, so why hadn't I?

Instead, at each turn, when confronted about the bar, the bruised knuckles, or the ambulance ride, I couldn't settle. Anyone asking about her triggered this insane, almost possessive need to keep her private. It made no sense–I made no sense. I didn't want the drama...But whatever magic she was packing was enough to drive a man insane.

It had to be the mystery of her that was so alluring–the brokenness under all that bravado that called out to something in me that just wanted to fix it. Ergo, solving the mystery should solve my problem. I needed to find out why she was in town and how long she would be staying. If temporary, I'd fuck her out of my system and breathe a sigh of relief as her taillights hit the highway. If she were staying for a while, well... I'd cross that bridge when I got there.

Up before dawn, I drove to the hospital, arriving as the sun peeked over the horizon. I debated whether to rush in and catch the night crew or wait and interact with the morning shift, then recalled how Chase's first visit to Moira made the small-town grapevine. Opting to avoid prying eyes and the gossip-mill reaching my work, or my brothers, I decided to avoid the ER full of personnel who knew me, and used the main entrance.

"Morning, Sam. I don't normally see you in civvies," Lou worked nights at the front desk and patrolled the halls like the retired cop he was.

"Hey, Lou." I shook his hand. "I'm checking in on someone I dropped last night."

"That's a first." He remarked, turning to his computer screen. "Name?"

"Rivera...Delilah," I stated. "She may not be in a room, though–"

"She's here. Up on a floor." My anxiety spiked. I considered her mildly concussed, but maybe there was something more profound if she'd been admitted. "You know if you are here as a visitor, and not family, I'm not supposed to tell you where she is."

"Yeah. I know. I just..." I paused, still chastising myself for not being more thorough with her. I missed something, which might have put her at risk, and that was unacceptable. "She was pretty rattled and didn't have any emergency contacts. I figured a familiar face might be nice, ya know."

"Mm Hm." Lou gave me a look that said I was full of shit. "Mighty generous of you to check on her...like your brother Chase, I suppose." He winked at the town's favorite story; Chase refused to leave a fire victim, who then became his wife, and they had babies, blah blah blah.

It was a dramatic and violent story shifting into small-town lore. If only they knew how close I came to losing my brother, my sister, and my two nieces in that last fire. I nearly broke performing CPR on Chase. When he pulled through, when we all saw the other side of that, it felt like a damned gift. Maybe that's why their success felt so out of reach for me.

It had grown into something mythic.

"Don't bust my chops here, Lou. This is weird enough." I admitted, shifting from one foot to another.

"I'm not *supposed* to tell you that she's in room 312. And you aren't *supposed* to know that visiting hours don't begin til 8 am." He glanced at the clock on the wall, which read 7:45. "And I can't turn a blind eye while I grab myself a cup of coffee." He stood with a chuckle as he hobbled off, cane in tow, and I said a silent thanks.

Hopping on the elevator, I mashed the 3rd-floor button and wondered what I'd say. Lila hadn't called me all week, despite having my number in her phone. That bothered me more than I liked, which tumbled into the jarring reality that I hadn't, until just now, considered if she even wanted me to come see her.

Would she be confused at my arrival, or furious at me for showing up unannounced? Maybe she'd smile when I walked in, and we could have an honest to God conversation.

That was the desire I clung to as I exited the elevator, noting the pleasant lack of staffing as the changeover occurred. Rounding the corner, I found her room and, without knocking, quietly peeked in to find it empty. Stepping further in, I noted the open and empty bathroom.

No one was here.

As I turned to walk out, my eyes caught a glimpse of blood on the bed. Droplets of bright red against the white sheet next to a wad of gnarled-up tape and a discarded IV cannula yanked too fast. There was no discharge paperwork either. Only an empty plastic bag on the floor next to a discarded hospital-edition gown and socks.

If properly discharged, the IV would have been cleanly removed, and the room would have been cleaned. I turned towards the voice of a nurse down the hall, 'Yes, officer, the doctor is discharging her early at the patient's request. If you need to gather details for your report, I recommend doing so now. She seems motivated to leave.'

Their footsteps echoed down the hall, and I knew I had to go. I didn't want to be caught early or get Lou in trouble, and Lila clearly wasn't here. Ducking into the stairwell across the hall, I descended quickly, figuring Lila had to be mere minutes ahead of me.

Maybe she knew the police would question her—nothing to worry about, since she'd done nothing wrong. So why avoid them? Was she scared of getting in trouble, or was she here because she was already in trouble? Was she running from some guy, and that's why she was so cagey with her identity and details the night we met?

Growling, I shook my head.

My imagination conjured too many details from Moira's fiasco with that shithead Jensen. Lila said she was passing through, so she likely left because she wanted to get on the road. By the time I hit the ground floor, I'd convinced myself I was a damned fool for coming here to begin with.

"Sam?" Moira, clearing the parking garage door across the lobby, hoisted her purse and glanced at her watch. "What are you doing here so early in the morning?"

"Hey, sis?" I hugged her, willing my heart to slow down. "You, okay?"

"Just a check-up." She answered. "I prefer to get in and out early so my day is free."

"And my nieces?" I made a dramatic show of scanning around for the babies.

"Chase gave me some solo time—even ordering me to grab a coffee on the way back." She rolled her eyes in feigned annoyance, but the smile on her face showed she loved it. "Decaf, of course."

"Ah, okay. Well," I looked at my watch. "I don't want to make you late, so - "

"FREEZE, buster." Her voice's rare edge stopped me cold. "The last time I saw you, you bolted like a murderous clown chased you." She squinted her eyes and continued. "All because I asked you about the woman you bloodied your knuckles over." She glanced down at my hand with an air of authority.

"Bruised. Not bloodied." I sighed with resignation. "And I was running from a nosy brother and equally - "

"Loving sister?" she countered with a smile. "Chase told me you've been cagey all week. And that you missing work was unheard of." She crossed her arms and continued. "And now you show up here, sneaking out a stairwell." Her hand swept down the front of me. "Not in your uniform, I might add." She narrowed her eyes and added, "And avoiding talking to me...again." Her voice softened. "Are you okay, Sam?"

"Moira," I waved over to the elevators and made a final plea to dodge her insistent questioning. "You're appointment - "

"Can fuck off straight to hell." I blinked at the language falling out of her mouth. "Or you can come talk to me while I have a lactation appointment to try and provide more milk for my ravenous daughters. Though Chase will lose it if you get up close and personal with my nips." She smiled at my wincing grimace, her raw honesty relaxing me. "I'm here... I'm listening....and I'm not budging."

Too tired to resist, and suddenly desperate to tell someone everything in my head, I spilled. I told her how Lila and I met the night the girls were born. I shared that we'd had a fun time at the bar, a night together, and I told her how I'd been losing sleep ever since. Then I shared how I'd come across her on the call last night, only to discover her hotel room and its state of half-lived-in chaos.

"And I stalked her here like a crazy person to try and scratch her out of my system, but she's already gone, and I don't know what the fuck I'm doing, and maybe I'm wasting my damned time on a woman who doesn't remember who I am beyond the Jackass from a one-night-stand."

I rubbed my hands down my beard, drained and relieved to have it all off my chest. For her part, Moira stayed silent, an open expression of kindness on her face, as I rambled. Having a sister around was pretty cool. Troy would have jumped in with interrogation, and Chase wouldn't have lasted two sentences without interrupting with enthusiastic questions.

"Go to her hotel." She said at last. "You need answers to get her out of your system. And if she came in last night but is already gone, chances are she's gone back there. So, your best bet is to go talk it out."

"God," I huffed at her decisive confidence. "You make it sound so easy."

"Look, Sam." She tilted her head as if talking to a small child. "I certainly don't have the history to be a voice of authority, given how Chase and I came together." She lifted her hand and rested it on my

135

shoulder. "But I know you well enough to know you are a good man. My husband trusts you with me and the girls, which is saying a lot, given how overprotective he is. But I know your integrity." I blinked at the unexpected compliment. "As much as this woman has you spun, going and talking to her is your quickest way to both show her who you are and also find out if she's worthy of all this energy you're giving her." She then cocked an eyebrow and added, "But when she starts talking...shut the hell up and listen!" Shaking her head, she laughed at me. "I've never seen a group of men so prone to interrupting, monosyllabic, short-hand as you and your brothers."

"Monosyllabic short-hand?"

"Your communication is efficient. But speaking as an outsider, sometimes y'all need more nouns to let the rest of us follow along." She patted my cheek again and tilted her head with a smirk. "So use your words...Funcle Sam. But give her space to think things through." Glancing at her watch, she added, "I'm only five minutes late if I go now, but I can -"

I cut her off with a wave of my hand as I pressed the elevator call button.

"Go. You helped. I'm good." I answered before realizing I'd interrupted her with three entire sentences in only five words. Her knowing smirk had me adding, "But...you aren't an outsider. You're 100% family."

"So, you can use whole sentences." She laughed as she got on the elevator.

"A 100% pain in the ass, little sister," I called as the elevator closed on her flipping me both middle fingers.

23

SAM

HOPING TO CATCH LILA before she discovered her car missing, I went to the liquor store. The clerk told me she'd already come and gone—cursing a blue streak at my note when she called an Uber. Surprised to learn she had such a lead, my sense of urgency ratcheted up several notches at the added frustration I'd caused her. I wanted her to feel safe with me, not angry because of me, and that...gave me pause.

Driving to the hotel, I considered all the unspoken things between us. We shared one hot night, one ambulance ride, and nothing else. That didn't count as a situationship even after our vulnerable moment in the ER hallway. Not when she'd never reached out to me between those two moments.

And yet... 'Just you.'

That's what she said when I asked if I could call someone. She had no person. I could be that person.

Arriving at the hotel, I walked into the lobby to a beautifully disheveled, wickedly angry, little Hellcat giving the front desk the what-for.

"Look, lady, I've had a helluva night!" Lila leaned on the counter, gesturing wildly at the fresh black eye on her cheek. "I *know* you gave me two room keys, and I'm *sorry* I've fucking lost 'em both, but I can't show you my fucking ID unless you let me into my fucking room where my fucking driver's license is inside of what sure as shit better be my safely stowed away purse or so help me god that Jackass is..."

"Ma'am, I apologize," The flustered employee cut Lila off, impressively holding her ground in the face of a customer using fuck like a comma. "There is nothing I can do until a manager arrives at 10 am; perhaps your husband has the other key."

I loved that Lila's fury made her tiny frame feel ten feet tall.

"Woman to woman, I don't give a flying fuck if 'my husband' has my key. You shouldn't give two shits that your manager isn't here. You have a fucking brain between those ears. Let's do this! Grab your little card and walk me the fuck up to my room, and I'll prove -"

"Sorry," I said, stepping in before the front desk clerk got her full ass handed to her.

Lila stiffened as I tugged at her belt until she leaned back into me.

"I have our room keys here." I showed both keys to Lila and smiled at the front desk attendant. "We had a little fender bender and got separated in the chaos. The missus tends to get cranky when she's tired." I grazed my beard along Lila's ear, sliding my hand down to lace our fingers together. It was as much for show as anything, but getting a feel of the woman who'd driven me half-crazy all week didn't suck. "We stayed out a little too long last night, didn't we, baby?" To my great relief, Lila didn't pull away from me—nodding in agreement even.

I calmly turned us towards the elevator, hoping beyond hope that Lila wouldn't create a scene. A subtle tug against my arm had me holding my breath as I turned back, preparing to explain to Troy why he might need to bail me out of jail.

"I...um." Lila looked at me, her face flashing with a thousand emotions: anger, confusion, and something that vaguely resembled relief. Then she turned back to the front desk, cleared her throat, and looked the woman in the eyes. "Sorry...about the yelling. I didn't know he - "

"It's no trouble, ma'am." The woman said curtly. "I am glad it worked out."

"Come on, babe," I whispered, tugging until Lila turned back to me, her face awash in confusion.

We didn't speak—just rode the elevator and walked the hall in heavy silence.

Not a sound between us as I held the door open.

Lila entered quietly, eyes dark and downcast, and it killed me to see her light snuffed out.

"I'm sorry about the confusion over the jeep." I broke the silence, keeping my voice calm. "I figured you didn't want it left behind with your stuff inside. I moved it to be safe and didn't get a chance to tell you before you left the hospital." I watched, waiting for that flash of anger to return, but she just sat on the bed, shoulders sagging as if the world were too heavy.

"Thank you." I might have missed her soft words if I weren't holding my damned breath. The hot-tempered sailor ripping the front desk a new asshole shrank to a bandaged, stitched, exhausted, and stripped bare Lila, and with it so shrank away all my questions and frustrations.

Where was my fiery hellcat?

She glanced at her hands, flipping them in examination. Then she grazed her fingertips along her bruised cheek before fingering the bandage at her hairline with a wince.

"Wait." I knelt in front of her, lifting her chin just enough to be eye-to-eye. "Lemme help you." I gently tugged the tape from her hair, inspecting two fresh stitches. "It's small. Clean stitches, too. Rinds must have done it; he's a wiz at hiding 'em." I offered a smile, but her face was so sorrowful that my chest ached.

"How ya feeling?"

"I'm so...." Her voice cracked, a tear slipping down her cheek. "I'm so tired."

The haunted burden in her eyes felt scarily like trauma victims I'd treated in the military. Bigger than being alone, sore, and shaken from a robbery she bravely...stupidly...thwarted. She wore a bone-deep exhaustion like a million miles of bad road.

She pulled at her coat with uncooperative fingers and slow arms. Standing, I helped her remove her jacket and long-sleeve flannel, baring her arms from under her thin t-shirt.

"You pulled your IV too fast?" I nodded at the bruise blooming in the crook of her elbow. She looked at it, shaking her head dismissively and scowling at her shoes. Her clumsy attempt at toeing off her boots was painful to watch. I knelt again, removing her shoes and noting the goose bumps on her arms.

"Why are you here?" Her question came out flat and lifeless. I considered a thousand different things I wanted to say in that moment. Still, her words from the hospital rang through my head again, and I couldn't bring myself to do anything beyond being her person.

"I'm here for you," I brushed away her tears with my thumb.

"Why?"

"To take care of you." I stood up, kicked off my boots, tossed my coat aside, and pulled back the comforter. "You are in shock. So we're gonna rest, and when you wake up, we can hash it all out."

I tugged Lila to her feet with almost no resistance. As I lifted off her shirt, I saw a fresh bruise on her ribs to match the one on her cheek. I wasn't wrapped like a cracked rib, but she had to be far sorer than she let on.

"Let's get you out of these damn tight pants and under the covers." She let me peel off her jeans without argument, using my shoulders for balance as she lifted each leg. Then I tucked her into bed, tucking the sheets tight around her to counter the adrenaline shock and its companion chills.

"You'll...stay with me?" A simple, loaded question.

I considered my words carefully, but looking down at her, seeing her so teary-eyed and exhausted with all that beautiful fiery light missing, simplified things. No matter what drew her here, or how short our time, I couldn't leave her.

She might wake up breathing fire or shedding tears–so be it.

Stripping down to my underwear, I crawled in behind her. Letting the warmth of my body answer her question. I buried my face in her hair, drawing in her scent, as she pulled my hand to rest on the softness of her belly. Even her feet slid back until they tangled with mine, and she sank deep into my bones. Being here like this, bodies intertwined, comforting her with my body, felt instinctual and right.

"Thank you." She mumbled before we both passed out.

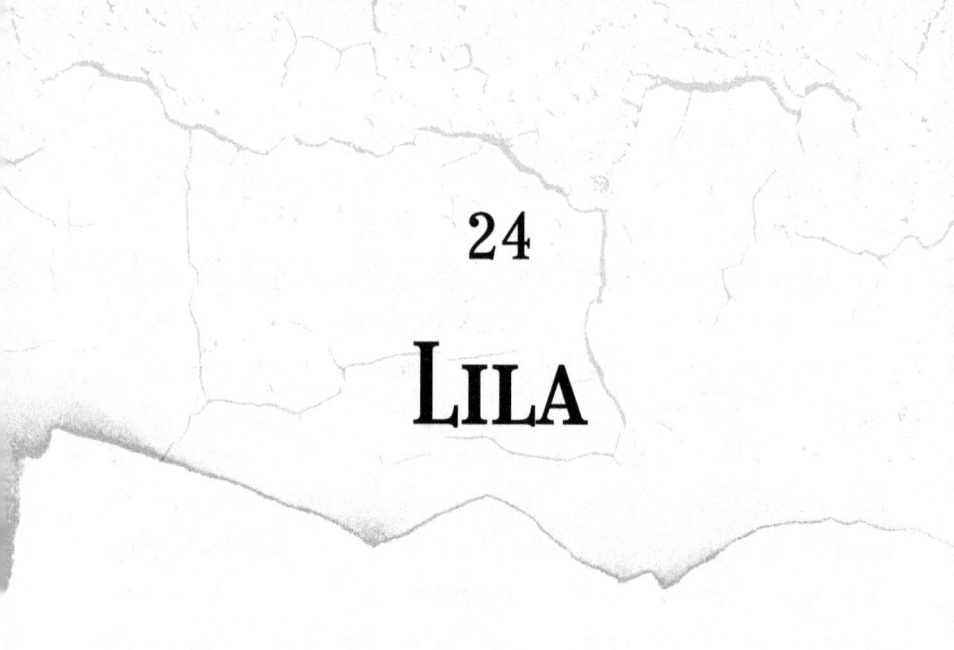

24

LILA

FOR THE FIRST TIME in as long as I could remember, I didn't wake up in a nightmare's grip. I wasn't cold, disoriented, or unsure of my whereabouts. My eyes opened naturally—easy as breathing. I was warm, and safe, and rested, and it...was...bliss. I slipped a hand out to check the time on my phone–6 pm. A groan protested behind me as a giant hand tugged me back under the covers.

"Stay," Sam, my do-gooder lumberjack, grumbled. I couldn't remember the last time I felt this safe. It was the most depressing thought I'd ever had, and it felt so, so good.

"If I tell you I need a shower," I whispered, wondering how awake he was. "You gonna let me get up?"

"No." He drawled, a smile lacing his tone. "You need more sleep." The soft bristle of his beard along my back was relaxing. I considered obeying his order if only to indulge the small luxury of a kind man who wanted to be with me.

His warmth was foreign—and soothing.

Lingering in his arms, falling back into dreamless sleep free from nightmares, was tempting. But the hospital's antiseptic stench coated my nose, along with the copper tang of dried blood and iodine. The pillow pressed my stitches into aching, my ribs begged to stretch, and the physical discomfort of it all pushed me to rise.

"I feel gross." I dragged myself to sitting, wincing at my head's pounding reminder of the concussion.

"You need more rest," Sam said, sitting up, resting his lips on my shoulder, and gently lifting my hair to examine me. "But your black eye is pretty good–no new swelling around the stitches." He took stock a little longer before sighing in resignation. "I suppose a shower can't hurt." His statement dropped without a hint of sarcasm or double entendre. "I'll start the water, then you can clean up while I call into work to talk my boss off a ledge for no-showing."

"Oh shit." A thousand pounds of guilt joined the storm in my head. "I didn't think... didn't know...when I asked you to stay...I should've - "

"Stop." A gentle command. So different from our first night together when he was primal and possessive. "I slept for shit all week. I was no good to anyone. I just failed to call in. I'm a big boy... it's not on you."

Before I could say more, he slipped out of bed and shuffled towards the bathroom, not bothering to cover himself in any way. The view of his phenomenal ass clad in the tight, black underwear, thighs flexing with each step, brought a fresh perspective, even as memory flashed to our night together–flashes of us pressed together in passion.

My phone chirped a text alert, and I reached slowly to avoid jostling my head.

Sgt. Troy Wilder: Checking on your vacation situation. My rental is available.

I stared at the screen, unsure how to respond. I still hadn't decided if I trusted Sgt. Wilder enough to meet him. I'd run his name through every database I could access and found he co-owned a real estate business with his family. The domain registration and city tax records matched—just "Wilder," no first names, but enough to confirm ownership. The company's digital footprint was thin: a few dated listings with solid reviews and consistent timestamps, which made it unlikely they were spoofed fronts. Social media activity was recent and organic, not bot-fed or paid-follower-inflated. All signs pointed to legit—but was that enough to trust that he harbored no connections with Marcus Brinks?

I texted carefully, trying not to close the door but not committing myself.

> Me: Is it possible to see a property link beforehand, or do you need a commitment?

> Sgt. Troy Wilder: I will do you one better. Let's meet at the property. I can meet you in an hour. No commitment necessary.

He sent an address, but it came across as pushy and raised all my alarms. Then again, he seemed genuinely interested in discussing discrepancies in internal affairs and didn't feel dirty. The mental back-and-forth grew irritating since I was typically very decisive. I chalked up the apprehension to fatigue and pivoted the conversation back under my control.

> Me: I need a bit longer. Make it 2 hours?

> Sgt Troy Wilder: Agreed.

He agreed to the time change so quickly that I suddenly missed my sidearm and the comfort of knowing that no matter what I walked into...I was packing heat. I chastised myself for not considering it sooner and made a mental list of things to do. I needed to get away from Sam, find a weapon, and reach the address Wilder sent beforehand. If I parked discreetly, I could walk in under the cover of the surroundings and scope out the area. Something I worried about pulling off in my concussed state–I wasn't going into this in top form.

"Water's ready," Sam's voice called me towards a hot shower like a siren. Wrapping my sheet around me, I walked into the bathroom and found Sam pouring bath salts into the giant tub.

"That's not a shower," I scowled at the steam-filled tub.

"Don't miss a thing, do ya." That cocked eyebrow and irritatingly handsome half-smirk threw me straight back to our night of unbridled fucking between slinging insults. As such, when he finally looked up at me, I prepared myself for the volley of fresh snark, but that's not what I got.

He was soft. His smile, genuine.

I'm not sure what emotion my face held, but he noticed it with a flash of concern as he closed the gap between us.

"Make no mistake, I'd love to go round two with you, Hellcat. Maybe even round three and four." He slipped my sheet off and spun me around to unhook my bra. "But you've been through the wringer. You've got stitches, a fresh shiner, and bruised ribs, and the last thing you need is me pawing at you." Bra discarded, I felt vulnerable and exposed. "If you want me to give you privacy, I will...no pressure. But between you and me, soaking in that tub with you sounds like a slice of heaven, and it might do us both good to share space without being fuck-drunk."

"Fuck-drunk?" My laugh bubbled up. "Boy, Shakespeare, you know how to make a girl swoon."

"No pressure. No strings." His smiling hazel eyes held genuine warmth and what I might have mistaken for concern. If I could recognize concern–lately, I only held rage or numbness—except that night with Sam. He gave me release.

"I'm not...I have a..." I fumbled for the right words to tell him I was now on a clock and expected somewhere, but I worried I would hurt his feelings.

"Shall we?" He swept a hand over the tub, and I paused for a count of three before accepting the invitation.

His easy charm, once again, rendered me a puddle of useless goo.

Stripping my panties, I stepped into the tub and sank into the steaming water, Sam watching my every move. His underwear hit the floor and I couldn't help raking my eyes over his beautiful olive-tanned body. I hadn't seen his muscular back up close before, and I couldn't help but admire the strength that feathered there. His broad shoulders flexed clearly defined muscles that cut an impressive path as they dipped towards his glorious ass. I imagined those muscles pumping into me, and a flutter low in my belly came unbidden.

"Getting a good look?" I'd blinked up, finding him watching me ogle him in the mirror. I could have died from embarrassment. "It's yours to look at, Lila." Before I could utter a word of snarky comeback about his arrogance or ego, he turned around, putting me eye level with his giant beast of a cock.

"Holy...." Words, normally quick on my tongue, fell flat at the sight of his already sizeable dick–growing before my eyes. Long and veined, it rose until it curved towards his navel, and I was frozen, fighting the urge to reach out and slip that thing into my mouth.

"I'm committed to being good here, Hellcat, but you keep staring at my dick like that and I'm gonna think you wanna do more than soak in this tub." The full blush that burned my cheeks came in a rush, and as if on cue, my head gave a throbbing ache that snapped me back with a hiss.

"I'm sorry," I winced at the pain. "I'm like 10 shades of not myself and - "

"It's okay." Sam cooed, stepping into the tub behind me. "You're allowed an off day after single-handedly stopping a robbery." His feet slid down the sides of my hips as he tugged me back, cradling me into his lap. "Come here."

Sam nestled me between his legs, guiding me until I lay against his chest. Gently, he released my hair from its messy bun and draped it over his shoulder, free of the water. The move relieved the pressure I hadn't realized was building from the weight of my hair tugging against my stitches, and I sighed at the release. We stayed like that, soaking in the steam, every muscle slowly unwinding. Sam dragged a warm cloth in and out of the water, caressing my shoulders, my neck, and across the top of my breasts. His sensual touch relaxed me, and I found myself growing increasingly at ease in his arms. Maybe that's why his next question didn't shake me.

"Why are you here, Lila?" A loaded question if ever there was one.

"Why am I in town? Or why am I in this tub?"

"Well now, both." His laugh sent breathy vibrations down the side of my neck.

"The second one is easier," I huffed. "You stole my car, and my hotel key, and forced me into bed with you."

"I did all that now?" He gently tugged my chin towards him, releasing me only after I gave him a small smile. "I'm terrible, aren't I?"

"Big sensitive baby," I teased.

147

"So why are you in town?"

On any other day, I would've given a quick-witted side step to steer the conversation away from me. Any other guy, I'd have kicked his balls out the front door—but this guy, this day, was different. I don't know if it was the concussion, or the bath, or the glorious day of sleep where I felt rested and safe, but the only answer that seemed right was the truth.

"I'm here to catch a murderer."

25

SAM

O F ALL THE ANSWERS I expected, murder wasn't one of them, and it took effort to hold my voice level as I processed her words to respond.

"I'm going to need you to give me a little more."

For her part, Lila's body never tensed or froze, leaning into me like this wasn't news to her—it was a weight she'd grown accustomed to. As if murder was so normalized that she was numb to the enormity of it.

"My dad and brother," she sighed. "They were cops."

Were.

"I was a cop too...cybercrimes division, though, not riding patrol like they did." I flagged that for later, but stayed quiet. "I'd started seeing a pattern coming across my desk. Missing persons, or homicides, but all involving the fringe of society...faceless people most wouldn't miss. But they connected weirdly. I started compiling information on a possible

Perp. A real piece of work. White collar, top-tier, power-playing kind of upper-crust, Grade-A, scumball. But I couldn't get enough to nail him."

Her voice took on an edge as she described the guy, and I caught a glimpse of a thousand-yard stare in her reflection.

"He was heavily connected to all the power players, and at each turn I'd get close, he'd slip right past me." Lila never slowed her strokes with the washcloth as she spoke, but her body was otherwise frozen. "I'd begun taking heat from my captain on the cold cases I was digging up. I tried to convince my dad about my theory, but he was...being a dad, I guess—told me to lie low and let it go."

She lowered her voice into a masculine mimic, "'Lila-girl, don't make waves. You've got a good thing going with your job. You're smart. Use your head and let this go.'"

The washcloth dipped into the water, running up and over my arms as she continued.

"I know my dad was worried for me, but it stung that he didn't trust my instincts. But my brother... he believed me. Said he'd hit the streets and try to get me more information as long as I kept my head down."

The washcloth paused as her voice dropped to a whisper.

"I tried."

I ached to say something, to encourage her, or to tell her she didn't have to finish if it was too hard. Moira's voice in my head stopped me, *'When she starts talking...shut the hell up and listen'.* So, I took the cloth and began caressing her with the warm water, as much to ease her as to hold onto my patience.

Eventually, she exhaled and kept going.

"I was off-duty one night when I got an anonymous call on my cell. A modulated voice with a courtesy heads-up about a robbery about to go down on my dad's route. The caller said two officers would be down if I didn't hurry." Her voice thinned, cracking as she kept going. I was at a loss as to what to do other than wrap my arms around her and ride it out. One hand around her chest, another around her waist, I held her as she spilled it all out. "I knew it was them—my dad and my brother. I called their phones, but they didn't pick up. I called the station to send backup, but I couldn't just sit there. I tracked their location on my phone, and ran to the scene as fast as I could, but I was too late to do anything and..."

Lila's breathing grew ragged, and her chest heaved as her words tumbled out.

"It was a liquor store hold-up. My dad took two to the vest, but a third clipped him above the neckline, and I tried to stop the bleeding, but my hands weren't strong enough, and his eyes were looking at me, but he was gone before I ever got there, I think...." Her story came faster and faster, the pressure of my arms doing nothing to protect her from the crash she was about to take. "But my brother...he was still alive. His vest took most of the shots, and I thought I had time, but his arm and leg were beat up pretty bad, and I held his hand, and...and he looked at me, but...he couldn't breathe...he could barely talk."

Her hands grasped my arms around her, and her whole body shook with the deep breaths she sucked in, but she pushed on.

So fucking brave.

"He was coughing, and blood came out of his mouth, and all he could tell me was I was right. I was right about Marcus. He had done this, and he'd killed my family to send me a message to back off." Lila sat up, hunched and heaving as she took in huge gulps of air in between broken words and phrases. "I pushed...too hard... and I fought my captain... and I always pushed, and I... my dad and my brother ...I couldn't get there in time, and I couldn't stop the blood, and they died because I wouldn't stop...I did that...I should have stopped -" Curling almost into a fetal position, Lila turned to her side as I pulled her against me, doing my best to whisper soothing words into her hair as I held her through wave after wave of full-body sobs.

The way she cried, the violence of it all, told me these tears were fresh and had never seen the light of day. It made me wonder how recent this all was since I hadn't heard about a shoot-out like this. Not that it mattered in the shadow of the single emotion that came careening at me out of nowhere. How hard would it be to track down Marcus and make him pay?

"Jesus Christ, Lila," I murmured when her sobs began to ease. "That's a hell of a burden for such tiny shoulders." I stroked her hair and tried to use my voice, my body, to anchor her into the present again. "I'm sorry that I made you go there...I never expected that. I'm glad you shared it with me."

A few more minutes passed, and she lay limp, silent as the grave and clinging to my arms as the water cooled and her tears stopped. If not for the occasional hitch in her breathing, I would've thought she'd drifted off to sleep. Of course, she would carry PTSD after witnessing this. And the liquor store hold-up that landed her on my rig...a perfect trigger. She was folding in on herself, and I scrambled for anything to bring her back.

"It kinda seems like this relaxing bath sorta backfired. How about we order some food?" She didn't speak, or couldn't, but she nodded in agreement.

That was enough.

26

LILA

I'D NEVER SHARED THOSE details with anyone. Even the therapist didn't penetrate the brick wall I'd placed around those memories. The brief morning flashes that clawed out of my dreams were unbearable enough, so I fought bringing any of it into the light of day.

But Sam.

The way his voice rumbled through his chest, his body wrapped around me, I couldn't explain it. When he asked, the words fell like rain, and with them a thunderous hail of emotions. Each truth dragged me deeper—guilt, shame, and self-loathing. Tears disguised as justice or vengeance raged until I hit rock bottom. Even my lungs stopped begging for air.

But then...Sam.

He never flinched as I shattered, holding me until the tears stopped and our fingers pruned. He spoke words I could barely hear, over a numbing buzz in my head I couldn't control, and I nodded agreement to things I didn't comprehend because at last I was empty enough to admit to myself just how profoundly lonely I'd been.

Agonizing grief in solitude.

Somehow, I was wrapped in a robe on the edge of the bed, and he crouched in front of me.

"I'm going to go downstairs and grab our food." His hands were warm, resting on my forearms with a squeeze. "I'll be right back, okay?" I heard him, but it wasn't until he gave my hand a squeeze that I looked at his eyes, saw the rock-steady concern. He waited for an answer. I nodded, and as the door closed, my phone chirped a text alert.

> Sgt. Troy Wilder: Did you receive the address I sent before? If you need directions, call.

I was late for whatever rental he wanted to show me—or, you know, murder me in. The cloak-and-dagger...all too much. I couldn't handle one more thing.

> Me: Sorry for bailing. I have arrangements for now. Thanks.

The three dots that appeared on my screen told me he was typing a reply, but I shut my phone off and tossed it into my bag.

I didn't have a single fuck left to give.

Whatever connection Sgt. Wilder offered me, whatever assistance he gave to catch Brinks, would be there tomorrow.

Or it wouldn't be.

Whatever.

I couldn't handle it tonight.

I couldn't handle anything tonight.

It was all too heavy.

Too real.
Too much.

27

SAM

I EXTENDED THE ROOM reservation a few more days and ordered takeout from my favorite hole-in-the-wall Chinese joint. While waiting in the lobby, Lila's story played on loop—colored by every gut-wrenching detail my EMT training could fill in.

Her dad took a hit to the neck. Bleeding out would have been fast...but messy. No doubt, when she arrived, the pool of blood would've been enormous, and she would've been covered in it to hold his neck. No amount of strength would have saved a jugular hit. She'd have been kneeling in her dad's blood and would've seen his blown pupils.

The hollow stare of an empty shell was brutal on strangers, but someone you love? Unthinkable.

Then there was her brother. He'd had a torn-up leg and arm, and blood coming from his mouth. A bullet likely clipped his lung. He would have lingered as his capacity to breathe diminished. That would have brought with it the awful, wet, rattling gasps of a man drowning from the inside out.

A shit way to go.

Seasoned medics could crack under less, and this tiny powerhouse carried it for... how long? She grieved like it was fresh. That kind of rawness—I'd only seen on trauma victims, right down to the shell-shocked look on her face when I left her sitting on the edge of the bed.

But the timeline...it didn't work.

I'd not heard anything about two cops dying. On the other hand, her lie about coming into town to see a friend made more sense. Who in their right mind would share something so raw with a guy from a one-night stand? So if she came to my town to catch this Marcus guy, then he was here... or she thought he was. And judging by the multiple laptops and the lived-in Jeep, she wasn't just passing through. But that meant her dad and brother were shot somewhere nearby—and there's no way I wouldn't have heard. Essex County wasn't that big.

Heading up the elevator, takeout in hand, I opened my phone to fire off a text to Troy, but hesitated. If I ask him about dead cops, he'd 100% climb my ass for details and want to know how I knew, which would lead to Lila. He'd want to know all about her, including her knowledge of it all, which would only open more questions. When I opened the door and saw that tiny fireball curled in a terry-cloth cocoon on the bed, I slipped the phone back into my pocket. Troy's instincts were only rivaled by his tenacity—and the last thing this broken woman needed was another Wilder in her space.

I needed more info before I brought this to Troy.

And Lila needed time to recover.

I needed to put her together first... then I'd dig deeper.

WILDER FAMILY GROUP CHAT

-3-

Me: I need to push spaghetti night a few days.

Troy: Reason?

Me: I just need to.

Chase: Bro...

Moira: Is it the woman?

Me: Yeah.

Moira: You took my advice and talked to her?

Troy: You're pushing dinner...for the woman?

Chase: Wait—has my wife met this mystery woman before we have?

Moira: So she's worth your time and energy?

Me: It's complicated. I need more time.

Chase: Is it the barfight girl?

Troy: It must be.

Me: Guys... I've never asked before. I just need a few days. I'll explain everything after.

Troy: You get 3. Then we talk—family business.

Chase: You good?

Me: I'm fine.

Troy: You sure?

Me: Yes.

Moira: I'm here if you need me.

Chase: We all are.

28

SAM

L ILA AND I SPENT the rest of that night in silence. She barely
ate, but was so exhausted that sleep came easily. My crawling
into bed behind her–never questioned. The next morning, I asked
her about breakfast, but she shook her head, wincing again at her
stitches and declaring herself 'not hungry'. Deciding enough was
enough, I grabbed both sets of keys and picked up something health-
ier than hotel pastries. When I returned, I found her nestled into her
makeshift desk, laser-focused on the laptops.

"Coffee?" She held out a hand in demand, never looking up from
her work.

"Smoothie." I slid a plastic cup into her hands, enjoying her
honey-brown scowl. "Caffeine affects like 10 different hormones in
your system, and you're freshly concussed. Show me a little more
appetite and hydration, and we'll see about coffee tomorrow."

"You're killing me." Lila sipped the bright red smoothie, scrunching her nose before shoving the cup at me. "I've been guzzling coffee since high school. Believe when I say my blood type is A-caffeinated."

She flicked her fingers at my other hand, demanding my coffee. Having anticipated this, I shared my herbal tea with anti-inflammatory properties. Not even trying to hide my smirk as she slugged back a mouthful of steeped raspberry leaf.

"Fucking hell! Don't tell me you're one of those health nuts. If that bag is full of granola, I'll bodily take you down...bruised ribs or not, Lumberjack."

"Calm down, Hellcat." I sat on the opposite bed and pulled a thick breakfast burrito from the bag. At that, she turned away from her laptop and peeled back the wrapper on a bacon, egg, and cheese burrito, eating a few modest bites before closing it up to sit on the bedside table.

"You gotta eat more than that," I prodded. "Protein helps recovery."

"Look, I appreciate the food, and..." She let her words trail off, the weight of a thousand unspoken emotions igniting the air between us. "I have work to do. I'll be okay. I'll give the front desk my credit card, but– "

"Front desk is handled." I didn't bother looking up as I pulled my burrito out of the bag.

"I didn't ask you to do that." Her words were clipped and the amber flash of irritation in her eyes, gorgeous.

"I didn't ask if you wanted me to." My dry response goaded her, begging a fight.

"I'm not some helpless damsel, you know." She stood, her tiny frame enveloped in the oversized robe. "One moment of weakness doesn't make me weak." It was an interesting turn of phrase...and I hated that I couldn't unpack it.

"You're right," I mumbled around a mouthful. "It doesn't." My flat agreement irritated the crap out of her, but I didn't need her blood pressure rising, so I let her off the hook. "Look, Hellcat, you're healing from the concussion, and my EMT training won't let me leave you alone. Like it or not, I'm hanging around." I hoped that deflecting away from the trauma would ease her irritation. "I have emails to catch up on. We can talk more later if you want." With that, I leaned against the headboard of the bed and began scrolling through emails on my phone, looking as busy as possible.

I meant it. I was staying until she was healed... or more, though hell if I knew what.

It took a moment before Lila crawled into her bed-desk with a huff–finishing her burrito and smoothie within the hour.

I'd never spent so much time with a woman before, but being near Lila eased a tension I hadn't realized I'd been carrying. She sank into her work, at home in her tech hovel, and it was mesmerizing. Her little noises, the faces she made, were oddly fascinating. Even the furrowed brow of concentration was endearing, as I remembered how it looked when it was angry. More than that, when she'd rise to move around, I got to watch as she stretched her arms or arched her back. Every bend she made had me imagining how she'd look if the robe hit the floor, and I had to rein in the near-constant hard-on.

To distract myself, I searched her name and came across a single mention tied to a news blurb about two NYPD officers—both with the last name Rivera—killed in the line of duty. Lila wasn't named directly, but the liquor store detailed lined up close enough that I figured they had to be her family. The article was a repost picked up by social media, so the original publication date was unclear. Still, it felt recent enough to sting. What I didn't find was any clear link to someone named Marcus...

or my town. A few hours later, Lila closed her laptop with a huff and sank into her pillows.

"Didn't find what you wanted?" I asked, hoping she'd open up and give me a few details without me having to pry.

"Don't worry about it." She swatted at me like a gnat, and the dismissal grated.

"Talk to me," I commanded softly, swinging my legs off the bed to face her. "Maybe I can soundboard it." I wasn't leaving her alone, but I also wasn't leaving without answers. This woman had worked her way under my skin, and whether she liked it or not, she was now going to deal with me.

"Forget it." Her voice held indifference, but the thousand-yard stare had returned.

I wanted to pull her out, but didn't know how, and it made me half-mad. She got up and started to walk away when I placed my hand around her wrist, gently halting her.

"I've been here all day. Fed you and watched over you. I've tried to give you time, but our last conversation really left you feeling wrecked. I feel terrible for ripping that open for you." She flinched like I'd slapped her, but I pushed on. "I'm gonna help, and I'm not leaving, so let me." Saying it out loud, I realized I meant every word. I wanted to put her back together, fix what was broken, and see her smi le.

"Help me?" She tried to pull away, but I held steady.

"You think this Marcus guy is here?" She shook her head in protest, but I pushed on. "I have resources in town. I can help if you'll stop shutting me out."

"I won't put you in the middle of this. It's dangerous." Her voice rose—panic creeping in the edges of control. "This guy–"

"Is an evil piece of shit," I finished, my other hand lifting as if to soothe a wild horse verging on stampede. "But he's just a man...and I can hold my own." I flexed my bicep with a smirk, the comedic relief landing well with her eye-rolling response. "I'm also stubborn as fuck." I slid my hands around to the back of her thighs, tugging her closer. "So, use me."

I hadn't meant any innuendo, but her face said she heard one.

"Sam," Lila breathed my name, fingers tracing my biceps to my shoulders. "I don't have the bandwidth for you." Her words said no, but she leaned into me.

"Your mouth is telling me something entirely different than your body right now." It took all my self-restraint not to slide my hands up to her ass, whirl her around, and have her underneath me. "I'm gonna need you to use your words. What do you need?" Lila pulled back enough that I feared she'd retreat from me again. Instead, her fingers wrapped around the robe ties, tugging the belt until it fell loosely around her waist, letting the robe slip to the floor.

Glory...Hallelujah.

The last time I saw her naked, she was fresh from the hospital—nothing sexy about it. Since then, she'd hid under that damned robe like a shield. The chance to now take in the gorgeous figure before me as she stood, fully bared, was a goddamn gift. Her warm, golden skin begged to be touched, but it was those full, perfect breasts that had my mouth watering. Full and heavy, I ached to slide my hands underneath them, to press my face between them, and take a mouthful of those pebbled nipples. But the bruise on her ribs was still visible, and I restrained myself from manhandling her when she needed more time to heal.

"You gonna admire my tits all night," Lila whispered as she stepped in between my knees once more, "Jackass?" She wound her fingers through my hair as her words echoed our first encounter. One she clearly remembered as fondly as I did. My balls ached for me to take her, claim her, as she lifted one knee to straddle me.

"Fucking hell," I growled, my hands sliding to her hips. "You're still healing, Hellcat."

"I need this." She whimpered, her arousal hitting my nose as she pulled me close and leaned down to kiss me. "Please." That single, raw word nearly undid me. My hands trailed up her thighs, the apex radiating heat. "Just take it all away." I understood exactly what she meant.

She didn't have the bandwidth to talk but needed something else to feel.

I let my fingers graze against her core, softly stroking her as my other hand held the rounded swell of her breast. Timing it just right, I sucked her nipple into my mouth as my fingers circled the outer edges of her swollen clit.

"Condom." She exhaled.

"Never leave home without 'em," I mumbled, working my way to her other breast. "But we won't need those." I halted her follow-up question by sliding a finger inside, cutting her words short with a gasp. "You don't need me fucking you while you heal." I pumped my finger slowly in and out, in and out, before pulling it free and circling her clit once more. "But that doesn't mean I can't take care of you."

I watched her face as I slipped two fingers into her, feeling her walls stretch around me as she tossed her head back, sending her wild mane of hair cascading down her back. She arched her back, pressing her mound closer to me, but I held back, keeping a simple rhythm of in and out, circling, then in and out again.

"Sam...I need..." The walls of her pussy fluttered around my fingers, and my dick raged as she panted and tugged at my hair. I wanted to feel her around my cock so badly that pre-cum spread in my pants, but watching her face as she surrendered to me was too intoxicating to stop.

"Tell me, baby," I sped up my strokes, in and out, in and out, circling and dipping into her tight heat. "What do you need?" Slipping out again, I returned to her core with three fingers, her juices sliding down my hand as she stretched around me with a moan. Halting at the knuckles, I let her body adjust to my fingers and placed my mouth just on the edge of her nipple. "Use your words, baby," I growled, letting my teeth graze against her nipple.

"God...Sam." She was coiled tension, radiating heat as she squirmed on my lap. "Please... let me cum."

My eyes on hers, I sucked in her nipple just as I rocked my hand beneath her, letting the heel of my palm press down on her clit and crooked my fingers to hit that soft spot deep inside of her once...twice...and that was all it took.

Tossing her head back, Lila cried out in climax as her walls clenched around my fingers, and I shot my load in my goddamn pants.

29

LILA

I'D NEVER HAD A man selflessly focus on my pleasure like Sam. He'd brought me to climax first with his hands, then once more with his mouth. Afterward, he fed me again and talked about his job and Marine Corps days, then tucked us into bed. He never asked for anything, save the robe which he tossed across the room and growled that he 'wanted us skin-to-skin'. I never considered arguing the point. Somehow, Sam kept the nightmares away—and for the first time in a long time, I remembered what good sleep felt like.

I wanted more of that.

I wanted to wake with my body's natural rhythms, bringing me to consciousness instead of the screaming chill of memories. I wanted to feel...something.

Slipping free of Sam's heavy arm, I snagged my phone and padded into the bathroom, finding the courage to take in my reflection for the first time in a long while. The bruise on my ribs faded, and the stitches hidden in my hairline showed minimal bruising. The shallow cut in my palm was itchier than anything else. My eyes weren't sunken or weary-looking either.

All hail the healing power of sleep and orgasms.

It was a relief to know I hadn't sustained more damage from the thug in the liquor store, and, considering my situation, I had a moment of clarity; my paranoia was nearly my undoing. When I'd staged the diner meet-up for Sgt. Troy, I'd been so focused on discerning if he was in Brinks' pocket that I overlooked how he'd tried to pull me into his investigation. I had been so hesitant to share my true purpose, but he'd wanted me to know more. If Sgt. Wilder was shady; he would have deflected me away from being in town, away from looking anywhere near Marcus Brinks, and certainly wouldn't have invited me to help him dig around about Internal Affairs, right? It was still a risk—but one that might pay off, and Sgt. Wilder would be a hell of an ally. Grabbing my phone, I fired off a text.

> Me: Is that rental still available? I want to stay in the area for a while.

> Sgt. Troy Wilder: Indeed. Let's meet at the same address today. Say 7 pm?

> Me: Perfect. See you there.

My adrenaline was pumping, my mind ticking off a to-do list. Only then did I check the time and realize I'd slept away the day in Sam's cocoon. I calculated that I'd have plenty of time to shower, buy a pawn shop gun for safe measure, and scope out the property before meeting the sergeant if I hurried.

Except Do-gooder Sam would surely try to stop me.

If I wanted to make the most of Wilder's offer, I had to stop letting a lumbersnack orgasm me into submission. I sifted through details as the steam filled the bathroom. Stepping inside, I let the hot water wash away the aches and pains until a familiar set of hands slid around my waist.

"I expected you to come back to bed." His sleepy voice was as sexy as it was untimely.

"Needed to stretch," I tried to ignore the bulge pressed against my backside. "And I have things to do today, so I gotta get moving." I hoped to keep my departure casual and not raise any alarms with this overprotective caveman.

"How're your ribs?" His fingers traced the bruise before I looked down.

"Better already. Doesn't even hurt to stretch." Sam turned his attention to my palm, lifting it to run a finger gingerly across the shallow cut. "A papercut," I said with a huff. "Honestly, I'm fine." Sam didn't stop his inspection, turning me to cup my jaw and slide his thumb gently across my cheekbone. "No pain," I added, knowing his next stop was the stitches. "I didn't even have a headache when I got up."

"No dizziness? Nausea?" He checked both eyes–full medic mode.

"Hey, Dr. Lumberjack," I placed my hand over his and rested my other on his chest, waiting until he looked into my eyes for real. "I'm okay. A day or two of sleep was the ticket. I heal quick." He looked concerned still, and I knew if I didn't put it to rest, he'd never leave...or let me leave. "You've done more than enough. I've got leftovers to eat. And I appreciate everything, but..." I stepped back and squared my shoulders. "You can go now."

30

SAM

"I CAN GO?" I smirked, masking the sting. "You sure about that, Hellcat?"

I planned to spend another day with her, maybe get her out for a change of scenery. And after making her cum twice—and sleeping with her fine ass pressed against my cock—I planned an encore. So, her telling me to leave hit like a ton of bricks.

"Like I said...stuff to do." She turned away, grabbing the shampoo—conversation over.

"So, you get a few good nights' shut-eye and suddenly we're done?" I snatched the bottle, irritation flaring.

"Hey, I was gonna–" She reached for the bottle, but I moved it away, filling my palm with citrusy liquid. Directing her with a fistful of that wild mane, I turned her back facing the wall as I lathered up her hair.

My cock liked this plan—my aching balls made it unanimous.

"So you think," I worked the suds through her tresses, starting from the bottom and working my way up. "Because you say you're done," reaching her scalp, I massaged my fingers into her head, careful to avoid the stitches while scratching the base and sides of her scalp. "That you can dismiss me like some errant fuckboi."

Lila let her head loll forward as the tension in her neck released.

"It's not like that," she softened as I took the body wash to her shoulders, leaning into me for added pressure. "I never thought of you like that."

The past tense only pissed me off more.

"I can stay another day and help you." She stiffened at my words, so I increased my pressure, moving lower on her back and around her hips. "We're not done."

"Sam," Lila whimpered. "You have a life." I slid forward to the soft skin that ran along her lower belly. "I don't. I'm not..." Her words were again at odds with her body as her hands slid over mine, guiding me until I cupped her mound.

"Kinda seems like you want me to stay," I growled, her slick ass shooting lightning down my balls. I dragged my beard up her neck, her head tilting to give me access.

Every kiss, every touch, had a voice in my head screaming: Claim her.

"I shouldn't want you." She whispered, breath hitching as I slipped a finger inside her. Her gasp when I tugged upward, my palm pressing against her clit, was everything.

"Lift your leg." She obeyed instantly, and I pulled her hips to me. "What should you want then?" I dragged my finger across her clit as I removed my hand from her, and bent my knees, positioning the head of my cock at her entrance.

171

"Wait..." One hand on the wall, Lila shot her free hand back, clawing at my hip to draw me back to her. "Don't go - "

God, if she could've seen my grin.

"You do want me." I placed her hand on the wall in front of her and increased the pressure against her entrance, still not penetrating her. "Admit it, Hellcat." I slid my hands down her back until my fingers wrapped around her hips, and I pushed the tip of my cock into her. "You want me to stay," push, "and take care of you," push, "a little bit longer," push, "don't you?"

"God...Sam," With every inch, she leaned forward until her palms rested flat against the wall, hot water hitting my chest and splashing across her ass. "Please."

"You know what I want." I burned to pound into her, but not until she fessed up and set aside the bullshit. "Use your words...tell me." I pulled back the few inches I'd given her.

"Yes...I need you." Her whimpering plea might as well have been a starting pistol as I slid back in to the hilt in one smooth arousal-soaked motion. "God, yes."

I moved in steady strokes—root to tip—careful of her ribs.

"I love watching you from this angle," My hips kissed her perfect ass, sending gentle waves across cheeks so sweet I wanted to sink my teeth into them. "I'm not done with you yet, Hellcat. You aren't done with me either." I pulled up tight against her body and ground against her, hitting those deep spots inside as I let my hand slide against her mound.

"I...I can't," Lila panted, her body shoving into me.

The idea of her pushing me away when we felt this good together was pure madness. It was that madness that had me leaning over her as I thrust, kissing and nipping at the skin of her shoulders. Half-feral and unyielding, it took all my restraint not to mark her as mine.

"Yes....more."

"I'll give you more," I breathed into her ear, slamming into her till her breath hitched. "I'll always give you what you need, Hellcat."

"Yes, Sam, God, I'm so - "

"Fucking Hell, woman...cum for me." I was dying to blow my load, but not before she did, and it was with a shocking pulse of her channel that she screamed the words I wanted to hear.

"Please, I need you!" With a cry, Lila clenched around me, and I held off as long as I could, realizing at the last second that I'd forgotten the condom. Pulling out, I released my load on her ass. "I...do..."

The water washed away my jarring oversight as she moaned through her climax, empty of my cock. I couldn't believe what I'd nearly done, and my brain was equal parts enraged and turned on at the potential to have cum inside her.

"I'm...sorry." Lila's apology snapped my focus back to her.

"Hey." I turned her to face me. "Don't apologize for needing me." The emotion surprised me when earlier she'd been a pillar of calm. "What can I do for you?"

"I just," she hesitated, and I heard Moira's warning to shut up in the back of my mind, so I waited. "I've only done this...alone."

She didn't mean life; She meant life since her family's death. Specifically, their investigation, which she ran on her own, had to be terrifying. Not knowing what to do and having no answers for her, I fell back on the thing I knew would help.

"Let's get dressed and grab some food?" I placed a kiss on the top of her head. "Fill me in on what's going on, and I'll see how I can help."

Lila didn't nod or say a thing, but she grabbed a towel and turned to leave. Knowing I'd pushed her plenty, physically and emotionally, I lingered, giving her space, before shutting off the water and grabbing my clothes.

"Thank you." Her voice was quiet, but held a resolve. "I don't... I've never." She looked at the bed, biting that gorgeous bottom lip of hers, and then up at me. "I don't know what to do with you."

"What to do with me?" I teased, aiming for levity, but quickly realized I missed my mark.

"We had one night." She speared me with a glare and held up a single finger. "One. And yeah, it was hot, amazing, mind-blowing, but still. ..one night." She started pacing, rapid-fire thoughts spilling out. "And as great as it was, we both expected a one-and-done kinda deal. You left before I even woke up."

My guilt kicked in at that little reminder.

"But you put me in this swanky hotel, and you delivered my car, and my purse, and the front desk thinks we're fucking married."

The way she was rambling, arms swinging, I realized seconds too late that I'd stepped into a minefield.

"Then the ambulance. Then the hospital. Now here—again." She flung a hand toward the bed. "But it's not hot animalistic fucking, oh no!"

Shit, do I say something, or jump out the window?

"It's tender and sweet and cuddles and sleeping," Her voice rose with her eyebrows.

I could pull up a chair and grab a snack.

"And it's 'no sex, just relaxing' baths and super personal questions and hold me while I cry and get me more food and..." Lila sighed, closing her eyes for a second as if to collect herself. "Sam...*why* are you *here*?"

"For you!" The words tumbled out louder than intended.

She opened her mouth, but I cut her off—not risking another tirade.

"I hate drama. But I wasn't looking for a one-night stand when you walked into Marge's that night. You had that smart mouth and that fine ass, and one night was never gonna be enough." I raked my hands through my wet hair, stalling long enough to line up the next truth. "You got under my skin with whatever wild spell you cast, and I couldn't think straight. So yeah, I planned to find you, fuck you until we saw stars, and exorcise the obsession."

Lila's brows knit—maybe pissed, maybe confused—but I stepped in closer anyway.

"Then I saw you again—on my rig, bleeding and broken, and it wrecked me. I needed to know you were okay. When you ghosted the hospital, I lost it. I didn't care if you ended up in my bed again—I just needed to see you safe." I slid one hand to her neck, the other hooked her waistband, as I tugged her flush to me. "Fucking hell, woman—when I saw you again, broken and bruised...I didn't care about scratching an itch." I pressed my forehead to hers. "I just want to fix what I can...and see that fire behind those eyes, again."

"No," she whispered, clutching my arms. "You can't—"

"However long it takes, to help you fight whatever demons you gotta fight.... for however long I get you... I'm all in."

"Sam...I..." A single tear slid free, and I caught it with my thumb. "I don't know what to do with you."

"Let's start with food," I said. "We'll talk after—"

Her phone chirped a notification, and she jolted like she'd been tased.

"Oh shit." She yanked her phone out, eyes scanning the screen. "He's already there! I'm late!"

"Late for what?" I tried to peek, but pocketed the phone. "Who's where?"

175

"A guy...a contact. It might be a lead on Marcus. I'm still vetting him." She glanced at me, torn and tense. "Sam... I've gotta go."

"Lemme grab my boots and I'll -" She tore out of my arms. "I can't miss this. I wanted to buy a gun, stake out the location, but—" She snatched her bag and bolted.

"A gun?" I hauled up damp jeans like a fucking chump, powerless to stop her. "No fucking way are you walking into a meet with someone you think's that dangerous." I scrambled to get my boots on, sensing she was about to leave me behind.

"I didn't ask you to come!" she shouted, snatching her keys and vanishing out the door.

"Lila... Fuck!" One boot on, the other in my hand, I scrambled after her, snatching my keys and wallet. When I reached the elevator bank, each one called away, I crashed through the stairwell door, flying down. Too late, she was already halfway to her Jeep.

"Wait!" I shouted as she reversed—jumping back, I slapped the rear window. "Goddammit, Lila!"

"I'm sorry, Sam." Her voice was muffled. "I have to do this."

"Fuck!" I roared, sprinting for my SUV.

She was flying blind into something so risky she wanted a gun—a meet with a maybe-lead on the guy who killed her family—in some unknown location. There were a thousand ways this could go sideways, and she wouldn't let me in—not even for backup. I was pissed, sure, but underneath anger, something more profound stirred. I didn't know what I was chasing...But I couldn't let anything happen to my Lila.

31

LILA

RUNNING FROM SAM WASN'T intentional. But I didn't have the capacity to process his commanding embrace, the way he read me like a book. Our time in the bathtub together gutted me. His tenderness and care disarmed me. His questions ripped open wounds I'd long buried, and I couldn't stitch myself back together. He was too much of a complication—I was too much of a mess.

Sam's declaration ... 'One night with you simply wasn't enough...I had to find you, had to see you safe...All I want to do is fix whatever is broken for you, for however long it takes. I'm all in.' Beautiful words that I didn't deserve—not after what I'd caused.

I couldn't risk it again.

Pushing Sam aside, I followed the GPS, white-knuckling the wheel and sifting through what I knew about Sgt. Wilder. He'd been upfront and professional with me from the get-go. He never gave off any signs of being dirty. That's why I risked reconnecting with him at all. Yeah, he clocked me at the diner—but he never threatened or cornered me. He invited me to learn more, even sharing information about the Internal Affairs discrepancy.

What else could that be but a good cop trying to do the right thing?

The highway gave way to a two-lane blacktop winding around tree-lined hills. The further I got from civilization, the more my nerves spiked. If all my instincts about this guy were wrong, I was screwed. Wilder held all the cards. He picked the location. He knew I was undercover. He'd had plenty of time to tip off Marcus Brinks, and Brinks didn't leave loose ends.

I slowed as I passed the drive, spotting Sgt. Wilder's lone truck. I decided to park a little further up the road, trying to slide my Jeep into a turnout on the shoulder of the road. Hiding gave me a chance to scout unseen before jumping in. I might be a little late, but it'd be safer, and frankly, it was my only play. This cop was still my best—and only—shot at Brinks.

If I were right, this could end my search for my family's killer.

If I was wrong, I was hiking straight into their killer's hands.

32

SAM

LILA DROVE LIKE A bat out of hell. Hopping into my SUV, I hit speaker on my phone and called Troy as I peeled out of the parking lot.

"Sam?" Troy answered on the first ring. "I'm about to step into a–"

"I need an assist," I interrupted.

"Are you okay?" Troy was stern, no doubt sensing my urgency.

"I'm okay, but..." I debated what to say—and what to leave out.

"Where are you? I can send a unit–"

"No. It's not me. It's..." I hadn't told my brothers anything about Lila. Yet here I chased after her to do what... save her from a murderer?

"I can't help if I don't know what you need." His voice all but painted a picture of him: arms crossed, squared stance, big-brother mode activated.

"Alright," I huffed. "Remember the chick from the bar?"

"The one you swore wasn't a thing?"

Fucking hell...here we go.

"Okay. Bullet Points. She's in town hunting a guy, Marcus, who murdered her family. She says there's a local contact who might help, but she's unsure if they're safe. She ran to meet 'em, and I tried to stop her, but she took off and damn it if I don't think she did that to keep me from trying to protect her when frankly it's the only fucking thing I seem to want to do since I met her, which makes no mother fucking sense."

I took a breath and jumped back in with a roar.

"And she's too fast and I lost her up the two-lane so now I need you to run her plates or whatever it is cops do to trail a person and tell me where the fuck she's gone before she gets herself killed and I lose the chance to kick her sweet ass back to the hotel for ditching me!"

I waited as impossible seconds ticked by, but I knew the longer Troy's silence dragged on, the more agitated he was. I tried to wait him out, but as I took the last turn I thought Lila had taken, only to find an empty road, I snapped.

"Look, man, I can't explain why I have to do this...just help me find her, and later you can lecture me about the pitfalls of one-night stands!"

"Is her name Delilah Rivera?"

"What? Yes! Did you find her... "My words halted. I hadn't told him her name or the license plate yet. "How'd you know that?"

"Is Marcus's last name Brinks?"

"What the fuck, TJ?" I strangled the wheel, irritated at getting hit with more questions but getting no closer to Lila. "What's going on?"

"I need you to meet me at the vacant cabin."

"I'm practically there now," I answered. "Dude?!"

"I'll explain when you arrive." That was all he said before the call ended, and my head exploded.

Turning into the driveway of our rental, rocks flying as I came to a stop, I found Troy standing, arms crossed, leaning against his truck.

"Where is she!?" I barked, scanning the porch of the cabin.

"Not here, yet." Troy glanced at his watch and then at the driveway behind me.

"What do you mean, yet, TJ?" I didn't realize I was yelling until he lifted his arms like he'd done a thousand times growing up when Chase or I lost our tempers.

"Calm down, Sam." Troy's voice went placating. "All is well, though Ms. Rivera doesn't realize it. I need to explain a few things."

"What doesn't she realize?" My heart was pumping like I'd run a marathon. "How do you already know her?" I spun around, expecting to find her standing behind me. "Where is she, Goddamnit!"

"She was the specialist!" Troy bellowed, the rare volume enough to snap me out of my spiral. "The NYPD officer on loan who salvaged Moira's laptop."

My adrenaline-soaked brain needed a moment to think back all those months ago as Lila's words surfaced, 'I was in the cyber-crimes division.'

"She was already here, in town?" I asked. "How come I never saw her?"

"I don't exactly debrief the family about work," Troy said. "And if memory serves, our dear brother was unhinged over a woman, demanding our full attention."

His eyebrow cocked up at me, and I rolled my eyes at him.

"I'm not like that." Moving on, I started pacing. "Did you know why she was here now?"

"Not until a few days ago," he answered. "I've barely talked with her. She cancelled our last meet-up. Tonight was to be our first real conversation. But there's more." He added. "It involves Moira."

"What about her?" My body stilled as a new kind of fear crept in.

"The man Ms. Rivera is hunting was Dean Jenson's attorney."

"Holy fucking hell," I ran my hands through my hair and down my beard before resting them on my knees. "The sleaze ball that got Jensen off after kidnapping Moira, and stalked her in the grocery store."

"One and the same," Troy confirmed. "There's more."

I stood up, eyebrows in my hairline, and arms out in shock.

"What...the actual...mother fuck!?" Lila's angry voice snapped our attention to the treeline where she emerged from the shadows.

"Ms. Rivera, I know this looks - "

"No!" She barked, cutting Troy off with the sharp rise of her pointer finger and a look that could level the biggest of bastards. Hurt briefly flashing across her face, she addressed me. "You talk first, Jackass."

"Lila, this," I rested a hand on Troy's arm. "Is my big brother, Troy. I called him when you took off tonight, hoping he could help find you, and he told me to come here." Her hand shook as she slid that raised finger to me in silent command—my turn to shut the fuck up.

"Now you talk." She commanded Troy, who cocked an eyebrow at me.

"Ignore her at your peril," I mumbled.

"I wanted to meet with you because your...side investigation...and mine crossed before." Troy began. "I hoped we could share information." He lifted a hand slowly as if soothing a caged beast, "I did not know you were with Sam."

"That's my fault," I added as Lila's breathing sped up.

"I wanted to meet in a place I knew we could talk freely, so I suggested here." Troy waved at the cabin behind us. "The one from our real-estate business, as I mentioned."

"NB Realty," Lila's eyebrows pinched, hand still raised, but her tone shifting down from the rafters of rage. "And you?" She looked back at me, hurt flashing again. "Keep talking."

"I didn't know anything about you meeting Troy, or about that attorney until - "

"Stop!" Lila's eyes went wide, her back ramrod straight. "How...how did you know Brinks was an attorney?" Lila took a defiant step forward.

"I told him." Troy intervened. "Just now, as he drove here for you. I knew Brinks from the arson investigation before - "

"How did you know I was looking for Marcus Brinks?" A new undercurrent of anguish lashed through her anger, and her breathing grew ragged. "I never told you I was looking for him." She lowered her hand, but I saw the clenched fists at her sides and could feel the rage she wrestled.

Things started clicking for me, and I began to see how all of this looked to her. She'd lost her family to an evil bastard who cost her everything. She was trying to catch the murderer all by herself. Now, after spending days in her most vulnerable state, she discovers me connected to it, making me a potential threat.

She wasn't mad...but terrified.

"That was me, Hellcat." I took a few steps forward, knowing that if she didn't calm down, that headache would return, or worse, she'd pass out. "I blabbed what I knew to my brother. He's a good cop. He put it together, but I promise -"

"So... you're a cop who knows Brinks." She said to Troy and then turned her face to me, "And you just happen to be the brother of the only person in this godforsaken town who can connect me to the bastard."

Her foot slid the barest step backward, and the air nearly crackled with the shift.

"And you," Her whisper was laced with pain. "just happened to be in the same bar I strolled into when I arrived in town?"

"It's not like that," I hated the sheen in her eyes. Hated that I wasn't safe with her anymore. I took a few more steps, hoping to reach her, to help her calm down at least, before she hyperventilated. "We...just this second," I gestured to Troy and myself, hoping to halt the vicious narrative in her brain. "Began to piece shit together."

"We planned to sit and - "Troy tried to speak, but that halting finger was in the air again.

"Your plan was to what?" Lila asked, a tear slipping down her cheek. "You said you didn't know I was looking for Brinks, so what, you wanted just to see how low I'd fallen since I was thrown off the force? You wanted to see what a disgraced, homeless cop looked like in the flesh? Maybe get a front-row seat to the symphony of pain that is my life!?"

"I assure you -" Troy began, but she cut him off.

"And what was your plan, Jackass?" She stepped towards us, and I half hoped she would come in swinging—anger so much easier than hurt. "Planning to run up here, swap stories about how we fucked all night, then you put me up like a paid whore?"

Her eyes were swirling pools of anger, and a hurt that my heart broke for.

"Lila, no." I lifted my hand to her cheek, but she turned away from me, eyes clenched. "Look at me."

I rested my hands on her waist, and after a full minute of breathing, she mimicked the move. Resting her hands on me, pressing herself against me.

It was the first moment of relief I'd felt since the hotel.

"You don't do drama," She whispered.

"You might be a tad dramatic, but you aren't drama, Hellcat." I started to smile, but Lila jerked back and scowled.

"Drama is all I fucking am...so I guess that lets you off the hook." She removed her hand from my waist, stepping out of my embrace. "Just a one-night stand...and no longer your problem."

She turned to walk away, and I tried to follow her, but Troy stopped me.

"Give her a moment. It's a lot to take in. There is more here than even we know, and - "His eyes darted over my shoulder, and I turned in time to see Lila climb into my SUV.

"What the," I patted my hip pocket as the engine roared to life. "She took my keys!"

I yelled her name, half running down the gravel driveway like an idiot—my brain slowly melting at how royally fucked this situation was.

"I see you have well met your match, brother." Troy jogged up behind me, grinning.

"This is terrible," I stood in the dust, breath ragged, watching my taillights vanish. "Just...fucking terrible. How the fucking fuck did I fuck this so badly?"

"Indeed," He answered with a smile. "Your a match in every way."

"What do I do?" I asked, looking to him for answers as I'd done my whole life anytime I was in over my head. "I don't even know where to begin."

"Now we go get her," he said. "And try to help her believe we're not the devil she's chasing."

33

SAM

I T TOOK TWENTY MINUTES to reach town, and in all that time, my only guess was that Lila might have returned to our hotel. Unfortunately, as I walked into the lobby, the front desk informed me they had reserved the room for the following day, and we had to vacate it. Up in the room, relief washed over me seeing her stuff still there–crazy irritation running a close second that the mad woman herself wasn't.

"The nicest hotel in town?" Troy eyed the room as I shoved her stuff into bags. "This is where you took a 'one-night stand'?" His use of air quotes felt personal.

"It's a long story. Just help me get her stuff, will you?"

"As we have established, she is not here," Troy slipped Lila's papers and laptops into messenger bags. "Where else would she go?"

"I don't know fuck-all about what makes that woman tick or how she's crawled under my skin, and I sure as fuck don't know where she took off to in my goddamn car." I slammed clothes into bags, driven more by worry than frustration. Lila was hip-deep in PTSD with this vendetta of hers. This misunderstanding could push her right over the edge.

"Sure you do," Troy prodded. "Think."

"Dammit, TJ," I barked. "I barely know her!" Troy's brow raised at the bellowed anger coming out of me, and I couldn't blame him.

If I didn't know her, why did I care?

And if I cared enough to be pissed, why hadn't I told my family about her?

"Brother." Troy rested a hand on my shoulder, slowing my mad dash. "Let's dispense with the pretense that she's a stranger." He turned and scanned the room. "It's quite evident she wasn't here for fun. It looks as if she rarely left." He turned back to me. "Trust your instincts. What do you know? Where might she go? Someplace she can feel in control, perhaps."

"The only other place I've even seen her is the liquor store and Scaled–"my phone rang. "It's Marge," I hit speaker phone as roaring bar noise filtered through.

"Your girl's here, Sam." Marge's scratchy voice rose over the den. "Three shots deep, and shaming the money outta some idiot's pockets at the tables. There's fire shooting from her eyes like she's about to break a stick off in someone's ass."

"Fucking hell," I threw everything else into spare trash bags.

"I could wait around til my baseball bat comes out, but figured you might want to intervene again?" Did even Marge know more about my feelings for Lila than I did?

"Slow her down," I growled. "Troy and I are on our way."

"Oh, yay." Marge deadpanned. "A madwoman, a pissing contest, and a cop. Just what this joint needs."

Tossing Lila's stuff in the back of Troy's truck, we drove the 15 minutes to Marge's while I pictured the myriad of ways shit might hit the fan. I imagined Lila furiously slugging shots, her gorgeous body draped over the pool table in a room full of drunks, flirting like a cat in heat after a few drinks. Then I added on the fresh slice of hurt she carried from tonight, and my blood boiled to think she might try to hate-fuck me out of her system with shit-fisted Carl.

No way. Not my Hellcat.

I stomped in, finding Marge distracted by some suit at the front door. I would need to circle back on that at another time. Lila stood at the same corner table as before, but unlike last time, she wasn't laughing, flirting, or joking. Her face was stone-cold as she pocketed ball after ball–running the table like a professional. The guy watching her was a mix of shock and anger, which gave me no small measure of pride. When Lila was down to the 8-ball, she leaned over, locked eyes with the guy, and sank it in one.

"That's going to be a problem." I heard Troy say, eyeing the same scene.

Rejoining his spectator buddies, the guy mouthed off as Lila swiped the money off the table, swiftly folding it into her bra without so much as a glance in his direction. My fists clenched when he reached for Lila's arm, but Marge walked over, bat in hand. The guy popped off at Marge, and Lila gave no reaction to show the storm she was hiding under the surface; her calm was as unnerving as it was rare. The idiot's buddies were goading him, though, and he smirked as his eyes raked over Lila's body. This got my feet moving.

"Hold." Troy stopped me with a raised hand. "That won't help."

"That ass looks like he wants to eat her for lunch," I started, but Troy nodded his head again.

"She seems calm." He said. "And Marge is in play." Troy slid his gaze to me then, his voice a little softer. "Lila lost control tonight. Having you bust in will only feed her helplessness."

Surprised by his insight, even as he pulled us around to a side wall, my gut told me this was not gonna be pretty.

34

LILA

I TORE DOWN THE gravel drive, hands slamming the steering wheel and anger streaming down my face as I racked my brain for the connection I missed. The headlights bounced off the blacktop in front of me as my head swam over my efforts to catch Marcus Brinks, who landed me in this town with Sam, who, until now, was the one thing that didn't drown me in memories of failure and loss. He let me feel something when I'd been all but a numbed-out zombie. He was the first one I'd felt safe with.

And now—ruined.

I'd stepped into their trap so damned easily, and still my body wanted him to come and hold me and make it go away, and thus did the merry-go-round of pain spin. I couldn't go back to the hotel. I'd smell the remnants of our time together, and I'd have to pack up and leave. It was too much, too raw, too soon. Driving to the only place booze, music, and background noise could drown it all out, I burst into Scaled Back on a mission to forget. Climbing a barstool, I slapped the counter to get Marge's attention.

"Hey there, Hellcat." She smiled, tossing that damn towel over her shoulder. "Wondered if you were still around."

"Don't call me that." I snapped. "I'll take a Bushmills neat, three fingers," I tossed a stack of twenties across the bartop. "Keep 'em coming." She grabbed the bottle, folding the cash into her apron, but never taking her eyes off me.

"Sam meeting you here, sweetheart?"

"Who?" I tossed back the glass in a single gulp and slid it back to her.

"Humph, thought you might've lasted past a single night." She mumbled, pouring a second glass and sliding it back. "Rumors had him hung up on you pretty good."

Nope...not fucking touching that one.

"I ain't here with Sam." I slugged the second glass, never feeling the burn. "Another."

"Well, if you ain't here with this Sam guy, I'll buy the next round." I glanced at the intrusive flannel shirt that oozed onto the neighboring barstool. "I'm Todd. I was meeting friends for pool, but I'm a little early."

He motioned to Marge for a refill of his beer and another glass for me. Her brows shot up as she poured them both.

"I'm not feeling social, Todd." I tossed back the third, glad that the hum of relief vibrated through my muscles. "Just blowing off steam."

"I hear ya." Todd lamented. "It's been a bitch of a week." He gave my elbow a nudge. "Mine's been work stress...you?"

"Man trouble, Todd." I looked him dead in the eye, hoping to get my point across. "I hate men."

"Maybe you've just been hanging with the wrong ones." He handed his credit card to Marge, who shook her head with a wry smile. "How about we blow off some steam at the tables?" The numbing buzz in my chest barely muffled his sing-songy nag. "I promise I'll go easy on ya."

Jesus, what was it with guys in this bar not taking a damn hint?

"Alright," I said, giving Todd the sweetest smile I could plaster on while plotting his demise. "Been a while since I played, though."

"I bet you'll be a natural." His predictable compliments fell like a thick fog in my brain. "Especially being short, you'll have a better line of sight than what my long legs allow."

That was his angle—short girl jokes?

"A bet, eh?" I tempted fate, ignoring Marge's glare in my periphery. "I'm down for a bet." I flashed my biggest doe eyes, fluttering my lashes. "How much should we play for...100?"

"I can't take that much of your money. Let's say 50." Todd led me to a table with a smile.

Hook.

Line.

Sinker.

Todd explained how to rack, break, and identify the stripes and solids. The blowhard loved his own voice so much he never noticed I barely muttered an 'uh-huh' or 'oh.' The first game was a clear win for him. I made sure to laugh as I handed over $50 with a coquettish pout. After another round or two like that, I decided not to take his money and called it a night.

I was too fucking tired for the fuckery of asshats–The sentiment alone stung my eyes.

"I'm cooked, Todd. Thanks for the game." He'd distracted me long enough that the booze did its job. I was too exhausted for anything beyond a good cry in the shower before bed.

"Hey, wait." His hand wrapped around my arm. "The guys won't mind if we played another round, would you guys?" His friends gave me an approving once-over, leering at Todd's conquest. "The least I can do is give you a chance to win your money back, sweetheart."

He did not grab me.

He did NOT just call me sweetheart.

"In that case," I made sure my smile masked the disdain in my eyes. "How about double or nothing?"

Zero flirting, zero fucks given, I ran the table.

Todd gaped at the realization he'd been swindled, his anger rising when I wiggled my open palm for his money. His friends goaded him into another game to earn it back, and I could only laugh when Todd slammed another hundred to the table.

Men in packs–absolute idiots.

"Your money, your loss," I shrugged. "Rack 'em, loser."

The music blared across the bar, and I let myself go, growing my winnings while a new shade of humiliation improved Todd's face. I felt no shame. I'd tried to let him walk away. But good ole Todd kept pushing, his friends doing him no favors with their unoriginal misogyny. I didn't care–it let me forget.

No Brinks.

No Sam.

No job.

No family.

I was doing society a favor by teaching assholes that they shouldn't judge a short-stacked, big-boobed book by its cover. When the last 8-ball sank, rage flashed in Todd's eyes. The hair on the back of my neck told me it was time to cut and run.

"It's been real, guys." I slipped the cash into my bra and slid my stick across the table. "But I'm baked." I started to leave, but Todd stepped in front of me.

"Whoa, whoa, whoa." His body blocked my exit. "Most girls would give a guy a chance to win his money back."

"Yeah, well, you've had like what...6 chances?" I gave him a quick once-over. "Maybe stop treating women like helpless damsels and you'll keep your money next time, k...*sweetheart*."

Todd's friends stood with him, sneering and blocking my primary exit. Retreating behind the table was my only option.

"Don't be like that, baby." His malicious grin set my teeth on edge. "We're having fun."

I was so over the bullshit.

"Don't get it twisted, Todd. I'm not your baby." Adding insult to an already injured ego, I stupidly tossed on, "And I'm not here to be bored by a whiney bitch who can't handle his stick."

Goading him was a mistake. He was bigger than me, and I was outnumbered. Not that my temper cared much for reasonable odds.

"This what you get off on?" His hands lowered, and his buddies closed in, forcing me to take a step back. "Coming here dressed like a whore and scamming guys out of their hard-earned money?"

The bullshit that dripped from the man's mouth was gross.

"I'll tell you what...baby," The endearment dripped with as much venom as I could muster. "How bout I be nice and buy you and your buddies a beer?" His buddies grumbled something unintelligible behind Todd as I stepped close enough to Todd that only he could hear my whispered words.

Because bourbon always did make me do dumb shit.

"Then you can drown your sorrows with your sad little pack of limp-dicked punks about how a teeny, little, shortie cut your fucking balls off at the tables with a stick bigger than yours."

"FUCK YOU!" Todd roared as his buddies jumped at his side. "No way you're getting out of here with my money, bitch!"

"Hey, baby," I said, fanning the cash like a bored debutante. "I was trying to be nice." I was practically begging him to make a move. "But if you don't wanna drink," With a snap, I folded the money and slipped it into my bra. "We're done." I spun on my heels, heading to a crowd to block Todd from causing a scene. Instead, he grabbed my arm, jolting me to a stop.

Fuck. Fuck, fuck fuck.

"Your gamble...your loss, Todd." The buzz of adrenaline and booze clouded the final remnants of my better judgment. "Take it like a man and get your fucking hands off me." I tried to jerk my arm free, but he stepped so close I had to crane my neck to look at him, my mask of boredom still in place despite my racing heart.

"You got five hundred of my dollars in your tits," Todd growled, bruising me in his grip. "Hand it over or play me for it—either way, you're not keeping it."

"I said I was done." I jerked my arm free. "I gave you an out." Raising my voice slightly, I squared my shoulders. "But you," I slammed both hands against Todd, forcing him back, "Just had to be a handsy piece of shit!"

"Everything okay, fellas?" Marge's voice sliced through the bar noise like a blade, her bat sitting comfortably on her shoulder.

"You know, Marge, no matter how much I try to be nice, some micro-peen with a hearing problem just has to push my FUCK OFF button!" Marge cut disapproving eyes at me, while Todd and his buddies looked back and forth between me and the bat-wielding bartender. His menacing glint had my unarmed status rising to the forefront of my mind.

"I have a better idea," Todd sneered. "How about I bend you over the table and take it out in trade?" He grabbed his dick and added, "The old lady can watch for free."

Marge's bat whistled forward, blunt end landing in Todd's chest with a thud.

"Last warning." She pointed the bat like a sword. "Take a hike, before I take you out like the trash you are."

"What the fuck are you gonna do, Grandma?" One of Todd's cronies chimed in

"You know, Marge," My adrenaline burned off some of the whiskey. "I came in here thinking my Give-A-Fuck was broken...but turns out my Go-Fuck-Yourself is fully functional."

"Walk away, girl," Marge growled at me. "I ain't here to ya-ya-sisterhood with you."

"Better listen to grandma," Todd smirked. "Run home so daddy can rescue his little girl." My blood was boiling at the slurs, the looks, all of it, but it was the next mumbled phrase that pushed me over the edge. "More like daddy's little whore."

My hands moved of their own accord—swiping a nearby bottle and smashing it over Todd's head. As his face jolted to the side, I slammed the heel of my boot into the middle of his foot, then drove the business end of my elbow up into his descending chin.

The hard click of chipped teeth was so goddamn satisfying.

"What the hell!" One of his buddies yelled. "You're gonna pay for that, whore!" They took a swing and missed, but it was my final straw.

"Now you flipped my Bitch Switch," I launched at the group as Marge started swinging.

Todd yanked me around the waist, lifting me mid-swing as my fist landed square on his buddy's nose. I scrambled to plant my feet, but his hand fisted in my hair, pinning my back to his chest.

"Big fucking mistake," Todd hissed in my ear. "I'm dragging you out back to earn my money back. I cocked my fist, ready to hammer it into his dick—when a roar ripped through the bar.

One second, I was bracing to fight–the next, Todd was airborne.

35

SAM

LILA EXPLODED—SMASHING A BEER over the guy's head before elbowing his face, then launching into the whole pack behind him.

"There's my Hellcat," I muttered, charging forward.

"That escalated quickly," Troy followed.

I prepared for one or two good hits before Troy's badge shut it down, but the douche yanked her by the waist, fisting her hair and pinning her to him.

She cried out...and I saw red.

Something primal roared out of me as I charged at the guy, splaying him out before he saw the truck that mowed him down. I swung until the crack of his nose soothed me. I barely registered the sting of a boot in my ribs as I grabbed its owner's foot and twisted.

This side-guy wouldn't be dancing tomorrow.

Movement beneath me snapped my focus back to the bastard who grabbed Lila, and I grabbed his shirt in both fists, slamming him into the floor.

"You don't touch fucking touch her!"

"Sam!" Marge nodded towards Lila, running into the fray like a savage. "Get her outta here!"

"I concur!" Troy yanked me off the bloody mess on the floor even as I snarled insults at the man who dared to put his hands on my Lila. "I'll settle this." I wasn't done, not by half.

"SAM!" Troy's icy-cold authority had my body obeying before my brain caught up.

"What!" I growled, fist cocked.

"Help Lila!" That snapped me to her—clinging to a guy's back, choking him out.

Beautiful.

Ferocious.

Seconds from getting slammed into the wall.

She couldn't take another hit right now, and that had me stalking over, socking the guy in the gut and crumpling him to the floor. Grabbing Lila by her belted waist, I pulled her free and set her on the ground.

"Come on, Hellcat." She spun to take a swing at me but stopped, hand frozen in mid-air.

"You!" she yelled, chin trembling, before squaring her shoulders. "Fuck off, Sam." She tried to turn away, but I held her back.

"We're leaving." I didn't give her time to argue, just dragged her towards the door as the bloody nose from the floor mouthed off...again.

"You're dead meat, bitch!" It was a testament to Lila's fury that she pulled us both to a halt when she faced the screaming man. "I'm gonna find you and get my money back one way or another!"

"Troy?" I nodded at the mess, trusting him to handle it.

Then I did what was quickly becoming routine. I hoisted an angry Lila over my shoulder, an arm across her knees, and pinned her sweet ass against my shoulder. As expected, my Hellcat needed the last word, pushing off my back and screaming across the bar.

"I hope in my next life I come back as the big-dicked karma fairy just so I can assfuck you with the come-upping you deserve, you limp-dick waste of skin!"

If I weren't so pissed, I might have laughed at the foulness falling out of her beautiful mouth. As it stood, I was the only thing keeping her out of jail. So I burst out the back door, unceremoniously dumping her into the passenger seat of Troy's truck, where she froze.

She didn't speak. She didn't argue. She just...stopped.

Unlike last time when she kicked and screamed right up until I shoved my dick into her, this time Lila was a quiet, seething force as I buckled her in. The drive was a practice of pure restraint as I warred within myself. I was a white-hot blaze of anger at her recklessness. Drinking that much, scamming and taking on a bunch of guys with nothing but her wits, her mouth, and enough rage to fuel a small nation's army, it was too much. I didn't know how to proceed. Just as I had checked her into that hotel, I had checked her out. I was primarily responsible for her current state, and despite knowing a great deal about her, there was even more I didn't know.

More to learn, more to unravel, more to explore.

More connecting us.

We parked in silence, and I debated how to start, but when I turned to her, everything fell away. Sitting next to me wasn't the ferocious ball of fiery sass I'd just hoisted out of a brawl amidst the most colorful insults I'd ever heard. Sitting, hands in her lap, was the most broken creature I'd ever seen wearing a mask of numb detachment. I gently ran my fingers through her hair, hoping human contact might bridge the cavernous divide. Instead, a tear slipped down her cheek, and that singular show of emotion told me she wasn't totally shut down.

My earlier anger gone–I ached to make it all better.

"Troy and I packed up the hotel. Your things are here." A brief flutter of lashes indicated she heard me. "We can stay here until we sort all this out." I caressed the side of her jaw, but she didn't react. Racking my brains, I knew she relaxed in showers, and we both smelled like smoke and booze.

"We're going inside and I'm starting you a shower. I'll grab your things and get you settled."

"Fine."

As she showered, I placed her things into the master suite, setting up the laptops on the desk in a similar fashion to the hotel. My attempt to convey that I wasn't the villain here. She exited the bathroom, wrapped only in a towel and a cloud of steam, wet hair pulled over one shoulder.

"This is my room?" She scanned the space distantly, seeing every-thing and nothing.

"Yes... I'll stay if you want, or sleep across the hall if you need privacy." I wanted to go to her, to wrap my arms around her, to claim her mouth and use our bodies to find equilibrium.

But more than that, I wanted her to know she had agency and options.

She needed to feel secure, and if my sleeping across the hall gave her that, then so be it.

"Get out." She was quiet, but resolute.

I waited...hoping she'd look at me, begging her to yield to me.

She didn't....So, I left.

36

LILA

THE ROOM WAS DARK, except for the moonlight cascading through the sliding door that opened onto a small balcony. The frigid cold temperatures outside held no sway over the warmth inside. I climbed into the massive log cabin bed, sinking beneath heavy blankets and the fluffiest pillows I'd ever touched. With the booze and the shower, this should have been the perfect prescription to pass out.

But the quiet...

Being a New Yorker, I was raised around noise. Subway trains, cars, bikes, people talking, it was always there, ever-present, even at night. A living white-noise machine of lights and people, and when I slept, I did so with a sound mind. Until death came, and nights became impossible. That's why I took up drinking before bed. Booze dulled the vivid replay, and I got used to a half-alive haze each morning.

But Sam.

All the new information fueled my brain into listing the thousand new ways I'd failed. No amount of nature-lux ambiance or exhaustion could give the sweet release of sleep. I contemplated a walk to the kitchen for liquor, but figured opening the door would invite conversation. I couldn't handle the conversation.

Not now. Maybe not ever.

Sitting with my back against the headboard, knees drawn up, I stared at the details of the clear night sky. The moon loomed huge and bright, like a silver dollar begging to be plucked from the sky. The few visible clouds were huge and fluffy and glowing in the moon's light. All of that sat on the darkest blanket of midnight blue I'd ever seen, and the stars... my god, there were so many—tiny ones and large ones, some twinkling and others frozen across the sky like glitter dust.

My dad loved the stars.

My father loved the stars so much that he went to the planetarium every week in high school. By the time he and my mother were married and he'd joined the police force, my grandparents had given him a telescope that sat in the back window of our kitchen for my entire childhood. Countless nights, we'd find Dad sitting in the kitchen, waiting for some celestial event, and he'd always invite my brother and me to join him. My brother mostly would, but I never stayed awake long enough. After Mom died, Dad looked at the stars less and less. One day, I saw him packing away his telescope. When I asked him about it, he just shook his head. *'I could only love the stars in the heavens when I had an angel on earth with me.'*

I don't know why that memory hit now, but it landed in my chest with the weight of a thousand planets, and I sank. When the tears started, I couldn't stop them. Frustration slipped out in silence—until the tears turned bold, pouring out in waves of memory that cascaded around me until I could no longer muffle my sobs. I pulled the blanket over my knees and buried my face to endure the bone-deep sorrow that rushed through me as quietly and small as possible. But the unbearable future of a lonely lifetime was too much, and when I heard the soft snick of my door opening, relief washed over me so strong it took my breath away.

Sam came.

"I said I'd stay away." Sam's face was solemn, his eyes pleading for me to welcome him. "But staying out here, hearing you cry, is more than I can stand." He wore long flannel pants, with bare feet and a bare chest, and my body screamed for the comfort of his muscular arms. "So I'm just gonna sit in that chair and you - "

"You can't see stars in the city," I choked out. "Did you know that? There are too many lights and too much smog. It has to be a special set of conditions and..." I tried to stifle the sobs, but my words stuttered. "My daddy...loved the stars and had a telescope and everything, and...he would've loved...seeing..." I looked out the window again, a gut-wrenching wail heaving me forward.

My daddy was gone.

Sorrow beyond measure rushed forth so unexpectedly that the very air I was gasping for was shallow in the wake of the next cry, the next sob, and the next heave.

The bed dipped.

Sam's strong hands cradled me in his arms.

My head burrowed into his chest.

"It's all so...." My words were broken. I was broken. "I can't..."

"Let the tears come... they'll heal you. But you are stronger than this, and you're never alone, now and forever. I'm here. I've got you. I'll take care of you." His voice was soothing, his body warm. "You don't have to say anything... I'm here, and I'll watch out for all the stars."

His words rumbled through me, and his fingers sent relaxing shivers down my back.

His voice caressed me to sleep—the steady thump of his heart in my ear.

WILDER FAMILY GROUP CHAT

-4-

Me: Hey guys, set an extra plate for dinner.

Moira: Who's coming?

Troy: Surely you jest.

Me: Lila's coming with me. You can all meet her at once.

Chase: Uh, what about the family meeting stuff?

Me: Involves her.

Moira: Not so complicated then?

Me: She's... mine.

Moira: Or quite possibly VERY complicated!

Chase: Holy hell...

Troy: Are you sure?

Me: I might be fucking it all up.

Moira: What does your gut say?

Me: She needs more than I can give her alone. Needs a family. You guys are the best there is.

Moira: INSERT ALL THE HEART EMOJIS HERE ▯▯▯▯

Chase: To clarify—this is the woman from the bar fight?

Troy: Which one?

Me: Dude.

Chase: There's been more than one bar fight?!?

Moira: Ignore your brothers. I cannot wait to meet her!

37

LILA

"*L*IL D....YOU WERE RIGHT..." *My brother's voice is weak.... too weak, there's no laughter in it. No, don't try to talk. The ambulance is coming. I can't make the words. Where are they, where are they? I'm trying to talk, but it's only wailing.* "Brinks." *He rasps, squeezes my hand, and I stop screaming.* "Follow...Brinks." *His eyes are distant and empty like Dad's.* "No...don't leave me....come back...come back...come... NO!.... don't leave me!" *But hands begin to pull at me, and people move in.* "No. Let me go. He needs me! He was talking. Just now." *I can't be alone, I can't be, I can't be, I can't be...NO!*

I began box breathing.

Sunlight flooded a room I faintly recognized; Snow-topped evergreens a jarring contrast to the lingering nausea of my dream.

Inhaling, holding for 3 seconds...or 5...who cares.

Sitting up, my body pulled at tight muscles as last night's fuzzy chaos stuttered to memory.

I ran.

I drank.

I fought.

Then, Sam...I fell apart.

Sounds of him floated from the other room, but facing him felt impossible. Instead, I stretched my back and stumbled into the bathroom with a head full of bourbon-tinged regret. Leaning on the counter, I took a hard look at my bedraggled reflection–hair sweaty, skin dry, eyes bloodshot and puffy. I swear I heard my dad's voice in my head, *'This too shall pass, Delilah-girl.'*

Sure, Dad...then more bullshit takes its place, and the merry-go-round spins.

Shaking my head, I turned to the shower, needing the heat and quiet to hide until I could face my consequences. The water began to cool before preparedness arrived. Drying off, I found shea butter tucked beneath the towel folded neatly on the tiled bench. The jasmine scent was a welcome treat after weeks of hotel toiletries. I dressed as slowly as possible before peeking into the short hallway, spying across the open-concept living room where Sam donned an apron. Coffee and bacon's rich aroma tugged me forward.

"Morning, Lila." Sam sounded kinder than expected, given how badly I imploded last night. "I hope I didn't make too much noise in here." He held no hint of anger or frustration in his words or body language. "The coffee is hot...I made you a plate," he pulled a warm plate from the oven. "It'll help soak up the last of the booze and give your stomach something gentle."

The plate he handed me was stunning. Fluffy eggs, thick-cut bacon, and two slices of sourdough toast smothered in butter. On the bar sat a second plate stacked with the most beautiful golden-brown pancakes I'd ever seen, and before my eyes, he began pouring syrup over the top.

"So, you're a carb-junky after a night partying. Noted." His face held a familiar half-smirk as he held up a fork. "Bon Appétit." I accepted the fork with a wary eye.

Where was the lecture, the ass-chewing, the get-the-fuck-outta-here?

"It's a helluva lot easier to get through it if you dig in." He said, bringing my eyes back to his knowing expression that had me wondering if he'd read my mind. "The pancakes," He nodded at the plate, and I bit my lip as I followed his eyes. "They won't jump willingly into your mouth."

"I'm just wondering if they're poisoned," I joked, hoping to deflect the wrenching humiliation twisting my gut.

"Not today." Sam laughed. "But if you thought they were, I've not done a proper job."

"I just..." My words trailed off, unsure of how to finish. What did I want here? What was I expecting? Did I want answers, or did I want to be gone? Did he want me gone? What about Sgt. Wilder...his brother?

"I can smell the gears turning in that head of yours, Hellcat." Sam rounded the bar and took the stool next to me, caging me in with his wide man-spread. "I'm sure you have eleventy-billion questions–"

"Eleventy-billion?"

"Yeah," He huffed, with a small smile. "A word I picked up from my sister-in-law. Oddly fitting for times when you can't count the amount of shit in your head." He took the fork from my hand. "Last night was a lot," Sam cut into my pancakes, "And we have a fuckton of shit to wade through." He took a small bite of the pancakes with a cocked eyebrow before continuing. "But for now, I need you to know two things." He began stacking several bites and dragging them across the melted butter

211

and syrup. "1–that you are safe here. I won't let anything happen to you." He lifted the bite and poised it in front of my mouth. "And 2–You're not leaving this motherfucking stool until you're so full you beg me to stop feeding you."

A laugh bubbled up at the demanding note he used to say such thoughtful and caring words. Any other time, my kneejerk reaction would've been to reject the food and sling bullshit lines about not needing a man to feed me. The truth was, at that moment, I couldn't think of a single argument that sounded right. I wanted him to feed me, protect me, care for me, and make it all go away, and in admitting that to myself, I knew last night had broken something in me that needed to shatter. As if a healing waited for me, that could only happen on the other side of pain.

And I was so tired of running from it all.

"Holy mother of God," I moaned around the buttery goodness exploding in my mouth.

"My Nonna made sure I was no slouch in the kitchen. My broth-ers, too. We each have our specialties, but I jam mostly on breakfast." He cut me another bite. "This pancake recipe started while I was in the Marines. Cooking helped occupy the time between ops."

"Ops?" I mumbled the single word around a forkful of content-ment.

"The Marines liked how we worked together. We got sent out for special work once in a while." He cut a fresh slice of pancakey goodness. "It was good work, but weird hours at times, and the downtime in between messed with my head. Cooking kept my mind busy...and made the MREs more palatable." Sam gave a little wink and nodded at my plate, the fork waiting for me to open wide.

He didn't continue until I opened again.

"My unit was down to be guinea pigs. Although the supplies weren't great, I managed to come up with a fairly solid start for pancakes. I perfected it once my term was up." After the fourth bite met my lips, he set the fork aside and lifted the coffee. "How do you take it?"

I had so much food in my mouth I could only gesture with my hands, waving my fingers back and forth as I shook my head.

"Yeah, I figured you take it black. Must be a cop thing." I might have bristled at the memories...but fuck me sideways, the bacon. The salty pork was wrapped in a peppery, sweet shell, and the combination made my toes curl.

"Candied bacon." He said with a smile. "It pairs well with pancakes and coffee, though I've never heard anyone react to it so colorfully." I moaned through the slice as he lifted another bite of pancakes.

This bacon was heaven.

I could marry this bacon...and make a good life.

Mr and Mrs Bacon.

"You are wasting your skills on that ambulance," I mumbled.

"I meant what I said. I hope you slept well. Last night was...heavy." He slowed enough to let me chew, but as I cut my eyes to him, wondering if the lecture was about to begin, a forkful of eggs appeared in front of me. "But we have some work to do today, and I need your help to get it all done in time. It's almost noon, so after breakfast, I'll need your help in here." His eyes drifted into the kitchen, and I followed his gaze.

The counters held small piles of bright red tomatoes and leafy green herbs, and a variety of meats stacked neatly to the side of a giant stockpot near the stove.

"More cooking?"

"There's this...dinner thing. I need to bring pasta. My Nonna would roll over if I sauced it from a jar, and her Bolognese requires a bit of time to cook properly. I figured we could get the base started after this, and then you could help me with the project I need to finish while it simmers." Sam moved the now-empty pancake plate off to the side.

"Oh my god, I ate all that?" I stared, shocked to feel full for the first time in what felt like forever.

"Think you can handle more egg? The protein helps." He slid the second plate in front of me, but all I could see were the giant floating hearts surrounding slices of candied bacon.

"Girl after my own heart," Sam lifted the bacon. "If you want, I'll make you some more."

"No!" I waved my hands in surrender. "I'm stuffed. Please, GOD, not another bite." Sam's chuckle was heartwarming and unencumbered, making me long to laugh like that myself.

"Come wash up, and we'll get started chopping the tomatoes and searing the meats."

38

SAM

I'D NEVER SEEN ANYONE cry as hard as Lila. But unlike when I held her in the tub, this hurt was my fault. I'd made her feel unsafe, made her run, and made her relieve a grief so fresh it broke her. My guilt kicked me in the teeth. I had to fix her. Holding her, watching her sleep, and feeding her now all felt instinctively right. Still, we had so much to talk through. And tonight's dinner could scare her off if I didn't handle it right, so I was banking on my Nonna to ease the way.

As a kid, whenever I felt anxious, Nonna would pull me into the kitchen. Between the hands-on work and the repetitive motion of chopping or slicing, words flowed easily. I invoked this trick now, hoping some of Lila's walls would come down. As we worked, I avoided anything complicated. I started with light stories, easing into my background. She listened, then shared some of her thoughts, even sharing some stories from her academy days. Those ended with her eyes glazing over, her voice dropping into nothingness. I worked around those as best I could to keep her moving forward, but when I finished the sauce, I could tell her reserves were low – her responses were dwindling.

"Grab your shoes," I said, wiping my hands on the apron and tossing it over the sink. "While the base simmers, we're gonna run that errand."

"For the project you mentioned?" Lila's eyebrows pinched together as she looked back at the stovetop and bit that adorable lip of hers.

"I'll explain in the car," I said, slipping into my boots and putting on my coat. "The heat is set super low to let the herbs and spices work their magic. We shouldn't be more than an hour."

If Lila had any thoughts or feelings about the quaint downtown of my hometown, she didn't voice them. It wasn't until we neared the residential section that she spoke at all.

"Whose house are we going to?" She nervously rubbed her thighs.

"First stop's work—just dropping off paperwork. Then we'll swing by my place." I kept my voice casual. "I need to get a few things for the cabin. It won't take long." I minimized my time in the ambulance bay, informing my boss that I would be switching to part-time hours for the foreseeable future and providing as brief an explanation as possible. I also took the current week off to 'settle some business'. It was short notice, not a great move on my part, but I had 3 months of unused vacation time, and I worked like a dog.

My supervisor assumed it was due to the arrival of my nieces.

An assumption I was happy to let him have.

From there, I headed towards my house, and again she was quiet, only furrowing that brow of hers when she saw the burned house next door to mine.

"It's my brother's old place." I reached for her hand, relieved she didn't pull away. "The winter slowed down our crews from clearing the debris. We'll rebuild for rental income or sell it outright, depending on the market at the time."

"Not Troy's, though, right?" She asked as I pulled her into my small living room.

"Nope. His house is on the other side of mine." Reaching over her shoulder, I pointed to a photo on my wall of my brothers and me in our military gear.

Nonna's favorite—each of us had a copy.

"This is Troy," I pointed to a younger version of Troy's stoic smile.

"Yeah." Lila deadpanned. "That dude I know."

"My other brother, Chase." I pointed to a significantly less muscled Chase, donning his military fade and a baby face. "His house is the one that burned."

"And you're all brothers?" she cocked an eyebrow up, sliding a finger along the photo from Troy to me, then Chase. "Kinda looks like the printer ran outta ink."

"Adopted," I huffed out. "Triplets no less." I waited for the standard quizzical expression I saw whenever someone learned about us, but Lila left it unremarked. "Wilder Brothers, three," I went on. "We came to Nonna's differently, but we're brothers through and through."

"Chase Wilder," Her eyes darted around the photo as if recognizing something. "I found records about a Chase and that woman...Vander something..." She bit her bottom lip, trying to piece together details. "Moira!" Her fingers snapped, and she smiled down at the photo. "It was in a newsreel. Connected to that slimy arsonist, right?"

"They're married now, Moira is my sister-in-law." I slipped the photo from Lila's hands and replaced it on the wall, shifting my hand to one of us all together at the wedding. "She and Chase are the proud new parents of my nieces."

"And Chase caught that sleazeball making sex tapes, and that led to arson, and - "

"Damn." I cut off her inquiry before she tripped into Brinks and caved in on herself again. "You've been a busy little detective." I gave her shoulder a nudge. "Come on, Nancy Drew." I led her to my bedroom and pulled out a few duffels from my closet.

"Before I met up with Sgt. Wilder...I did a dig to see if he could be trusted." Her voice was so matter-of-fact; I was pleasantly surprised to see she wasn't even remotely sheepish. Most people would feign embarrassment if they'd been discovered spying on someone. Instead, she was curiously eyeing a shelf of collected souvenirs.

"Uncle Buck's Gator Bayou?" She wrinkled her nose at the miniature resin alligator wearing sunglasses.

"From Bossier. I drove to Louisiana for Mudbug Madness 2 years ago." I pointed to the toy skeleton riding a bicycle next to the gator. "I made that trip a two-fer and hit The Bone Yard in Tennessee on my way back."

"And the carved zipper?" Lila waggled the granite miniature of a Zipper. "Was that the same trip?"

"Nope. That was Vermont last year. "World's Largest Zipper!" Her eye roll was adorable.

"You seriously travel just to see weird roadside shit?" she asked, crossing her arms with a smirk. "Most single guys just shoot pool or play poker for a hobby."

"I like road trips," I tossed a packed duffel bag to the floor. "I like seeing the country, meeting new people, and trying new foods. It's an adventure." I bit back the boredom of doing them alone.

"Your brother seemed clean, ya know. But info on all the mess with him, Chase, and that Jensen guy was spotty." Lila pivoted to our original topic, scanning my room as I shoved clothes into another duffel. "I knew he had two brothers, and figured Chase had to be one since the name Wilder wasn't common. But...I never saw you coming." She mumbled that last part, and I let it go.

I never saw her coming either.

"So, you figured Troy was a pretty okay guy to at least try to meet, and that's what preceded the cabin meet-up," I confirmed. "Where I blew in outta nowhere and fucked all your plans like a...what was that clever turn of phrase you used... oh yeah, I remember." I snapped my fingers with a smile. "Like a big-dicked karma fairy." My joke took all of two seconds to register before a heated blush rose from her neck to her cheeks, glowing the most gorgeous tinge of pink as she sighed and shook her head at me.

"You know," she laughed, genuinely–the first full smile I'd seen in days. "That guy had it coming. I legit tried to give him an out like 3 times before he pushed my buttons."

"I'm sure he did, Hellcat." I tossed the second duffel on the floor and scooped up an empty one. "Any drunk hitting on you has gotta be asking for an ass-whooping."

"That includes you, Lumberjack?" The flirtation in her voice shot down my spine.

"I wasn't drunk," I gave her ass a playful slap as I passed by. "Besides, you hit on me."

"Whatever, Jackass." She smiled again and watched as I grabbed the duffels and headed back to the living room. "Sam?"

I froze at the softness in her voice, waiting as she nipped that bottom lip of hers.

"Why didn't you tell me about the connection? That you knew me and that your brother was a cop and..." All the courage and words seemed to flee on an exhale as she stood, frozen, a few moments before squaring her shoulders. "Why didn't you tell me?"

No trembling chin. No tears. She'd flipped a switch and was a picture of determination. And still, I could see her hands pressed into her thighs, and the way she shifted from one foot to the other. She needed me to alleviate all her worries.

"Like you said, we'd had one hot, amazing night of mind-blowing sex. And, much as I hated to admit it, I pulled the douche move of bailing before you woke up." I stepped toward her, aching to hold her but needing to be slow. No pressure. Not now. "You got under my skin, but I had no way to reach you. You had my number—I didn't have yours." She blinked at that, but I kept going, not wanting her to feel bad for the oversight. "I wasn't mad. That night wasn't planned. But when I pulled you onto my rig, everything changed."

I took another step.

She didn't back away.

"When I found you at the hotel, you were broken, Hellcat. You didn't need some caveman crashing in with answers. You needed someone to look after you. So I didn't offer a bunch of information. I didn't ask the hard questions. And maybe that was wrong. If it was... I'm sorry." I offered her my hand, palm up. "But I'm not sorry for what we shared, or how you needed me then. I'm not sorry for trying to help you. Or track you down." Her fingertips barely brushed mine—but it was enough. "I'm not sorry I followed you to the bar—or that I tossed your sweet ass over my shoulder and brought you home."

I closed the last bit of space between us.

Her hand in mine–her eyes on mine.

"I hadn't shared you with my family either. No names, anyway. I love my brothers and Moira, but they're nosy as fuck. I wasn't sure what this was. Troy keeps his police work separate whenever he can. I never knew that the specialist helping Moira... was the same New York City Hellcat who was wrecking my whole goddamn world."

"Sam," Lila breathed as tears pooled in her lashes.

"I'm not done," I commanded gently, stopping her emotional spiral. "I told you I wasn't ever looking for a one-night stand, and I meant it. I've been there and done that. I was ready to stop road-tripping alone even before you came along." I lifted my free hand to cup her jaw, my fingers tangling in her mess of soft waves. "I wanna fix whatever I broke and get that damn fire back in those gorgeous eyes. Then I aim to keep it there as long as possible."

"But I'm - "

"Still not done yet, woman." My lips grazed hers. "For however long it takes to help you feel safe," I let my nose slide along hers, drawing her scent into me. "However long you need to stop making me fucking chase you," she let out a breathy laugh, and I rested my forehead on hers. "However long it takes for you to get it through your stubborn head that I'm yours, and you are mine, I'm. All. In."

"I'm...a mess." A tear slipped down her cheek.

"I'm not scared of messes."

"I'm...so lost."

"I'll buy a map." I held her firmly in place.

"I'm a grieving, disgraced, ex-cop with no job prospects who's squatting in some guy's house I barely know after spreading my legs on the night we met." Her brutally low self-assessment was a gut punch. "I'm not worth the baggage I'm carrying, and your family has been through – "

"I'm. All. In." I growled. It was a lot, and I knew it was fast, but I was done being at arm's length with her. If it killed me, I would earn her trust.

"You are worth it. Don't question me, and don't you dare speak like that about yourself again."

She exhaled, wrapped her arms around me, and rested her cheek on my chest.

When she nodded her agreement...it felt right.

39

LILA

THE DRIVE BACK WAS companionably silent, giving me time to process that, for the first time in a long while, I didn't feel alone. Sam's calm, gentle commands soothed the thunderstorm of doubts in my head. My stomach was relaxed and my head silent. Sam's fingers laced together with my own, anchoring me in the moment as he rested them both on my thigh.

I didn't want to run and hide.

I was comfortable in this space, in my skin, breathing the same air as him.

At the cabin, he hauled the bags inside, and I followed with the box. Turning down the hall, he paused at the space between our two doors. I saw a flash of his profile as he took in my room, his eyes dropping to the floor as he turned to enter the room across the hall. Leaning against the door to his room, I watched him toss the bags on the bed, unpacking them with jerky motions. A small but noticeable shift.

"Do you...want some help?"

"No." His soft, monosyllabic response felt clipped, and I suddenly doubted everything. Maybe all this comfort I was feeling was one-sided. I didn't want to run and hide from him, but maybe Sam needed space from me. It sliced through me to even think it, but I wouldn't deny him some time, given how horribly I'd treated him before.

"Oh...okay." I set the box down and turned, figuring I'd find a drink and chill in my room for the night. "I'll let you—"

"I'm not..." His voice halted me, and I heard him take a few breaths, as if schooling his frustration or unease.

Not that I could bring myself to face him.

"I meant all the things I said." His hand grazed the side of my arm in invitation to face him. The simple move felt Herculean, but I managed to turn enough to lean against the door jamb, reflexively crossing my arms like a battle shield. "But I also know that you've been through a lot. I'm trying to respect your space, and last night you didn't want me in there. But then you cried, and I barged in, so..." He swept his hand across the room. "I'm just putting my stuff here to give you space."

"I...understand," I lied, still unsure if he wanted to share a room with me or if I even cared since my only desire was to crawl into bed with him. "I'll give you time to unpack." The showdown last night must have been as jarring for him as it was for me. I owed him a level of privacy, and I'd be damned if I couldn't find enough goddamn courage to walk away now. Turning to leave, I wondered when my black pit of despair would return in the absence of Sam's arms around me, while knowing at my core that I deserved that loneliness.

"But know," He spoke softly, halting me again and closing the space between us. Tugging my arm, he spun me back to face him, caging me against the door jamb with his eyes scorching through me. "I can't listen to you cry and be alone. It's too hard. So, if I hear you in there tonight, know that I can't help myself." Sam lifted his free hand as if to grab my neck or cup my cheek, but then he paused. "I won't...I don't wanna push you and -" His fist clenched, the restraint in his knuckles mirroring my inner battle, and all I wanted him to do was put those hands on me so that I could take his frustration away, too.

"Hey," I whispered, uncurling my arms to rest on his chest. "It's okay."

"Lila." Sam's hand rested on my shoulder, fingers applying just the barest bit of pressure, and I soaked the sensation into the marrow of my bones. He closed his eyes, unable to even look at me, and it was then that I realized he was restraining himself even now. Holding back his own need to touch me out of some godforsaken need to give me a space I no longer wanted. I didn't want space or distance–I wanted him.

"Sam...Push me." His eyes snapped up, locking on me for one second, two, before I repeated myself to make sure he heard me. "Please...push me."

Sam crashed into me in a claiming kiss. Not one born of lust or alcohol like our wild first night–this was a sensual unraveling, my body melting into his as my soul begged for more. Sam's tongue slipped a request across my lips that I longed to answer. Deepening our kiss, tongues exploring one another, he nipped and sucked on my lips, devouring me as the whole world disappeared and all I could think, all I could feel, was Sam.

Never breaking apart, he hooked his hands under my knees, lifting me and carrying me across the hall into my room. I braced for the drop, but Sam knelt on the bed, sliding us to the center and lowering me gently. Only then did his lips move down, nipping and sucking across my collarbone into the tender hollow of my neck. Still kneeling between my legs, he sat back and stripped off his coat and shirt. I had only a moment to admire his bare chest before he was leaning over me, unbuttoning my shirt and adorning each newly bared spot with a fresh kiss. I unraveled a little more when he lingered at the swell of my breasts.

"Sam." I whimpered, aching to press so close together that the end and beginning of us would be lost forever.

"I've got you, baby," he growled, sliding my pants off in one smooth motion. "Now take that bra off and let me see those gorgeous tits." He stood back and unbuckled his belt as I unclasped my bra and tossed it to the floor. His eyes darkened as he took me in, nipples hard at the sudden burst of cool air and arousal. "Oh, how I dream about those." He drawled, his hand gripping his massive cock right in front of my eyes–staring but not touching me.

I ached at the distance.

"Sam," I pleaded, needing his weight, his heat. So much so that I leaned back on my elbows as my head fell back, heaving my breasts towards the ceiling in temptation. Hoping my vulnerability and his desire made an intoxicating mix he couldn't resist, I let my knees fall to the side, baring my drenched sex to him as I repeated those firing pistol words at him. "Push me."

"Fuck, woman." Sam's voice was ragged as his body dipped the mattress again, his mouth trailing kisses up my leg, across my thigh, right up to the very core of me, and just as I thought he might give me his mouth, I felt the cool breeze of his deep inhalation instead as he dragged his nose back and forth across my sex. "You smell like heaven."

He moved again, and I barely had time to miss his mouth between my legs before his tongue circled my nipples. His hands cupped and squeezed my breasts, sending lightning bolts to my core. I moaned as need grew in me, bucking my hips as his fingers pinned me to the bed, and I'd never wanted anyone more. He licked and sucked his way down my belly, and I let my fingers tangle in his wild and unruly hair, tugging slightly to get him where I needed him.

"Greedy girl." He laughed, resisting my efforts to lower him to where I was begging for friction.

The desire was boiling up in me, and my brain was chanting his name, begging for release, and screaming how badly I needed this...needed him...when words came out unbidden.

"Sam. I need..." Insecurity choked off my words, and I froze.

40

SAM

"**W**HAT IS IT, BABY?" I hated the new tension beneath me. "Tell me what you need." My cock was granite, and I ached to be balls deep in this gorgeous creature, but none of that mattered if she didn't feel safe. I'd suffer a cold shower and finish the fucking spaghetti sauce with a smile on my face if that's what she needed from me.

"I don't know, I..." Lila whimpered. "I can't..." Her words stumbled—like spreading her legs was easier than voicing her needs; A conflict I was unaccustomed to with her. I wanted to be able to anticipate her needs, but I didn't think she knew what she needed, and it was driving me insane. I burned to find whatever caused this wild, voracious force of nature to suddenly cave in... and murder it. The anger is even more acute if the cause was me.

"Whatever it is, Lila, speak it," I commanded between kisses. "'Cause I wanna bury myself in you—every inch." I drew her eyes to mine. "But I won't be mad if you need this to stop. I won't be upset if you need time or space." War waged behind her eyes, and as much as I wanted to roar my protection at her, I waited. Trust had to come in her own time; I couldn't force it. "I'm not going anywhere, either way. I'm good. We're good. There is no point here where you can't tap out...but please tell me what you need so I can give it to you."

"I need," Lila breathed, sitting up and tugging my face to hers. "I need you...to just make it all go away." Before I could confirm what she meant, her fingers wrapped around my cock and squeezed, causing my eyes to roll back in my head with a groan. "I need you in me, Sam...and on me...I need you everywhere." Brushing her lips against mine, she whimpered, "Please."

"Good girl," I growled into her ear, pulling her close and pivoting us until her head lay on the pillows. "Lie back and let me take care of you." Mercifully, she obeyed without hesitation, allowing me to slide down her body–welcoming the stretch as I placed my hands on her inner thighs, spreading them wide to admire her glistening cunt. "So gorgeous."

Leaning down, I used the tip of my tongue to slide from the top of her slit, down one side to her opening, and then back up the other side in one slow loop. Lila moaned, arching off the mattress and gifting me the breathtaking view of the slope of her breasts. Spreading her open with my fingers, I flattened my tongue and lapped her juices from bottom to top once, then twice, before returning my devotion to her clit. Licking around that bundle of nerves twice, I sealed my mouth around it and began sucking, flicking it with the tip of my tongue.

"Ah...Yes!" She grasped the headboard, arching further as I applied gentle pressure with my beard against her entrance.

She was close, but I wanted to make it so good for her that she saw stars. Slowing my efforts, I dipped two fingers deep inside as she gasped.

"Fucking hell, you are so wet." I hummed against her as I pumped in and out, "You're gushing for me." Lila arched again when I crooked my fingers against that spot on her inner walls, pressing rhythmically in time with my licking.

"Oh god," she breathed. "Your mouth...it's so...." Her climax built again as her movements grew erratic and her thighs tensed over my shoulders. "Please," she cried out, "Don't...stop!"

But I did stop.

"I'm not done with you yet." I removed my hands and mouth from her, loving the way she groaned at the loss. "I wanna taste every drop of you." Rolling us both over, I grabbed her waist, spinning her until her knees straddled my head. "Sit on my face, Hellcat." I had almost edged her to death, yet the command made her hesitate as she held herself hovering just inches away, denying me a chance to drown in vag-halla. "I want your thighs shaking around my ears when you lose control." I gave her ass a light slap. "Now sit."

I tugged her hips until her pussy sealed over my mouth, humming approval at the full weight of her world-class ass on my face. Within minutes, she was shaking and trembling so hard I was easily able to suck in air between each rocking tilt of her glorious hips. She was close, and I nearly halted her again—until her hands slid down my stomach. Sixty-nine wasn't in my plans, but fuck if I'd be the fool to turn it down.

The moment my girl circled the tip of my dick with her tongue was christmas-fucking-morning.

I held onto her hips, sucking at her sex while she moaned around my shaft. My balls tightened when she reached what I thought was her limit with a gag, but then Lila shifted. Lifting her hips a little, she relaxed her throat and reached both hands around to cradle the back of my thighs, taking me deep down the back of her throat.

I tried to steady my breathing, slow the climax, but she popped my cock from her mouth, licked my balls, then swallowed me again—giving me the best damn head of my life. Her cunt on my face, my dick down her throat, it was nirvana and I could have died happy.

Heaven...stars...death by blowjob.

Glory, hallelujah, what a helluva way to go.

I was the living embodiment of restrained frenzy as we devoured one another, groaning and grinding, and her entrance fluttering again. I was too close to blowing my load, and there was no way I was missing the opportunity to look at her face as she came once, if not twice, before me. With painful delight, I edged us both again when I lifted her off of me with a groan.

"Ride me, baby. I wanna watch you cum." Lila looked half-mad with need and didn't hesitate as she eased herself down around me with a pornographic moan.

"Oh god, it's so..." Her breath hitched as I thrust up inside her. "Please, Sam, let me –"

"You feel too fucking good," I grabbed her hips, sliding her back and forth, guiding her into a grinding motion. "Take your pleasure from me."

"Yes. Oh God." She was panting and whimpering, desperate for release after being edged so many times. "You feel so... God, it's so deep!" She was breathtaking—rocking, bobbing, her gorgeous tits moving with wild grace.

Beauty carved in golden light.

A goddess ushering this lucky bastard into bliss.

"I was made for you, baby." Thrusting up and up and up, grinding against her clit, I pounded relentlessly. "You were made for me...the way we fit... it's – "

"Perfect!" She screamed, her walls fluttering around my shaft. Grabbing my hands away from her hips, Lila guided them to her breasts. I squeezed them softly at first, then harder, then harder still as she ground down around my cock. "Oh God...yes...please don't stop!"

"Fuck yeah, baby." I pinched her nipples, giving her the bite of pain she needed to fall over the edge. "Cum for me, baby, Cum with me!"

"Yes! Yes! Yes!" Lila's orgasm clenched my shaft in waves as she rode me through her pleasure. "Sam, please... don't stop." I couldn't get enough of watching this woman scream my name, so just as she began to come down the other side of her climax, I bent my knees enough to thrust up so hard I lifted us both off the mattress. "OH, God! Yes! Yes! Yes!" her cries sounded fractured, and it was music.

"Yeah, baby. Fuck!" I growled my orgasm at last, sending her into the stratosphere one last time as I savagely bucked and emptied into her, and she collapsed into a boneless heap on my chest.

The spray of her wild hair blanketed me in darkness as I squeezed my arms around my girl, the back side of my orgasm a blissful flood of adrenaline. Stroking her back, relishing the feel of her in my arms, it took a few seconds before the blood drumming in my ears slowed enough to hear a soft sob.

"Hey." I rolled us to the side, scanning her up and down. "I didn't hurt you, did I? God, tell me I didn't hurt you." I began looking for bruises or ...God help me, blood. I knew I was big, but she'd taken me before, and she was with me the whole way. Wasn't she?

"No... I'm okay," she whimpered, sliding my hand up to her face, placing a kiss on my palm as she smiled. "I've just never had anything like that, or like you, and..." The flood of tears came again, and she lost the ability to finish her statement, but her touch, the way she folded into me, told me enough.

Every bottled-up emotion poured out of her.

Lila was satisfied, on a bone-deep level, maybe for the first time.

"I've got you." The words were small, but I meant them more than anything.

41

SAM

I FELT MORE PEACE, lying there with Lila, tangled in sheets and limbs, than I'd ever felt before. Her emotional climax was as intense as her orgasms; she dozed lazily while I processed this new rush of feelings. 'I've got you.' That was what I'd said to her at the end. It set her mind at ease, but it was an incomplete statement. Having her with me, in my bed, in my arms, in my life, was so much m ore.

More intense. More intoxicating. More complicated.

There was no going back for me. I had her...but she had me too. I had irrevocably fallen for this woman, but I couldn't tell her that yet. My intensity would no doubt scare her off. And there was a dinner full of hard conversations ahead of us. I eased out from under her and went to start the shower, hoping to give her just a few more seconds while the water warmed up. At the trash can, I reached my hand down to pull the condom off and found only skin.

"What the..." I whispered down at my dick and confirmed my fears, then did a sweep of the floor in case the condom slid off amidst the remnants of our time together.

The floor was bare.

"What the actual..." All the way to the bed—nothing.

Then the bucket of icy realization crashed over me.

"What...the actual...fuck?" I whisper-yelled, my brain exploding with the utter mind-fuck that in the heat of the moment, I'd never wrapped it up.

Me!

The man who whored around so much, I bought condoms by the case. I got tested regularly for every disease known to man as a matter of habit. The guy who was never without a condom in my car, on my bedside table, in my wallet, the one who'd double-bagged it a time or two.

Me.

A panicked rush of 'how and why' barreled through the truth that I was so focused on her pleasure, so gone in the moment with her, that when it came down to it, I raw-dogged that Goddess and I...loved it. Shock at the oversight bedamned, something instinctually deeper lay in wait.

Something primal.

I'd buried my seed in her—marked her. I wanted to climb to the rooftop and beat my chest like a fucking caveman and scream my territorial ownership to the goddamn stars that this fantastic, glorious, phenomenal woman was mine.

What in the fuckity fuck?

Starting the shower, I tried to reconcile the poster boy for feminism with the caveman grunting for Lila to be barefoot and pregnant. It was ten shades of fucked, and I had to tamp this thing down fast. Lila needed to get through whatever she was going through. We needed more time together as a couple and, for fucks sake, I needed to introduce her to my family and ... I don't know, date her, get engaged, marry her.

Ya know...the usual stuff you put before a baby, dickwad.

I was such an idiot, but oh God, she got caught too, neither of us realizing. I wasn't one of those guys who shot off like a pressurized jizz-pistol. But she didn't prompt so much as a cursory ask about birth control or testing. Then I remembered our last encounter in the shower when I'd also unintentionally nearly taken her bare.

If this happened twice, could I call it unintentional?

And how many times had I told her how I never left home without them? Maybe she was trusting me to be consistent, which I should have been. It was my job to be safe and consistent for her.

What in the goddamn hell was wrong with me?

Grateful that I had been thoroughly tested, I felt confident she either didn't play the field much or would at least be responsible enough for regular testing, so I wasn't worried about myself either. But God, we had oceans of ground to cover now.

A cold chill shuddered through me as I remembered her hurt at discovering the mere connection between Troy and me. What had it taken to talk her down from that betrayal, and it didn't even involve her uterus. When I imagined her anger, her rage, and how that might be the death knell to her letting me help her through this time, my stomach clenched. The cart was fucking lightyears before the horse. But Lila didn't need anything else on her plate. I had to get my head on straight so I could help her through tonight. So, shoving all thoughts aside, I went back to the bed to get her awake and moving.

"Come on, baby. We gotta get cleaned up for dinner." Lila rolled over, wild hair fanned out, sleepy eyes cracking just enough to glare—then close. I glanced between her thighs, and my stomach sank. How would I hide this from her long enough to get her through tonight?

"I'm cold... you're warm...come back to bed." Her short, incomplete sentences, combined with the commanding hand that slapped the mattress next to her, were arguably the cutest thing I'd ever seen. Still, tonight was too important to skip, so I tugged her towards me.

"A shower will wake you up, then we'll get some of that amazing pasta you helped make." I hoped the enticement of food would motivate her.

"Fine, you go, I'm sleeping." She tipped an adorably crooked half-smile across those lips of hers as she flipped me the bird and rolled over. "Bring me a doggy bag."

My little Hellcat.

"Alright... don't say I didn't warn you," I slid her closer to me on the mattress, her back arching into me as if to spoon before I ripped the sheet off and hauled her over my shoulder.

"Sam! Jesus!" She smacked my bare ass—so I returned the favor, hand bouncing on those perfect cheeks.

Walking into the bathroom, I glance at her cum-glistening snatch in the mirror, my seed leaking out, and my cock jumped to attention. Resisting the urge to slide my cum back up her thigh and shove it inside again, I groaned—fully spiraling into my shiny new breeding kink as I hauled her into a shower to wash away my mistake.

42

LILA

COOKING WITH SAM. SEX with Sam. Showering with Sam. These
were the things that grounded me as the little house of cards
I'd built for myself went careening into the void. He made me sleep,
nightmares be damned, and fed me until I nearly burst. Kept me talking
but never pushed. He demanded things from my body, but wasn't demanding of me, a distinction I needed for the strength to breathe in this
bubble Sam created. In his arms, I could hide from the mess I'd made
of my life and get lost in the ecstasy he brought me through—stolen
moments where I shared his breath, as he stole away mine. Ensuring I
was cleaned and properly cared for after he left me dick-drunk was just
another Sam-bonus. No one had ever been so thoroughly gentle after
wrecking my body.

And now, the fucker was blowing it up...with spaghetti.

He waited until we began loading food into the car to share his
plans. Not a simple 'dinner thing' as he'd first eluded, but a weekly

family tradition where I'd meet them all just one day after my brain was raked across an emotional cheese-grater. One of the myriad things in the shitstorm of my life that I had been blissfully hiding from in my little booze-soaked, pancake-glazed, shower-sexed bubble that Sam made for me

.

Jackass.

The drive to his brother's place was short. Sam talked the whole way, telling me that this was no big deal. He even tried to tell me that they had people drop in on this family dinner all the time. I briefly contemplated dumping the heaping pot of pasta across his face, but before the urge grew actionable, his thumb brushed my thigh. That calming connection sent reminders of how safe I'd felt during our time together, so when we pulled into the driveway, I clung to that gesture like it was the last inch of rope dangling over the edge of a live volcano.

"They're here!" A woman's voice shouted when we reached the porch.

"That'd be the sister," I said dryly as the door opened to a giant of a man, holding a baby, with the biggest shit-eating grin I'd ever seen. "Jesus, you're huge!" The words fell out of my mouth purely by knee-jerk reaction to the wall of muscles in front of me.

I ignored Sam's eyeroll as I took in the brother, Chase, who I recognized from the picture. Taller than Sam, muscled to high heaven with a military fade and a baby face that showed dimples you could swim in. He was definitely bigger than the photo in Sam's house. He had what appeared to be an assortment of ink peeking out from the various edges of his snug-fitting t-shirt. He wore head to toe black, right down to clunky biker boots, and it all fell away with the tiniest pink baby burrito in his arms.

A boyishly menacing look, all things considered.

"You must be Lila." He stepped aside so we could enter. "I'd shake your hand, but River here needs a little help holding onto her pacifier still." His eyes, when he looked at his daughter, were pure love.

Sam chose that moment to walk between us, scowling at me as he did.

"The sauce ain't getting any hotter out here, dude." Sam strolled into the kitchen, his brother following him until he'd settled the food. Then, with a clap of his hands, Sam spun around and commanded, "Gimme my girl".

Seeing Sam holding the baby was just unfair.

It was clear Sam was a barfly; his home, though cozy, screamed bachelor pad. The way he maneuvered my body made it clear he was an experienced lover, making his tenderness with me surprising enough. But him smoothly cradling that baby as if it were the most natural thing in the world, pivoting the little girl until she stared at him, had my ovaries practically throwing eggs overboard with a swoon.

"Uncle Sam missed his girls. Yes, he did. Are you eating and sleeping good for Mama?" No annoying baby voice, Sam spoke in his usual smooth timbre with a twinkle in his eyes that had the little girl as mesmerized as me. Watching them made my heart sink just a little to imagine how my brother might've been with my baby one day, and suddenly, all this family togetherness was too much.

I wasn't in the right space for this. I had to focus on my goal and get my Brinks' investigation back on track. A long-avoided sorrow began to snake around me, and I started calculating ways to make a hasty exit. As if knowing I was sinking, Sam tucked the baby into the crook of his arm and walked over to me, extending his other arm on my lower back.

"Hey, guys, this is Lila. Lila, that's my brother, Chase," he nodded to the tatted-up giant. "And over there is his wife, Moira." I followed his gaze to a bubbly blonde with a huge smile exiting the bedroom holding a second pink burrito.

Bright and cheery, post-partum bedamned, she practically sprinkled fairy dust in her wake.

"I am so happy you are here, Lila!" She handed off the other baby to Sam as if holding two newborns was as easy as breathing. Then...the woman hugged me. "Sam hasn't shared much with us yet, but what he has told us has all been great."

"Oh...uh..." I looked at Sam for help, but the traitorous bastard was lost in the confetti hearts floating from his besotted baby-eyes. "Thanks, I guess?"

Her embrace lightened a little as she stepped back enough to hold me at arm's length and take a long look at me. She was clearly a new mommy, exuding all the signs of sleepless nights, slightly disheveled hair, and the tell-tale wardrobe of a 4th-trimester body that had only recently been vacated. She was beautiful. Her smile was so open, so genuine, and her blue eyes sparkled like whatever she saw in me made her the single happiest person on the planet. My traitorous brain took that moment to remind me that my entire wardrobe was black, like my icy soul, and I had no reservoir of glitter to offer this woman.

A hole to fall into would've been great.

"And hiding back in the corner," Sam's eyes never left the babies as his voice resonated through my awkward half-hug, "Is Troy."

"Smooth, brother." Troy's voice carried from where he'd been sitting as he lifted a hand in a soft half-wave. "I was offering the poor woman room to breathe, unlike you all, who have attacked her with hugs...and babies."

Troy was growing on me.

"Who doesn't love hugs and babies!" Moira exclaimed, tossing her blonde waves over her shoulder to flash a pinched look at Troy. "Hugs and babies are the best."

"Fancy." Chase caught Moira's attention and tilted his chin down to where her hands were still holding mine. As her gaze looked back up at me, whatever expression I wore must've been akin to a bag of hissing snakes. She dropped my hands immediately and stepped back with an apologetic look on her face.

"Oh. I'm sorry. I'm coming on too strong. It's just... I'm so excited there's another woman here, I've been the only one for so long, and these guys are great, but their monosyllabic shorthand is maddening, and I rarely get to leave the house these days, and - "

"Hey, baby," Chase caught Moira's attention again, eyes darting to Sam, who scowled at her with some unspoken conversation. "Wanna help me with the pasta?"

"Right," Moira sighed before departing for the kitchen, butterflies and tweety-birds in her wake.

Sam and his dueling babies returned to my side.

"See." He whispered. "Casual." He gave me a wink, nudging me towards the living room to one of the couches. "Let's go sit."

"You big fucking liar," I whispered. "You said people joined these things all the time, but the pretty pink princess over there is practically shell-shocked to see another human."

"Hey now," He shot a stern admonishment frame in a smirk. "Watch the language around the babies." He sat next to me, still holding the two bundles, and added. "I may have over-stated the number of times someone joined us, but only because I didn't want you to say no before giving it a chance. If you are miserable, we can leave, but...there are things we need to discuss as a family that might hold answers for you."

I opened my mouth and then closed it again, wondering what they could be discussing that had to do with me. How did they even know what my questions were? Did I even know what questions I had?

"It would mean a lot to me...if you stayed. Think it over while I go change one of the girls." He stood and handed over the other baby to Moira, who'd been hovering within earshot.

Of course, the man also did diapers—Jackass.

I could hear the chatter in the kitchen, the weight of their eyes boring a hole in my head, and I wondered. Did they know about our one-night stand? Did they know about the liquor store? Did they know how or why I was here? Had Troy told them about my getting fired? Did they know who I was in the whole arson case? I rubbed my palms on my thighs, resisting the urge to bolt like the house was on fire, and stared at the hallway where Sam disappeared.

Come back. Come back, come back, come back!

Despite my efforts to resist melting into a pile of insecurities, I could feel my badassery slipping away. Just as I started to rise out of my seat to run bodily out the door, a beer appeared.

"I thought the occasion called for liquid courage." Troy's voice cut through my racing thoughts, smooth and low, like he knew the storm in my chest. I looked up to find his judgment-free face holding out a beer for me, another of his own in his other hand. "I know how very... overwhelming we can be." I took the offered bottle on instinct and watched as he sat on the opposite end of the couch. "I wouldn't blame you for calculating exit strategies."

His insight was stripping, and it made me take a closer look at him. Troy wasn't just calm—he was measured. He didn't just observe chaos—he cataloged it and moved pieces to restore order. Handing me the beer at precisely the moment I thought to leave, sitting as far away as possible on the couch to join me, but not crowd me. Any decent cop could recognize basic human emotions. Still, Troy exuded an air that suggested he was a deep study of the human experience, hinting at a deeper well of experience he drew from.

"You're not wrong," I breathed, drinking deeply.

Where Sam was raw edges and reckless charm, Troy came off like quiet precision. Steel beneath a suit. Even the way he sat, posture perfect, tie smoothed, showed a man who commanded his energy in a fist so tight you could fall apart in his wake, and he'd be unruffled.

I bet he was hell in the interrogation room.

"I need to apologize, personally, for how things went down last night. I can imagine how very intense it must have been for you to find Sam and me together. Especially if you hadn't already connected those dots."

Overwhelming, jarring, intense...he had a thesaurus of ways to describe fucked.

"I know it will take more than words to give you a sense of security, but know that I am glad you are here. Both at dinner, but also for Sam." The last line was delivered with an odd sort of softness in his tone that I could only account for by his love for his brother.

"Hold your vote on that last one," I said, my eyes focusing intently on the label of my beer. "I'm pretty sure he got the short end of the stick."

"Nonsense," Troy's monotone voice was at odds with the kindness he offered. "You're doing the best you can. It's all anyone can ask."

"Which, all things considered," I chugged another gulp, hoping it washed down the loathing that rose to smother me, "is pretty fucking sad."

43

SAM

I CHANGED RIVER IN record time, worried even a minute away would let Lila get in her head. But as I walked out of the bedroom, I found her sitting on the couch, drinking a beer with Troy, the barest hint of a smile on her face. Everything in me sighed in relief, and when I looked down at River, a truth clicked into place.

I wanted what Chase and Moira had.

More than sex and emotional rollercoasters, I wanted a wife. I wanted a family, and I wanted it...with Lila. I'd promised to help her through this. I had told her I was all in, but I suddenly realized just how deep that went.

"Everything okay with River?" Chase asked from the kitchen, drawing everyone's eyes to me.

"Yeah. She just needed an outfit change. No big." I crossed the room, standing in front of Troy.

"I was just telling Lila how glad I was that she came." Troy tipped his beer in her direction before reaching for River. "But I feel the need to hold my niece...if you would be so kind."

"Don't let him fool you," I winked to Lila, "Uncle Troy only wants the girls after they're clean and dry."

"She looked like a deer in headlights," Troy murmured as we swapped baby for beer. Troy returned to the kitchen, and I held out my hand to Lila.

"Have you seen the view from the balcony? It's pretty spectacular." Leading her out to the large wooden deck hanging off the edge of the cabin, I made a mental note to keep alcohol away from her for a few weeks. "I'm sorry if I made you feel ambushed," I slipped behind her, caging her in as she leaned against the railing.

"I'm fine."

"Let's try that with a little more honesty, Hellcat," I wanted her truths, all of them, even the hard or ugly ones.

"Fuck off." She breathed, the corner of her mouth tipping the barest hint of a smile as her body melted into me.

"So, we've decided to be a brat?" I growled into her ear, her laughter my reward for pushing her past her comfort zone. "Be honest, babe. I can't read your mind yet."

"It's just your family, your brothers...I had that." Her head dropped, but she continued. "I had dinners and inside jokes." She pulled away, leaning forward to inspect some fascinating detail in the railing. "I haven't been in that space for so long, and I wasn't..."

She didn't need to finish her thought for me to know her only goal, her singular focus, from the moment they were killed until now, was to catch the man responsible. She'd nested in that pit so long she didn't know how to crawl back out.

"Look at me." I nudge her around. "I won't pretend to know what it's been like for you. If I suddenly woke up one day and my brothers were gone, I'd go completely off the rails." She started to shake her head, but I kept going. "The fact that you have kept your head above water, kept going, is nothing short of a miracle." Her eyes turned down again, but I hooked a finger under her chin until she returned her tear-filled gaze to me. "I want to help piece together a little bit of a foundation for you...And I think my family can help. We're gonna go in there and talk about a lot of things, and it's gonna be hard, maybe scary, and definitely intense." Lila's body sank against the rail, and she placed a hand on my stomach as if to distance herself from my words. "But you won't be alone, Lila. Not with me here...and frankly not with my family if you let them in."

If breaking her came from losing her family, then healing her could come in the hands of mine.

"I barely had a plan when I got to this shitty little town. Much less processed, what to do after you and your brother blew up my world—now I'm being served babies and spaghetti and a pretty pink princess, and I just..." She waved an irritated hand around before huffing out, "It's just all so fucking intense. Everything. All the damn time!"

"We'll figure it out," I said, cupping her cheek and pulling her to me until our foreheads touched. "But first, take a few deep breaths with me." Anxiety screamed through her silence, like her world had grown too big and too loud. Taking a deep breath, I guided her, "We've got right now, just the two of us, so soak it in."

Lila breathed in and out, pausing long enough for her shoulders to relax again.

"I'm not sure Chase is gonna be able to rein Moira in from absolutely smothering you with all her best intentions, though." A surprising laugh bubbled up from her as I held that space, and it was everything. "So take a moment to make it all smaller with me, bring it down...and breathe."

Standing there, my family at my back and her in my arms, was perfection.

"Okay." She sighed, turning her face to me with renewed focus. "I can handle the princess of excitement, but I'm not promising I won't clock someone. I'm still low-key pissed at both of you."

"It's okay." I whispered, letting her wrap that badass armor around herself, "We've probably got it coming."

I led her back inside, where the smells of fantastic food filled the air. Once seated, my brothers led the charge with their best manners, offering graces and airs and dancing on eggshells to make Lila feel at ease. I knew Lila didn't need fake, but I didn't know how to snap the guys out of it without making a scene. Of course, I forgot our secret weapon—Moira.

"Okay, Jesus, enough already!" She flung her hands in the air before crossing them across her chest. "You three are the worst."

"Babe?" Chase held a baby in one hand, spaghetti half-raised to his mouth. "What do you -"

"You are all being completely weird." Moira leveled her blue eyes at my girl from across the table. "I know I came on a little strong earlier because I was so happy to meet the person who has Sam so torn up."

"I'm not - "Moira silenced me with a raised finger, never taking her eyes off Lila.

"But I recognize that look." She lowered her hand, and her face and voice softened. "I've lived that shell-shocked look of someone whose whole world was upended one too many times." Chase dropped his fork and reached over to stroke his wife's shoulder.

She smiled some private message for him, then stood and circled the table.

"I don't know the details of your story, but it's painfully clear that no one has said the right thing for you yet. That one thing, whatever it is, to help you release the breath you've been holding since you're whole world came down around you."

Moira nudged me out of my chair with an elbow, stealing my seat and lifting a napkin to Lila's cheeks for tears.

"So, I'm going to blast past their awkwardness and just tell you the words I needed to hear...to begin accepting my place with these three exceptional weirdos who just want to help." The room went reverently still as Moira took Lila's hands. "You are welcome here...and very wanted. You're not a mess to clean up. Not a catastrophe dropped in our laps. You are strong and capable, but right now you need to know...you don't have to be." Lila's lips parted as she breathed through a silent sob. "Not with us."

Moira flicked her own tears away as she continued, commanding in her gentleness.

"You are safe, Lila. Safe with me, safe with my husband and my daughters and their big, dumb, uncles who might be in desperate need of tactful communication skills..." She flashed a smile at the room, "But who are the most trustworthy men I've ever met?"

Lila's shell cracked, one tear at a time, as Moira's words lifted her rawest self to light, and I didn't dare break the spell my sister was weaving.

"My husband literally pulled me from a burning building, saving my life. His brothers saved me all over again with their acceptance and loyalty. These men broke a cycle of abandonment so completely that my daughters will never know the isolation I did. And they did that not by being strong," she nodded at Chase, "Or being efficient," She cast a glance at Troy, "or even by being doggedly persistent," her head tilted back to me, and I saw a small laugh bubble up between Lila's tears. "They saved me with their intention...and their integrity. Their yes is yes...their no is no...and if they say they'll never let you fight a battle alone, then you won't. Plain and simple." She gave Chase that same quiet, knowing smile. "Even if that means they have to chase you down on a city bus cause your stubborn ass was too independent for your own damn good."

"How..." Lila began, pausing as a shudder broke loose. "How did you get past it?"

"A little trust...a lot of courage." Then, Moira wrapped Lila in a warm embrace, lingering until Lila's body relaxed and her arms lifted to return the hug. "Two things I know you have in abundance if you've made it this far."

I raised my eyebrows at Chase, who just shook his head with a puff of air filling his cheeks. Troy lifted his baby-free hand in surrender. We'd never been around this kind of energy, this kind of emotion, and it was a moment that we knew was significant. Still, we hadn't the slightest idea of what the fuck to do with it. When my gaze returned to the girls, Lila wiped her cheeks as she sat back.

"Okay then." Her scratchy, tear-filled voice held quiet resolve as her armor slid back into place. "You said this dinner was meant to hash shit out as much as to eat, admittedly, really good food." She squared her shoulders and leveled her gaze at Troy. "So, let's hash shit out."

44

SAM

M OIRA RETURNED TO HER chair, Troy squeezing her hand as she passed him before clearing his throat and smoothing his tie. Once she was seated, he took a breath to nod at Chase and me, the unspoken 'it's time' zinging between us.

"Given our collective communication failures, I propose we lay all our cards on the table."

"Ditch the cloak-and-dagger. Agreed." Lila nodded, eyes narrowing. "You first."

"Of course." Troy didn't hesitate, instinctively knowing Lila needed blunt honesty to trust him. "There is a bit to cover, I will try to be brief. First, Chase and Moira, Lila was the specialist who helped with Moira's fire-damaged laptop. That's what first put her, a New York cyber-crimes expert suddenly interested in a local case, on my radar. So when you were suddenly recalled," he nodded to Lila, "I dug deeper and found you'd been let go from the NYPD cyber-crimes division." Lila shifted slightly, but Troy pressed on. "I'm not trying to embarrass you, merely explaining your exit tipped me off to look deeper."

"Because of Internal Affairs?" We all looked at Lila before returning our eyes to Troy.

"Yes. The IA paperwork didn't add up, given your impeccable record."

"And this connects to Moira's case again somehow?" Chase asked.

"Jensen's attorney, Marcus Brinks, was the reason I came then...and the reason I'm here now," Lila answered. "Marcus is responsible for the murder of my family."

Her voice was confident, but I saw her palms flatten against her legs even as I saw Chase and Moira's jaws come unhinged. I couldn't remove the heaviness of Lila's confession, so I settled for caressing her shoulder–a reminder that I was with her.

"There's more," Troy looked back at Moira. "Marcus Brinks is the man who had a brief interaction with you at the supermarket."

"The sleazeball gave me the heebie-jeebies...over oranges," Moira said with a noticeable shiver.

"Rightfully so," Lila huffed with disgust. "He's a master of skeezy loopholes—he gets one-percenters off the hook like it's a damn hobby."

"Also," Troy continued, "Brinks was the keynote speaker at a fraternal order Dean Jensen was a part of. One, he attempted to recruit Chase's boss, Chief Brandt, into."

"Apex," Chase confirmed to Troy's nod.

"Apex?" Lila stiffened. "I've not seen anything about that. What's Apex?"

"Nor would you," Troy said. "On paper at least, Brinks' name is clear. But he spearheads several financial donations through outside investors, to organizations spanning the entire state, including a recent surge of Apex-funded investments here in town at the schools and - "

"The library!" Moira interjected. "They donated those awful flowers before it burned."

"Geez," Lila huffed. "They got a fire kink too?"

"I suspect that was all Jensen-led, since he was largely in play at that time. However, the Apex connection to Brinks was enough for my boss to sanction a covert, off-the-books investigation. Keeping above board and quiet until full evidential support." Troy opened his hand, palm up. "But my sources ran dry until you showed up at my diner."

"I am so confused right now." Moira leaned forward, looking at Lila. "You were chasing the attorney here, Brinks, but Troy is chasing Apex?"

"And you thought I'd be your new informant." Lila tipped her chin to Troy and crossed her arms. "With information on Apex, you couldn't get through official channels."

"I was wholly unaware of your urgency at finding Brinks, nor your ... personal history." Troy's face softened. "I can't imagine how hard the past 18 months have been. I am deeply sorry for your losses."

"18 months?" I spat out the words, caught off guard by the timeline. "You've carried this for that long?"

A slight nod, eyes cast down, a hint of pain. All I wanted was to pull her into my lap and hold her. Her pain felt so raw, so fresh, but she'd been bearing this for almost 2 years. I felt awful for my outburst, but all I could do was pull her to me, my lips pressed to her temple in silent solidarity.

"That was what you lost?" Moira's face was a painting of sadness. "Two of them?"

"Guess it's my turn." Lila clasped her hands in her lap, resignation wafting off of her in waves as the mask of a hardened warrior slipped into place.

"My mom died when I was a kid...some freak aneurysm...so the bulk of my life was spent with just my dad and my brother. Dad was a cop with the NYPD. My brother joined up right out of high school, and I was recruited after a stint in college. My brother became a beat cop, like my dad, but I had a knack for computers, so cybercrimes scooped me right out of the academy. One day, I started connecting dots on cases that seemed unrelated."

"Except Brinks," Troy confirmed, and my girl nodded but pushed forward.

"His clients all fell in Manhattan's elite: finance guys, CEOs, politicians—anyone with money and power. Brinks' name was synonymous with expensive loopholes. Fuckin' bets were placed on the man. You knew that if someone got booked, and Forbes reported their income, Brinks would be the thorn in your side."

She sighed, her eyes taking on a distant stare before she continued.

"A friend from my old neighborhood was my first tip. We'd gone to the same high school, but where I had a solid home, she wasn't so lucky. She became an escort—high-end clientele, good money, mostly safe. She made good bank until she ended up dead. My history with her earned me the opportunity to assist with the case, and I found a year's worth of emails. She'd been communicating with other women, trying to warn them away from something. The emails stopped 3 months before her murder, so I dug into the messages only to find that the women in question were all also dead."

"And that was your pattern," Troy added quietly.

"The start, at least," Lila confirmed. "I dug into the other women's tech print, social media, and the like, connecting more dots and piecing together a theory. These women were being wined and dined and swooned...then suddenly found floating on the Hudson. And lo and behold, every one of their cases had some tenuous link to a penthouse with Brinks on speed dial."

"You presented this to your Captain?" Troy asked.

"Yeah...loudly. But you know the drill." Lila huffed. "No evidence, no case. All I had was a tech trail, a theory, and a line of bodies no one cared about."

"No one cared about them?" Moira huffed. "How?"

"Like my friend–no family, no friends, most of them runaways or orphans. No one looked for them. Pretty faces that could earn a buck with their bodies and a file that read 'a john got aggressive.' Case closed."

"But you didn't give up on your friend." Moira grabbed for Chase with oceans of unspoken emotions that only those who knew her orphaned background could understand. "You fought for her, didn't you?"

"And the women like her." Lila shook her head as if trying to clear the emotions behind her eyes. Sighing deeply, she squared her shoulders once more. "I created files: names, addresses, dates of social engagements, where their lives crossed. Then followed the paths to see who or what held the purse strings."

"You don't think the money was its own string?" Troy questioned, and Lila shook her head.

"It didn't add up. Too many unrelated cases with only one connection keeping their noses clean." She pointed at Troy. "Marcus Brinks–but he didn't have the leverage for all that." Leaning back in her chair, her face fell. "So I started looking at Marcus personally, wondering what kind of guy could be involved with that many evil bastards and who held the other end of his leash. That was my mistake," her voice trailed off, her hand sliding to mine under the table. "Sometimes when you look for the devil, he starts looking back."

The intensity of her grip spoke volumes. She was diving deep and needed an anchor. Squeezing back, I clung to her. I would be the lifeline, feeding her oxygen to keep her from drowning.

"He screamed down the pipeline to my captain, and Cap barked at me to leave it be."

"That'd be the write-ups on record. Disciplinary actions for insubordination." Troy sprinkled in details for the room, as Lila nodded along.

"All it did was fuel my stubborn ass." She huffed a sardonic laugh of disgust. "I knew Brinks was shady as fuck with the kind of woman-hating sex parties he attended. That man is sick." Another laugh accompanied a fresh tear. "And not to put too fine a point on it—I was way fucking right." She breathed the final words so quietly, I might've been the only one who heard them. "For all the good I did anyone." I caught the next tear with my thumb, winding my free hand around the back of her neck and squeezing until she glanced at me.

Silent words between us as I inhaled, and she matched me. Breathe in...breathe out... I'm with you.

"The night my dad and brother were killed, I was warned...a voice modulated tip from a burner I couldn't trace. But I know–I know–it was Brinks."

"A liquor store hold-up," I filled the space while she took another breath, hoping to spare her the full weight of sharing. "Both men shot in the line of duty. She saw it all."

Chase and Troy both shut their eyes, understanding fully what I wasn't sharing. Watching death was never pleasant...watching someone you love die, unspeakable.

"Dad was on my case to let the Brinks thing go. He wanted me to keep my head down and stay focused on my career. But my brother promised to keep his ears open. He'd been putting something together and told me he found information to share that weekend when we had dinner at Dad's."

"But you never got that information?" Troy finished, direct but gentle.

Lila paused her story, the scene no doubt flashing afresh in her memory.

"My dad," her breath hitched, as he eyed her hands as if searching for their blood. "Gone before I arrived on the scene. And my brother...only got out two words before he died...Follow Brinks."

Silence swallowed the room.

Troy's face held the distant look indicative of his mental gymnastics. Moira wiped away tears. Chase, scowling at the table, no doubt wishing he could inflict pain on Brinks on behalf of the whole world. All of us felt the burden she had carried alone, and each of us, for reasons of our very own, silently picked up the mantle with her.

Unsure of how to bridge the weight of the moment into something with a forward momentum, I pressed my lips to Lila's shoulder, willing comfort and strength into her and wondering if she knew how amazing she was, and how supported. Chase broke the silence.

"Brinks brought you here, through Jensen. And that's how you helped my wife."

"That misogynistic bastard was a real piece of work." Lila nodded, wiping her cheeks. "He earned the ass-whooping that put him in a coma for the deep-fake gaslighting he worked."

"Little Badass," I said with a wink to Moira.

"That was you!" Lila's sadness gave way to genuine surprise. "Good on you. I hope you wore those bruises like a badge of fucking honor."

"She saved me, ta-boot," Chase added, kissing his wife's head with a smile that I noted didn't reach his eyes. "And our girls."

"Indeed, my dear sister's courage brings our family no small amount of pride." Troy smiled at one of his nieces before continuing. "But this does bring me to another piece of news. For this, I need to put my niece to bed, as should you." He nodded to Chase as they both stood.

45

SAM

W E SETTLED THE GIRLS and grabbed fresh drinks. Chase and
Moira took the love seat, Lila and I the couch, while Troy
perched on the stone hearth, wearing his focused scowl that meant business. Without pretense, he dove in.

"Dean Jensen is gone." His words rippled like a stone in a still pond;
everyone's jaw collectively clenched or fell open as the ghost of that man's
evil deeds whooshed through us.

"Oh," Moira whispered, hand on her chest. "I... wasn't expecting
that."

"None of us were." Chase's angry glare bore down on Troy. "Why
didn't you tell me?".

"Hey, hey, hey," Moira's hand shifted to Chase's leg. "He's telling us
now."

"I know, it's just—" Chase huffed, a mix of anger and something else
shifting across his eyes.

Jensen was an albatross around Chase's neck. Troy and I spent months helping him come to grips with what happened in that last fire. But Chase felt he should've overcome duct tape, multiple stabbings, and bleeding out to take Jensen down. It was heart-wrenching to see him beat himself up over something no one could've handled better. This anger, though, was more than he couldn't shield his wife from the shock of Troy's news.

"I assure you, my omission was well-intended," Troy continued. "But there is more."

"More?" I asked, concerned that this added to Lila's already emotionally taxed state. "What more can you say about a dead guy?"

"He didn't say dead." Lila's clipped words cut the tension, her head cocked to one side as she eyed Troy. "He said...gone." Leaning forward, elbows on her knees, she added. "Kind of a big distinction, don't you think, Sergeant?" Her stance and intensity mirrored his—two bulls facing off.

"One that brings us full circle." Troy tipped his glass at Lila. "The alert on Jensen's death reached my desk as part of the arson investigation, but the paperwork held...discrepancies."

"Lemme guess, this is where I come in." Lila pushed.

"Normal channels for disposal of a body in criminal proceedings are for the officer in charge to be notified, along with the next of kin. The officer in charge confirms the time of death, signs off, and closes the case file, notifying anyone involved," he nodded to Moira and Chase, "that the case is closed due to the primary suspect's demise."

"No criminal, no case," Lila deadpanned.

"Indeed," Troy nodded.

"But that didn't happen?" Moira's eyebrows bunched into a scowl.

"I was never notified. An automated system alert indicated that the file had been closed. Everything processed and handled by Internal Affairs. The same IA agent who handled the disciplinary action against Ms. Rivera...and who doesn't seem to exist."

"It's Brinks." Lila jolted, sitting ramrod straight. "That rat can work every damn loophole with dirty IA in his pocket! Why would IA even be involved in body disposal?"

"My suspicion as well, especially given that a single IA agent can't cross easily into so many jurisdictions. Alas, my sources have dried up." Troy's hands went wide. "And with the case closed, I'm at an impasse."

"Brother," I chimed in, understanding the risk a little more. "If Internal Affairs kicked Lila from the force, and there is even a hint that they are connected to whatever the fuck else is going on up here...then you gotta back off. Like...yesterday."

"Jesus. Sam's right." Chase added. "Your job is at risk. Maybe more if Lila's story connects." He flashed an apologetic look at her. "But if Jensen is dead, then the case is closed, and we can all move on...so, let's move on."

"No!" Lila shouted, all her attention on Troy. "You can't quit. Marcus Brinks got involved with Jensen for a reason, and I couldn't figure it out on my own, but you have more information." She stood, emphatically gesturing. "We can pool our info. Brain dump what you have to me about Brinks and Apex. I'll get more intel and–"

"Stop!" Troy shouted, hands splayed out. "I *cannot* hear however that sentence ends."

"We can't stop!" Lila turned to me, eyes panicked. "I can't stop. I have to nail that bastard!"

"Whoa, babe, come here." I offered my hand, urging her to sit back down. "I don't think that's where TJ's going with this." I shot a warning look at Troy, and his nod told me he got the message—land this fucking plane.

"My theory," Troy began pacing, "Is that you and I share a missing link. You didn't have Apex, and I missed Brinks' history. But...there is one more thing."

"Jesus fucking Christ!" Moira threw up her hands. "Just spit it all out at once and stop drama-bombing like a doom-fairy with pockets full of shit-glitter?!"

"Dear sister...because of how much it pains me to hurt you." Troy set his glass down and walked to the coffee table across from Moira and Chase. Sitting, he took her hands in his own. "I inquired at the hospital, personally. Jensen's body didn't pass through the morgue."

"What does that mean?" Chase leaned forward, his arms never leaving his wife, but his free hand clenching into instant, white-knuckled rage.

"I can't be sure, but I have no confidence that Jensen is actually dead." His words sucked all the oxygen from the room as we peeled back the hidden meaning in each syllable. Jensen was gone, but not dead—thus, out there. The man who nearly killed my sister, my nieces, and my brother walked free...and able to strike again.

Moira went pale—Chase red-faced.

"Fucking hell." I huffed in disbelief. "How is this possible, TJ?"

"I've brought everything I have thus far," Troy looked to Lila, "Boxed and sitting by the door. As far as anyone on the force is concerned, the case is closed. I must act accordingly. Especially being assigned as police liaison to the mayor's new Town Development Committee. Scrutiny will be my bane for the foreseeable."

"Understood." Lila nodded, her clarity lost on the rest of us. "The Cabin gives me a solid cover. On paper, I'm not here. I can dig in...string a trail together."

Lila's eyes flicked in my direction, and warning bells began sounding in my brain.

"Agreed," Troy confirmed, nodding at me with a sadness shadowing his eyes. Before I could unpack that, Lila spun on her heels and leveled me with a resolute look.

"We're done." My jaw dropped at her sudden detachment, squared shoulders, and a little volume in her words. "Pack your shit. Get out tonight. You're gone."

I leapt to my feet like a stray dog being kicked.

"How the fuck does this shitstorm turn into you throwing me out?"

"Lila's story is the cautionary tale you should be looking for answers in," Troy tried to interject. "It's for your safety and - "

"No!" I snapped, anger boiling into frothing fury as I stabbed a finger into TJ's chest. "No fucking way."

"Yes, fucking way," Lila commanded, a sheen of tears my only hope she wasn't sincere. "I gotta dig in here, and I can't do that if you are under my goddamn feet. I want you out...tonight."

My jaw ached from the force of my gritted teeth as I did my best not to scream across the house. Her words were harsh and acidic, but her face held pure anguish in her eyes.

"I'm not going anywhere."

"Sam, it's time."

"The fuck it is!" I growled

"It's past time!" She made a show of storming off, but I stepped into her path.

"End of the goddamn Discussion?" Toe-to-toe, crossed my arms, blood boiling as I blocked her retreat.

"We had a good run, Lumberjack. God knows you lay good pipe, but I gotta dig in here." She hoped a little shock and awe might back me down in front of my family. All it did was fuel me to dig in harder.

"I'm. Not. Leaving."

The surprise about Jensen, and the utter shock that my brother would condone this, were both drowned out by the pure anger that Lila still considered doing this alone. Troy and Chase glanced at one another, mouthing something, but I locked my eyes on Lila; everything falling away.

"Jesus Fucking Christ," she started again.

"No." My voice was deceptively calm as I narrowed the space between us, daring her to butt heads with me, prepared to toss her over my shoulder and drag her back home and show her exactly how I felt about this situation.

"Sam," my name was a plea.

"I said no, and I meant it," I laced my fingers with hers.

"Please," she whispered, chin trembling, before she took a deep breath and squared her shoulders, preparing to come at me again. "I won't work with your brother if you are underfoot. You want me to help him, you gotta go."

"Sam," Troy interjected, but I silenced him with a raised hand, never taking my eyes off my girl.

"You listen and listen good, Hellcat. I'm. Not. Leaving. You're mine, and I'm yours. And that means your battles are my battles."

"You don't understand." Lila touched my arm, her tear-filled eyes dissolving my anger. "Please."

"However long it takes, to help you fight whatever demons you gotta fight... I'm. *All*. In." I repeated the words from before, meaning them on an entirely different level now, and she knew it because she let the tears fall, holding my gaze.

I wouldn't yield.

I wouldn't bend.

I would be her rock...or her weapon.

"I can't...risk you." Lila put a hand over her mouth and gasped at her whispered confession. "Not after... and your family..." Her words broke, sobs rising as the weight of her resistance cracked. "I'll break...if you..." Sobs choked off her words, and she leaned into me–her body giving me what her words couldn't. She was afraid for me...for all of us. Wrapping my arms around her, I let the tears come again as I rested my head on top of hers and tried to let my warmth soothe her.

Looking around the room, I saw Chase and Moira having a silent conversation of their own, and Troy, taking all this in, sat waiting to voice his thoughts.

"Say your piece," I growled, my frustration simmering still that he'd condoned her booting me to the curb.

"She's in the best position to move the needle on this," Troy stated. "And by setting myself aside, I maintain plausible deniability and can monitor things from within. But" he shifted his weight from one foot to the other. "It's not without risk." He looked at Chase and added, "If Dean Jensen represented Apex–his caliber, their model–no one is safe."

Then it sank in: me holding Lila, Chase with Moira, Troy's words hanging in the air.

The race none of us wanted had just begun.

Again, it was Chase who broke the silence.

"I won't lie—the idea of any of you being involved in this makes me wanna lose my ever-loving shit. I've got a wife and daughters. I can't imagine a world where they are remotely close to danger like this." He pressed Moira's hand to his mouth, a gleam of tears in his eyes.

"But," Moira finished, "we also can't live in a world where people like Dean walk around scot-free." She looked at Lila and smiled. "So, we stay smart...but we do what's right." I could have kissed my badass sister for the lifeline she'd cast Lila. We'd stay smart...and together.

"Then it's settled." I tilted Lila's head back. "You're *not* doing this alone."

"You...stubborn jackass," Lila answered with weary tears, despite a smile lingering in her eyes.

"A jackass that won't tolerate another eviction." I winked. "Hope you enjoyed blowing your one shot at that." She responded with an eye roll, and I leaned down and growled into her mouth through a kiss that I hoped muffled words meant only for her. "And I'll address that bratty sass when we get home."

The night wrapped up quickly after that.

Chase helped Lila move the boxes of files to the car while Troy, Moira, and I cleaned up the dinner remains.

"You're all in?" Troy nudged me with his elbow. "Not unexpected but still fast."

"Tell me about it." I agreed. "This woman's like a freight train."

"Be careful." Troy's tone held that stern brotherly instruction laced with an edge of something loftier. "Her emotions seem to be tied to you in a big way."

"I can take it," I reassured.

"You misunderstand." He dried his hands and turned to me. "You are a steady man in a storm. I don't doubt you or your intentions with her. But she's walking shell-shock. If you aren't careful, you'll become her emotional avatar."

For a brother of few words, his landed in my chest like an anvil. We both had training in PTSD recovery, me for my medic work, and he for his police efforts. But I hadn't considered the aspect that I could become the wall Lila used to shield her from the world, and I immediately wondered how to avoid it, or if I even needed to. I wanted to be here for her...in whatever way she wanted.

"I like her." Moira chimed in. "I think she'll be okay. She's tough."

"Hey, I wanted to ask you," I turned towards her. "Earlier...when you two had your ya-ya-sisterhood moment, Lila asked you how you 'got past it'. What did she mean?"

"The fear," Moira answered. "When you lose everything at once, you either believe it was your fault, or..." She nodded towards where Lila waited outside. "You believe you never get to have anything good ever again." She slid an arm around Chase, seeking his comfort. "Some of us work our ass off trying to earn everything, never accepting help." Then she sighed, gazing back at me. "Or we run from the chance of ever having it again...because loneliness feels easier than loss."

WILDER FAMILY GROUP CHAT

-5-

> Me: Just wanted to say thanks.

> TJ: For?

> Me: Tonight was huge. On a lot of levels.

> Chase: Understatement of the century.

> Moira: How's Lila?

> Me: Quiet.

TJ: Understandable.

Chase: I like her.

Me: She's been surprising.

Moira: Not that surprising.

Me: Meaning?

TJ: Headstrong. Good fit. I approve.

Me: Thanks???

Chase: Tread carefully, brother.

Me: I know. She's been through hell. I'm open to tips here.

TJ: He means be careful with you.

Me: Throwing my own words back at me now?

TJ: Proximity complicates things.

Chase: He knows, Grandpa. ;-)

Moira: Ignore them. Listen to me. Her head's chaos right now. Don't add your crazy, pushy, alpha-hole-ness to the mix.

Me: Damn. Don't sugarcoat it.

Chase: Alpha-hole-ness?

Moira: AND NO SEX-BOMBING HER.

TJ: Dear God, make it stop.

Moira: I saw that look in your eyes.

Chase: Baby... damn.

Me: I'll give you all my money if you never say sex-bomb again.

TJ: Add mine to the pot.

Moira: Just be her calm. Be her center.

Chase: My wife is smart.

TJ: Savagely so.

Moira: And when she talks...

Me: Yeah yeah. Got it. Shut up and listen.

46

LILA

I WOKE THE NEXT morning to a sleepy, growling Sam kissing down my spine.

"Now to deal with that Brat that kept trying to leave me last night."

Deal with me, he did.

Sam tied me up and edged me so close that I saw stars. He explored every inch of me with his lips, tongue, even beard... growling proprietary demands about claiming the entire time that. Had he let me walk afterward, my legs would surely have given out. Alas, his caveman brand of aftercare put any doubts to rest that I hadn't pushed him away as he cleaned every inch of me. Somewhere during all that, he declared he'd be permanently staying in my room.

Presumptuous as he was, I wasn't sad about it.

I set up the adjoining bedroom as a workspace and began sifting through Troy's notes. Papers littered the bed, dresser, and floor—Sam called it a rat's nest. A day or so later, he dragged me into town for a load of office supplies, folding tables, and a magnetic whiteboard. While I unpacked groceries, he transformed the space into a proper workroom, which is where I spent every day thereafter.

Sunup to sundown, I pieced together a picture—my Brinks files and Troy's Apex intel.

Troy's work was impressive, despite numerous holes in the data. Only one eyewitness connection linked Marcus to Apex, and there was no online roster of Apex members. Marcus's trail of NYC clients didn't reach up to this small town, and the file on Jensen didn't reach down to NYC. A veritable Swiss cheese of missing information with one screaming truth that I'd already suspected: Brinks wasn't the architect—just the fixer.

Someone else pulled his strings, and no one dared to type that name.

Apex sold itself as a wholesome nonprofit: outreach, youth leadership, community growth, and other fraternal douchebaggery. The glossy pamphlets, provided courtesy of Fire Chief Jacobs...pure vanilla schlock.

The financial records Troy pulled from the county tax office showed donations of vast sums of money to the Board of Education, as well as the city's Library Reconstruction Fund. It seemed warm and fuzzy until you saw Apex attached to the sudden repayment of back taxes on a local business in what appeared to be a buyout. Troy didn't list them all, but jotted Scaled Back's name in the margins. The single financial record I found was a wispy thread, alluding to anonymous donations routed through a Political Action Committee for some New York Senator. PACs weren't just shady money; they were the fuck-your-life kind of shady money.

Dirty...but ultimately useless to me.

Troy documented Moira's statement about the fire at Chase's house, including Jensen's plan to put Apex on the map in return for the Chief position in the fire department, possibly earning money from helping them move product. The word 'product' was circled, and Troy scribbled the word Drugs with a question mark. I made a note to investigate that angle. If drugs were being moved, I'd find arrest records, evidence logs from raids, or autopsy records. That could tie into Apex's school outreach efforts, if they aimed to recruit kids from underprivileged families into criminal cash flow.

Unoriginal...but effective.

A slip of paper taped to the fire report held one sentence typed in all lowercase letters, reading, 'membership gained with emphatic assertion.' As there was nothing else to be found in this odd sentence, I made a note to ask Troy about it the next time I saw him, although I didn't know when that would be. I couldn't reach out to Troy for fear of putting his job at risk, or worse, putting him in the line of fire with Brinks by associating with me. Troy's safety now my stumbling block. I couldn't run off vigilante style without considering Sam's family, including Chase, Moira, and the twins—a daunting task to satiate my need while worrying about someone's family.

Someone else's family, I reminded myself. Not mine.

Mine was dead.

I tried poking around the IA server for that ghost agent, but their security was tighter than most. Not impenetrable—but solid enough to make me cautious. I limited my time inside each day since routing my signal through spoofed locations was a major time suck, and I was determined not to get sloppy.

Meanwhile, I looked for Jensen's body.

Even without proper case-closing paperwork, body disposal came with documentation. I searched the morgue and hospital records for Jensen's transport or final resting place, only to prove Troy correct; there was absolutely nothing. I made a note to visit the morgue in person, hoping that my unknown face might prompt someone to slip up and provide new information, leaving me with more questions than answers. My to-do list grew, as did my frustration at slogging through incomplete data, partial records, dead ends, and stonewalls. Some days, I'd end my work with a frustrated slam of a laptop, and others, anxiety pushed me to angry-typing til Sam pried my fingers from the keyboard.

I was missing something critical – a single person or place.

But Sam...my anchor. Every morning, I woke renewed—thanks to the nights spent in Sam's arms. He shattered me over and over in new and inventive ways. As sore as I imagined I would be, his aftercare rose to the occasion. Gourmet meals filled my belly, earth-shattering orgasms satiated me, Lord almighty could the man work a loofah. Then he'd dry me and carry me back to bed, sometimes continuing the care with a massage before tucking us in for the night.

I slept peacefully across his warm chest, acclimated to a healthy circadian rhythm. And, there were smiles. Unspoken movements, sharing space with ease, were accompanied by honest conversations. Sam talked about how he and his brothers came along, and how their Nonna insisted that they stick close together and look out for one another. He shared funny stories of youthful missteps, as well as the times his brothers had to bail him out from one shenanigan or another. When I shared, Sam listened, accepting what I could offer, and I did have stories to offer.

I had a past–I just wasn't sure about my future.

Sam's connection with his family was something I didn't think I'd ever get again, and I didn't dare put them at risk. As much as I found myself craving Sam's touch, I vowed to move carefully as I tried to snare Brinks. I grew protective of this growing connection I'd been grieving, even if it wasn't meant for me.

Sam's family was a gift.

I wanted to protect him, protect them all, and...protect myself too—a thought I had long abandoned on this kamikaze mission of mine. I couldn't let myself believe 'right now' would ever be 'forever.'

47

LILA

THE FOLLOWING SUNDAY, I strolled into the kitchen to find Sam making a giant salad and announcing that our dinner plan was at Chase and Moira's cabin.

"Again?"

"Did I not mention we do this weekly?" He cocked an eyebrow, that mischievous grin of his making it clear he knew he hadn't.

"Nope." I shook my head emphatically.

"It's not gonna be like last time." He set the food aside, stalking towards me.

"You mean how we spent hours unraveling so many secrets, even the pretty-pink-princess started swearing like a sailor?" I lifted my hand in protest. "Uh-uh. No way, pal." I pivoted around the couch, out of his grasp. "You aren't sweet-talking me, Lumberjack."

"Lila." He purred my name in that smooth timbre my body recognized all too well.

"I mean it!" I snapped. "I'm still emotionally hungover from the last dinner."

"We're going," Sam prowled to intercept me like a wild animal.

"You're *ruining* pasta for me." I knew that look. I think I sorta loved that look.

"Come here." He growled, chin down, eyes narrowed in on me like the last gazelle on the prairie, limping in front of a feral lion.

"You wanna go so bad? Fine! Go without - " Sam lunged, scooping me over his shoulder with a swift slap to my ass. "You, Jackass!"

"Here I thought that bratty mouth knew its place." He marched to our bedroom. "You must need a refresher on who's in charge if you think you're skipping a meal, woman?"

"Woman!" I slapped at his ass with all my might, knowing he barely felt my strikes. "Put me—" Sam flipped me onto the bed, knocking the air out of me before I could finish the sentence.

Conversation...orgasmically over.

We arrived noticeably late and sex-rumpled–the ripping from Sam's brothers dashing any hopes of a subtle entry.

"What's the matter? Chase elbowed Sam's ribs. "Need more time to primp, princess?"

"At least I have a routine." Sam eyed Chase's all black attire. "What's yours again? Shower, shit, and shave?"

"Come now, brothers, let's not resort to childish taunts." Troy asserted that older-brother vibe. "As if either of you can compete." He ran his hands down his crisp button-down shirt, complete with creased slacks, suspenders, and the leather holster across his back, sans guns.

Did this guy ever not look like a narc?

"Ignore the testosterone throw-down." Moira snagged my elbow, tugging me towards the bedroom. "They'll settle soon enough. I could use a hand." I followed her less out of desire to help and more out of necessity. She was surprisingly strong. "The girls are going to wake up any second now, and efficiency is key to avoiding meltdowns." She dragged me toward two tiny bassinets, each with matching pink bow-topped burritos nestled inside, asleep

"If they're sleeping, shouldn't we...let them?" I took a step back.

"Don't worry," she whispered. "They're on a great schedule and will stir any minute now." As if on cue, the first baby girl began to squirm, grunting as she fought her fluffy bindings. "Yep...Blue is always up first."

She swooped in, unwrapping her daughter in the kind of smooth, practiced motion seen in morning, noon, and night, dedication. Her daughter smiled at her, stretching and scrunching her teeny body into the sweet kisses her mother lavished on her cheeks. At the changing table, Moira had her into a dry diaper so fast I barely registered all the steps; Her fluid movements a stark contrast to my awkward stiffness around children.

Being the youngest, I didn't grow up around little kids. My dad and brother made a great home, best described as frat-house adjacent. I was perfectly comfortable performing kegstands at a football game, or playing poker, but babies...blegh. Kids were like tiny, erratic, drunk people. Given a chance to hold one, I would politely decline and run for the hills.

Not Moira, though.

Her ease as she maneuvered Blue, speaking and cooing lovingly to her baby, holding her daughter close to breathe in her scent, made it clear she was a natural mother.

"And like clockwork, there's River," Moira sighed. I looked over and found the other pink bundle struggling to break free from the swaddle. "Hold Blue for me?"

"Oh...uh." I opened my mouth to protest, but my arms were full of baby before a word escaped. Looking at the tiny thing, her wide blue eyes scanning my face like she was memorizing it for a sketch artist, I panicked. "I'm not really...um..." I looked to Moira, hoping she'd realized she'd handed her baby to an inexperienced dolt. "I'm not very experienced with babies," I confessed at last, not missing the small smile I was being gifted by baby Blue or the way it tugged at something knotted up in me.

"Oh, I wasn't either at first." She smiled, scooping up a scrunching River. "Can you believe, Sam taught me to swaddle?"

"No shit?" I said, then winced as I looked down at the baby as if they understood me. "Sorry, kid."

"Uncle Sam was the most natural thing you'd ever seen. He taught Chase about the kangaroo method...River's favorite," She nuzzled the baby's cheek with her nose, "And has been super helpful for me as I transition the girls onto formula."

"Who knew he was so paternal?" I said dryly, ignoring my ovaries tossing buckets of eggs overboard as tribute.

"You're better at this than you think." Moira joined me, nodding at the baby in my arms. "She likes you." I glanced down to find her still studying my face, tiny fingers curled around my pinky. Broad and gummy and pink and perfect, her smile drew me in. She had her mother's delicate features, and as I glanced over at the other baby to see the similarities, I couldn't help but smile back at them. "How was your week?" Moira asked, moving into the telltale sway that good mothers have.

"Fine, I guess. I pieced together the data Troy collected with my own. Nothing new to share, but I hope to dig in more tomorrow and _ "

"I meant," Moira interrupted with a wry smile. "How was your week...with Sam?" She drawled out Sam's name with a sing-songy quality.

"Sam is," I sighed down at the baby in my arms and let the moment draw me away from Moira's scrutiny, searching for a word that fit since 'Sam's a long-schlonged sex god who dicks me down so thoroughly I can barely walk but it doesn't matter because the guy's gotta kink for carrying me around...how's Chase?' might embarrass the princess of prim and proper. "Sam's good, I guess. It's all fine."

"Oh, come on," she whined. "Is he completely smothering you yet?" I gave her my best eye roll of agreement. "Ha, ha," Moira pumped her fist in triumph. "Knew it. If he's anything like Chase, he never leaves you alone and is constantly feeding you, ammiright?"

"Oh my god, the man and his food," I said, happy to share something straightforward and unemotional. "Every time I turn around, he's making me a four-course breakfast or buying bagels. Twice this week it was taco runs, and I swear to God if it weren't for the nightly sexcapades, I'd bust outta my pants." The words fell from my mouth before I registered them, and I blushed as I watched for Moira's reaction. To my great surprise, her brows lifted in approval at my inappropriate outburst.

"No shame in that game, sister." Moira teased, lowering her tone into mocking secrecy. "You did announce the man laid good pipe."

"At this point, I think he's laying federal infrastructure." I laughed, relieved to have a moment of levity. "And the aftercare..."

"Oh my God, Chase too. So incredible!" Moira added. "I didn't hate it, but also...sometimes..."

"Just let me roll over and pass out, already!" I finished as we both laughed and swayed with the girls. I loved how the rocking motion seemed to settle me, too, and I wondered if this was Moira's grand plan to get me talking.

Annoyingly insightful must be a Wilder family trait gained even in marriage.

Our conversation continued, the moment lingering into a tenuous friendship, and it was nice to talk about my situation with Sam, with someone who wanted nothing more than girl talk. Having primarily hung out with guys growing up, I'd often found the drama of other girls a bit too much. That lack of girlfriends was never as apparent until I was hip-deep in grief with no one around to hold me up or let me cry.

Standing here now, holding a baby and gossiping about boys felt odd...but easy.

"Ya know, I meant what I said last week... about you being safe with us." She looked at me with gentleness. "I know how hard it can be to trust that without concrete proof...something life doesn't often give us."

"You're not wrong," I agreed plainly. "I still can't wrap my head around how I'm here."

"It's true what they say, everything happens for a reason."

"True. For instance, the reason my life is a hot fucking mess is because I made a shitload of terrible choices....Consecutively...One after another after another..."

"Stop! You aren't a trainwreck of bad choices." Moira scolded, tilting her head to the side sympathetically. "But that sentiment is exactly why I want to share something with you. Something the guys would never dare, but might give you a little foundation to build some trust on."

She looked at the girls, one at a time, her eyes lingering on each of their faces as if the words were so heavy she needed to draw on her love for them for the strength to bear it. I was about to reassure her she didn't need to share anything with me when she took a deep breath.

"Dean Jensen is the biological father of my girls."

I was unprepared. Mouth gaping, my swaying halted, I could only watch as Moira smiled at her baby, leaning in to smell her before turning back to me.

"I found out I was pregnant the night Chase rescued me." She settled her baby on her shoulder, snuggling her against her neck. "I was an absolute mess–lost everything in the fire, had no friends or family, no job." She offered a small half-smile and added, "And then...babies."

"I had no idea," I mumbled, sifting through the times I'd seen Chase with the girls, the way he melted into a gooey pile of doting daddy.

"I was homeless, jobless, pregnant, unwed, and alone...after being raised in 8 different foster homes before falling into the arms of a man who catfished me in every way possible. I was a hot mess."

"Hey, I saw some of the emails from that dirtbag. He worked a deep-fake like a pro. He committed to that long con. That much time...that many details....would've fooled anybody."

"Oh, I know that...now," Moira gave a meek smile. "But I didn't at first. I felt like I'd made eleventy-billion mistakes. Adding eleventy-billion more each step I took. But then...Chase."

She stepped just outside the bedroom door and leaned against the hallway wall. I followed her and watched the guys from across the room: Chase dishing up pasta, Troy pouring wine, and Sam setting the table.

"All of them." She whispered, just for the two of us. "They accepted me and my girls and never flinched. I was their sister, and these girls were their nieces. None of the baggage I brought into their world mattered. It only mattered that Chase loved us, and so they loved us too."

"Wow. That's so..." I couldn't find the right words to express how magically rare and unique that gift was. The joy I felt for Moira and her daughters, and the immense pride on their behalf, about Sam and his brothers, was a thing of beauty. Looking into the kitchen, I locked eyes with Sam. He smiled and elbowed Chase, who found Moira's eyes.

"Isn't it, though?" Moira sighed, a dreamy look of contentment crossing her face, love leaping across the space between them. Turning to me, she added, "And it could be, just so, for you too...if you let it."

48

SAM

THE WEEK AFTER LILA'S second family dinner, something shifted.

She moved with ease, like she'd finally exhaled. It was little changes at first; bags finally unpacked and toiletries put away; then I woke up to the smell of coffee and found her sitting at the kitchen table in my giant Henley, scanning her phone–a fresh cup waiting for me as if she'd made it every day.

No dragging her out of bed or forcing her to eat. I felt welcomed in her orbit, and I craved more of it. It also brought a peace that let me return to work part-time without worrying she'd take off. Since she enjoyed diving into research in the mornings, I used those hours to maximize my time on the rig. Clocking in before 7 am, I aimed to be home by 1 pm, if not noon.

Though Lila's wild and fierce nature was strong as ever, her submission in bed became my drug. I got lost every night in the way she moved, her scent–our bodies exploded like a match to gasoline. And feeling her against me, sweaty and begging, every fiber of my being wanted nothing more than to be the shelter against every storm life threw at her. Lila was a blazing inferno of unadulterated lusty goodness, and my brain lived in a haze of carnal lust that short-circuited all higher functions.

I daydreamed about her belly round with my baby even as I showered her body with soaps, oils, and lotions after every round of lovemaking. My guilt about the conversations we should be having was overridden by a desire to protect her from my crazy, pushy, alpha-hole energy. So, after every roll in the sheets, I'd haul her to the shower and promise I would do better next time.

I was on a clock to come clean, too. I didn't know when her cycle was due, but we'd been together over two weeks. I needed to get ahead of this, but the 'how' was my stumbling block. Finally running desperately close to losing my shit, I reached out to Chase.

"Knock knock." Chase's voice bellowed through the living room as he nudged open the front door, carrying a weight bench. "Where do you want this?"

"Out there," I flicked my chin to the back deck. "I'll set it up kinda like yours, but ya know...half the fucking size 'cause I have a life."

"What the hell?" Lila asked, peeking her head out from the war room where she worked every day. "Oh, hey, Chase. What's this for?"

"Moira needed Chase to clean some of the gym stuff off the deck," I answered before Chase could, "I told him he could store it here til their house was ready." Chase shook his head with a laugh, but waited until we'd made three more trips with assorted gear before calling me on the lie.

"Alright, spill. You asked me to bring this shit, and I've never seen you hide anything from anyone ever." He followed my gaze as I watched Lila stroll into the kitchen for a bottle of water. "What gives?"

"I'm so spun, man. I royally screwed up."

"And you came to me...over Troy?" Chase's eyebrows hit his hairline. "That's a first."

"Dude, Troy's got a shit-ton of pressure on him, and the last thing he needs to be worrying about is the fuck-up I've gotten myself into," I answered, running both hands through my hair before scratching them down my beard. "I don't even know how to start digging my ass out of this one."

"Can't be that bad," Chase offered as encouragement, "But go ahead. Tell your big brother." He thumped his chest like a gorilla. "I'll impart husbandly wisdom."

His Troy-like tone mocked me.

"Fuck you," I said, punching his arm. "This is serious, dude."

Chase spun, having secured the weights to their rack, and sat on the bench. I sighed, waiting until Lila returned to her office before continuing.

"Lila is..." My brain stopped, one sentence in, stumped. Jesus fucking Christ. "She's so..."

"'You had a fight?" Chase gave me that half grin of his. "But she's still here, so how bad can it be?"

"Jesus. I don't even know how I got here, but I have to tell her." I stalled, knowing once I said the words, I couldn't unring this bell; Chase would have reasonable cause to kick my ass. We all had a hard rule: No glove, no love.

Be respectful...be smart.

"I wanna help, but I'm gonna need more words." Chase's expression turned concerned. "Whatever it is, we'll get through it, man. Just spit it out."

"A few weeks ago, that first night in the cabin, Moira and I were fucking, and I took her raw," I said, ripping the band-aid off and spitting it out. "I didn't know I'd done it at the time. Caught it afterward, when there was no condom to toss."

"Oh shit," Chase's eyes blew wide. "Is she pregnant?"

"I dunno, but there's more." Chase cocked his head back and spread his arms out in confusion, as I barreled forward into the full depth of my depravity. "She didn't know. I hauled her ass to the shower and cleaned her up. And that got me so hot and bothered I took her again...bare." I ran my hands across my face, turning from the house to look out at the trees, muttering. "Like a man possessed."

"Holy Fucking Hell." Chase started pacing the length of the deck, waving his hands around. "What the fuck. Like, seriously, what the actual fuck. Jesus, Sam. What...How – "

"I know!" I roared, snapping my eyes inside and lowering my voice. "I don't know what came over me, and I don't know how to fucking deal. So, brother-up and help me out here."

"Okay...okay." Chase took a few deep breaths, sitting on the weight bench. "I mean, I sorta get it. I loved seeing Moira pregnant and growing the girls and being with her, bare–hot as fuck." His voice calmed, "So I get how you could get caught up. We were foster kids, dude, and growing a family feels..."

"Mythic." I finished softly. "But I got the cart so far before the mother fucking horse."

"What does she say about it?" Chase asked, and I couldn't hide my cringe. "Fucking hell," He stood, anger clear in his eyes as he walked to me and growled. "Tell. Me. She. Knows."

When I couldn't look him in the eyes, he started pacing...and cursing.

"I've tried talking about it ten different times at least," I admitted, my head so low I might as well have lain down on the ground. "But she seemed so overwhelmed, and I didn't want to add to that. I should've told her that first night, but you saw how wrecked she was then. I barely got her to fucking dinner, much less into a conversation that may or may not involve a baby, and that is IF it's possible. She might be on birth control. I don't know, but we haven't had that conversation either!'

"Jesus Christ, Sam!" Chase's voice was a screaming whisper.

"I've told myself over and over to wrap it up since then, to be more careful, but I couldn't. There's a part of me that wants to fill her–"

"Wait...you're STILL doing it!?!"

"I know. I *know* it's fucked up. I know it makes me the worst of all mankind. I know she might not even BE pregnant. I know that knocking her up isn't the way to keep her." The words fell so fast then, confession lifting the block of tension sitting on my chest. "And each time I clean her up, I swear I'll stop, but every night all I can think of is her in my life, pregnant with my baby, and us making a family so big we need two goddamn minivans!"

"What the fucking fuck!" Chase whisper-yelled so hard the veins in his neck popped as he punched my shoulder. "When the hell did you develop a breeding kink and at what point did your brain check the fuck out of your fucking skull so fast you forgot everything Nonna taught us about respecting women!?"

"Apparently," I growled, swinging my hands wide. "When I met that infuriating goddess!" I prepared to take my lumps while trying to resist the urge to punch Chase back despite knowing he was dead on. "I have no goddamn clue when her cycle is due, but it's gotta be any day now, and I'm terrified as fuck that if I tell her, she'll bolt - like Usain Bolt

- and I'll never catch her again. And dammit, Chase, if she leaves me...I'll break."

Chase paced, sighing and huffing, fists clenching and unclenching, in a ball of controlled anger I deserved at the agency I'd removed with my insecure, primordial, caveman, bullshit.

"Dammit, Sam...the timing." Chase dropped to the bench in a huff. "I love my girls and wouldn't change a thing about them. You know that."

I nodded.

"But I won't lie that if I had a chance to do things differently..." He didn't finish his sentence. He didn't have to. Moira was a surprise to us all, but she came with a level of complexity none of us were prepared for. "Her pregnancy, combined with all the danger and the risk...I mean, you saw how crazy I was."

I could see the agony in his eyes. He loved his family, but their being at risk was suffocating. I looked into the cabin, to the closed door where Lila was, and I suddenly understood a little more. She wasn't in a good headspace, and this Apex-Brinks mess didn't exactly invite picket fences and tire swings. And I, like a dick, had selfishly added to the pile.

"What can I do?" Regret flooded me. "How can I keep her and fix this?"

"Shit, dude. You played your hand. You gambled, but you gambled with her, too. Now you gotta let the cards fall where they may." He leaned his elbows onto his knees. "I suggest leading with how madly in love with her you are." His face softened a little. "And maybe toss in how insane you have become since she's entered your life because of how magical you think she is, and that's why you lost control of your mind...and your spooge." He gave a small huff of laughter and shook his head, "And wear a cup—'cause she's totally kicking your dumb ass from here to Timbuktu and frankly Troy and I might line up to watch."

"I'd happily take the beating as long as it meant she was still mine." I shook my head at my idiocy. "I haven't even taken her on a proper date yet."

"No shit?" Chase asked.

"Zero shits," I confirmed.

"Okay...new plan." Chase's eyes held a fresh excitement. "This Friday, take her out. Moira and I have been talking about getting out. Chief and Carol are dying to watch the girls, and it'd be great to get out with my wife since she's about to be cleared by the doc. I wanna reconnect a little." His face lit up. "We'll double date. It'll give Moira a distraction from leaving the girls for the first time, and give you and Lila a buffer to connect somewhere other than your dick."

"Friday?"

"Yeah. Pick someplace she'll be comfortable." He said. "And let Moira do her magic to lighten the mood. Then work around to fessing up, and hope Lila doesn't castrate you while Moira holds you down."

"That's the best I can hope for...to keep my balls?"

"Dude, it's literally all you can hope for at this point. So pick a spot she likes!"

Finally, an easy choice; There was only one place I'd seen Lila let loose.

49

LILA

WAKING TO LUMBERBEAR SAM growling at me to stay put was becoming my new normal.

"Fuck coffee. Bed warm. Woman soft."

He spoke fluent caveman—and I kinda loved it.

Having a private chef plate up those heavenly pancakes was another perk. All I had to do was hint that I was craving them, and he leapt out of bed like it was on fire.

Then the adorable jackass ruined it.

"Chase and Moira are going out tonight." He said after he'd finished his plate. "It's their first time since the girls arrived. Chase thinks it'll be hard for her to leave 'em, so I told him we'd make it a double."

"A date?" I pointed to the door, as if the outdoors were poisonous. "Like you and me...out...there."

His smile was annoying.

"We've moved ass-backwards so far. From fucking, to shacking up, and now we sit here in this ... situationship. We've skipped a few steps and need to talk that out, put a label on it." He turned my barstool until our legs intertwined. "Tonight, I'm taking you out. We'll laugh and hang out with my brother and his wife. Get to know each other like a normal couple in love."

And then I lost the power of speech.

The big oaf planted a kiss on my forehead, strolling away as if he didn't drop a bomb with his casual use of, 'in love'. He even let me stew in silence all afternoon...so maybe he knew. I was crazy about Sam, but part of me feared it was just bedroom chemistry.

'Tab A fits Slot B' didn't make the leap to love any safer.

Did it?

The sweet kisses he placed inside my palm as we drove into town reminded me of a million other sweet things he'd done. Even if he hadn't said the words, he'd shown it in every action he'd ever done. He'd even said he was all in. All that was left was to decide...was I? I mean, I was crazy about Sam. I could hold onto that...right?

"Alright enough." Eyes locked on the road as he drove, his voice was commanding. "I can tell you're spun by this date, but it's not heavy. I promise." I nearly snarked out a comment about his earlier use of the word Situationship and Label, but he barreled forward. "I wanna get to know more about you; what you love and hate, what's your favorite food, or what was your worst date ever."

I was crazy about Sam.

I was crazy about Sam.

I was crazy about Sam.

I chanted the mantra on repeat, bolstering my courage to open up.

"Music. Cats. Sushi. Billy Crups." My words bubbled out like word salad.

"Gimme more nouns, baby."

With a deep breath, I tried again.

"I love music. It settles me, it motivates me, and I miss having it around." He nodded, so I continued. "I hate cats. Bossy assholes think their owners are staff–Dogs reign supreme." He gave a little laugh as I went on. "I would sell my soul for good sushi. It's pretty and packaged for rapid eating, and the flavor varieties are never-ending, and if you can't use chopsticks, you don't deserve to eat it."

"And that other man's name on your lips?" His menacing voice was so hot. "Better be the worst date ever."

"Settle down, Lumberjack." I smiled, relaxing a little as my thumb traced a scar on the back of his hand. "I was 19. He kept referring to me as 'his bitch' and got handsy before we got to the restaurant. I managed to make it through dinner, dancing around his advances, but fired off a text to my brother, who showed up and clobbered the guy."

I allowed myself to swim in that memory of my big brother swooping in to save me, relieved when the usual pang of grief didn't slice my heart in two.

"Sounds like I would have liked your brother."

Sam's words were gentle, almost begging for me to share more. But my head was too full, my heart too fragile, to unpack all those bittersweet memories, especially with Scaled Back coming into view.

50

LILA

"Don't worry," Sam said, squeezing my knee. "I'll let you walk out this time."

His joke was the perfect tension breaker as I remembered my two other visits to Scaled Back—neither finest moments. Exiting our cars, Moira hugged me, whispering that Chase was wrecked about leaving the girls. I watched as Sam gave his brother a reassuring pat on the back and stifled a laugh. The poor guy looked like he might vomit.

Marge nodded from behind the bar as Sam led us to a corner booth, sauntering over with menus and her trusty towel slung over her shoulder.

"Sammy, boy." She nudged Sam with her hip. "I see you finally brought in this big oaf and his new bride to see me." She turned and smiled broadly at Moira. "Congrats on the girls. Funcle Sam can't shut up about how beautiful they are. A gift they clearly get from their mama." Chase and Moira both beamed their thanks before the whole table went quiet as Marge leveled me with a look. "Now...Hellcat," She leaned over, pointing a finger at me. "I've seen you in my bar twice, and both times ended in a brawl."

"I know." Heat flushed up my neck. "I'm sorry. I didn't intend - "

"I don't need an apology," My mouth went dry under her scrutiny. "I'm here to say...good for you."

All our mouths fell open.

"It's never a woman's fault if the good Lord sees fit to put her together like a book full of sin, but that sure as shit doesn't mean she is obligated to spread her pages for every putz who wants an easy read." Moira gasped, a huge smile spreading across her face that damn near mirrored my own. "You ain't afraid to stand up for yourself, and I respect the hell out of that. I like knowing you'll put this one in line." She winked at Sam, who shook his head with a grin. "Maybe try to keep her on a leash, tonight, kiddo?"

"If only I could." Sam leaned back, slipping his arm around my shoulders.

"So, you *were* in two bar fights!" Moira grinned, reaching for me. "I begged Troy for details, but he clammed up. I've been cooped up with the girls for weeks and weeks; I *need* vicarious thrills. Spill the tea!"

"I'm gonna call the Chief and check in." Chase excused himself, slipping quickly out of the booth and opening his cell phone.

"Pour guy," I said, hoping to deflect Moira. "He's a wreck, isn't he?"

"So, how did you get out of the fights?" She turned her attention to me once more, undeterred, and I wished the ground could open beneath me. "No...how did you *start* the fights?" Embarrassed, I was unsure how to begin.

"This one has a helluva right hook," Sam beamed. "Must have been all that cop training, right?"

"I mean, that was some of it, sure. But," Remembering Sam's desire to know me better, I pushed myself to open up. "My dad and brother taught me self-defense. Once I got to college, they felt it was unacceptable for me to ever be helpless. So, every weekend, I would either spar with my brother or practice wrestling moves with my dad. By the time I got into the academy, I walloped everyone, trainers included." Moira's face took on a pensive expression as Sam leaned in and kissed my ear, mumbling, 'I definitely would have liked your dad and brother,' privately for me to hear.

"I'm gonna grab us some drinks and find Chase." Sam announced, "Beer's all around?"

We nodded as he left, and I noticed Moira still held a distant expression. I assumed she missed her girls and wondered how to bridge the gap when she spoke.

"I don't mean to make heavy revelations a habit," her voice lost all the enthusiasm from before. "I have a favor to ask, and I feel like you need to know where it's coming from before I do." I nodded, leaning closer as she lowered her voice. "Did you see the police report from the fire that took out Chase's house?"

"Yeah," I nodded, relieved to talk about anything else. "You badass'd Jensen into a coma."

"Right." She gave a half smile, cheeks flushed red. "Before that, though, before the fire started, before Chase came home, something...happened." She nervously tucked a lock of hair behind her ear. "Something I left out of the report...Something I didn't want the guys to...." Discomfort radiated from her body, but she pushed on. "We had just gotten married, literally that day. We came home to pack before going on a surprise honeymoon Chase planned. He stepped out to get dinner, and when he left...Dean showed up."

I'd seen enough battered women testifying to know that this was about to be bad. The wringing of hands, eyes down at the table. I stayed silent and took her hand.

"He was furious...ranting about ruined plans and throwing his weight around. But there was a moment when he threw me on the bed, handcuffed me, and..." She paused, gulping again and slowly letting the air exhale from between pursed lips. "He tried...to force me...but he never got all the way. Thank God Chase came home when he did. But," Her glassy eyes were focused, in a moment of pure, earned courage as she pushed on. "I hated how helpless I felt; hated that I couldn't fight him. I couldn't defend myself, but more than that, I hate how much I still find myself replaying that moment, not the fire, but the minutes before...over and over and..." She paused, breathing at the ceiling, fighting tears.

"Hey...you did fight him off. The guy had a massive head wound. That's no small feat."

"Dumb luck." She huffed dryly. "I panicked, scrambling to keep Dean's attention off of Chase." Her tone shifted, something darker tinting the seriousness of her repeated statement. "I. Got. Lucky."

Suddenly, she let go of my hand and sat back, face hard with resolve.

"Teach me to fight—to defend myself. Or my girls, if it came to that."

"Well, well." I smiled, crossing my arms. "Look at the set of balls on the pretty pink princess." Moira smiled all the way up to her eyes, and I couldn't have been prouder. "That man worked you over but good. You have every right to be meek, scared, and stuck in that trauma. But here you sit, determined to fight back, to make sure you and your girls never have to feel that way again. Do you get how ballsy you are?"

"Is that a yes?"

"That's a hell yes," I could only laugh at Moira's squeals and hand-clapping.

"Please don't tell Chase, I'm not ready to - "

"Managed to pull Sad-Dad back with a temptation of pool." Sam's jovial voice cut Moira's request short, but I understood what she needed and gave her a reassuring nod as the guys sat down. "What were you two gabbing about?"

"Lila agreed to help me lose the baby weight!" Moira exclaimed, sending Chase's eyebrows to his hairline.

"Whoa, babe, you don't need to lose a single–"

"What she *means* is I've agreed to do a little training with her....for muscle tone," I emphasized the words, nudging her under the table. "She does not need to lose weight, but I can't spar alone, and extra mommy muscles never hurt with how fast those girls are growing, right?" I tipped my glass at her, and she mimicked my movement.

"Oh, god," Chase's face went pale. "They are growing so fast."

"Okay...I'm stopping that." Sam stood up, "Let's hit the tables before this big baby starts crying again."

The following two hours were the most fun I'd had in ages—enough to forget the loss, loneliness, and vendetta. Shooting pool, Sam leaned on the wall and wrapped around me, felt right. He and Chase teased each other like siblings do, and Moira and I laughed at their antics.

I was just a girl, on a date, with a guy.

Even Sam denying me a bourbon chaser for my terrible beer, teasing about carrying me out, couldn't dim the light I felt as happiness tinged the edges of my world.

"No closing the tab tonight, Sammy-boy." Marge clapped Sam's shoulder as we cleaned up the table from our last game. "This one is on the house...Bars sold."

"What?" Sam exclaimed, as Chase and Moira both sang choruses of 'Oh no' and 'Sold to Who?' "I told you to talk to me before you made any decisions."

"I know you did, but they doubled the offer. It was too sweet a deal to pass up." Marge scanned the place, memories welling in her eyes. "I fucking love my bar, but I'm old, kiddo, and the new numbers set up my retirement. It's high time I parked my ass on a warm Florida beach."

"Wow," Moira added, opening her arms to hug the woman. "It's so sudden...but you're gonna love Florida."

"Yeah, Scaled Back is a staple around town," Chase added. "Can you tell us who bought it, or what their plans are?"

"Some non-profit outfit outta New York, Apex. I pushed back their first offer, but one of their bigwigs showed up two days ago, looked around, and doubled the offer on the spot." She twirled her bar towel off her shoulder and gave Sam's shoulder a playful swipe. "Too good to resist."

"Marge." Sam pleaded.

"Who's the guy?" I blurted, all my alarms ringing at how fast everything moved. "The bigwig...his name?"

"Lemme grab his card." Marge turned away, and Sam made a point to tell Chase and Moira to head on home to the girls while we wrestled Marge into letting us pay. It was hugs all around before Marge waved goodbye to them and handed Sam the card.

"That's the guy, Marcus Brinks." My blood ran cold. "He wasn't warm and fuzzy, but with the money he was offering, I wasn't looking for a prom date."

"Jesus, Marge, you can't trust -" I started, but she waved a hand.

"It's done, sweetheart. Money's in the account. Movers come this weekend. I'm staying with my sister down in the Keys 'til I settle." She lifted her faithful baseball bat. "I can't think of a better person to take this over than you." She smiled, dropping the bat into my hands, then turned to Sam. "I'm gonna miss ya, kiddo." She hugged his neck and walked away as I turned to him.

"He's Here!"

WILDER FAMILY GROUP CHAT

-6-

Me: APB - Brinks is officially in town.

Chase: What? We just left you!

Moira: Oh No. How's Lila?

Me: Marge told us after y'all left. Lila dove straight into her war room.

Troy: What am I missing here?

Me: He came as an Apex rep 2 days ago. Doubled the previous offer on Scaled Back. Marge folded.

Troy: You're sure it's him.

Me: He left a business card.

Troy: Did he have anyone else with him?

Me: Not that she said.

Troy: Interesting.

Moira: Interesting???

Troy: He's not listed on any active cases.

Me: And...

Troy: Why would a criminal defense attorney broker real estate for a nonprofit?

Chase: Unless the location is significant.

Troy: My theory as well.

Chase: Lock her down, Sam.

Me: way ahead of you

Troy: Moira and the girls as well.

Chase: Texting Chief about a leave now.

Moira: HOLD UP! Did you 3 decide, in 3 sentences… to LOCK up me and Lila?

Chase: Not LOCKED up

Moira: Without even asking??

Me: It's not like that.

Moira: Just assumed we'd be okay shoved in a corner while you 3 measure your dicks?

Troy: We mean to keep you safe.

Moira: And I MEAN to keep my goddamn freewill!

Moira: Besides, if we've learned anything, being smothered by you 24/7 isn't enough.

Chase: She's not wrong.

Troy: She rarely is.

Moira: SHE'S RIGHT THE FUCK HERE!

Me: Whoa, okay…we're listening.

Moira: Lila is already planning to train me to defend myself.

Troy: Not unwise.

Moira: And Troy will get me a gun and take us for target practice.

Chase: The Fuck!

Me: What the Fuck!

Troy: I agreed to no such thing.

Moira: I'm right and you know it.

Moira: You hate it…and you'll do it.

Moira: RIGHT Troy.

Moira: TROY.

Troy: …Fuck.

51

SAM

I FUCKED LILA INTO a boneless heap that night, but she woke with intense nervous energy. Before I left for work, she'd hacked Apex's purchase of Marge's bar, mumbling about the dark web. That evening, I tried to help her relax after a day of going laptop blind, but I understood that feral energy better now.

I knew what Brinks took from her and how he shaped what happened to Moira. We all hated the bastard, but it was visceral for Lila. That, and my guilt about our sexcapades, made me determined to respect her space as the days rolled forward. I slipped snacks in front of her and tried to stay out of her way until Chase and Moira began coming over in the afternoons. Their presence pulled her out of the haze in the most fun way. Each afternoon, I would shove the furniture aside while Chase set up the babies in the kitchen, and we'd settle in for our new favorite entertainment.

Wife Boxing!

Lila put Moira through the paces of strength, conditioning, and light sparring — the instructor role an impressive side to my girl. Continually encouraging, pointing out things Moira did right, and how she was a natural at certain moves and had a surprisingly strong backhand. They'd go back and forth for an hour or so, taking water breaks to discuss the areas Lila wanted to help Moira improve.

Despite her princess rep, Moira was a quick study and never backed down. Not when something was complex or new, or when her body wouldn't move the way she wanted it to. When Lila landed a few carefully timed strikes, my sister rolled with it. Moira took the critiques in stride, using them to spur her on. By the third session, Lila finished their time with a 2-minute sparring round, coaxing and coaching Moira as they fought. At session 5, the 2-minute interval had grown to 3 minutes. By the next spaghetti night, Troy demanded a demonstration, which they happily gave, despite sore muscles.

That meal ended with Troy gifting the girls guns—and Chase and me getting aneurysms.

"Jesus Fuck, Troy!" Chase tossed his hands in the air. "I thought this wasn't happening."

"Then you weren't paying attention." Troy admonished. "Your wife was clear, and Ms. Rivera was all too happy to recommend something that fit."

"This one is the best!" Lila flashed an excited grin as she showed the gun to a near-giddy Moira. "It's a Sig P365. Smaller grip, lightweight, comfortable trigger... about as point-and-shoot as it gets."

"As you are not a licensed user, I will purchase your choices in Lila's name for now," Troy interjected, "I'll help train you so that when you have a license, you'll be ready." Moira squealed as Chase's face dropped to the floor.

I didn't blame him. As much as I trusted Lila's experience, even I hated that she wanted a gun; a reminder of just what we were up against.

"Hey, man, come help me with the dishes," I nudged Chase off the couch. Once we were out of earshot, I added, "I don't like this either, but can't ignore the threat."

"You think I don't fucking know that!" Chase whisper-yelled, his fists white-knuckling the edge of the sink. "Like I don't replay that night every goddamn day? I left for tacos, and that psychotic piece of shit –"

"Hey, I get it." I rested my hand on his shoulder, but he flinched and took up pacing the kitchen. Moira told Lila that Chase's agitation had been growing. I could see it now. His face held all the rage of a wild animal tossed in a cage too small for its own good.

"Or at least I get some of it," I added, wishing I could ease the ache I saw my brother carrying. "But we got there on time because of your text and–"

"She's having nightmares, Sam." Chase's voice grew ragged with the effort of keeping his volume down. "When Jensen's body went missing...they started up. She won't talk about them, but I know that's why she asked Lila to train her. That's why she wants a gun. Cause I didn't stop him from–"

"Bullshit, this ain't your fault." The shine in my brother's eyes cracked me open as he turned away—his entire countenance brittle and embattled.

"You don't understand...I saw her...When Jensen first pulled her from the bedroom..." Chase leaned his fists against the counter, arms flexing and releasing as he fought to keep control. "Her clothes were messed up, man...his belt hanging off him and..." He leaned over, green like he might vomit, and my stomach dropped. Silently, I begged the universe for this story to end any...other...way.

"That piece of shit had her handcuffed to our bed...my wife...and he bit her and hit her and..." His voice rose, but he didn't look up, and I could only sit, willing my strength into him as he struggled past a blind rage I felt in my soul. "He bloodied her lip, and had his filthy mouth on her and hit her, and fuck my whole goddamn life, Sam–she won't admit it but I think he raped her." Months of anger and pain finally broke loose from inside that muscled wall he put out to show, and the angry tears that fell. "She won't tell me...I can't fix it, but goddamn it, Sam, he raped her, and I wasn't there to stop it, and now he haunts her dreams...and their guns...and...."

I moved without thought, embracing him as my own bile rose at a confession that would've had any of us unhinged. The fact that my herculean brother held it all together for so long was staggering. I was desperate to take it away for him, but had no idea how.

"No." Moira's whisper drew us around to find Moira, flanked by Lila and Troy, who held her up as tears streaked her cheeks. "He didn't." Her voice was calm, despite the horror of Chase's words, and she spoke with quiet resignation. "He threatened...very nearly did...but you came." She took a step towards her husband. "You got there in time. You stopped him before he could do more than threaten."

"Baby...the nightmares." Chase stumbled forward, and Moira met him. "You wake up screaming his name–"

"Because I couldn't spare you the hell of walking into that." Moira cupped his face in her hands. "I was scared for our girls, and I panicked, and the only thing I could think was..." She gave him a slight scowl as she swallowed, then pushed forward; so damn brave. "I agreed with him. I told him he could have me, and it made me sick, but I didn't know what else to do, and that's what haunts me." She ignored her tears, wiping Chase's instead. "You think I didn't see you beat yourself up over that fire, Chase Wilder? It's broken my heart that you endured this because of me. I didn't want to tell you anymore, but I swear I would've if I'd known you built such a terrible picture." She moved her head, making sure she was in his fallen eyeline. "That's why I asked Lila to train me. Not because I think you failed me, but because I don't want to feel helpless, or make you witness that ever again." Chase wrapped his arms around her, enveloping her with his body, and she mumbled into his ear, "You always make me feel safe and protected, Big guy. So put this guilt down."

Lila turned away from the scene.

Troy and I followed.

Not a dry eye between us.

"Did you know?" Troy asked, his voice breathless. "That he..."

Not even he could speak it.

"I knew he wrestled something," I shook my head, "but...God no."

"She's brave as hell," Lila whispered, watching River and Blue in their bassinets. "Using everything in her to fight back." She looked at Troy and me. "I'm giving her physical strength, and the guns will give her a sense of power. But the emotional stuff, it's harder." She nodded her head at the two of them embracing in the kitchen. "They'll be okay." Then she looked down at the babies, "We could give them some time, though. A few nights here and there...to reconnect without the girls around. It could help."

"Great idea, baby," I loved the idea of time with Lila and the babies.

"Agreed." Troy's eyes cut hesitantly to the girls, "I'll bring pizza and beer?"

"Chicken shit?" Lila jabbed. "You get diaper duty."

52

LILA

"HOLY SHIT!" I HAULED my laptop out to the kitchen as Sam careened out of our bedroom. "Holy fucking shitballs!"

"What!" Sam grabbed my shoulders, looking behind me before scanning me up and down. "What's wrong?"

"It's him!" I shoved past him, dumping the laptop on the table, reaching for my cell. "I've gotta call Troy!"

"Wait." Sam jerked my phone away, thrusting his at me. "No connections between you two...remember."

"Un-fucking-believable!" I dialed Troy, pacing the kitchen.

"Sam?" Troy's steady baritone was calm, unaware of the bomb I was ready to drop.

"It's me. You at the station?"

"I am stepping out for a meeting," Troy answered, vague enough not to alert anyone in earshot.

"You'll never believe it...I can't fucking believe it...holy fucking balls!" I listened to his footsteps, distant station voices, and, finally, the closing of his truck door.

"Go." He commanded.

"Marcus Brinks is Internal Affairs!"

"What?" Troy and Sam answered in stereo. Putting the phone on speaker, I continued.

"I've been working the IA servers for a week—covering my trail ten ways from Sunday with ghost IPs and signal bounces. Today, I finally slipped into the agent file tied to that paperwork. No photo. Name was 'on record' but redacted. Only usable data was a driver's license and SSN from tax docs."

"So you hacked Social Security?" Troy asked.

"Too much work. I hacked the Toll Authority." My blood was racing as I recounted the pathway to Brinks.

"They've got license plates, tags, and camera logs like bloodhounds. And any self-respecting New Yorker knows a guy like Brinks has a toll tag account to dodge traffic on the Brooklyn Bridge."

"Okay... but how does that get you to IA?" Troy pressed.

"That IA agent's license number matched a toll tag tied to Metro North. From there, I tracked it to a car registered under a shell corporation with political ties. Used the plate to cross-search DMV and toll booth footage until I got a clear shot of Brinks crossing the Kennedy Bridge." I spun my laptop around and pointed. "98% profile match."

"Oh damn. It's him." Sam leaned closer. "She got a booth photo."

"Can you tell where that car was last seen?" Troy asked.

"Two weeks ago was the last log, but he was headed north. If he followed that path, he could go straight to us, but that's not 100% and–"

"Send me the License number, make, and model. I'll dig around town." Troy paused and then added, "This is good work, Lila. I don't know that I would have thought to use Toll Booth cameras."

"Wait, Troy, I don't think you fully grasp the 'holy fuck' of this 'holy fucking shit'," I slapped my laptop shut. "I can't send you this license. I can't send you anything. Not now. We confirmed he's IA, and I know what he'll do."

My head leapt, lightyears forward, to all the permutations of how Brinks could just as easily find me...and them.

"She's right, brother," Sam added. "He can make all kinds of trouble for you."

"Surely you don't suggest I ride the bench," Troy argued.

"There's more to learn here," I said. "We don't know why Apex wanted Marge's bar. But now we know a sketchy Apex connection is in the PD's back pocket. You gotta lay low, if for no other reason than to be on the front line of whatever shitstorm is coming."

If no other reason than to stay out of his line of fire.

"Chase has to be benched, too," Sam added. "Jensen is still out there. You both gotta be careful."

"More than careful." I leaned forward, my head pounding as memories flooded through me, and I tried to craft a way to pull them all out of this before Brinks targeted them the way he'd targeted my father and brother. "Brinks is wicked evil, but not stupid. If you so much as sneeze wrong, he'll cite you for not using a goddamn tissue and smoke you out of a job." Closing my eyes, I shook my head as the blood rushing in my ears began to drown out everyone. "Or worse...look...Troy, you can't give him an inch. You have to be above reproach. You have to - "

Sam's hand on my back zapped me like an electric shock. When had I started crying?

312

"Troy's been training for this his whole life," Sam teased while caressing me.

My head was awash at the new connection, what it meant, and how very much history felt like it was repeating itself, putting good cops in the line of fire.

"I need to handle this here," Sam said into the phone, setting it down as he pulled me into his chest. "I got you, baby."

"We'll talk tonight," Troy sounded distant and wobbly. "I'll text the range's location."

"Keep it on a swivel. And update Chase." Sam said, hanging up the phone.

"You did good." Sam stood, legs spread, arms crossed around my body as he spoke in low, soothing tones that somehow tugged at me. "Now breathe with me."

He made an exaggerated inhale, slowing his exhale down.

"It's not enough," I croaked, air drying my throat from...panting? I wanted to run, hit something, anything to shake the ants under my skin. "I can't connect him to the bar, or why that bar mattered, or why he's in IA to begin with, and if I can't find that, he can–"

"It's enough for now." Sam lowered his face to my ear as he gripped my fisted hands. "Give that big brain a rest." His voice rumbled through me, soothing the panic attack growing beneath my skin as he pried my fingers open. "Come on, baby, like we practiced. In for a four, then hold it."

Again, he gave an exaggerated inhale, squeezing his arms around me and adding a slow rocking sensation.

"I can't let him–"

"And we won't." Sam cooed. Inhaling again, his hands mimicking the up and down of settled breathing, beckoning me to join him. "Breathe with me."

Finally, I registered his command as the tension in my body yielded...to him. We stood like that, breathing and swaying for a span of a dozen heartbeats.

Or a lifetime; I lost track.

"I'm sorry," I whispered, the familiar tug of exhaustion arriving. "I'm not sure why...or when..." I couldn't explain losing it over a grainy photo without sounding crazy. "It's research, not a big deal–"

"Your body knows its triggers, even if you don't." He lifted my face, tucking my sweat-dampened hair behind my ear. "But look how well you did. You stopped, you breathed, you cut it short." I started to roll my eyes, but he tugged my attention back with a crooked finger under my chin. "You got a little power back today."

I hated that I lost it—but damn, it felt good to find a little slice of the me who'd been buried in the past.

"Let's celebrate the win. I brought you a gift. It's on the bed. Put it on and meet me on the deck." Sam turned, strutting back to the office in full assurance that I'd do as I was told. Walking to the bed, I found a giant fluffy robe lying next to a pair of fluffy slip-on boots, and the tiniest collection of triangles I'd ever seen strung together into a string bikini. Glancing out the window at the snow, I shook my head.

What in the hell were we doing in bathing suits in the mountains in winter?

Curiosity overcame hesitation, and I found Sam standing on the deck–a matching robe stretched across his back.

"I'm warning you, Lumberjack. If you try to bikini-blizzard-dash me, I'll use my new gun on you," I scowled at the cold nipping my legs.

"Trust me, you're gonna love this." He grabbed my hand and led me down the deck steps to a stony path that stretched beneath snow-laden trees into a clearing where a wooden deck surrounded a huge steaming hot tub.

"Oh wow."

"My brothers and I own both the cabins you've seen, plus the one in the middle. We plan to attach one of these to each to boost the rental rates, but our place got it first." He dropped his robe, showcasing his magnificent body dressed only in black swim trunks. Lowering himself into the water, he stretched his hand out to me. "You've more than earned a little something special after all the hours you've put in, baby." He motioned impatiently at me, adding, "Now lemme see that bikini."

"About that," I pulled my eyes off the breathtaking scenery and shot him a wry glance. "I'm not sure how you thought this thing was gonna fit with all that I'm packing." I slowly untied my robe, sliding the belt through my fingers while holding the sides closed. "In case you haven't noticed, I've got a little more va-va-voom than broads who typically fan around in tiny strings."

"Woman, there isn't a single part of your body I haven't worshipped," Sam rumbled, his voice a growl. "Now drop...the...robe." The bass in his words held a dominance that made me shiver for reasons entirely different from the cold.

"I dunno." I teased. "My fluffy robe is so warm and cozy." I cocked a half smile at the emotions that slipped across Sam's face.

Amusement, arousal, affection, and something...deeper.

"Water's warm." He said. "And I'll keep you warmer still. Now...off, woman."

How long before he'd go feral, I wondered?

315

"What if I catch a cold?" I lilted into a coquettish whisper, letting one shoulder slip from the fluffy collar, and fluttering my lashes.

"I'm professionally trained to tend to your every need." He looked half-mad with want. "Now show me that sweet ass before I rip the robe off with my teeth."

"Oh, fine," The robe sighed into a heap around my feet. "If you insist." The air was freezing, but it was worth the torture for a few seconds as the visible bob of Sam's throat was soundtracked by a groan.

53

SAM

HOLY. BIKINI. FANTASY.

I'd seen Lila in shredded denim and spiked boots.

I'd seen her in tight t-shirts and leather jackets.

I'd even seen her in bare feet and my baggy shirts.

Then, one day, I saw her in plain, white cotton panties. Their pale contrast to her beautiful, tanned skin sent my lizard brain into overdrive, and I immediately shopped for the bikini. I knew I'd love seeing her like this, but when she let that robe fall, I realized how woefully shallow my fantasies had been. Her lush tits swelled out of the top, and the tiny bows holding the bottoms onto her round ass were precariously snug. I wanted to unleash that perfect cunt from behind its tiny triangle of fabric, with my teeth.

"Mmm, the water is nice." Lila purred, dipping low enough to get her shoulders wet but not her hair piled atop her head. "Usually, these things are so hot I can hardly stand 'em."

Insert bucket of ice water here.

I'd intentionally set the temperature to a level safe for first-trimester pregnancies, crossing my fingers that the icy-cold walk would make it feel warmer. Not unlike the times I swapped her drink for non-alcoholic beer without her knowing. Or the sudden health nut in me that refused to allow lunch meat into the kitchen. All things I did 'just in case'–the overwhelming hole I'd fucked myself into made us a baby.

"I can't believe you've been hiding this place all this time." Lila floated over, turning her back to me as I tugged her into my lap.

"Honestly, things have been..." I let my words trail off. Things had been about 50 shades of fucked up with the dramatics, emotional intensity, and entire life upheaval. But, things had also been a magical kind of wonderful. Meeting, falling, claiming, owning, and living to serve this unprecedented woman was my definition of bliss.

"A merry-go-round from hell?" She smiled as she teased, and I couldn't help but let it invade my senses as she pressed into the bend of me, her legs floating to the top of the water until her toes tipped the surface while her body melted into me.

"It's been amazing seeing you in your zone. You're a force to be reckoned with, Ms. Rivera."

Mrs. Wilder had a far nicer ring to it.

"Lack of intensity was never my problem," Lila scooped a handful of snow off the side of the tub and watched it melt into the steaming water. "It's how I've always been. Instead of Laser Focus, my dad called it 'Lila Focus'." I loved it when she trusted me with pieces of her history.

"Lila-focus. That's way more descriptive." I laced my fingers through hers, cupping the last of the melting snow between our palms. "I also love the way you've helped my family, looking out for Troy, training Moira."

"Meh," She leaned her head back on my shoulder, our arms lowering into the water and folding around her soft belly. "It was nothing. They're good people, doing good things. Who wouldn't help?"

"We only had our Nonna before. And Moira was a foster kid." I leaned my face into her neck, inhaling her scent. "I don't think you realize how much we appreciate you being here. We know what it means for you." I planted a kiss on her shoulder, and she hugged my hands closer in return. "You have been a surprising new addition to the family." I felt her body tense as she pulled my hands away and turned to face me.

"We're gonna have that talk now?" The clipped tone was telling.

"That...talk?" I willed my face into neutrality–my heart leaping into my throat. She was about to call me on my shit—the lack of condoms, all of it.

"Yeah. We haven't labeled our little situationship...but you just called me family." She watched her hands play through the water's surface as she continued. "We've danced around this long enough?"

Jesus Christ...bullet dodged.

"You've been letting us dance around it," I teased, trying not to spook her as I took a moment to recenter. "Let's start with the easy part. I don't love 'situationship.' "

"You have something else in mind?" Her tone was light, but her face was direct. On anyone else, it would have seemed almost challenging if I didn't know it to be the armor she wore. I loved her willfulness, and I was truly over dancing around this thing we had going on.

"You're mine. I'm yours." I shrugged but kept our eyes locked. "So yeah, let's call it what it is. Girlfriend, Lover, ye ol' Ball and Chain–whatever label you like is fine by me. As long as it's clear that it's exclusive...mutual...and permanent."

"Ball and chain?" Lila's mouth curved into that adorable crooked little smile. "You can leave that one off the table."

I loved that she chose levity. But when she cut her eyes to the side, taking in the scenery, I could tell she was hesitating to say whatever else was on her mind. I'd practiced waiting for her, but my impatience wore thin with the emotions I battled.

"Use your words, baby."

"Ugh. I hate it when you say that." She rolled her eyes at me and floated away. I reached out and snagged her fingers, holding her there. "I can't keep my mouth shut when you say that."

"Speak your mind. Good or bad." I tugged her closer. "Don't hide from me."

"How long?"

"What do you mean?" Lila bit her bottom lip in answer. "Speak your piece, Hellcat."

"Before you dragged me up to this cabin, you said you were 'all in for however long it takes', and you declared in front of your whole family that 'you're not leaving'. Then the other night, you said we should go out and act like any other 'couple in love.'" Her air quotes rubbed me the wrong way, but I held my tongue. "You've been fucking and feeding me like a man possessed, but also spouting the merits of my work on the case for Troy, and today you said whatever label we put on this, you wanted it clear that it was exclusive and..." she drew in a breath, then squared her shoulders and narrowed her eyes at me. "And permanent."

In one breath, she'd single-handedly called me out on all my rawest emotions and laid me bare. For all the effort I'd put in trying to resist this sex-bomb, it was clear I lost the battle...and she realized it long before I did.

"What happens when the case is closed, Sam?" I thought we were talking about us —our feelings or relationship status —but she jumped the track, which threw me. "I came here for Marcus. You brought me to the cabin because of Marcus. And now I'm working each day to find him, and now find Jensen, and help Troy take down Apex." Her voice cracked as she added, "So what happens when the case is over, and...you don't need me?"

"So that's what's got you spun," I sighed, connecting the strings woven together in that beautiful brain of hers. "You think you are only here for work, and that when that's done ... we're done. Is that it?" I drew her to me, cupping her face as her legs wrapped around me without resistance. "Let me put this to bed for you, Hellcat. We might not have had the most traditional beginning, but you are permanently stitched into me. Woven into my family. When I said I was all in, I meant it. Me, my heart, I'm completely...irrevocably...in love with you."

"Jesus, I can't...." Emotions welled in her eyes, but she gave a subtle shake of her head. "It's too..." A fresh sob surfaced, her body tensing, under the weight of unspoken words.

My chest squeezed, fearing she was about to hand me my walking papers in the wake of the declaration I'd made. I held her, forehead to forehead, hands around her back, praying the truth in my touch would be enough to keep her here.

"I can't... lose you...or another family. I won't survive it." Tears streaked her cheeks, and she wrapped herself around me to let them loose.

The worry I'd been choking on washed away as her cries brought the sweetest relief. It wasn't a declaration or a label in the traditional sense, but Lila wouldn't be so afraid to lose...if she hadn't grown to love.

"Baby, you aren't losing me...Ever," I murmured, emphasizing that last word with a squeeze as if my body could brand it into hers.

"It's all so much." Shaking her head again as she spoke, her breathing hitched between the soft sobs. "I shut it all off when my dad and brother..." I squeezed her tighter to me, willing my peace into her and wishing I could short-circuit the hurt she was reliving. "And now you come blowing through, ripping me out of myself, and I'm so raw that I can't – "

"Shhhh, baby. You don't have to say anymore." I kissed her neck and ear as I held her. "It's okay that you aren't sure where things are for you right now. I'm here, rock solid, and I'm not rushing you." I lingered in the moment, letting her tears slow while grazing my beard along her jawline.

Her words said she was overwhelmed.

Her tears said she was scared.

They all told me she loved me.

But her body pulsed alive in my arms.

"What do you need, baby?"

"Please." She rocked her hips against me, jolting my cock to attention. "Make me feel."

My girl needed more than words. I could give her that. Leaning back, she placed those gorgeous lips of hers on mine, her tongue begging for purchase, and my mouth all too eager to give it. A slow dance, a tug of the strings, the warm water caressing our skin, and I was lost in her body and the bond we cast between us.

Everything else would wait.

WILDER BRO'S GROUP CHAT

-1-

Troy: An oddity has occurred.

Chase: What's up?

Troy: Maple Hill tenant received white roses. No note. Just a vase on the porch. Oxford Dr. tenant received a set as well.

Me: Weird coincidence.

Chase: Wait…WHITE roses?

Troy: Indeed.

Chase: That's not random.

Me: What am I missing?

Chase: Moira hates white roses. Jensen used to love-bomb her with them.

Me: That asshole again.

Chase: Apex sent them to the library. She found one in the crib before the fire.

Me: Fuuuck. So we're fighting florists now?

Troy: I knew they were a hot button for her. But not the full details.

Chase: Thought it was a Jensen thing…he was supposed to be dead.

Me: So…he's searching for her with flowers?

Chase: We can't tell Moira. She's barely holding it together as is.

Troy: Hence the text excluding the girls. There's nothing concrete yet.

Me: Even you think Jensen's sniffing around again…no coincidences here right?

Chase: Or Brinks.

Me: Goddamn it.

Troy: It's one delivery. It could be a fluke.

Chase: But you don't believe that.

Me: Not for a goddamn second.

Troy: Heads on a swivel. Eyes open.

Chase: And if you find another petal—burn it.

Me: No one touches our girls.

Troy: Oorah

54

LILA

S AM WRECKED ME IN the hot tub, and again in the shower, showing me his love with fingers and tongue and unspoken thrusts of unyielding devotion by cleaning and feeding me. By the time we headed to the address Troy provided, every fiber in my body felt peaceful and ready for whatever came next. Pulling up after dark, Troy waited out front of the deserted shooting range in his usual crisp dress shirt, suspenders, and slacks, with his piece firmly in the holster.

"Chase texted...they'll be late," Sam stated when we exited the car.

"He's stalling," Troy added.

"Does he not like guns?" I asked, remembering his emotional display at our last dinner. "Or is all this still from the other night?"

"Remember when I told you Chase feels our adoption the most?" Sam asked, and I nodded. "Nonna adopted Troy as a newborn. Technically, I came to the family when I was 6...from a friend-of-the-family situation. I was never in the system. We never felt what Chase did." Sam nodded to Troy, who picked up the story.

"Chase was scrawny then, and skittish." Troy gave a wistful smile as he reminisced. "Bounced around to a few foster homes that were clearly unsavory. He struggled the most with feeling secure....like he belonged." Entering the shooting range, Sam continued the story.

"Building a family with Moira, to love and protect the way he never felt as a kid, is everything to him." Sam shrugged. "So when Jensen attacked on their wedding night..."

"He thinks he failed her." I finished, my heart bleeding from old, familiar cuts.

"On his first official day on the job," Troy resigned, pain in his eyes.

"And the training and the guns..." my words trailed off, no longer needing to name the salt in the wound. "We gotta shift his focus."

"How?" Sam grabbed a vest and goggles.

"There's this thing my dad did when I'd get hung up on something I couldn't control."

"The downside of that Lila-focus?" Sam winked.

"Total double-edged sword." I shook my head, clicking my clip into the gun.

"Hey, guys," Chase and Moira strolled in, hand in hand. "I would say sorry we're late, but I figure this will be our new norm now." Moira hugged me. "What are we shifting?"

"Troy, we need blank paper and a marker." I slapped the button to bring all the target systems to the front of the firing bays. "My dad always made this process more productive for me. I wanted to show you guys, if you don't mind."

We walked out of the control booth and met Troy, who handed me a ream of paper and a big, fat, black Sharpie.

"Anyone can shoot generic targets, but sometimes life needs a little Zen." I scribbled Marcus Brinks' name on my paper and capped the marker. "My dad used to tell me, 'Lila-girl, focus on what you can control, and let go of the rest.' " I attached the paper to the target system and slapped the button to send it down the lane, lifting my earplugs and seeing the others do likewise. "That," I pointed to the traveling name, "Is what I can't control. I can't control where it's going, I can't control where it's been." Then I held up my gun, "This is what I can control. My breathing, my grip, my stance, my aim."

I gave Sam a little wink, spun around, and unloaded the clip into the still-moving target. When I finished, I popped the clip free, placed the gun smoothly on the counter, and called for the target to return.

"Growing up, I sometimes let all the shit I couldn't control pile up until everything felt too big." Moira's gaze told me the target arrived, and I turned to see the paper shot to shreds, name barely legible, bottom half tattered and gone altogether. "Dad would bring me to the range to help me remember to let go of what I couldn't control and focus on what I could."

I handed a sheet of paper to each person.

"Fuck me, that was hot." Sam cocked an eyebrow. "But I'm never getting on the receiving end of your wrath."

"Damn straight, Jackass." I teased with a bump of my hip before I turned to Moira. "You don't have to tell us what you write. Write as little or as much as you need to, then attach it and send it away. And when you're ready," I looked at Chase to finish.

"Put a little violence in our Zen?" Chase's face took on a mischievous grin

"With a song in your heart, Boyscout." I smiled, turning to help Moira set up her target.

For the next hour, we unloaded bullets like they were going out of style.

Initially, it was handwritten notes, but soon we transitioned to traditional targets. I worked with Moira on grip, stance, and aim. At the same time, Troy and his brothers competed against one another on bullseyes, distance, and the like, swapping stories from the Marines.

"Don't be surprised if you are sore tomorrow," I told Moira while the guys cleaned the area. "The kick-back can feel like you got hit by a car if you aren't used to it, but it's temporary." My shoulder throbbed at the lack of practice time I put in recently, so I knew she'd be feeling it.

"Are you kidding? I'm sore now." She laughed, rotating her arm. "But thank you. I can't wait to have one of my very own and do this all the time. We could go together!" Her eyes lit up, and I prepared myself for the squeal. "Like a girls' day. Mani's, Pedi's, and bullet-yoga!"

"Sure...that could be fun." To my surprise, I meant it.

Suddenly, two giant hands spun me, pulling me into an oxygen-sucking, brick-wall of darkness.

"Thank you." Chase's voice was gruff and muffled in my hair. "This .... was good." He squeezed until I tapped out.

"Dude," Sam gave Chase a jolt to the ribs. "Give my girl some air."

"Sorry." Chase sheepishly stepped back.

"He gives the best hugs." Moira beamed, interlocking her fingers with his as the two of them turned to leave.

"Who knew that wall of muscles was such a teddy bear?"

"He's nothing if not a ginormous man-baby." Sam teased. "This was great, and you're sexy as hell with that sidearm."

"For the record, the last part of that sentiment is his own." Troy chimed in as we left. "But it was a fine lesson, Rivera."

"You know," Sam said, holding my hand as we drove. "Your dad was a pretty smart guy." The warmth of hearing dad's memory coming from Sam's lips spread all over me. "That thing with the shooting range was epic. Pretty sure my brothers and I needed that just as much as Moira." Knowing I'd carried a tiny piece of dad's legacy into Sam's family bloomed in my heart–two parts of my life finding purchase in one night.

"Do you know what everyone wrote on their papers? I only saw Moira's." I said, wondering what Sam wrote.

"Chase's was pretty obvious...Jensen." Sam nodded, and I hoped this helped him come to grips with his guilt. "Troy wrote Apex, which surprised me. He doesn't usually let a case get under his skin like this."

"He likes shit buttoned up," I said. "And Apex is definitely not buttoned up." Then I slipped a half grin at him, "And you?"

"Nope." He said with a mischievous grin on his face. "Not telling."

"Oh, Come On!" I said, lifting my hand to my chest in a pleading manner. "This whole thing was my idea; you can't leave me hanging."

"Tell you what," He bargained. "Let's finish out the week, and I'll tell you at the next spaghetti night."

"Seriously?" I sat back with a huff. "Does every revelation require pasta and a live studio audience? A girl could develop a fear of Italian food."

"Least I'm not announcing how much pipe I lay to a room full of strangers," He teased, and the blush that rushed over me was enough to shut me up. I was never going to live that down.

The night did wonders for me. I'd been so tied up in Brinks that I forgot to focus on what I could control. Safe and hidden, we had the upper hand on Brinks. He couldn't find me and, more than that, he couldn't hurt Sam or his family, whom I was growing so attached to that my chest ached.

They were all skilled, trained, prepared, and together, and that...was enough.

55

SAM

MY NEXT DAY ON shift, I slipped out of bed before sunrise, threw down a quick workout to burn off nervous energy, and headed over to Chase's. I knocked lightly to avoid waking the babies, but when Chase opened the door, I realized it was a moot point.

"Thank God, man, get in here." Chase hurried back to the kitchen, where an angry set of beautiful girls screamed it to the cheap seats. "Moira's grabbing a shower, and I overslept. Take River for me." I stared at the red-faced bundles of infant rage, no clue which was River. Painted toenails were useless under footy-pajamas. Grabbing the one who seemed angriest, I pulled out all my best Uncle Sam tricks.

"What the hell did you do to my nieces?" I bounced and jiggled, using my free hand to try to soothe the other one with a spare toy that might as well have been a pile of garbage for all the good it did.

"I was late with breakfast." He shook two bottles and tossed one to me along with a burp cloth. "My girls don't like being hungry, and daddy hit snooze." He lifted the other baby and cooed at her as he placed the bottle into her frantic mouth. "Daddy's sorry he was late." He smiled at his daughter, a face full of love. "Blame your pretty mama for keeping me up last night with her talented mou - "

"I beg of you not to finish that sentence in range of my niece's angelic ears," I said, astounded at the sudden onset of quiet as both girls went to town on their bottles.

"Thanks for the help, man," he sighed, eyeing my uniform. "Why are you here before work? Everything copacetic?"

"Two things," I said with a sigh. "Wanted to check on you after the range."

"Great...and the other thing."

"Try a little less bullshit, Boyscout."

"No, really, I mean it." Chase sighed at my cocked eyebrow. "I won't lie that shit's been weighing me down, and I still feel like..." He didn't finish his statement. I didn't push.

You didn't get over that kind of rage in a single evening.

"But last night helped. It gave Moira and me a starting point to talk through shit. I'm...better." He shifted his face to resignation–he was done sharing.

"Alright. The other reason is," I took a breath, bracing for his reaction. "Where'd you get Moira's ring?"

"Seriously!" Chase's face split into a broad, toothy grin. "This rocks! When are you gonna propose? Have you told Troy? Will you do at Margie's bar?"

"Jesus, he's worse than your Nonna," I muttered to my baby, who blinked agreeably.

"But you talked it out with Lila, about all the things you told me, and she's cool? Ya'll are set... she's all in?"

"Who's all in?" Moira blessedly halted Chase's questions.

Truth was, I wanted Lila to know I loved her, no matter what. I loved her and I wanted her, and I wanted her with me, regardless of whether I put a baby in her. I still planned to have that conversation as soon as possible, but I needed to time it right. I hoped a ring would prove my commitment.

"Sam's buying a ring!" Chase blurted.

"Dude." I rolled my eyes as Moira clapped and squealed. "You have no chill."

"Oh, Sam, I just love her." She pulled me down for a hug and whispered, "I love her for you."

"Can you two at least try to maintain some semblance of cool? I haven't bought a ring yet, or figured out when or how... I'm just planning." I turned my focus back to Chase. "Text me the details?" I stood and handed my niece to her mother.

"Did Blue eat for you?" she asked, tossing the burp cloth over her shoulder and propping the scrunching baby up.

"That one was Blue?" I said in surprise, looking at Chase, who shook his head as well.

"I can see little differences," Moira replied. "You can't?"

"It's like they took you're DNA and went copy, paste, paste." Moira laughed and rolled her eyes at me as I turned to leave, mind reeling at the dozen ways I wanted to propose to Lila.

I'd dug myself deep, but loved her deeper. I prayed one would cancel out the other...and I wouldn't lose her altogether.

56

LILA

*T*HE FUNERAL WAS DONE. *The mourners gone. The procession that brought us all in left. I remained. I stood alone in the dusky light, casting a long shadow over two freshly covered graves. They were both given full department honors and laid to rest with all the pomp and circumstance. Daddy was given the added military honors due to his time in the army; their coffins were draped with police and American flags, which were folded and presented to me. I hugged them so tightly, my locked elbows ached in protest. The honor guard gave final salutes; the haunting sounds of drummers echoed away; taps sounded somewhere in the distance. I remained. I didn't like the guns; their intended respect chambered through me like fresh wounds. Flashes of blood and bodies whipped past my mind in a numb haze. My captain brought his car close enough for the final radio call from dispatch to reach me. He stayed longer than most. The longest. But even he left when the rain began. Still, I remained.*

The muted flashes lingering in the morning light left traces of sensation.

Hair clinging to my face.

Cold rain pelting my skin.

Echoes of mumbled words I couldn't grasped, lost altogether by the time I showered.

Sam must have left early. Or the shooting range triggered something. It left a lingering sour in my mouth until hot coffee and determination burned it away.

I steadied myself for the day ahead, more determined than ever to uncover the truth about Brinks and his involvement with IA. Last night, I set my ghost laptop to run a full scrape of the New York State Office of Internal Affairs—live servers, data warehouses, and offsite backups. This morning, I planned to comb through the pull, filtering out noise, anomalies, and redundancies to see what stuck. Entering my war room, I found a sticky note on my laptop.

'Hit play and enjoy.
Sam'

The screen displayed a popular music app, signed into an account already paid up for a year of premium service–a single station titled, 'Bad Bitches', loaded and waiting. As instructed, I hit play, and the entire room filled with the energizing voice of Lizzo thumping from speakers tucked into the four corners. I almost squealed and clapped as the tunes infused me with energy and focus, leaving my whole body tingling with excitement. That thoughtful, caring, bear of a man brought me music.

I couldn't wait to show my appreciation when he got home.

The first order of business was to determine how a former criminal attorney landed a gig with Internal Affairs. At their core, IA was a professional standards division within the police that was responsible for investigating allegations of misconduct, policy violations, and similar matters. The size of the various IA branches and their internal structures varied by department and by district. However, consistently, IA agents were only police officers. So, how the hell did a shady attorney have jurisdiction over both my NYPD termination and a suspect's body in this upstate county?

This was the itch I scratched as hours ticked by.

A complete data analysis would take forever, so I started digging through my data, searching departmental employment rosters for Brinks' name or Agent ID. The investigations and complaints unit had no record, nor did the auditing division or training department. I even checked into their administrative support and found nothing. I decided to let the internet do a little legwork for me and found a passing news story that barely made a blip on the media radar at its release.

'In a move to boost public trust, Internal Affairs has announced the phased launch of a new Community Outreach Unit. Designed to bridge the gap between law enforcement, government, and civilians, the unit will address internal concerns and promote stronger police-community relations.'

I then went back into the mined data. I searched for 'Community Outreach Unit,' getting a hit in a departmental memo that evaluated officers of the court, who were in good standing, as part of the community outreach initiative.

It was Disneyland for Marcus Brink!

Anyone employed within the court system was considered an officer of the court, which meant that anyone, from a sitting judge down to the courtroom stenographer, could now be judge, jury, and executioner over the state's police. It meant the same judge who decided guilt or innocence could kneecap a case before it reached court.

Doing what my brain does best, I decided to sniff out who the hell greenlit that memo. That kind of boneheaded decision reeked of upper-level meddling. If it involved court officers, then someone in state government pulled the strings. The Senate, the governor's office... take your pick. Both had the juice to nudge policy when it suited their agenda. But who looked at this flaming pile of conflict-of-interest and thought, 'Yep, this'll boost trust'? The judicial branch writes the laws...cops enforce them. When those lines blur, the whole system starts to rot, and the decay was getting whiffy.

And what the fucking fuck did this have to do with fucking Apex? "Fuck!"

My head pounded with frustration when a text from Sam alerted.

> **Sam:** Hey, gorgeous, get that ass up and eat. I can smell the gears grinding from here.

> **Me:** Anyone ever tell you you're kinda a busybody?

> **Sam:** I'd like to get busy with your body. ;-)

> **Sam:** Salad's made in the fridge. See you at home. XO

Smiling at his use of the word 'home', I stood and stretched, my entire body screaming that I'd sat for too long. I glanced at my watch and grimaced. It was nearly 2 o'clock. I always lost hours in research mode; my brain relentlessly following every rabbit trail no matter how off-track it took me. I wasn't hungry, but I knew Sam would nag like a little old lady if I didn't eat. I headed to the kitchen when the doorbell rang.

My heart stopped.

Instinctively, I reached for my hip before remembering I still didn't have a gun—silently cursing Troy for holding it until my civilian license came through. No one was supposed to know I was here. Chase and Troy both had keys and never bothered knocking. Moira would text ahead, then barge in with sing-songy greetings and my two favorite burritos.

"Flowers for a Ms. Rivera," a feminine voice announced.

Sliding soundlessly forward, I peeked out the peephole to see a young woman, maybe 20 years at most, holding a giant bouquet. I contemplated opening the door, but before I could, she set the delivery on the ground, snapped a picture with her phone, and left. I waited until the car was out of the driveway before opening the door and bringing the arrangement inside.

A dozen white roses nestled into an arrangement of mossy green eucalyptus and baby's breath permeated my senses. I set them on the counter and looked through the petals, finding a card that held a single line.

I'm so very glad you are here.

Floating down the hall, I shook my head at my big lumberjack's romantic side. I'd never been sent roses, and my heart fluttered as I imagined Sam picking them out and telling the florist what he wanted on the card. I looked around for a place to put them, then decided my war room needed a little cheer.

57

SAM

MY SHIFT WAS SLOW, giving me time to browse the ring site Chase sent and the few posts he forwarded. The latter included an article entitled 'Which diamond is best suited for your future wife?'

My future wife.

Words I'd never considered before Lila, but they felt right. I wasn't nervous about proposing. I wanted to get the right ring, say the right things, and do it the right way.

There was the rub.

I could do everything perfectly and she might still, rightfully, kick my teeth in for knocking her up...or not? I didn't know when her period should start, but it had to be soon. I knew women's cycles could be affected by any number of things, like stress, diet, hormonal fluctuations, and more. God knows Lila endured a carload of stress and grief. Before me, her diet was booze and garbage. I worked hard to turn both things around, but there was so much ground to cover. I pocketed my phone with a growl and stood to inventory the rig, brooding, deep in thought, when a text came through.

> Lila: I'm so very VERY glad I am here. <3⬚

I went back and read it a second time, and then a third–She'd sent a heart emoji.

Lila wasn't exactly the flirty, heart-eyes-over-text type. She kept feelings close, even in writing. I often worried I was too pushy with my daily check-ins. But there, in simple letters, was an unprompted message and a heart emoji.

Heart. Emoji.

That was my sign.

When I got home, we'd make dinner together, maybe revisit the hot tub, and I'd profess all my love for her. Then we'd talk through everything and she'd be furious, no doubt—but... heart emoji.

We'd make it. We'd be okay.

Grinning like a lovestruck idiot, I started typing a response, but the alarm sounded for a call. I pocketed my phone again and rallied my crew to a construction site injury at the new library.

Wrecking crews were clearing debris when a skid-steer tipped, pinning the operator. It took an hour to get the machine upright so we could rescue him. When we left, I clocked the banner strung along the temporary fence surrounding the area and texted it to Troy.

'Renovations and expansions courtesy of The Apex Society. '

> Me: Feels criminal to let these guys work here.

> TJ: Technically, they have no reason not to.

Me: I call bullshit.

TJ: Agreed. Any progress?

Me: I'll find out when I get home. I'm headed to the station; it'll be an hour or more.

TJ: Understood.

Cleanup took longer than usual. I was covered in mud and grease and had to restock the rig. Paperwork took twice as long since job-related injuries involved extra red tape. By the time I clocked out, it was closer to 5 than my usual 2. I was itching to get home, to dive into her text and learn what prompted that heart. I wanted to feed her, fuck her, tell her how much I loved her, and how sorry I was for being such a caveman. That last part was a small lie since I wasn't entirely sure I was sorry.

If it worked, and she was pregnant...

Driving home, I contemplated our time together and how different my life was. The bachelor's life had been my way for so long—laughs, lays, no strings. I wasn't totally clueless. I knew losing my parents impacted me. I lived with a silent pressure to be grateful for what was in front of me, to hold it close because it could be gone in an instant. But seeing my brother get married sparked a desire for more. More than fun, more than easy, more than casual, and more than temporary.

Enter fierce, complicated, perfect Lila.

She had a mind like a steel trap, a tenacity that wouldn't quit, and an iron will. She didn't walk into my life; she detonated in it, like flicking a match and tossing it into gasoline. I sparked to life for her before I even knew her last name. And it wasn't just lust—it was everything. I burned for a life I never realized I wanted: wife, kids, the whole damn picket fence. And, God help me, I just prayed I hadn't torched it all before I ever had a chance to build it.

I had to come clean tonight.

If she were mad, I could take it.

If she were sad, I would shoulder it.

Lila deserved the truth, and whatever happened, I was ready.

58

LILA

"COME ON, FANCY PANTS...SHOW me what you got!" I taunted Moira.

"I don't want to hurt you now, Hellcat. You've been sitting pretty in this cabin getting soft?"

Moira and I bantered back and forth, teasing each other's nicknames and circling, sweating through our leggings with ponytails hanging on for dear life as sticky tendrils clung to our faces. The pretty pink princess did not come to play. We'd been at it for over an hour, and it was the most fun I'd had in days.

"You're nesting in basics...try some combos but remember, don't give away your moves." I clapped the pads together. "Now, quit stalling, Fancy Pants," I yelled at her growing smile. "Come on!" Moira leaned in for a 1-2 punch, and I dodged, sending my kick-pad into her stomach for effect.

"See...I knew you would follow with your left cause you dropped your shoulder. Don't let me do that again." In my periphery, I saw Sam walk in, drop his bag, and join Chase.

"They've been at it like this for over an hour," Chase commented.

"No shit?" Sam replied.

"Zero Shits." Chase gave a good wolf-whistle to Moira as she did a punch-kick combo that I narrowly missed. "Kick her ass, baby!"

"Okay. I'm coming for ya, Princess." I lunged in and out, trying to catch her off guard. The girl had killer footwork, and I wanted to build on that. "I'm coming and I wanna steal you away. What are you gonna do?" I asked, helping her to prepare for my attack mentally. I faked left and lunged to the right, grabbing her arm and swinging her around until she leaned against my body, my practice pad jammed into her side. "If I had a gun, I'd own you." I released her with a laugh. "Don't leave an opening from any angle."

"Don't drop the shoulder. Don't fall for fake lunges," Moira chanted, "And don't let the angry Hellcat have a gun."

This was a favorite part of the day for me. Sparring with Moira burned off my anxiety and the stress of research. My body felt stronger than it had in months. Not to mention, I loved our chats during breaks when we'd play with the babies.

"Oh-ho, the pretty-pink-princess has jokes. I must be going too easy on you." My smile widened as I planned my move. "Maybe I need to try a little harder."

"Only if you think you won't break a nail," Moira volleyed back.

"You gonna let her talk to you like that, babe?" Sam jeered.

"You're supposed to be on my side, Jackass?" Sam winked at my withering glare, and I refocused on Moira.

I wanted to lean into her agility and see if I could knock her off balance. I planned a solid lateral move and prepared. I shifted, feigned left, then lunged beneath her elbow. Moira spun, too fast, ducked, then slammed a punch into my gut. I went down hard, a breathless 'oof' rushing out of me as I hit the floor and rolled. Moira whooped like a champ, arms in the air, chanting, 'Who's the pretty princess now?' while Chase broke into the Rocky theme like a frat house mascot.

Then Sam.

Sam sprinted across the room; No hesitation, no smirk, no sense of play. He dropped to his knees beside me, one hand gripping my shoulder, the other hovering over my body like he didn't know where to touch me.

"Are you okay? Lila—talk to me. Are you winded? Do you feel…" His face was pale–voice shaking. His eyes darted from my face to my stomach and back again.

"It was a punch, not a drive-by." I blinked up at him in confusion.

"Jesus, Baby!" Sam shouted as his eyes shot up to Chase, almost pleading.

"I'm okay," I huffed, laughing and failing to stand as Sam pulled me half onto his lap. He wasn't hearing me–eyes scanning me like something was wrong.

Like I might break.

"Oh God, Lila. Did I hurt you?" Moira knelt next to me, her hands over her mouth. "I'm so sorry. I should've held back; I didn't mean–"

"I said…I'm fine." I glared at Sam, then turned to Moira. "You did good." I looked down at my stomach and saw no bruising to indicate an injury that would warrant Sam's reaction.

"But you don't know." He growled. "There could be internal - "

"Hey, Samoa," Chase cut his brother off, an odd look on his face. "If she *says* she's fine, then - "

"Then she's fine!" I growled, pulling against Sam's hands to get up. Moira, looking as if she might cry, reached to help me up. Ignoring Sam's weird vibe, I focused on her.

"That was a solid hit. Your footwork is fantastic. Next time–"

"Let me at least...check you out or - " Sam's tone was tangled—angst, anger, panic, I couldn't tell. His eyes carried a terror that made no sense. "Lemme take you to my rig. I can–"

"Your rig!?" I pushed him away with a laugh. "Have you lost your mind?" Moira and I had been sparring for a while. He'd seen me take a stray headshot, even. Sure, this had me on the floor, but only because I was off balance–momentum carrying me. "What the hell has you so spun?" I started removing pads as I smiled and cocked my chin at Moira. "Give the girl props for a good hit, but don't get it twisted. I'm A-okay and I'll get mine later."

Moira smiled, but it didn't reach her worried eyes, and that pissed me off. Sam was ruining this moment for her.

"But what if you're not!" Sam's bellow rippled through the room, and I was so over it.

"Hey!" I lowered my voice to a yelling whisper and narrowed my eyes. "Whatever landmine just tripped is yours...not ours." I motioned to Moira and me before thumping my finger into his chest. "So get a grip!" I shoved him back on the last word to make my point before taking Moira by the elbow and turning away from the guys.

"How about you and me leave the giant man-baby to sulk while we get a celebratory drink."

"Are you sure?" Moira asked, eyes pleading with worry.

"It's the only time I'll let you get a leg up on me, princess. Take the win...and the bourbon." Finally, she sighed in relief.

Then Sam ruined everything.

"What about the - "

"Dude!" Chase stepped to Sam's side, growling. "No." The undercurrent in Chase's voice had Moira instantly on alert.

"There could be a - "

"Not. Like. This!" Chase's jaw clenched so tight you'd think he was grinding stones with his teeth. "I'll get my girls out...then you two can hash shit out."

"Not like what?" Moira asked, turning to face them with a look that earned its Medusa name. This wasn't a landmine—this was bigger.

"There is a what?" I added, splitting my gaze between Chase and Sam.

"I'll explain on the way home." Chase glanced at his wife, eyes wide. "I'm getting the girls in the car. We're going." He moved to gather up the babies things as Moira crossed her arms in resignation. He knew something and had kept it from her, too.

"The hell we are!" Moira looked at Chase with a look that took all of two seconds for the man to cave. With a sigh, he slumped on the barstool. Only then did Moira address Sam. "What...is he talking about?" Sam tried to avoid her, but she stepped into his line of sight and asked again. "What...did you do?" Seconds ticked by, dragging on the tension in the room as we all held our breath.

Sam stood frozen, fists clenched so tight I could see the ropes of muscle bulge in his forearms. His nostrils flared like he was trying to control his temper, but his eyes showed something sorrowful and filled with regret.

"I wanted to talk to you, baby. Tonight, in fact...to explain everything." The word 'everything' had all the hairs on my neck standing on end, despite that EMT tone he'd activated. He was using all his soothe-the-savage-beast tricks on me because whatever this had an 'everything'...meaning more than one thing.

This was a multiple, thing, kind of fuck-up.

"I rehearsed all the way home...put all the cards on the table and come clean so we could move forward."

Cards. Plural. This was a greatest-hits playlist of fuck-ups, and my brain began formulating a list of terrible, gutting theories.

"Come clean?" My heart sank at the possibilities. Had he cheated on me? God knows he'd had the opportunity–I'd been stuck here, and he showered after every shift. Bile rose, and my mouth was moving before my brain could filter the words. "You cheated." I stepped forward, squaring my shoulders. "You fucking cheated on me, you bastard!"

"No...God...Baby." Sam stepped towards me, but I retreated in equal measure.

"Don't 'baby' me. Lemme guess," I waved a hand around the room. "You planned to keep it on the DL 'til you got home, saw me get knocked me on my ass, and your guilt kicked you in the fucking teeth?"

"Is that true?" Moira's question was aimed at Chase, but Sam answered.

"No, Jesus. I didn't cheat on you." Sam reached for me again — I pulled back.

"He didn't cheat," Chase answered his wife, and then added to me. "He'd never."

"But whatever this is, you knew about it." I fired at Chase, my anger beginning to buzz as the familiar rush of adrenaline simmered beneath my skin. "You two had fun playing Alpha-hole Confession Hour while I was stuck in the goddamn dark?"

"And me with her, apparently." Moira snapped.

"This is on me," Sam addressed Moira, lifting a hand towards Chase. "I did this, not Chase. I went to him for advice, but this is 100% not about anyone else but Lila and me." He held one hand on his chest, reaching the other across the cavernous divide between us. "Please, baby, hear me o ut."

"Then sack up!" I held my hands out in challenge. God knows I was mad enough to take a swing at this point. "What the fuck did you do?"

59

SAM

I T WASN'T SUPPOSED TO be this way.

We'd make dinner, make love, and when she was good and boneless, I'd confess that my inner caveman was unapologetically an ass. She'd be mad, but she'd forgive me. This mistake would be a blip in the rearview of a fantastic life. Instead, she took one punch to the gut, and every instinct in me screamed that my imaginary baby was at risk, and I lost it. Now, instead of getting engaged, I faced cheating allegations.

How did I fuck this all to fucking hell?

"First, you have to know I didn't intend for things to go down like this," I tried like hell to calm us both with an even voice.

"Great," Lila huffed. "Keep talking."

"I meant to tell you sooner, but things have been intense, with so much going on, and I thought - "

"Got it. Bad timing." She cocked her head, angry, honey eyes slicing through me like a knife. "Keep. Talking."

"You and I started rocky–only just labeled things." I hoped reminding her of that might soften the blow. "And I meant what I said. I'm yours. Body and soul. 100%. No matter what." I paused, hoping happier memories would sink in to soften the murderous rage simmering in her gorgeous eyes.

"Keep. Fucking. Talking." Her glare could've burned a hole through my head for all the intensity she drilled into that barely whispered command.

I had danced around enough–she was out of patience.

"I, uh…" Emotion choked me, and I had to clear the boulder from my throat. "When we…" I halted again.

How did you talk down a live grenade after you pulled the pin?

"Baby…I haven't used a condom. Not since we moved in here." I blurted it out in one rambling rip of the bandage, and once I started, I couldn't stop. "The first time was an accident, I swear, and I thought I'd wrapped it but didn't realize it was missing til after." I stepped towards her, relieved when she stood unmoving. "I was gonna come clean, make it a one-time thing." Another step forward, and still she didn't move.

"But that first dinner was intense, so I gave you time to settle in. But the next time we were together, something…shifted. All I could think about was how crazy I was about you and how much I wanted you in my life, forever, and holy fuck woman, when we were together, my higher brain functions stopped because of how well we fit." I stepped close enough to touch her–words tumbling out. "You're my perfect match in every goddamn way. And I want all of your forevers, and then it happened again." I paused, reaching for her, hoping she'd reach back and put me out of my misery.

She wasn't moving, wasn't running, wasn't yelling.

This had to be good.

"And...you knew?" Moira's tone pulled my focus. I turned to see her scowling at Chase. "You knew he'd done this...took this choice from her...and didn't say anything?"

"Don't be mad at him, please." My head was exploding, realizing I'd been so wrapped up in Lila that I selfishly hurt their marriage by dragging Chase into my shit.

"No, Moira. Be mad at him." Lila's words were short and clipped. "Be very mad. Mad feels right." She never took the murderous stare off of me as she spoke. "Be very, very mad."

"Way ahead of you." Moira snapped, shrinking away from Chase in a way that punched me in the gut.

"To be clear," Lila closed her eyes, a mask of calm dropping into place. "You decided it would be okay to load me up with your jackpot sauce...and not tell me. That about right?"

"No! I mean..." I stammered, all the air in the room seemingly sucked out. "It's not like that- "

"Oh?" Her eyes popped open. "It's. Not. Like. That?"

I...was a dead man.

"I think it's exactly like that!" Lila stepped towards me, flinging my hand aside and jamming her finger in my chest. "You figured me an easy way to a bigger nut by hiding your dude soup in my fine china."

"Please. Baby—"

"Oh, poor Lila. She's a mess." She emphasized each phrase with a wave of her hands, as if in mock performance. "She gets in too many bar fights. Big, strong Sam needs to swoop in and save her pathetic ass." She stepped closer, backing me up as her volume increased. "Surely she won't mind if I explore a breeding kink by dropping a little white rain in her lady-vein!"

"I've never looked at you like that," I shouted, only to be heard over her screaming, hoping my words would magically help her see how rock steady my love was. "I've only seen you as the–"

"Spunk monkey?!" She interrupted, her arms swinging wide.

"No, Jesus!" The words slapped me. "I see you as the–"

"The rim job for your cock shot?" She stood close enough to smell the sparring sweat, and my body ached to reach out and hold her and make her see that we could get past this. I was losing her.

"Lila, baby, please...I've only ever seen you as - "

"Oh, I know!" She thrust a finger high in the air, her face spreading into a broad, toothy grin as if presenting an award-winning idea. "The bun baker for your baby batter.... Is that it? Big. Daddy. Sure Shot!"

"THE LOVE OF MY LIFE!" The words came out with such force that the whole room jolted. "Fucking hell, woman, I've never looked at you as anything other than an absolute force to be reckoned with. Hell on heels. Smart and gorgeous, and my absolute match in every way." I started walking towards her even as she backed away. "I love your fire, and I crave your soft. I live in your wild, and I breathe in your calm. And I know I have fucked this up, but I've never wanted anything more in my entire life than you."

I sucked in air, my heart beating with such ferocity that I worried it might leap from my chest for the honor of dying at her feet.

"Never leave home without, em...eh Sam." Her voice cracked, and I felt it slice in my soul.

"Please.... Let me fix this." She jerked away from me like I was the shit-fisted asshole on a barstool, and really, I was no better.

"No." Her face fell, voice strained like the night she told me about her family's death. This was hurting her...I hurt her...like that.

"Lila," I whispered, my eyes stinging at the loss I saw barreling down on me. "Tell me what to say. I'll do anything."

"No." Her chin quivered as tears spilled down. "I can't..." She looked at Moira, her eyes wide with panic and her breathing rapid. "I can't be here."

"I'll drive," Moira yanked the keys from Chase and wrapped herself around my girl.

"No. Don't go. We can talk this out," I begged.

"Talk to Chase," Lila said, flicking a wounded glare at my brother, who looked gutted. "And while y'all are talking behind my back, you can both bend over and kiss my ass."

"Lila...stop," my eyes went wide.

"You've. Done. Enough." Moira stopped me with a scowling disappointment I'd never seen before tonight–now I'd seen it twice. "I've got her, now."

60

LILA

MOIRA DROVE WHILE I replayed every brutal moment, minute by minute.

Sam's reaction to Moira's hit, the way he scrambled to explain, then blurted out the one thing I was starving for. He might not have cheated, but he'd betrayed me all the same. He called me the love of his life while confessing to a guttural invasion, and I couldn't reconcile it.

How did I not feel it when...how did I not know or...but then the aftercare?

Sam was always tender, loving, and, above all, thorough. Was that his way of hiding the evidence? I thought through each moment again and again, then rewound and played it back once more. Our relationship, our history, his confession, and each time, my understanding of the situation sank deeper into the abyss, even as Moira held my hand — silent comfort from someone as angry as I was.

I worried about her and Chase.

Would this be what broke their family?

"This is about Sam and me." It was suffocating. All of it. "I don't want you to be mad at–"

"Oh, don't worry about me and Chase," Moira said coolly. "He's in a heap of trouble, and he can stew in it, but right now," she squeezed my hand. "I'm here for you." Her kindness was too much; already halfway to forgiving the man she loved while holding me together in a solidarity of friendship that...

God, would I lose her, too?

On some level, I knew. I'm not an unintelligent woman. We were having way too much sex for any one couple without having 'the talk.' Body count, protection, consent, boundaries, STDs, these were all the important things I'd always talked about before taking a guy to bed. Yet it all just went out the window with Sam. He came careening into my hurricane and anchored me with sheer force of will, and at some point, in the wake of his arrival, I...let him.

I let him lead me.

I let him take care of me.

I let him be the hiding place for my pain.

I used him, and I didn't ask questions because I couldn't.

"Let's take a beat." Moira's voice broke me from my reverie, and I looked up to see us stopped in a parking lot. "You've been with Sam for weeks. I know the hurt of all this is raw and new, and you have valid feelings right now....but we need to put a bigger question to bed."

I looked out the side window and saw the pharmacy's sign.

"Let's buy a test and go from there. I'll go with you while you take it, and I'll read the results if it's too much." She squeezed my hands. "Whatever you need."

Holy shit, she was right. I could be pregnant already. I started doing period math and realized I had no idea when my period was due. My normal "clockwork" bloody-buddy had become increasingly unreliable since my family's murder.

"I never stopped to ask about the important shit...what the hell was I thinking?" I leaned forward until my head rested on the dashboard.

"Well," Moira gently rubbed my back and giggled. "You weren't."

"You're a helluva pep talk, you know that?" I said dryly.

"Sam wasn't the only avoiding responsible adulting." She sat back in the seat. "You and he are both... intense. And considering that Chase and I started in a burning building... that's saying something." Moira rubbed her hand down my back again, a gesture both kind and calming. "You've been grieving. Carrying so much for so long." Her kindness turned sing-songy as she continued. "So, this one itty bitty thing slipped your mind."

I turned to give her another questioning look.

"We'll call it a mulligan!" She grinned like I'd won a game of poker and not maybe created a whole-ass human.

"Oh my god, you're the most optimistic person I've ever met." An unbidden sardonic laugh huffed out of my lungs. "I might be pregnant, and you're calling it a mulligan?" She laughed, too, and before I knew it, we were both captured in peals of tear-inducing laughter.

"Come on, Hellcat." She nodded as she opened the door. "One step at a time. Let's go see if I get to be Auntie Moira."

WILDER FAMILY GROUP CHAT

-7-

Moira: We're at the pharmacy.

Me: Is she okay? Can I come there? Tell her I'm sorry!

TJ: I take it we have a situation.

Moira: Understatement.

TJ: I'm listening

Chase: The girls left.

TJ: To a pharmacy?

Me: I messed up … Bad.

Chase: They're both mad…Baby, please come back.

Moira: I'll deal with you later, Big Guy.

TJ: And the pharmacy?

Me: Oh god…is she?

Moira: We don't know. I convinced her to take a test. She's in the bathroom now.

Troy: Dear God!

Moira: I'll get her to come back. But we gotta finish this first.

Me: I should be there.

Moira: Give me time.

TJ: There is an element of security we should discuss.

Moira: Are you tracking us?

TJ: Trackers are on all the cars, yes.

Moira: So, do your cop thing...I'm focused on Lila.

Me: Jesus Fuck. Let me come there.

Moira: If you show up, I'll punch you in the nuts before she ever gets the chance!

Chase: Besides, Moira took the car seats. We're stuck.

Me: FUCK!

TJ: Sam, you can't keep her if she doesn't want to be kept.

Chase: He knows.

Me: I can't lose her!

Chase: We know.

Me: I fucked this up so bad.

Moira: Give us space. Let me work.

61

LILA

THE BATHROOM'S LINOLEUM FLOORS made a bleak backdrop for my task. Although the instructions were overly elaborate and felt daunting, the pictures were straightforward—pee on a stick—wait. Moira shoved a disposable cup at me, proclaiming, 'Trust me, the dip test must be easier if you are nervous.' Exiting the stall, I set the stick on the counter and washed my shaking hands, feeling like my world was knocked off its axis.

Seconds crept by as I sifted through each missed opportunity I had to take responsibility for myself. Instead, I recalled the hotel bathtub where Sam cared for me after I left the hospital. He was tender and caring as I sobbed out my tale—too exhausted to hide my emotions. His response... 'I'm glad you felt like you could share it with me...All I want to do is fix whatever is broken for you. I want to see that light come back on behind those gorgeous eyes of yours.... I'm all in.' How many times had he scooped me up, carved out a chunk of his world to keep my demons away, and what did I offer in return? Cold distance, a temper, and fuck all.

My timer buzzed—three minutes up—and I felt the weight of my next breath. I reached for the test but halted at a knock on the door.

"My timer just went off," I called to Moira; no doubt been pacing outside. I sighed in relief, flipping the lock, grateful I wasn't going to be alone for this. "I was about..."

My heart stopped as I stood face to face with the icy-blue eyes of my nightmares.

"No!" I reacted on instinct, fruitlessly shoving the door against the polished black shoe wedged into the opening.

"Now, now, Officer Rivera." Marcus Brinks' sugary drawl grated against the sneering venom in his eyes. "My apologies. It's just Delilah now, isn't it?" He took a half step forward, pushing into the ladies' room. "Shall we be friends...Little D." My stomach twisted at the overly enunciated nickname dripping from his thin, pale lips.

"H-How...did you find me?" I made the mistake of stepping back, searching for air that wouldn't carry his scent to my nose; instead, I let him grab my elbow. With a harsh jerk, he pulled me against his body, and my guts went watery.

"My dear," he leered at my breasts from under translucent, bushy eyebrows, reminding me I still wore my sparring clothes and nothing by way of protection. Close enough, his stubble grated my cheek, he whispered his oily truth in my ear. "What makes you think I ever lost you?"

Before I could so much as wretch, he yanked me from the bathroom, spinning me to face the drugstore from the back hallway, pressing against my body with one of his hands, clamping firmly against my mouth. I readied to throw my strength into escaping, but froze at the sight of Moira in front of me.

"Before you do anything rash," Marcus whispered in my ear. "Do consider."

Halfway down the baby aisle, Moira lifted newborn bibs and toys, smiling and taking pics on her phone, oblivious to the man standing beyond her who made my blood run cold.

Tall and grizzled, with a salt-stubbled beard, he had slicked-back dark hair that barely hid a gnarly scar on his forehead. He wore a dingy grey t-shirt and a biker jacket with worn edges. In his hand, he twirled a single white rose, while eyefucking Moira's spandex-clad backside.

No...God no!

I thrashed, flinging out my hands and feet to run to her, to spare her from the man of *her* nightmares...Dean Jensen.

Alive. Here.

"Fear not, my associate has a flair for dramatics, but even the wildest of dogs can be trained."

Moira texted someone and then glanced at her watch. Any minute, she'd turn and see him, and her world would come crashing down, and I was helpless to stop it. Marcus removed his hand, resting it against my throat in an unspoken threat–My silence for her safety.

"It would be a shame if her husband arrived a hair too late to save her from being ravaged the way I know my hound would like...now wouldn't it?"

"Ok," I dug my nails into the arm of his black wool trench coat. "I'll go with you, just...let her go."

"Like I said," Marcus gave a self-satisfied huff. "Even the wildest of bitches can be trained."

Whatever signal he gave, Jensen scowled at before slipping around the outer aisle and walking past Moira. As he neared us, Marcus jerked my hair, spinning my whole body towards the pharmacy's emergency exit. When we hit the fading daylight and the door clicked shut, I threw everything I had into a heel slam—my only shot.

Cursing, Marcus shoved me, scattering me to the ground. I scrambled to run—to flee—when a boot came down and the world went black.

WILDER FAMILY GROUP CHAT

-8-

Moira: 911⊠

TJ: Report.

Moira: She's gone.

Chase: Chief and Carol are almost here—we're coming.

Moira: There's no time. She's in danger.

Me: Danger? She didn't run? What the actual fuck?!

Moira: I went to check on her—she was gone. She left the pregnancy test... and on the floor was a white rose.

Chase: Baby—don't follow her. Please.

Moira: a WHITE. ROSE.

TJ: I'm en route.

Moira: It's Dean. I know it. I can't let him hurt her.

Me: Moira...Wait.

Moira: I won't leave her with that bastard.

Chase: Goddammit, STOP—I'm coming!

TJ: Sister...Do. Not. Do this.

Moira: Track me, Troy. I'm going.

Chase: No!

Me: MOIRA!

Chase: BABY!

62

LILA

*A*TTENTION ALL UNITS, ATTENTION *all units.*
This is Central Dispatch with a final call.

It is with great sadness that we mark the End of Watch for two of our own: Officer Jesse Rivera and Sergeant Dominic Rivera. Both officers made the ultimate sacrifice in the line of duty, serving their community with courage and honor.

Officer Jesse Rivera—your tour is complete. You are now 10-42. Rest easy, your brothers and sisters in blue have the watch from here.

Sergeant Dominic Rivera—you are 10-42. We thank you for your years of unwavering service and leadership. You will never be forgotten.

Gentlemen, your dedication, bravery, and sacrifice will echo through this department forever. In your honor, we now observe a moment of silence.

...

Thank you, Officer and Sergeant Rivera.

May you rest in peace.

Central Dispatch, clear.

Sorrow beyond words shredded my heart as agony sliced through my shoulders.

My head was thick, heavier than a hangover, and slow.

My eyes wanted to open, but my brain couldn't find the switch.

Distant voices murmured, but they weren't Sam.

Sam wouldn't be far away.

Unless Sam wasn't here.

No... I'd left Sam.

Sam.

Sam!

Adrenaline lifted the fog, bringing echoes of the boot and a hair tugging on dried blood at my temple. Struggling to clear the cobwebs, my father's voice took center stage in my mind. *'When you're in a jam, baby girl, go back to basics.'*

Opening my eyes a fraction, I saw my hair curtaining my face in privacy.

Basics... Right... what do I see? I can see my lap...because my head is hanging forward. I flexed what muscles I could and assessed my body, noting the cold, metal chair I sat in. Tugging my hands, I felt the burn of bindings and fresh shoulder pain.

I'm half tied up, but it doesn't feel like metal handcuffs...it's not rope....

Not moving my head, I took in what I could–dingy concrete floor, my chair bolted to it. I carefully dragged my feet, just an inch.

My feet aren't tied up. That's good...I can use that.

Mental clarity made the mumbled voices clearer. I recognized the louder of the two. Brinks's words were short and clipped. He sounded furious that Jensen screwed up.

So they're here, and I'm here. Where is here?

I could smell a familiar tang of salt and grease. It was nauseatingly persistent, like leftover fried cheese and warm beer—a disgusting reminder of bar bender dieting before Sam's parade of healthy, home-cooked meals.

Sam. Sam. Sam.—how much I'd changed since the first time he'd hauled me over his shoulder at Marge's, just to have his way...

A flash of recognition snapped me back.

I'd seen this dingy concrete twice, hanging upside down as Sam hauled me out of a brawl.

I was at Marge's!

Tugging at my arms again, a dull ache dug into my breast. I'd tucked my cell phone into my sports bra at the pharmacy—they never searched me.

I have a phone....that's very good!

The minuscule amount of things going in my favor was enough to chase away fear and get my brain focusing on what I could control.

Yes, Marcus Brinks found me, but I was away from Sam.

I traded myself for Moira, so she was safe.

I was alone and unarmed, but there were only two of them.

I had my wits, my feet, and if I could work a hand-free, a cell phone.

One free hand—that's all I need to call for help.

Slowly, I twisted my hands. Whatever was holding me was thin, smooth, and pliable. My guess was plastic zip-ties. Tough to stretch, but not impossible. I began slowly, one hand at a time, pulling until the burn was intense before switching. If I could loosen them even slightly, that would be enough. I could fire off a text, and Sam could track my location and -

"Well now, lookie who's awake." A man's voice I didn't recognize waltzed over, his thick black boots stopping at my feet.

The boots...I recognized.

"Seems little Miss Detective was eavesdropping, boss." He fisted the back of my hair, snapping my head back so hard I cried out at the pain in my neck. "You know you're in a fuckload of trouble." He emphasized 'fuckload' by jerking my hair.

Double vision rode in on a wave of nausea.

"Doesn't look like much, does she?" Jensen was so close, all I could see or smell was the cheap liquor fogging out my oxygen. "Kind of a tiny little thing...tits aside."

Arrogance dripped from his whole body, and I recognized his type: guys who assumed they were bigger and brighter because they had a dick. Their downfall was always ego — One shot, and they'd unravel like fragile babies.

"Underestimating me was your first limp-dick mistake." My voice was barely audible, strained with my neck pulled tight, but I pushed on. "Moira told me how pathetic you were in the rack, too." His eyes darkened. I'd hit a nerve. "Said you couldn't find the G-spot with a fucking road map."

Jensen, predictably, reared back to take a swing at me, and I clenched my eyes tight.

"Dean. No!" Moira's voice cracked my heart, distracting Jensen mid-swing.

No, no, no, how was she here?

"I need that one." Brinks' voice surged like a dry heave. "Contain your baser urges until I am done with her."

If I'd had anything in my stomach, I would have lost it on the spot. As it was, my stomach convulsed enough that Jensen stepped back in disgust.

"Whoa, boss...she really doesn't like you." Jensen released my hair, giving me my first full view of my location.

Emptied of dining and pool tables, Scaled Back was a shell holding only the barstools on which Moira was perched and a few chairs. Tear-streaked, pony-tail half undone, Moira appeared largely unharmed.

Next to her stood Marcus Brinks, shining like an evil new penny. His crisp black suit cut a dark stain against his pale, wraith-like appearance. I wondered if today was the day I'd finally catch him in the act—hands dirty.

"You greasy piece of shit," I tugged against my restraints as I spat at Brinks. "You said you'd let her go if I came quietly. We had a deal!" Brinks flicked an annoyed glance at Jensen, and I realized then what he was so pissed about. The tiniest weak spot I didn't miss. "Or did your dog disobey his master?"

If I get the two of them bickering, Moira could make a run for it. The insult landed, evident by the swift backhand Jensen delivered before again fisting my hair to spit his tantrum in my ear.

"You're not in much of a position to be mouthy now, are you, sweetheart?" He twisted my face and slammed his mouth against mine so hard my lip split between our teeth.

"Enough, you idiot!" Brinks snapped. "Control this one and let me deal with the wayward Ms. Rivera."

Brinks shoved Moira off her stool so hard she fell sprawling at my feet. Scrambling to her knees, she flung her arms around me, burying her face into my neck.

"The guys know," she whispered, seconds before Jensen dragged her to a second bolted chair, zip-ties at the ready.

How much they knew...she couldn't say.

"Kinda feels like old times, doesn't it, baby-mama?" Jensen preened, securing Moira's wrists.

"Only if you have a camera to capture your impotence." Moira sneered. "Too bad you won't get to add this to your spank bank, eh...beta?"

Atta girl–fuck him.

"That's right. I almost forgot." I let a smirk lift the corner of my mouth. "You let a pregnant woman put you in a coma." I snickered before adding. "While cuffed to a chair and surrounded by fire!" I barked out a laugh to Brinks, "This is the dog you leashed to do your bidding?" Genuinely, another laugh bubbled up at Jensen's appalled expression. "Kinda seems like you're scraping the bottom of the barrel."

"Goddamn, you and your whore mouth!" Dean reared back, and I prepared to see stars.

"Enough." Marcus's voice was calm and steady, but tinged with violence enough to halt Jensen's assault. "I advise you to keep your mouth shut, Ms. Rivera."

"I mean, I could," I gave a disinterested shrug, tugging again at my bonds, "but you'd read the subtitles on my face."

Brinks' eyes flashed something akin to amusement.

Good. Notice my face, not my hands, you evil prick.

"My but this past year has changed you, Ms. Rivera." The soles of his glossy black shoes echoed as he stalked closer. "You always had admirable tenacity, but this fiery temper is new."

"Yeah, well, you're not the same person you were a year ago either. You're an even bigger asshole now."

I gave the bar a once-over, shifting my weight around restraints that sang of busted blood vessels and bruising. Knowing that the guys were coming, I threw a careful curveball to buy more time.

"I wouldn't put much stock in your interior decorating career, though." I cocked an eyebrow at him and took my shot. "Maybe stick to Internal Affairs."

Only the near-imperceptible twitch of his lip, the barest second of his body going stiff as a corpse, told me I'd hit a nerve.

"Hm." His thin lips pressed into a tight smile, completing his psychotic facade as he crouched, eye to eye with me. "Gone is the girl concerned with making good marks for her captain."

"Fuck you." I drawled. "People's approval was never my concern." I was feigning more confidence than I felt to keep him focused on my face, and not my hands, which twisted and tugged at the slow-yielding ties.

"What do you want with us?" Moira cut in.

Brinks never let his eyes leave mine as he answered.

"I'd very much like you both dead." The casual threat sent a chill down my spine. "You've caused unacceptable shipping delays. It's costing us a fortune."

Easy murder.

Cool delivery

"You won't touch us!" I said it for Moira's benefit more than mine as I tried to work out what Brinks wasn't saying. "We're married to the entire town's emergency services."

"You think I won't off you right here, bitch?" Jensen snarled, yanking Moira's hair.

Seriously, did this guy get his jollies from hair-pulling?

"Ya know, the minuscule amount of thought I've given to anything you might do got lost somewhere between 'I don't know' and 'I don't give a fuck'." I let myself enjoy Jensen's insulted expression for a heart-beat, then returned to Marcus with an eye roll. "Could you at least spare me the beta's stupidity? I mean, seriously. That waste of skin is likely the real reason your shipments have been fucked."

It was clear Brinks held no love for Dean Jensen. I worked that angle in hopes that one of them might spill details we could use to nail Apex to the wall.

"You bitch!" Jensen roared, but Marcus silenced him with a raised brow. A terrifying display of the control that sent a shiver skittering down my spine. If Marcus had this much control over someone as violent as Jensen, what else was he capable of?

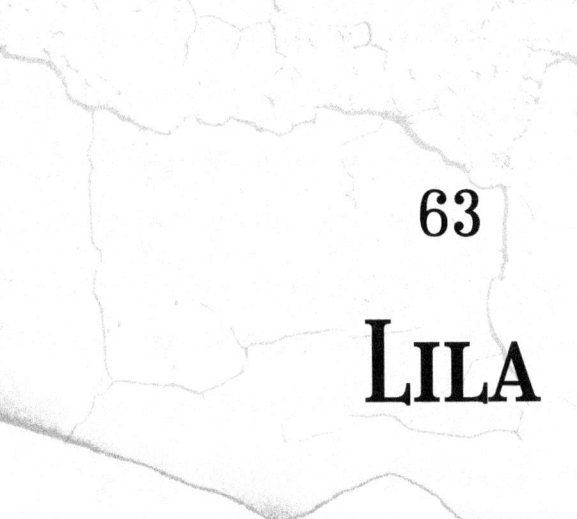

63

LILA

"H IS METHODS ARE CRUDE, but he has his uses." Brinks smiled at Moira before glancing again at Jensen. "Thanks to your little coma, I've secured a ghost for behind-the-scenes work."

"You're a monster." Moira spat.

Brinks shrugged, flicking invisible lint from his sleeve.

"Though you've created a bit of a kink in my plans for this town, so general annoyance aside, I'll need to be smart about your removal." His hand slowly reached forward, tenderly stroking a strand of my hair behind my ear, then caressing my cheek. Whispering so only I could hear him, he breathed, "You always were smart for such a looker." I could taste his cologne in my mouth, but before I could formulate words past the bile in my throat, he shoved his hand between my breasts and yanked out my cell phone.

I was a fool.

So focused on riling up Jensen, working my hands free, I failed to notice my cell phone had become visible. One moment of distraction cost me a major advantage. Now I could only watch as he paced between Moira and me, slapping the phone against his palm in contemplation.

"Jensen," *thwack*. "In your time with the mother of your children," *thwack*, "did she strike you as a good liar?"

thwack

"Moira here? Naw. She's a good girl, isn't that right, sweetheart." Jensen tenderly stroked her cheek with the back of his hand. "She's got no poker face."

thwack

The quivering of her chin belied the ferocious anger in her eyes. Hold onto that anger, girl. Keep your power.

"Yes." *thwack* Brinks sneered at Moira, as if noticing filth on the ground. "Does seem a bit mousey, doesn't she?" *Thwack*. "So then, it'll be you, Ms. Rivera." *Thwack*. "You will call the Wilders and tell them you've left for good."

The noise stopped.

He flicked an eye to Moira.

"Her, too. Get them off your tracks...and sell it, my dear." Brinks pulled out his phone and swiped to the photos. "Far more than your life depends on it."

My heart stopped.

There were photos of Chase, Sam, and Troy–Pictures of them at work and working out at the gym, Moira at yoga, and Chase at the fire station. He had snapshots of Sam and me at the bar, the Cabin, in the hot tub.

378

A sob escaped me when he slipped to a photo of the babies — going to the pediatrician, cuddling their mother at a yoga class, being proudly shown around the fire station.

All of them, now, in the crosshairs of a man I brought here.

"How?" I couldn't contain my shock. "WHEN?" I was meticulous in my research, taking care not to leave a trail.

Brink's looked practically giddy.

"You've known where I was this whole time?"

"I admit I momentarily lost you. But then Sgt. Wilder accessed your employment record. As the respected IA agent who fired you, I was notified. Then there was the liquor store receipt..." I closed my eyes at my stupidity. I used my credit card that night.

I had done this to all of them. I drew the devil straight to me, and Sam, and his family. I looked to Moira, her face twisted in terror as Marcus showed her the photos, too.

"I'm sorry." I cried to her, but she was shaking her head, lost in terror only a mother could know, and Marcus's sneering face said he knew just how much it tortured me.

"I am so *very* glad you are here, now." My skin crawled at the familiar phrase.

"You sent those flowers?" The delivery I had thought was from Sam was nothing more than an arrogant bait meant to tease or terrorize. "Okay. I'll call them. But you promise to let the girls go...let all of them go." Marcus didn't bother answering beyond a half-tilted smirk as he pocketed his phone.

"Now, which brother shall we dial?" He flipped my phone to my face for unlocking, and swiped the contacts open.

Chase would be unhinged over his wife's disappearance.

Troy would be in unrelenting cop mode.

But.... Sam.

I trusted them all, but Sam was the one I wanted...needed.

The one I trusted to hear what I wasn't saying enough to catch a secret message, maybe.

"Call Sam," I began formulating a plan. "We're temporary as is. I can sell him on my leaving."

64

SAM

G LARING RED AND BLUE lights surrounded the pharmacy by the
time Chase and I arrived. We slammed the car into park, and Troy
met us at the door. Chase blew past him, busting into the pharmacy
screaming Moira's name.

"Where is she?" I bellowed, but before Troy could respond, Chase
ran back out.

"Where the fuck is my wife!" He screamed at everyone—a sentiment
I viscerally understood.

"Brother." Troy held up her cell phone, and Chase's face went white.
"We found this near the back exit."

"No. Not again. No!" Chase took the phone, staring as if it held every
answer in the universe; his face was a ball of fury.

I was right behind him.

Tracking that phone was our only hope of finding Moira, and I was
kicking myself for not having tracking on Lila's phone.

"TJ, give me something...anything." Running my hands through my hair, my heart pounded out a rhythm I'd never felt. "You have other trackers, right?" Panic, adrenaline, and a deep-seated rage begged for violence.

"I had the car and cell phone both tracked to here." Troy raised his phone, GPS icons blinking at our current location. "And here they both are."

"I can't... Oh god." Chase bent at the waist, the hood of Troy's car keeping him from collapsing entirely. "I can't lose her again..." Troy was stoic, but I saw the hurt in his eyes as he rested his hand on Chase's shoulder.

"There's an APB on Jensen, Brinks, and the car Lila discovered in her work. The entire town is looking." Troy looked at me, with as much resigned anger as I'd seen him wear in a long time. "All we can do now is wait."

His face lost all the cop-cool he usually wore.

He was just my brother.

"Jesus fuck. TJ. You don't understand." My voice was unrecognizable. "They were here because of me. I did this. I..." I swallowed the choking panic–the world felt too hot. "She's my.... everything...and she might have my baby...fuck, TJ...." I couldn't get enough air, and it was all too loud, too big. "I can't lose them!"

"I don't think you caused this," Troy rested his other hand on me, and I was never more grateful for his presence as I felt the world closing around us. "The girls stepped out and were suddenly taken? It doesn't track."

"They were already here." Chase scratched out, wiping his eyes and standing straight. "Moira said there were roses. Jensen was waiting on them."

"A white rose was in the bathroom," TJ nodded. "Another in the aisle."

"Roses?" I pulled the florist card from my pocket and handed it over. "I saw some in Lila's office before we left. I was so focused on finding her, I hadn't had a chance to look into it. Dammit!"

"Courtesy of The Apex Society." Troy read the typed message on the back before reading the handwritten message on the front. "This was Brinks?"

"That's Jensen's trick," Chase wiped his face on the sleeve of his shirt. "He always sent roses to Moira. It's how she knew he was in the house that night." A sob broke through. "Jensen's got her, Sam...again."

I didn't know what to do other than hug my brother...so I did. Every ounce of his words in my soul felt the earth-shattering weight of what we'd lost.

I had done this.

Even if Jensen and Brinks knew where they were beforehand, I had crossed a line with Lila and, in her justified anger, she bolted and took Moira with her. My brother's wife, the mother of his children, and the love of my life and possibly the mother of my baby, were both gone, and it was my fault.

"I gotta fix this," I looked at Troy over Chase's shoulder. "I gotta do something." Taking the keys from Chase, I walked back to the car.

"You cannot drive like this," Troy grabbed my arm.

"I can't sit and do nothing!" I yelled as Chase rounded to the passenger side. "You have the pharmacy on lockdown, and APBs everywhere?" Troy nodded. "I'm trusting you to let me know the second they find anything."

"You know I will," Troy answered quickly.

"We'll check the old haunts—places Lila might've run, or Jensen might've reused."

It took all of two seconds for Troy to see our resolve before he released me.

"Be careful, brothers."

Chase and I peeled out as I was pulled between blind panic and wrenching guilt. I knew Chase was revisiting old ghosts that threatened to ruin him on a base level. I wanted to apologize, but no words felt adequate, so like a coward, I drove in silence.

Until he spoke.

"You didn't do this." Chase's unearned mercy cut deep.

"I never thought my shit would roll into you and Moira. You gotta know - "

"I do." Chase cut me off. "Moira and I are okay...or we would've - "

"You will be." I stopped that dark train of thought in its tracks. "We'll find them. They can't have more than half an hour lead. Your wife already hospitalized Jensen once, and my Lila is ferocious. No way they're making this easy on–"

My cell phone rang...and I nearly ran off the road.

65

LILA

I HELD MY BREATH as Brinks opened my phone's contacts.

"Let her go," I pleaded, cutting my eyes to Moira. "She's innocent in all–"

"Not a chance," Jensen interrupted with a fresh tug on her hair and a hand over her mouth. "We got plans, don't we, sweetheart?" I closed my eyes to block out her tears. My mind went to work.

They knew we'd been taken—but how much more, I didn't know. I had to convince Brinks that I was following orders, while also letting Sam know our location. But if Sam let on they were looking for us, we were as good as dead–Brinks in the wind long before the cavalry arrived.

"Make it count," Brinks put the phone on speaker.

It rang only once.

"Lila, Baby, Jesus!" Sam was frantic.

"Stop talking!" I paused a half second, my mind moving 90 miles an hour. "Listen to me." I kept my tone as level and commanding as possible.

"I can't do this shit anymore. Not you, not us, not even your fucking family. I'm out."

"Lila, you don't - "

"I said stop talking, Jackass." I couldn't give Sam an inch that might give us all away. "This is your problem. You never shut up and listen." Sam always listened. Please, baby, hear me now. "Let me talk for a change."

"Fine." I could hear his teeth grinding. "Talk."

"You and your brothers, you've gotta good thing going in this town. But frankly, it's just a-fuckin'-lot." I strained to keep emotion out of my words despite my heart breaking. I was signing my death warrant if this failed–Moira's too.

"Keep. Talking." Sam clipped out.

There...my words from before...did he understand?

"And all this shit you have been throwing at me, the shooting range, the double dates, the hot tub...I see through you." I huffed a laugh to sell it for Brinks. "You three go to the gym together and the store together, and there isn't any room for anyone else in your little trio, is there?" I quickly added. "And I don't have time for the fuckery of asshats, Samson."

That throwback to our first meeting, and the clue to my location, all wrapped up in the use of the full name he shared with me that first night. Brinks jerked his head towards Moira, reminding me of my secondary task.

"And poor Moira, you guys sold her on the whole picket fence, but she isn't cut out for it." Jensen shook his head; not buying it. "Orphans rarely make good mothers, Sam."

Moira whimpered–I broke her heart.

"Lila. Don't go like this." Sam didn't sound hurt; he sounded murderous. "We've gotten so close...baby, we're...so...close." His words felt oddly spaced, and I hoped they were a clue.

Brinks twirled his finger for me to wrap it up.

"No, Sam. We're not close, we're through. Tell Chase not to bother looking for Moira either. She and I... we're gone."

Brinks ended the call, slammed the phone to the concrete, and stomped it to pieces.

66

SAM

CHASE PUT MY PHONE on speaker, texting Troy in his other
hand, while I skid to a stop. I barely contained myself, but
Lila cut me short each time I spoke. I expected her to sound sad or
scared, but all I got was pissed.

Something more was going on.

Chase heard it too, nodding at me to keep her talking as he texted
Troy. I tried to piece together what I knew had to be clues. I kept
getting pulled to that first night, when she'd blown into my life and
changed me forever. God, how I loved my life with her in it.

I couldn't lose her.

Her final line, insulting Moira as a mother, sealed it for me —
the whole call was a trick. Still, her words cut deep, and Chase's face
was carved in rage. I snatched the phone before he said something
we'd regret.

"Jesus fuck. Lila. Don't go like this. We've gotten so close...baby, we're...so...close.." I tried to keep her talking, hoping for more clues, while telling her we were searching for them.

"No, Sam. We're not close, we're through. Tell Chase not to bother looking for Moira either. She and I... we're gone."

The phone went dead.

Chase stared at the phone in abject terror.

"No. No. No! Where are you?" He screamed, frantically hitting the redial button, but it went straight to voicemail. "FUCK!" Chase lost it–screaming, thrashing, slamming his hands against the dash.

"Wait a minute," I yelled over my brother's hurt, trying to piece clues together.

"Where's my wife, Sam?"

"I think she tried to tell us!" I shouted at him. "Call Troy!" Chase dialed, holding his shaking phone between us.

"What do you know?" Troy answered.

"They called. They're alive, but Lila played angry–I think she tried to throw Jensen off, but I can't figure out the clues," I said.

"SitRep," Troy commanded–Marine Corps shorthand rising.

"She said she was leaving me 'cause we were all too much." I started. "She listed the shooting range, our double date with Chase and Moira, and our time in the hot tub," I added quickly. "All things BEFORE today's fight."

"And outside... She'd been followed?" Troy confirmed. "Hence the flowers."

"But she mentioned us three at the gym, and other random shit," I added.

"Perhaps we've been surveilled as well," Troy interjected. His words made sense; the calm and level one between us. I trusted his gut. "What else?'

"She said something... It's important, I think." My hands hurt from gripping the steering wheel. "She said, 'I don't have time for the fuckery of asshats.'"

"A Lila turn-of-phrase if she was good and mad," Troy said. "What else?"

"She said Moira hated being a mother," Chase spat. "She wanted to leave me."

"Bullshit," Troy said quickly.

"We know," I said. "But they're together."

"So, they're alive, together, feigning anger at the lot of us and trying to say they don't want to be found." Troy summarized. "But a bar-brawl quip is the lynchpin you think is key here?"

"Bar brawl!" Everything clicked into place. "Troy, you're a fucking genius!" I slammed the car into drive, spraying rocks behind me.

"You're moving. Where to?" Troy asked, his car door slamming in the background.

"She's at Marge's." I slammed my hands against the steering wheel, angry at the precious minutes lost. "Fuckery of asshats. Jesus, it's from shit-fisted Carl and the night we met. FUCK, and she called me Samson. Goddammit, TJ... She's at Scaled Back!"

She knew I'd remember that night.

She was counting on it...counting on me.

"I'm 15 minutes out," Troy's siren sounded. "Wait for me."

"No fucking chance," Chase barked, hanging up the phone. "Haul ass!"

67

LILA

"**I** DID WHAT YOU asked." I twisted my wrists, pushing past all pain.

I laid out every clue I could think of for Sam, hoping he'd find us in time. But if he didn't, my next best option was to free my hands and fight our way out.

"Do what you want with me, but let her go. I've been the pain in your ass for so long, you'll have more fun with me anyway, right?" I sneered at Marcus, playing off his earlier remark.

"No!" Moira barked. "We stick toge–" Jensen jerked Moira's head back with a yelp.

"That's enough outta you, sweetheart." He salivated at her tits as he spoke. "You're in a heap of trouble as it is." Releasing her head with a grunt, he turned to Brinks. "How 'bout you and I work out our issues with these two, then deposit their bodies for the Wilders." Jensen huffed a laugh at me, clicking his belt free. "Maybe face down in a hot tub for Loverboy."

"You're a dumbass prick." I snapped, catching a glimpse of Moira, who gave Jensen a defiant glare.

"Why do you think he was just the lapdog?" Moira snarled. "All bark... no brains."

"Enough!" Brinks snapped, pulling his phone from his pocket. "This must be handled delicately as they are embroiled with local civics in a very family way." He flicked his eyes at me with a look of pure disgust. "I need to make a call." He dialed a number, walked into the front office, and closed the door behind him.

I never saw the test results in the bathroom. Did Brinks?

Is that why he looked so disgusted when he said, 'family way'?

Or was it that I lived with Sam, and Moira was married to Chase?

I looked down at my belly, wondering for the first time if I had a tiny passenger on board—created from me and Sam. Someone who hadn't asked to be here, but who needed me, nonetheless.

"Marcus ain't around to hold me back now, is he, sweetheart?" Jensen gave Moira's face a gentle caress with one hand while the other grazed between her thighs.

"You're the reason God created the middle finger." She spat.

"More like a walking example of what happens when Plan B fails." I chimed in, feeling my wrists move in their binds. "If only your mother had swallowed."

"I don't think hanging around that one has been good for your attitude." Jensen straddled Moira's legs, crushing her under his weight. His proximity forced her head back, and he took full advantage, cupping her breasts with a squeeze that had to hurt. "Even with little Miss

Kickboxing's training, you haven't snapped back from my babies, but I'm loving these new tits."

"Get a tissue, dickwad." He turned his ugly face towards me. "You've got a little bullshit on your cheek." He rolled off Moira, slowing my efforts with my restraints.

I was so close to slipping one hand free, but he stepped too close to risk it yet.

"Maybe I need to teach you the same lesson I gave Moira, about how men expect to be treated." He stalked over to the bar, slipping his gun into the back of his pants. Lifting a bottle of unlabeled hooch, he filled two shot glasses to the brim, shooting one back with a hiss from the cheap swill's burn. Based on the smell I enjoyed earlier, those weren't his first shots, and I hoped he'd drunk enough to make a mistake.

Unfortunately, this shot made him brave, and he strolled towards me, loosening his pants.

"No thanks," I sniped. "I'm not into limp pity fucks."

"You say that now," he said as he moved so close I could smell the dank musk wafting off his pathetic package when he tugged it out and started stroking the flaccid tag of flesh.

"Leave her alone, Dean!" Moira's shout drew his attention, and I lunged at the only thing I could reach.

Slipping one wrist free, I flung my hand forward and grabbed hold of his balls, fingers wrapping the sack as all five of my nails dug into his flesh. My hand his cage, I felt the sinew of him shift as my nails clamped down. Dean's eyes popped wide open as he gaped down at me, fists drawing back to punch me until I squeezed.

He froze.

"Gimme your gun," I slipped my other hand free and held it palm up, ignoring the agony shooting down my arms.

Jensen gaped at the hand locked around his package, rivulets of blood seeping around my nails as I let them slice into the leathery skin of his sack. I loved the powershift of his panic, but Marcus could return at any second.

"Come on, asswipe," I tugged at him, digging my nails deeper. "Work those few remaining brain cells." He released a squeak of pain. "Gun...now...or I start popping grapes."

Jensen's hands shook as he slowly brought his gun around and laid it in my hand.

"Good dog," I stood slowly, forcing him a step back. My arms shook, and I doubted I could keep a steady aim, but his balls made a nice leash. I shoved the gun into my pants and commanded, "Now, you're gonna set Moira free."

"You....bi - " Another squeeze silenced the insult, and gifted me his tears.

"You this dumb on purpose?" I led him to Moira by his bloody nutsack, then tightened my grip. "Cut her loose or sing soprano." Jensen crept along, tears and snot streaming as he pulled a pocket-knife from his pants. I glanced at the office door—we were on borrowed time.

Snatching the knife, I gave Jensen's jewels a crushing squeeze. A split second of meaty resistance gave way to a grainy pop as something crumbled inside, sending the sleaze heaving wordlessly to the ground.

"We gotta run." I cut Moira loose. "I don't know if Sam got my clues."

"They were good clues." She pulled at her ties as I snipped the first one. "And Lila?" Her piercing look halted me for a split second. "I know you didn't mean those things you said about me and the girls." My heart lunged into my throat at her swift forgiveness, and I couldn't help but pull her into a brief hug.

"Let's ya-ya this sisterhood back home. We gotta - " Fire flashed across my scalp as my head snapped back.

The knife went scattering as searing pain shot down my neck.

"Ah ah ah, Ms. Rivera." Brinks pulled my hair until I strained up to my tiptoes. "I step away for a moment, and you start misbehaving."

I pulled the gun from my pants, but he grabbed my hand and twisted until the skin on my wrist burned and my palm slowly opened. Then, so quick I struggled to follow his movement, he snatched the gun and yanked my hand to spin me around—a sickening pop brutalizing my wrist.

"Making an even bigger mess of my plans now?" Brinks gripped my throat as Moira screamed, scrambling to get her other hand loose from her chair.

"Revenge...not my plan..." I clawed at his fingers with my one good hand, the other throbbing uselessly against my chest. "You'll fuck yourself...on your own."

I tried to kick at him, but he squeezed tighter.

My brain screamed for oxygen.

"Seeing as you lost me my faithful dog," He sneered at Jensen, whimpering in a pool of vomit. My field of vision narrowed. "Seems disposal of you two will be wholly on me before I can move to more lucrative prey." He pulled me so close that the moist taste of him coated my tongue when he hissed. "Though I confess, I find myself inclined to enjoy the process before moving to clean-up."

"You bastard, you're killing her!" Moira shouted from somewhere far away.

Brinks pulled me against him, his grip on my throat loosening enough for the tunnel vision to recede as air seeped in and I registered the unmistakable pressure of a growing hard-on.

"One last hurrah before this bachelor ties the knot." His mouth came down on me, reopening my split lip as my stomach lurched hot sick up my nose. If Marcus noticed the tang of vomit, he never showed it as he tongued my bleeding lip and squeezed my throat again.

Just enough air to stay awake–but not to fight.

My feet barely touched the floor.

My broken arm throbbed.

Tears blurred my vision.

Moira's screams faded.

I was lost.

I hunted this monster for so long and failed so hard. I dragged Sam—and maybe our baby—into the fallout. But I could see my dad and brother again.

Darkness pressed around me with a roar.

68

SAM

MARCUS BRINKS' CAR SAT in Scaled Back's parking lot. Slow rolling past, I circled the long way around, parking near the rear exit. Before the wheels stopped turning, Chase lunged for the door, and I grabbed for him.

"We gotta be smart here." I understood his panic, but we needed reason. "We don't know if they're armed, or where the girls are." I reached back and pulled Marge's baseball bat from the back seat. "This is all we got."

"I can't wait around for the cops," Chase snapped.

"Agreed," I nodded, releasing his arm. "But I'll go through here," I tipped my chin at the back door. "I know where Marge kept the hide-a-key for deliveries. You take the front. If they try to make a run for it, you put those muscles to good use and - "

"Oorah?" Chase held out a fist.

"Oorah."

The key was hidden in a pile of crates stacked off to the side. Working quickly, I unlocked the door, slipped inside, and closed the door painstakingly slow to avoid the metal hinges screeching. Once inside, I maneuvered through the darkened storeroom towards the sounds of scuffling. My anxiety ratcheted up when I heard Lila's voice, and I quickened my steps to the blackout curtain separating the storeroom from the bar.

"You bastard, you're killing her!" Moira's cry made my blood run cold. Caution gone, I stepped out just in time to see Marcus Brinks grabbing Lila.

Grabbing Lila and kissing her.

Holding my Lila by the throat.

Choking my Lila.

All higher brain functions ceased.

Pure, unadulterated rage surged, and time stopped.

Marcus was a dead man walking.

I loosed a primal scream as I charged, causing Marcus to release my girl. Lila grasped her throat, panting, but alive. He swung an arm out from behind her, pointing at me, but I didn't stop. Swinging Marge's bat, I put all my weight into targeting the bastard's head. Something sharp bit at my side, shoving me down to the right, but I didn't stop. This man deserved no mercy. Rage fueled my slightly off-balance run, but I swung with everything I had in me.

I missed my mark, but hit the target.

Marcus got to keep his head, but he'd never walk on those knees again.

I hit the floor at the same time he did, already planning my next strike, as his head bounced off the concrete with a satisfying crack. Only when his eyes darted away from mine did I notice a gun sliding into my periphery.

"Sam! Sam!" Scratchy and hoarse, my Lila called me. "Jesus, Sam!"

She crawled in a limping triad, past a busted bottle of some foul brown liquor, her hand tucked beneath her. I needed to assess her injuries, but my body wouldn't move.

"Baby," I cupped her face in my hands. "You're hand, baby, what did he do to you?"

"Oh my god...Sam." So beautiful, my Lila. "You're bleeding!"

"I ain't afraid to bleed for what I love, baby." I stared into her wild and fiery eyes, which were so gorgeous even when crying. "I love you, Hellcat." I took in her head and her lip, and fresh anger pushed me to try and rise again. "You're head...I need to - "

"Lila!" Moira's voice cut through my fog. "I can't reach the gun."

When Lila shifted, I saw Moira held in place, one hand still tied to a chair. She stretched to reach a gun, but didn't see Jensen dragging himself toward her. I tried to lift again, frustrated that I couldn't.

"Look-out!" I shouted as Jensen grasped her ankle, clawing up her body as she thrashed and kicked.

I had to get up...to help...but my muscles wouldn't obey.

"Sam. No. You've been shot. You can't." Following my girl's eyes, I looked down and realized what was holding me down. Lila leaned all her weight on my side, blood leaking from between her fingers. The lack of pain was a bad sign.

"No!" Chase's roar rattled the walls.

He yanked Jensen back, screaming a rage I hadn't heard since that day he mowed the guy down in the pharmacy parking lot. Straddling the man, Chase rained punches down, punctuating his words with each blow.

"You." slam "Won't" slam "Touch." slam "Her." slam "Again!"

The wet crunch of splintering bone sang as Chase unleashed months of pent-up guilt into the monster who truly deserved it.

Oorah.

"Chase!" Moira screamed. "Chase...you got him! Baby, stop!" Chase paused long enough to take in the bloodied mess below him, then turned to his wife. "Come here, Big Guy, get me off this chair." Her command got him moving. "My hero."

He cut her free, pulling her into his lap, kneeling like a man at the end of himself as he pulled her arms and legs around him–his face buried in his wife's chest in a muffled cry.

I wanted to feel Lila around me.

"See, baby," My head lolled back to the concrete. "I told you...we've got you. We'll always have you."

"Sam. I don't know what to do. Tell me what to do!"

She was crying, and she sounded terrified.

I wanted to make her feel safe....I just needed to rest for a minute.

"Sam...Samson...LUMBERJACK?"

The floor was fucking cold. It was making me tired.

"No, no, no...STAY...Tell me what to do!"

I gazed up at her–loved, and lucky, and at peace with her hands on me.

"Come on, Jackass. Be that smug EMT guy!"

Something in her tone called to me– the fog lifted. She needed EMT Sam.

"My bag...in the car," I glanced at the blood on her hands.

"I can't leave. You're bleeding too much." Lila's voice cracked. "Chase!"

"Pressure," I answered, pain burning through my breathing. "Troy's coming."

Chase was there, applying a painful amount of weight to my chest as my girl moved to cradle my head.

"I'm so sorry I ran. I'm so sorry. I was mad and stupid, and I didn't think." Lila sobbed, and I tried to wipe away her tears, but my arm was so heavy. "I'm sorry." She leaned her face into my palm, bridging the distance. "I'm sorry, Baby, I'm sorry. I can't lose you. I won't lose you!"

"No, stop -" A stabbing pain clipped my words–coughing brutally, my big ass brother cracked a rib.

"Sam's shot." Chase, on his phone, sounded distant. "You need to hurry."

"No!" Lila looked at my body and back at me. "I love you, Sam. I love you and you're gonna so fucking pay for that shit you pulled back at the cabin, but not until we get the fuck outta here. So, stop with all that goddamn coughing that sounds like you're dying."

Her sob came again—big, heaving.

"You are not dying, Samson Wilder; do you hear me? I love you and you love me, and we maybe made a baby that you gotta help me raise, do you hear me?"

"No dying today, soldier!" Chase bellowed.

"You...whore..." Brinks' voice, guttural and strained, came from behind Lila. I saw his hand slip from his back, gripping a second pistol. My eyes went wide, and I reached to pull Lila away.

A shot rang across the room.

Our eyes snapped to Moira–arm raised, gun smoking in hand, and laser-focused.

"Not looking so mousey now, am I, asshole?" Then she blinked, face softening again as she looked at me and Lila, "That's quite enough outta him."

Chase gaped, replacing Lila's hands on my wound and pulling his wife into him, slipping the gun from her hand. Slowly walking to the bloody and battered body of Dean Jensen, Chase stared at the man who had haunted his life.

A man who was still somehow alive enough to lift a shaking middle finger.

"You....don't..." Jensen choked on a bloody cough. "...have the stones..." Chase stared, dead-eyed, measuring the life left in the man who'd done so much damage to our world. He flicked a quick look at Moira, who gave a subtle nod.

"Big words from a man who's kinda slurring his speech."

Lifting the gun and firing, Chase released three rounds.

Two in the chest–one in the head.

Oorah.

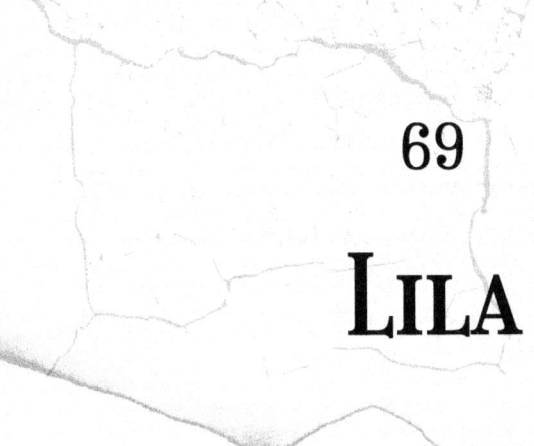

69

LILA

TROY BUSTED IN — a flurry of officers behind him.

He evaluated the scene for all of two seconds before issuing orders.

His presence instantly put me at ease.

There was little time to discuss what went down in the face of Sam's injuries.

Chase rattled off what he knew to the EMTs, who blanched only a second upon seeing their colleague bleeding out on the floor. Then they worked with practiced efficiency.

Moira and I were attended by a second team, who addressed our bruised wrists and split lips. She had a sprained neck and some scrapes and bruises, but otherwise was no worse for wear. Chase insisted that the hospital staff check her over, but the EMTs paid more attention to me and my tally sheet.

One concussion courtesy of Jensen's kick to the head.

Sprains to both shoulders from the chair.

Mild whiplash from the fucker's hair-pulling.

Bruises, scrapes, a partridge in a pear tree...I stopped listening.

I only had eyes for Sam and the crew working him over.

I couldn't breathe fully until I saw Sam loaded into the ambulance safely. At some point, I must have voiced a desire to ride with him, but excruciating pain reminded me of why I couldn't, when I was forced back into a gurney.

Chase promised to watch over him.

Moira and I were loaded into the second rig with Troy riding along.

"I am sorry that I led him to you." Troy started, but I shook my head.

"He never lost me. It wasn't your fault." I wanted to say more —the anguish on Troy's face was brutal —but fatigue won out.

The last thing I recalled was Moira holding my hand.

The next time my eyes drifted open, I was in a hospital bed, again.

Sam slept next to me in the vinyl hospital chair.

Letting my eyes adjust, I scanned the room to find Chase and Moira on a small couch along the wall. Her bruises bright and angry–His knuckles bandaged and bound. Troy leaned against the door–stoic and stalwart.

I couldn't wrap my head around all the events that had unfolded since I'd met them all. I brought more trouble than they deserved, and they had every reason to cut me loose after what they'd endured. No one would have blamed them for saying it was all just too much. Yet here they were–watching over me despite hurts they no doubt suffered.

Then there was Sam–head lolled to the side, arms crossed in front of him. I could see his shirt cut open, framing his wrapped ribs. It broke my heart to see him so damaged because of me.

"Hey." The room twitched when I tried to speak, my voice raspy and weak. Chase leaned forward, nudging Sam awake and helping him sit up.

"Sam." My voice was no stronger the second time around.

"Hey, baby. I'm here." He took my uncast hand in his, bringing it to his mouth and rubbing his beard against my knuckles. "I'm here."

"You're side?" I breathed more than spoke the question, instantly aching at how close I'd come to losing him...all of them.

"Bullet missed the good stuff. I'm fine." That flicker of a boyish smile made my throat tighten with emotion.

"Bullshit." I croaked through a rush of tears. "You...were shot...."

"He's down for the count," Troy interjected. "But he's not wrong—he got lucky."

"He's got some staples." Chase shrugged with a weary smile. "This family doesn't count that shit unless you have major surgery and/or go comatose for 24 hours, which," He glanced at his watch and shook his head. "Even you didn't meet the bar for real concern."

His joke was a light that cut through the guilt closing in.

"The bar is pretty high around here, I'm afraid," Moira added. "But it bears saying...this wasn't your fault," she glanced at Troy and added, "Or yours. You both need to set that down."

Before I could say more, Moira tapped Chase's chest and nodded towards the door.

"These two need a minute, guys. Let's go find some food." They filed out, leaving Sam behind.

"No way that chair works after taking a bullet," I rasped.

"We're not doing that," Sam's tone was direct but gentle as he brushed one hand against my cheek. "I'm not wasting a single second with you. Not again." I took in his eyes, clear and focused, as he held my gaze. "I'm gonna say the hard shit. You're gonna listen. When I'm done,

I'll hear everything you want to say. Good or bad. Happy or mad. Got it?"

The emotions already swelled within me to the point I couldn't form words, so I nodded my head, fighting back the tears.

"My entire existence, body and soul, was irrevocably changed the minute you walked into my life. I don't know how I managed to think I was happy with the shell I was before. And I know our relationship had unconventional beginnings–I know," He closed his eyes, jaw feathering as his throat bobbed, "I made a monumental mistake. But there isn't a single thing I would change, not a single thing I can bring myself to regret, cause it means I got to have you."

He rested a hand on my belly, and I lost control of the tears.

"No matter what the outcome of my actions, I don't regret one second with you."

He drew in a deep breath, letting his eyes linger where his hand sat, and I could see all the hope, all the pain, all the pure love in those eyes before he blinked his focus back to me.

"I'm in love with you, Delilah Rivera. You are my weakness. And my strength. You're my everything. No matter what...I'm all in...if you'll have me."

He watched me, patient as always, one hand on my belly, the other holding my fingers against his lips. His courage was awe-inspiring as he awaited my verdict.

Would I leave him, or could I forgive him?

The decision had long been made for me.

"You...were supposed to be a distraction," I mumbled, his lips curling in a smirk.

Taking a deep breath, I began again.

"You swept me off my feet, literally. I'm so tangled in you that I don't know how to ..." I paused, taking in a few breaths, and I noticed his eyes had turned almost sad.

I slipped my hand from his fingers and cupped his cheek.

"I knew you would come for me. That's how much I trust you. Even now–after everything." He shut his eyes, leaning into my hand. "Seeing you shot, because of me, shattered something. I never meant for this to threaten your family or–"

A sob took over, and it renewed the ache in my throat and my head. I had to slow my breathing before I could begin again.

"This place started dark and twisty for me, but you...brought me back, and I don't wanna go back to who I was before." A tear slipped down his cheek, and I brushed it away with my thumb. "So yeah, you made a mother fucker of a mistake," He huffed a laugh, and it made my whole heart smile. "I am completely, hopelessly, madly, deeply, in love with you and - " The words no sooner left my mouth than he was standing, pressing his lips to mine in a kiss.

Gentle, insistent, loaded with all the things we felt, and we stayed that way as eternity fell away.

Love shared without words.

Sam released me, gasping, as he pressed his forehead to mine, his tears falling against the tip of my nose.

"I thought I was too late...When I got there and he had you by the throat...your feet barely -" a sob choked off the rest of his words. "I thought I'd never get the chance to–" A ragged breath escaped between sobs. "I don't know what I would've done - "

"I'm okay," I whispered, wishing I could wrap my arms around him. "We're both okay."

"I know. You're right. We'll heal. All this will heal." He agreed quickly, his voice raspy with emotion as waves of relief and exhaustion wafted off him. "In a couple of weeks, my staples come out, and your cast will come off, and it'll be like this never happened."

"More like...36-ish weeks." I guided his hand to my belly and pressed him close to me. I couldn't contain the smile that spread across my face as understanding bloomed in Sam's eyes.

"We're *both* okay." His eyes, his smile, and his entire body radiated pure joy as he looked at our hands.

"Pregnant?" His eyes brimmed with tears. "When did you - "

"I saw the test in the pharmacy bathroom and told her in the ambulance." Moira's bubbly voice floated in from the door—her face beaming. "I didn't mean to eavesdrop, but we've been *dying* out here for you two to make up already!"

"I confess I saw it as well when we arrived on the scene," Troy slipped the test from his pocket and laid it across my lap. "I palmed it before anyone else could see...congratulations, brother."

"I didn't get to know until just now in the hall." Chase hooked a thumb over his shoulder, his face spread into a smile so big I could have counted all his teeth. "A baby!" his fist pumped, punctuating his statement.

"A baby." Sam breathed. "But your injuries? And the way he choked - "

"She's strong, Sam." Moira rested a hand on his back, her voice gentle but unwavering. "The doctors confirmed a strong heartbeat." She quickly added, "But JUST ONE!"

She and Chase laughed at that.

"Our baby," Sam whispered, trying to pull me close—but the movement seemed to hurt as he flinched with a hiss.

"Allow me," Troy joined me on one side of my bed, Chase on the other.

They carefully sat me up, Moira climbing onto the foot of my bed with her legs tucked under her.

Sam pulled me into his arms...followed immediately by Troy, and then Moira, and finally Chase's big-ass arms encircling us all.

A family.

My family.

My everything.

EPILOGUE

SAM

TWO WEEKS LATER, SURROUNDED by my family, Marge, Chief Brandt, and his wife, Carol, I changed her name to Delilah Wilder.

I want to say it was the no-frills, straightforward affair that Lila asked for. But with Moira at the helm, it turned into the grandest little shotgun wedding you've ever seen.

My nieces had tiny white dresses that matched their mother's, complete with little headbands and bows made to match Chase and Troy's, who held the girls in their arms. The cabin was rearranged and redecorated with an inordinate amount of flowers in every shade of purple, which I learned was Lila's favorite color. Chief played his guitar as Lila entered the main room wearing a stunning black, beaded gown.

I didn't even try to stop the tears as she walked the aisle, arm in arm, with Moira.

When my girl made it to the large window turned altar, she whispered, 'I hope those tears aren't cause you expected a fluffy white dress?' to which I happily replied, 'You. Look. Stunning'.

Suspecting she'd go non-traditional, I surprised my bride with a sleek platinum band rimmed in small white diamonds that served as the frame for a sizeable black solitaire. All the expressions that crossed her face when she saw it, from surprise to misty-eyed bliss, set my world at peace. Of course, my black band had a single white diamond set down in it, and in keeping with Wilder brother tradition, it was engraved on the inside.

'Property of Hellcat.'

Our ceremony was short and sweet, but we did slip away for a few weeks for a road-tripping honeymoon. I had a loose plan in mind, but left things open enough that we had plenty of space to explore anywhere my wife wanted to go. That is, after we first drove into New York City to visit her father's and brother's graves.

She hadn't been since the funeral, and I wanted her to have closure. I took the risk of surprising her with a loving but somber day, and we lingered a long while; I cleaned the site while she arranged flowers and a framed photo from our wedding.

My heart broke to hear her tell them about her new family.

I was honored to have joined her, to pay my respects to the men who'd helped shape the incredible woman she was, and I said as much before stepping back and giving her space with them.

When she finally stood, she seemed lighter.

We spent that night in a hotel, ordering room service and sharing family stories from her teenage years, followed by cheesy movies and a long bubble bath. It wasn't the fireworks one would expect from a honeymooner's hotel room. Still, it was the exact way my girl needed to be loved in that moment, and I was happy to give it to her. Then we took a day to arrange for all her stuff in storage to be delivered to my old house, letting my brothers take point on the receiving end, so our real honeymoon could begin.

We drove down the coast, stopping and lingering anywhere my girl desired, and I was gifted a glimpse of my bride unhurried, relaxed, and blissed-out. Turns out my wife rather enjoyed my penchant for weird roadside attractions, including an Elephant named Lucy in New Jersey and Pedro, the 104-foot-tall roadside mascot, in South Carolina.

Sightseeing by day, and exploring each other by night–our honeymoon was fucking awesome.

Our healing injuries and her 1st trimester fatigue meant we had to take things slow and easy in the bedroom for a while, and I found I enjoyed the change of pace with that too. It gave us a lightness we'd not experienced before–he chance to share what we'd skipped from before.

By the time our trip ended, I was in love with an entirely new side of my wife.

Her sexy temper was still there, especially if grumpy mama-bear was woken up too early, but I got more of her intoxicating laughter—loud and full, accompanied by that wild mane of hair tossed back. Being married made her ridiculously happy, and a ridiculously carefree and happy Lila was my favorite kind.

I vowed to see that laugh every damn day of our lives.

Returning home, we chose to stay in the cabin. My old house was a glorified storage unit, and the cabin provided a far better space for the baby. I had a plan to build us a house, but I wanted to surprise her with it later.

412

Coming home also meant I had to share my wife with her new best friend and sister.

She and Moira had already grown close, but the ordeal they shared bonded them even further. I put my foot down on sparring sessions until after the baby arrived, so they began taking Yoga with Carol and visiting the shooting range multiple times a week.

It was Moira who helped Lila put away her war room before the wedding. Together, they closed the door on a dark chapter of Lila's life. I don't think I'd ever loved my sister more than I did in the moment she helped my wife to let it all go.

It should have come as no great surprise that, while we came home to an empty cabin, we woke up the next morning to a houseful of family cooking brunch.

"Guys..." I called out, dragging my pajama-clad ass out of the bedroom. "Didn't occur to you I might be enjoying my wife this morning?"

"It's nearly noon. Besides...No way she's getting freaky with the way she's been feeling." Moira quipped, hugging me. "Welcome home, Sam."

"How'd you know that?" I asked, genuinely curious since the morning sickness hadn't kicked in until halfway through our trip.

"She texted me," Moira twisted her face into a subtitled 'Duh'.

"She at least loved my pictures of all the weird roadside attractions." Lila came up behind me, wrapping her uncast arm around me.

"I never said I didn't love them." I placed a kiss on her head. "I just didn't quite get the appeal of selfies with every single one of them when we could just buy a souvenir."

"Girls feeling better?" Lila asked, and I turned to Chase with a questioning look.

"Doc said it was run-of-the-mill Rhinovirus." Chase gave a sappy, sweet smile to his daughters, and my heart skipped a beat to think that'd be me soon. "They're all good."

"I brought that tea for you to try." Moira flitted over with a steaming mug of something that made my wife pornographically moan at first sip. "Told ya it was magic. Ginger is perfect for morning sickness."

Cock-teasing sounds aside, I was happy to have something that gave my girl some relief, even if it did smell like feet. I would tolerate anything if it meant she could eat a little more.

"Glad to see you both home." Troy hugged me and leaned down to offer one to Lila. "You look well, new sister."

"What's the latest?" Lila asked.

"You owe me a foot rub!" Moira yelled triumphantly, pointing a finger across the kitchen to Chase, who was frying bacon. "I told you Lila would be the first to talk shop!"

"Thanks a lot," Chase winked at Lila. "You just couldn't wait until after breakfast?"

"Ignore them." Troy said, "They've been insufferable since you all left, and they had time to re-sort themselves."

Lila and I sat on the couch, and Troy joined us.

"But they're okay," My guilt nagged at me from the fight my actions caused.

"Yeah," Lila answered, and Troy nodded agreement. "Her nightmares stopped, and Chase earned his way back into her good graces for keeping your bullshit secret." She nudged my shoulder with a playful wink. "They're okay."

"Do I wanna know what it took for him to earn that?" I asked Troy.

"Indeed, you do not." He answered. "Know only that I have spent more than a few quality nights with our darling nieces, but only once made the mistake of returning them without calling first." I grimaced at the unbidden visual as Troy turned to Lila, "And to answer your question, there isn't much to share."

"Marge's Bar?" I asked.

"Apex has disavowed any knowledge of Jensen and Brinks, claiming they broke into the bar illegally. With no records connecting them to Apex, and both of them being deceased, their respective cases were closed. Apex is, on paper, a non-issue."

"You don't buy it?" Lila's eyes narrowed as she leaned forward.

"Sharp as ever." Troy nodded. "Have you considered applying to rejoin the force? I've begun having the IA files attached to Brinks overturned, your dismissal chief amongst them. We could use your mind."

"Thanks, but...I don't know." Lila shrugged. "I'm not sure I'm suited to it anymore. I originally joined with my dad and my brother, but now it feels..."

Her words trailed off, and Troy and I both knew to let the space hang unfinished.

Financially, my wife didn't need to work, something I was able to share with her during our honeymoon. I told her, too, that I liked the idea of her staying home during the pregnancy, resting and recovering from everything before delivery and newborn nights began. She had as much time as she needed to sort her feelings and figure out what she wanted to do after the baby arrived, and she knew she had our full support with whatever she chose.

"Nonetheless." Troy finally added. "I'm enjoying a reprieve from a case that has hung over this town and my family for too long. Things have been, dare I say, boring." He held up his coffee.

"Here here," I said, tapping my mug against his.

No sooner had we taken a sip when a text caught Troy's attention:

Sentinel Alert: Fire alarm event logged at 211 E. Pineview Ln at 4:37 PM ET.

Alarm cancelled onsite.

Reply 1 to request local dispatch.

Reply 2 to confirm receipt and close this notification.

For assistance, call Sentinel Monitoring at 1-800-555-0199.

ACKNOWLEDGEMENTS

WRITING IS SOLITARY, BUT stories reach readers because of a team of people who love the characters as much as the author.

To Jonathan House and the Candlelight Creative team—thank you for artwork that brought Matchstrike to life exactly as I imagined. To Laura Matney at The Writer's Life, LLC—don't you dare ever leave me. You make me sharper, braver, better, and I promise Sam will always survive for you. To Aimee Ravichandran and the Abundantly Social crew—thank you for wrangling the whirlwind of rapid release with me (yes, I know I'm a handful). And to Rex—chaos coordinator, sanity saver, best assistant ever.

These books may bear my name, but your fingerprints are all over them.

About the Author

RHONE ATLESHEN IS A multi-award-winning author writing under a new name to explore the darker corners of the thriller world. After more than fifteen years crafting stories across genres, Rhone launched this brand to focus on what truly haunts the page: domestic danger, emotional reckoning, and villains you love to hate.

Known for strong voice, cinematic pacing, and deeply flawed characters, Rhone's work delivers adrenaline-soaked tension with explosive payoffs—and sometimes a little spice. Whether writing psychological thrillers, romantic suspense, or twisted moral dilemmas, the common thread is always this: the bad guys burn in the end.

READ MORE RHONE

The Apex Society Trilogy
Gaslight (Book One)
Matchstrike (Book Two) — You're holding it.
Burn (Book Three) — Coming December 2025

Learn more at rhoneatleshen.com or follow
@RhoneAtleshen on socials for updates and sneak peeks.

Sneak Peek: Burn

Book 3 of the Apex Society Trilogy

I ARRIVED AT OUR rental to find the front door slightly ajar, and all the lights in the house on. Walking up the two small steps, I could hear a woman's voice inside, the sounds mimicking the repetition of someone soothing a child. The rental agreement never mentioned a child, and I wondered if there were possibly others inside that weren't planned. The closer I got to the door, the more I could hear pacing footsteps and even intermixed shushing sounds.

"Ma'am," I called out, perched a few steps back from the door so as not to startle the woman inside. "I don't want to alarm you. I am Sgt. Troy Wilder of the local Police Department." The steps halted. "This is a courtesy visit regarding a fire alarm. I am here to make sure everything is okay." I waited a heartbeat, staring into the cracked door and willing it to open. Seconds crawled by before a light, airy voice called out... forced but near-carefree.

"I told the company that called...I-it was a false alarm." The woman spoke clearly enough, but the hesitation had me clenching. "There was no fire. I just...lost track of my dinner. It's fine." A baby began to cry, and shuffling footsteps sounded until the woman's voice was again heard murmuring until the cries subsided. My brothers and I exchanged a quick look of unspoken agreement, all of us sensing something was off.

I nodded towards Chase to step forward.

"Ma'am, I'm Lt. Wilder with the Fire Department. I'm glad it's a false alarm, but since I'm here, I could take a peek. Ensure the stove and oven are working correctly." I strained to hear any noises that might give probable cause to enter the premises.

My frustration gnawed at the silence, so I jerked my chin at Sam.

"And I'm Sam...an EMT. If that false alarm caused any scrapes or burns, I'm happy to patch you up. Free of charge." Relieved as I was to pull up and not see smoke, the open door and disembodied voice had that protective urge inside me clawing to the surface.

"No one is in trouble," I couldn't resist adding. "But I need to see on you."

It was a slip, far more personal sentiment than I'd intended, but accurate. I did need to see whoever was inside. The woman...the child...I needed to see them safe and unharmed. I'd always been driven to protect, to guide, to surround those I loved in a way that never fully made sense to me. When I was younger, I channeled it into my role as eldest brother. In the military, however, it took a different shape. Spreading to encompassing anyone in need around me, growing to be this wide and thin veil of longing that felt uncontrollably large until I found an outlet.

A random encounter with a one-night-stand who gave me an off-handed label as a joke–Dominant.

I was ravenous then, learning all that I could, and embracing the only thing that had ever made all my urges make sense. My desire to protect, to possessively surround, wasn't a flaw...it was a beast...and I'd need to learn how to cage it.

"Do you have a badge?" The woman's voice called to me, and I looked up to find her peeking around the door's edge. Her face was partially hidden, and the black-curtained lashes and the hint of visible hair gave me no indication of her identity. Still, I inventoried what I could.

Jet-black hair.

Ice-blue eyes.

Lilting voice.

And smart...insisting on a badge.

"This place isn't mine. I'm just renting it. I don't want to get in trouble with the owner by having people over without permission."

"Good girl." The praise fell from my lips without thought. It was careless, but it fit the pride I felt that she'd taken control of her safety in that small way. Praying that my brothers had missed the faux pas, I handed over my badge, focusing on the bloodied dish towel wrapped around the hand she offered. "I'm the property owner. The alarm triggered a courtesy alert—no authorities were called." I pointed to the business card, gently sliding it free to show her the NB Realty logo and my name and title, which matched the information on my license and badge.

Another minute passed as she scrutinized my documents before pulling the door back a little more, gifting me a full view of her. She was tall and willowy, with a flawless, fair complexion that stood in stark contrast to the dark hair framing her breathtaking face. She clutched my badge and ID with one hand, but in the other, she held an infant swaddled in a blue blanket. Wrapped as he was, I could only see the shock of dark hair that matched hers, tufting out from under his small hat.

"That has the makings of a mighty fine gash." Sam's voice floated around me, but the woman hardly took her eyes off me. "I brought a small first aid kit, and I could clean it up for you." She briefly flicked her gaze to Chase and Sam before settling those blue eyes back on me. Her expression gave away nothing save the dissociated cast that looked too war-weary to belong to a carefree young mother. Wanting nothing more than to ease the fear that was wafting off of her, I took in her predicament again and tried to offer a compromise.

"We are happy to see you on the porch, though I would advise an extra blanket for your child." She tugged the baby closer, as if afraid I might take him from her.

"And I can call the PD to verify your badge number?" Her chin raised in beautiful defiance as she ignored the fear that demanded she continue making safe choices.

"I encourage it." I smiled. "Officer Kramer should be answering tonight if I recall the duty roster. She's easy to speak with. I can provide the direct number for you if you like, or you can use my phone to - "

"Okay." She tucked my badge and ID into her pocket with a wince, drawing my eyes again to her bloodied hand. I had no grounds to enter the premises forcibly. Still, all my instincts were telling me that this woman needed my help, and I wasn't leaving until I had answers.

"My hand does hurt." Stepping back, she opened the door in invitation even while hugging the infant closer to her. "But afterwards, you can all go."

The simple one-bedroom cottage was in an odd state of disarray, and my cop instincts were dialed all the way up. For a place suffering a burnt dinner, the place lacked the hallmark aroma of charred food. I could tell Chase had also noted that the empty stovetop and sink contained no dirty dishes. The kitchen looked hardly used, in fact, save for the floor surrounding the small table. A vase had shattered, covering the tile with puddles of glass and broken flower stems. Sam nodded towards the small drops of blood swirling near the back door, and the woman followed his eyeline.

"I was in a rush...from the smoke alarm...and knocked it to the floor." She held her bandaged hand with an awkward shrug, "I hadn't had a chance to clean it up yet with all the phone calls and drop-in visitors."

The pointed note of irritation in her voice rang false, and that grated on me.

"As I mentioned, my name is Sam. And you are?" Sam sat at the small table, opening his medic kit and gesturing to a chair across from him.

"I'm J - " Her name stuttered in the air between us, and she cleared her throat, adjusting the pacifier for the baby in her arms.

Another lie.

"I'm Jane." My eyes swept past the unpacked suitcase in the living room. Then I watched Sam slide aside grocery bags to make space to work at the table. Bags holding diapers, infant clothes, and a bib–all in their original packaging. Jane noticed my eyeline, too.

"I ...just checked in yesterday. Hadn't had a chance to unpack fully to find my things." Too many things didn't add up—the empty stovetop, the fresh bags, the blood drops leading to the back door. This wasn't just a tenant fumbling dinner...she was on the run.

"If you are like me," Sam gave the baby a jovial smile, "There's no point in unpacking when you just have to repack later, ammiright?" He gingerly unwrapped Jane's hand, applying antiseptic that had me mentally preparing for her hiss of pain. She...Jane...never flinched, her eyes constantly following our movements with an impressive display of focused dissonance.

Shock, perhaps?

"I hope you are otherwise settling in well?" Jane nodded at Sam but never took her eyes off me as I walked to the laundry room for the broom and dustpan. I used the time to visually survey the rest of the house, noting the lack of a travel crib or bassinet.

"The place has been great. Very comfortable." A thin smile accompanied the compliment.

"It's a jagged cut, but not deep. You don't need stitches, but derma glue would help hold it closed while it heals." Sam applied his skills effortlessly, and I found myself grateful that she wasn't in any pain under his care. "I can then bandage it and give you the address to the local urgent care clinic in case you see signs of infec–"

"I'm leaving tomorrow." Jane half-shouted the response, jerking her eyes back towards her hand as if she'd just remembered Sam was in the room. The forced breath she took did little to sell the smile she forced. "But...I'm sure it'll be fine...thank you."

"So soon?" Chase asked, returning from the back room with a subtle head shake. No fire source found. "You've only just arrived."

"Yeah. I have had a change of plans." She watched as I slowly began tidying the broken glass into a pile. "I'll get on the road early and head to my final destination."

I bent to grab some large pieces of glass, uncovering a florist card hidden in the debris. Flipping it to read the note, I felt my jaw lock tight as my vision narrowed down at its small typed letters.

"Your flowers," My voice was a symphony of practiced calm, hiding the storm brewing beneath my skin. "They were a delivery?"

"A gift...from a friend." Jane's voice grew distant as I took in the pile of broken red flags still sitting at my feet. Tiny lies, discarded to the ground in defense of what? "It was clumsy of me to knock them over."

Chase moved to my side, noting the atmospheric shift, and I casually fired a text to the family group chat. Chase stiffened, and I held the card out for Sam to read; all of us were sitting amidst a pile of broken white roses, with a ticking time bomb in our hands, inscribed,

'Courtesy of The Apex Society.'

The Apex Society isn't finished.
Book 3 brings the reckoning. Order *Burn* today.
https://amzn.to/3JfevQg

www.ingramcontent.com/pod-product-compliance
Lightning Source LLC
Chambersburg PA
CBHW070833260626
47170CB00007B/2352